SOME FACES IN THE CROWD

short stories by

SOME FACES
IN THE
CROWD
BUDD
SCHULBERG

IVAN R. DEE
CHICAGO

www.ivanrdee.com

Library of Congress Cataloging-in-Publication Data:
Schulberg, Budd.
    Some faces in the crowd : short stories / Budd Schulberg.
        p. cm.
    ISBN-13: 978-1-56663-772-5 (pbk. : alk. paper)
    ISBN-10: 1-56663-772-4 (pbk. : alk. paper)
    I. Title.
PS3537.C7114S66 2008
813'.52—dc22
                                    2007041201

for Vicky, Stevie and Davy

SOME FACES IN THE CROWD

YOUR ARKANSAS TRAVELER

I

That was a nice little summer job on KFOX until he came along. I'd spin the platters and dead-pan the commercials, I'd read the news off the AP wire—I was a kind of transmission belt between Fox, Wyoming, and the outside world. For seventy-five a week. Just making enough to keep me in nylons and pay my way at the local beauty parlor. And doing enough to satisfy a nagging conscience.

But this isn't getting us to Lonesome Rhodes. The time is one quiet weekday morning when I have the shop pretty much to myself. There's just me and Farrell who sits there with all the little knobs and gets us on the air, hangover and all. The boss is off somewhere taking his ease. Joe Aarons, our staff-of-lifer, is out telling tradesmen their businesses will cave in if they don't hurry up advertise on KFOX. OK? Ready? Blow the trumpets. Sound the cymbals. Enter Mister Rhodes.

He's big and he's Western, but he isn't stringbean like Gary. He's kind of big all over, like a husky fullback three years after he broke training. He's got a ruddy, laughing face, the haw-haw kind. He must be well into his thirties, but he's boyish. He stands there in an unpressed brown suit and cowboy boots, shifting from one foot to another, shy-like, though something tells me deep down he is about as shy as a bulldozer. I spin one—one of my old faves, Berrigan's "Can't Get Started" and I duck to find out what brings to our wireless castle this happy big one I see through the glass.

"Ma'am," he says, "my name is Rhodes, Larry Rhodes. They call me Lonesome."

"Who calls you lonesome?" I say.

He grinned a nice warm grin. Too nice. Too warm. "Lonesome, that's my professional name, ma'am."

"Oh, a professional. What are you a professional at?"

"Singin', ma'am. Folk singin'."

Now I know that these days you are supposed to love folk singin'. If you don't drool over "Barbara Allen," if you don't swoon to the "Blue-Tail Fly" or "The E-ri-e Canal" you are considered un-hep, unwholesome and perhaps a trifle unpatriotic. Well, I plead guilty.

I look at the big clock in the broadcasting room and I see the impatient second hand sweeping on to my next cue. So I run in to tell the waiting world of Fox, Wyoming, and environs that if they want the finest dinner they ever had for one dollar thirty-five what are they waiting for, hurry their lassies down to the Little Bluebird Grill. Then I spin Fats on his own "Ain't Misbehavin'" and I come out for another peek at Western man on the hoof.

He beams on me. "You must be a mighty smart little gal to be handlin' this here raddio station all by yourself."

"My good man," I said, "I am able to read without laughing out loud any commercial that is placed before me. I am able to pick out a group of records and point to the guy in the control room each time I want him to play one. And that is how you run a rural radio station." "Haw," observed Lonesome Rhodes.

"I might add," I said, "that we are not in the market for live entertainment. Assuming that is what you represent. Except for the news, and once in a while an interview with a celebrity who wanders into our corral, we live on wax. We spin for our suppers."

He chuckled. Yes, warmly and nicely. He shook all over when he chuckled. He looked like Santa Claus rolled back to his middle thirties.

"You're a real five-gaited talkin' gal," he said. "Now you jest set yerself down an' try to keep still and give old Lonesome five minutes of yer invaluable time."

The way he said it and the size of him grinning down at me were not unpersuasive. What he offered was limitless confidence in his own charm. Now that you've seen him thousands of times you know what I mean.

"I brought along my *git*-tar," he said. "How can you send away from your door a fella who goes to all that trouble jest to entertain you?"

As a matter of fact we were hooked into a national soap opera called "John's Office Wife," so I was on my own for the next half-hour. "All right," I said, "entertain me."

He opened the guitar case and a *Racing Form* fell out. "How did you do yesterday?" I said.

He shook his head and shrugged and then he grinned. "I had a tough break. Shy Lady was ready to make her move, but she couldn't find racing room."

"All right, sing," I said. "Let's have 'Home on the Range.'"

The guitar case was a large one and it also held a change of clothes and his toilet articles. "I made this myself with an old cigar box, a piece of piano wire I found in a junkyard and a little spit," he said, caressing the instrument. "Back in my home town, Riddle, Arkansas, they call me the Stradivarius of the cigar-box *git*-tar. Them folks got a heap o' culture in Riddle." He put his ear down to that god-awful-looking thing and began to tune it elaborately.

"This isn't Carnegie Hall," I said, "and I only have twenty minutes."

I hate guitars. I used to hate banjos, but I think I hate guitars more. Except for Segovia or Vincente Gomez.

"I will first sing that old folk song 'We'll Have Tea for Two if You'll Bring the Tea.'"

A Western clown, I thought to myself.

He poised his fingers over the strings and announced, "I should say at this point that I do not know how to play the *git*-tar. I sent for a home-study course, but not having a home the lessons never seem to catch up to me. A folk singer without a *git*-tar is like soft-boiled eggs without a spoon, kind of embarrassin', so I carry the *git*-tar along t' keep up appearances."

I made a fairly good job of not laughing. But he had something. To look at his big hearty puss and the way he enjoyed himself, it made you want to smile.

He started to sing one of my favorite hates, "Little Red Wing." It was only slightly awful, but it was rapidly getting worse. He broke off after a few bars and said, "If you think this is good I wish you could hear my Cousin Abernathy sing it. He does it through his nose and on a nice damp day he gets an effect that's darn near as good as playin' a comb through toilet paper."

He talked that way all through the number. He kept reminding himself of funny stories from that outrageous home town, Riddle, Arkansas. He said the riddle was how it could call itself a town when it had so few people in it. He said there was only one family in the town, his own kin, the Rhodeses. Population 372 and one half. He said the extra half was for his Great Uncle Bloomer who had two heads. "But he only had two hands and one mouth so we figured he was only entitled to one vote and one jug of corn a day. But believe me that fella's got two good heads on his shoulders. It took two of 'em to get the last word with my Aunt Lucybelle." He said there was so much intermarriage in Riddle, Arkansas, that he figured out one time his mother-in-law's kid brother was actually his step-daddy. How he, Lonesome, ever came out so normal and intelligent he would never know, he said. He said in Riddle they called him The Perfessor because he was the only fella in town who ever got through the third grade. "And I was only fourteen at the time," he said. "The only other member of my family to be associated with an educational institution was my Great Great Uncle Wilbraham. He's been at Harvard for years. My daddy says he occupies one of the most important bottles· in the medical lab, but I wouldn't swear to it because Daddy is always boasting about his kin."

And all this time in bits and snatches he's singing "Little Red Wing."

I didn't know whether it was wonderful or ghastly but I'll admit I didn't dial out. He finished with a great throbbing chord. "That is the lost chord," he said. "I picked it up in a saloon in Jackson Hole one night and I never have been able to find anybody who would own up to it. . . . Haw haw haw," he chuckled from deep in his belly. "You bring the money, Mama, I'll bring the fun."

Well, I don't know. He was outrageous. He was boisterous and effective and he had a certain animal charm that made me feel uneasy.

He was just winding up when our boss came in. He's a rich man who owns a chain of rural newspapers and affects cowboy boots and a white ten-gallon hat like Gene Autry. He is just as crazy about folk singin' as I loathe, despise and abominate it. He takes one good look at Lonesome and what he sees appeals to his Amuricanism.

Now I happen to feel strongly about America, from General George to General Ike, but our boss, Jay Macdonald, loves America as if it were his own private potato patch. In his mind, he and America are practically interchangeable. You know the type. Well, he wants to know if Lonesome can sing "Bury Me Not on the Lone Prairie." Mr. Macdonald says he can always tell when it is sung right because the last line trailing off into the mournful silence invariably makes him reach for his handkerchief. Well, Lonesome gives it to him, with all the stops out. Right down to the last phrase of gooey self-pity on the Lo-an Pray-reeee. . . . Old Macdonald reaches for his hanky. I see this Lonesome Rhodes is no fool. He has played it very straight. Macdonald stifles a sob and says, "Dammy, I love that old song. A real true-blue Amurican song." Lonesome whips out a coarse red handkerchief and sheds a tear or two of his own.

"A-course I don' know too much about this here raddio busyness," Lonesome concedes, in what has now become a household phrase, "but it seems to me a raddio station in a hunert-per cent Amurican community like Fox could do with a bit of its own old-fashioned Amurican singin' an' talkin'."

With eyes still damp with patriotic emotion, Macdonald allowed as to how that was so. And next thing you knew, he was allowing as to how a half-hour spot must be made in the daytime schedule for my new fellow-staffer Lonesome Rhodes.

Well, I can't build any fake suspense about a name that has become as world famous as Lonesome Rhodes'. Most of you have read *Life* and that *Time* cover story and a dozen other articles on how it all happened. Lonesome got on there for half an hour singing "Little Mohee" —just that one song for the whole program because he kept interrupting himself with funny stories, family anecdotes, homilies, recipes for pineapple upside-down cake

the way his Maw made it in Riddle, Arkansas, and anything else that popped into his cagey, folksy, screwball
mind.

The next day I have a new job. I am answering Lonesome Rhodes' fan mail. Seems as if half the population of
Fox, Wyoming, is in his pocket. More letters in one day,
says our boss, than we had been getting in three months.
And I had to answer them in Lonesome's lingo. "I sure
am tickled yer out there a-listenin'."

The boss ups him to three times a day for an hour.
Lonesome just gets on there and drools. Anything that
comes into his head, that's what the people want to hear.
He's got the popular touch. A man of the people. The
way he wraps himself around that mike you'd think it
was his best girl or his favorite horse. He says, "Top o'
the mornin' to ya, Ma—mmmm, that coffee smells good!—
wish I had time to come over an' give ya a hand with
them dishes," and at least three dozen housewives plunk
themselves right down at their kitchen tables and write
him letters about how well he understands them. Sometimes he kids the commercials and sometimes he reads
them as if he were on his knees proposing. Rarely the
same way twice. He's smart. That's what's wrong about
him. I'm seeing quite a lot of him on the air and off, and
he isn't at all the simple, fun-loving oaf he pretends. He
drinks too much, and he's indiscriminate with women. I
see the way he eyes all the girls when we go out together.
He's not a wolf, he's King Kong. He has to prove what a
helluva fella he is every five minutes. And he seems madly
in love with Lonesome Rhodes. The little success he's
had in Fox doesn't surprise him at all. "It's my natural
magnetism," he explained, "my God-given magnetism."

"That magnetism wasn't even keeping you in beans a
few weeks ago," I reminded him.

"That's because I didn't have you, Marshy," he said.
"You haven't got me now."

Not that he hadn't tried.

"But you're what's keeping me here," he said. "I was always a wanderer. My feet get itchy after a few weeks. With the singin' an' the talkin' I'm always good for a few bucks wherever I go. I play the fair grounds and the barrel-houses. All I need to kill the people is to stay in one place. I never knew a woman good enough to stand still for. Until I found you, Marshy."

So it seems I had the love of Lonesome Rhodes. I was also responsible, in an indirect way, for elevating him from folk singer to political sage. It happened at the bar of El Rancho Gusto. The local sheriff, who was running for re-election, had had a snootful and in the dim light of the lounge he mistook me for Yvonne de Garbo or somebody. A pass took place. Lonesome Rhodes rose to defend my honor. Lonesome had had not one drink but one bottle too many and his aim was inaccurate. I sometimes wonder if his fist had ever connected with the jaw of the candidate, would he have gone on to his fabulous career. Missing the would-be sheriff left him with a king-sized frustration.

Next morning he worked it out of his system on the air. He said this fella who wanted to keep on being sheriff of a great, thriving, forward-looking community like Fox, Wyoming, didn't even deserve to be sheriff of Lonesome's home town, Riddle, Arkansas. Or maybe, he said, that's exactly what he did deserve. In Riddle, he said, the way they picked their sheriffs was they figured out which fella could best be spared from useful labor. In some places, he said, the village halfwit has to be put on town relief. But in Riddle, as an economy measure, they made a sheriff out of him. He said that is pretty much what Fox would be doing if they re-elected this poor fella of theirs.

The following day I had to answer fifty letters from listeners suggesting that Lonesome himself run for sheriff.

He answered some of them on the air. He said he would have to decline the honor as he had never gotten around to learning how to read and write and he had heard that this sort of erudition came in handy if you were going to be a sheriff. He said the only difference between him and the other fella was that he, Lonesome, admitted he didn't know nuthin'.

He kept this up day after day all in good clean fun until he had that poor man crazy. And the people loved it. In fact he could just stand there picking his teeth over the microphone and the fans ate it up. For instance, one day he said into the live mike—and he wasn't kidding either: "Marshy, I'm tired today, didn't get my beauty sleep last night, hold the mike while I caulk off for a minute or two." And he handed me the mike and closed his eyes. I could have killed him. I got out a couple of letters I was answering and read them to take up the slack. But when I was half through, he mumbled, "Shhhh, Marshy, yer disturbin' my sleep, le's keep it absolutely quiet." So thirty seconds of dead time went out over KFOX. Anybody else would have been fired. But when Lonesome Rhodes did it he got fan mail.

On election night the sheriff, whose margin last time had been 362 to 7, found himself licked for the first time in sixteen years. The fellow who won, an undertaker named Gorlick, got more votes this time than he had in the last four campaigns combined. (His seven votes in the last election had come from members of his family.) Lonesome introduced the new sheriff on his program next day by saying that Gorlick obviously was an unselfish public servant, for the better sheriff he was the less business he'd have for his undertakin' parlor.

That and some more of the same was how Lonesome got his first break in *Time*. I could hardly believe it when a local photographer phoned the station to tell us *Time* had called him to come up and get a picture of us. I say *us* because Lonesome was making a kind of assistant celebrity out of me. If he couldn't find something—in a playful mood he might pretend he had mislaid the commercial —he would call into the mike: "Marshy, Marshy—where is that forgetful girl? Neighbors, if there's anything you don't like on this here program I want you to remember it is Marshy's fault, so send your letters of complaint to her." I was always the patsy, the fall girl. So *Time* said they wanted me in the act too. The still man came up to the studio on time, but Lonesome wasn't around. That had become one of my headaches. Getting Lonesome to the studio on time. He was just a small-town star, but he was developing a talent for big-time ways. Twenty minutes before the morning show I'd find him in his room. The only way I could wake him was with a cold wet washrag right over the big, lovable, exasperating face. Lonesome Rhodes. My life work.

The *Time* piece had it pretty accurate. They called Lonesome Rhodes a younger, fatter, coarser Will Rogers in the American grain of tobacco-chewing, cracker-barrel, comic philosophers, a caricature of the folk hero who has always been able to make Americans nod their heads and grin and say, "Yep, that fella ain't so dumb as he looks!" It was hard to tell whether *Time* was putting the laurel wreath or the knock on him. You know the style. But it didn't matter. Lonesome was in. The next day I got a call from Chicago. It was the J & W Agency and they wanted Lonesome. Right away. Five hundred a week. There was nothing like him on big-time radio, the man said. A simple, lovable, plain-talking, down-to-earth American. I said Mr. Simple-Lovable would call them back.

I found the great American just where I expected to find him, in the sack in his room with a half-empty jug of blended by the bed. I said, "Get up, you slob, destiny is calling."

"Collect?" he said.

"Chicago," I said. "J & W. Five hundred cash money a week. One hour every morning. Week-ends free. And all you have to do is be your own irresistible self."

He looked at me with those big, bloodshot, roly-poly eyes. "What do you think we oughta do, Marshy?"

"*You*," I said. "You can find yourself a new slave in Chicago."

"I'm gonna marry you in Chicago," he said. "I'm a-gonna make a honest woman of you in the Windy City, little gal."

Among his many bad habits was his way of creating the impression, through careful innuendo, that we were a team, biologically speaking. This was a figment of his imagination and designs, but since when have people ever accepted truth when nasty rumors are so much more fun? "Why talk of marriage when your heart is wrapped up in somebody else?" I said. "How could I ever replace Lonesome Rhodes in your affection?"

"Marshy, I've known some pretty good-looking broads in my get-arounds, but they always took me apart. You're not going to win any beauty contests, but you put me to-gether. You get me up in time to go to work. You get me on and off. You keep in touch with my public. You cue me when I start repeatin' myself. You always tell me when I'm gettin' close to the line. I lean on you. So you say yes and we'll go to Chicago and make it hand over fist and you'll be the rich Mrs. Rhodes. I can't afford to lose you. You're the smartest good-lookin' gal I ever got hold of."

"Take your hand away," I said. "This is business. Shall I tell them *yes?*"

"If you're in it."

"Well, only as a job," I said, "a job I can quit when I've had enough. You understand?"

"Okay," he said, "I'll take my chances."

"So I'll tell them yes."

"Only not for five hundred. Lonesome Rhodes is not a three-figure man."

He had started at seventy-five like me and was getting a fast century now.

I called back J & W in Chicago and gave them Mr. Rhodes' estimate of his own value and they said even with that publicity from *Time* a four-figure bill was too big for a starter. I ran back to tell Lonesome (in his bathrobe drinking beer now) and he said, "I better get on the phone and talk to 'em myself." It took him an hour to pull himself into his clothes and get down to the station where he had me get on the other phone and take down what they said so he could hold them to it. Where he got that adding-machine mind I don't know, but he was never a cowhand when it came to finance. This is what Lonesome Rhodes, that simple know-nothing troubadour, suggested: That he work gratis for nothing for two weeks. At the end of that period if they want him to continue they pay him his thousand a week including back pay for the trial period. And at the end of twenty-six weeks an option for fifteen hundred for the next twenty-six weeks. "A-course I'm not tryin' t' run your busyness, gents," he Arkansighed, "a'm jest tryin' t' give ya an idea what a fella figures he's worth. Oh yes, an' transportation. Transportation fer my li'l ol' pardner Marshy Coulihan and yours truly."

So we flew in to Chicago and now Lonesome was on coast-to-coast. The show was called "Your Arkansas Traveler." It was pretty much the same routine that had made him the idol of Fox, Wyoming. With one important exception. That sheriff election had gone to his head. He wasn't content just to sing his old songs and tell funny stories about his family in Riddle, Arkansas, any more. He had to hold forth. It is one of the plagues our age is heir to. No longer do disc jockeys play the music. Now they lecture you on how to solve the traffic problems of New

York and improve the United Nations. That's the bug that was biting Lonesome. He was rushing in where not only angels but a majority of fools would fear to tread. I did my small best to talk him out of it and get him to know his place. But he was male-stubborn and he knew so little that any meager idea he had came to him as a world-shaking revelation that had to be shared with his public. I suppose the doctors would call it delusions of grandeur. It seems to be one of the main symptoms of the dread disease of success.

He had only been going a few days, for instance, when he interrupted the singing of "Barbara Allen" with the announcement that he was pretty sick of that song anyway and he would rather talk about the street-cleaning problem in Chicago. He said that Chicago reminded him of Riddle except that Riddle was a one-horse town and Chicago was a ten-thousand horse town and the difference between one horse and ten thousand horses ain't hay. The next day a Citizens' Clean-Up Committee was formed with Lonesome as honorary chairman. On his program next day Lonesome sang "Sweet Violets" in honor of the clean-up campaign and he said it gave him a funny feeling to be connected with "sech a projeck" because his Grandpaw Bascom used to call his paw a sissy for insisting on changing his clothes every year.

It was only a matter of weeks before Grandpaw Bascom and Cousin Abernathy and Great Great Uncle Wilbraham and the rest of Lonesome's so-called family had become public property. The famous comic-strip artist Hal Katz came to Lonesome with a deal to do a daily and Sunday strip around the Riddle characters, featuring a Lonesome-like folk singer to be called Hill-Bilious Harry. What was in it for Lonesome was a thousand a week and a percentage of subsidiary loot. So by the time the option was taken up, Lonesome, our overgrown Huck, wasn't exactly going barefoot. He was pulling down twenty-five hundred a week, not a bad living for a country boy. Lonesome was not impervious to money, either. *Au contraire,* he was decidedly pervious. He began spending it as if he had had it all his life, only more so. He lined up a pretty fancy flop at the Ambassador East and bought himself a powder-blue Cadillac that just said "Lonesome" on it. A monogram would have been too ritzy, he said. Right away he had one of those Swiss 18K calendar watches and a closet full of suits all a little baggy and country-cut but good goods. He was a folk singer, remember?

He went in for me, too. He never kept his promise about my being strictly business. He always figured the natural charm would finally overcome me. I was his one-'n-only, his indispensable can't-live-without. One night the phone woke me up and it was Lonesome getting ready to jump out the window if I didn't marry him. He said he felt confused about all the success and that I was his anchor. His anchor to reality is what I think he said. That is not exactly a compliment but I said I would think it over. I don't know if I was in love with him. Call it 90 per cent disgust and 10 per cent maternal. Oh yes, I'm the maternal type as well as the professional woman. To tell the solid truth, I was always ready to give up the high rank and all the loot whenever I found the right man. At first a girl thinks kids would be too much trouble, and then that maybe there's something to it even if it is trouble, and later that her life will not be complete without them, and finally that it is the one thing in the world she really wants. I was hovering around stage C the morning that Lonesome called. I told him to ask me at a more reasonable hour and when he was stone sober. And not to muck it up with suicide threats. What was a down-to-earth simple-grained one-hundred-and-ten-per cent Amurican doing with that psycho out-the-window talk? He

said, "Bless you, Marshy, you do me good. Even when I'm
the greatest, you'll be right alongside me."

"Lie back and get some sleep and do yourself some
good," I told him.

The sponsors were awfully happy with Lonesome. He
was the hottest salesman on radio-TV. He'd open with
"Look down, look down that lonesome road," and then
he'd slide into "Hiya, neighbors, this is yer Arkansas
Traveler," and he'd have the people eating out of his
big and sometimes trembling hand. He'd say, "Shucks,
folks, I don't know if you'll like the stuff, maybe you got
funny taste, but *I* love it, it's what makes my cheeks so
rosy," and the assistant geniuses of the advertising companies would shake their heads and acknowledge Lonesome as a full-blown number-one genius. A dry cereal
called Shucks came out with his picture on it. He got the
idea of forming Lonesome Rhodes, Inc., so he could keep
some of the gravy. It turned out he was nuts for cars—he
was on a vehicular kick—so he bought a Jaguar to keep
his Cadillac company. His Nielsen kept climbing until he
was almost as popular as Jackie Gleason and Bishop Sheen.
And when it came to getting his stuff across he could
more than hold his own with both those boys. "He's got
it." That was the only way the advertising brains could
explain it. "He got it," they'd say, and they would all
nod their heads with a sense of accomplishment and go
out to a long lunch of martinis.

Lonesome branched out from sanitation problems to advice on rent controls and diplomatic appointments. And
became not only a political pundit but a good Samaritan.
He built up a little department for himself called "My
Brother's Keeper." During the four and one-half minutes
for BK, as we called it, he would appeal for some personal
cause. For instance, a little boy was dying in Meridian,
Wisconsin, and his blood wasn't one of the two usual

types. Lonesome told the story with all the stops out and asked for blood. Half an hour after the broadcast there had been nearly a thousand calls from all over the United States. That's what they call penetration. Lonesome was just lousy with penetration. A widow in New Jersey with nine kids had her house burn down and Lonesome asked for the dough to rebuild it. "Nobody send more'n a buck," he said. "It's us ordinary folks got to do this thing." Us ordinary folks threw in about twice as much as they needed to replace the house. Lonesome thought up a gimmick for that, too. He organized the Lonesome Rhodes Foundation. Anything over the amount he asked for specific cases went into the pot. It was a tax-exempt setup and some big names kicked in, some out of pure generosity, I suppose, and maybe some for the publicity value of having Lonesome say, "Thank you Oscar Zilch, you're good people," over the air. The foundation became kind of an obsession with Lonesome. To listen to him you would have thought that no other charities and no other humanitarianism was being perpetrated in America. Celebrities who, for one reason or another, failed to come through for the foundation became the targets of public and private abuse from Lonesome Rhodes. He would do everything from questioning the legitimacy of their birth to hinting at their involvement in the latest Communist spy ring. BK and the foundation did some good, I will admit, but at no small cost to those of us around him who had to put up with the emotional wear and tear of his playing God in a hair shirt.

It was about this time, near the end of his second twenty-six weeks, that Lonesome took his first fling into international politics. Until now he had contented himself with just telling us how to solve our domestic problems. But suddenly—I think it was from getting indigestion after eating some tainted shrimps in a Chinese restaurant—he went global. He warned the Chinese that if they didn't stop messing around with us in Korea he'd stop sending his shirts out to a Chinese laundry. Back in Riddle there was a Chinaboy who aimed to marry into Grandpaw Bascom's side of the family, he said. Grandpaw told the Chinese he couldn't marry in until he went 'n cut off his pigtail. The Chinaboy said Hokay and went out to the barn and cut off the tail of Grandpaw's favorite hawg. "That's why I sez even when ya think ya got an agreement, never trust a Chinaman," Lonesome said.

I tried to tell Lonesome I thought the story was pretty irresponsible, when we were still trying to work out a truce that would save American lives. But darned if a couple of senators didn't write in and congratulate Lonesome for his brilliantly witty analysis of "our naive if not criminally mistaken foreign policy." Lonesome was invited to address Veterans United and the Daughters of the Constitution and to write a daily column of political jokes for a national syndicate. I don't know how many thousands wrote in after that Riddle Chinaboy joke telling Lonesome he was right and that we should break off negotiations in Korea and that this country would be a sight better off if we had a level-headed, plain-talkin' fella like Lonesome Rhodes as Secretary of State.

I tried to tell him, "Lonesome, you're fine as long as you gag your way through Old Smoky and tell your jokes about Cousin Abernathy in Riddle. But don't you think before you go handing out pronouncements on China that you should know just a little bit about what you're talking about?"

In the voice of the people, Lonesome said, "The people never know. The people is as mule-stupid as I am. We jest feel what's right."

I made a futile effort to explain: he was no more the voice of the people than I was, with my corrupted Vassar accent. In the sheep's clothing of rural Americana, he was a shrewd businessman with a sharp eye on the main chance. He was a complicated human being, an intensely self-centered one, who chose to wear the mask of the stumbling, bumbling, good-natured, "Shucks-folks-you-know-more-about-this-stuff-'n-I-do" oaf.

Like the time Lonesome made a really fine, moving talk about the noble institution of marriage. He had been singing "The Weaver's Song" and he cut into that tender ballad to ask everyone who might be contemplating divorce to try just a little harder to see the other side of the argument. "Never leave a first love just to have the last word," he murmured to the accompaniment of a few soft chords on that makeshift guitar. The response was fantastic. Some five thousand couples wrote in to tell Lonesome they were "reconsidering" and he promised the reconciled couple who wrote the best letter on why they made up that he would have them on his program and blow them to a whirlwind week-end in Chicago ("Second Honeymoon") at his own expense (tax deductible). Easy for him to say. I had to read, sort out and grade the darn letters. Such drool you never heard. Lonesome was described as a cross between the Lord Jesus and Santa Claus with the better features of both. Lonesome was getting so benevolent it was coming out his ears.

Forty-eight hours after Lonesome had come out unequivocally for marital bliss I was in my apartment working through the pile-up of letters when the phone rang. It was a woman I had never heard of before who said her name was Mrs. Rhodes. "Lonesome's mother?" I asked in my sweetest maybe-daughter-in-law-to-beish voice. "No, his wife," was the answer. "I wanna see you."

I must admit I was a little curious to see her, too.

She was about forty, in the process of getting fat, but you could see that she had been attractive once in a showy, third-rate way. Being a snob by instinct and a democrat by conviction, I tried to reject the word "coarse." But it hung over us like a low fog dampening our conversation. "So you're Lonesome's new tootsie," she opened. "Well I hope you have more luck keeping him home than I did."

"I am simply a business associate and personal friend of Mr. Rhodes," I said, cool, collected and unconvincing.

"Come off it, miss," she said. "The floor manager on your program is my brother-in-law's first cousin. He writes me what's been going on."

"I must say that it is gracious of you to inform me that Mr. Rhodes is married," I said. "I think he might have done me the courtesy of telling me himself."

"Mr. Rhodes never did nobody no courtesies," said Mrs. Rhodes. "If you want my opinion, Mr. Rhodes is a no-good bastard."

"I have no doubt your opinion is based on considerable experience," I said.

"Not only is Mr. Rhodes a bastard," Mrs. Rhodes went on, "Mr. Rhodes is a crazy bastard. A psycho-something or other. His skull thumper told me."

"Skull thumper?"

"His mind doctor," she explained. With her index finger she described a series of sympathetic circles against her temple. "Bells in the batfry."

"I see. And may I ask just exactly what is the purpose of your visit?"

"Get Larry to shell out three thousand a month and I'll divorce him. Otherwise I not only won't divorce him, I'll make it plenty hot for the both of you."

"I am not engaged to your husband," I said. "I mean I —I suggest you discuss this matter between yourselves."

"Larry thinks he has to have every broad he sees," said Mrs. Rhodes. "And as soon as he has 'em he calls 'em tramps and leaves 'em for something new. It's part of his psycho-something or other."

"A very interesting diagnosis," I said, thanking my

little stars I had never succumbed to the jovial, overgrown lap-dog passes of Lonesome Larry. "But I still suggest this is a matter between you and Mr. Rhodes."

"He's a two-timing no-goodnick," she said. "I caught him red-handed with my best girl friend. He broke my jaw."

"It seems to be working quite effectively now," I said, and showed the lady to the door.

I don't know why, it didn't really concern me except that Mrs. Rhodes' husband had proposed to me and I was curious, which Mr. Webster defines as habitually inquisitive. I called him at the Ambassador and told him I had something on my mind. "Marshy, come on over," he boomed. "Come over an' have a drink an' hear the good news. You'll be proud of me."

"You," I said. "You hypocrite. You pious bigmouth. You oracle, you."

"Marshy," he said, and he tried to laugh it away. He could commit murder with that haw-haw-haw and everybody would think he was being a laugh riot. "You just need a drink, Marshy honey."

"Something is cockeyed wrong with the world," I said.

"Why for? Why for, my lovely marshmallow?"

"The way people listen to you," I said. "The way they believe you. It's fake, it's mirrors, it's false bottoms. You and your Cadillacs and your Grandpaw Bascom. A man of the people. My derrière."

"Marshy," he said, "you're tired, you've been working too hard. You need a vacation. We'll go to Sea Island."

"Damn it, we're not a *we*," I said. "I hate you, hate what you stand for."

"What do you stand for?" he said, and the easy laughter was gone from his voice now.

"I—I don't know. Something better. Something true somewhere. I can't explain it very well. All I know is I hate phonies, sham is for the birds."

"Take it easy, Marshy. You're the boss. I carry the ball

but you call the signals, you know that. Now just come over and relax with some of this good Irish drinking whiskey. Let Uncle Lonesome put a friendly arm around you and tell you how rich an' pretty you're gonna be."

Well, I went over. I tell you I wasn't in love with the man, just involved with him in some perverse professional way. He wasn't alone, he was with Tommy de Palma. De Palma was one of those advertising-agency boys. Bright. Quick. Immaculate. In the next life he'll make a good pilot fish for sharks. I don't mean to go into de Palma but I can't resist one short take: he's the kind of fellow who attaches himself to a celebrity, acts the part of the responsible friend, solemnly warns he is going to tell the truth even if it hurts, and then plays back in slightly off-beat fashion all the things the great one wants to hear. Essentially it's a business relationship, but it poses as rather an intense personal friendship. Tommy de Palma, the account executive who handled the Lonesome Rhodes-Peerless account, was now Lonesome's best friend.

Tidings of great commercial joy were being toasted with that bottle of Jameson's.

"Marshy, the busher days are over, we're moving in on the big stuff. New York! New York! Big frog in big pond department."

The plan had size, all right. Lonesome was going to do two different big shows, the ballad-singing "Arkansas Traveler" thing, and a biweekly news commentary to be called "The Cracker Barrel," Lonesome Rhodes the hayseed philosopher jest talkin' things over with his Cousin Abernathy, his Grandpaw Bascom and his Aunt Lucybelle. "We'll chew up everything from the UN to tax evasion and back to Riddle," Lonesome said. "And we'll make a lousy fortune, Marshy girl. We ain't a-goin' t' work through no advertisin' agency, neither. Why give them 15 per cent of five G's a week? We'll be our own advertising agency. Tommy here'll head it up for me.

It's gonna be Rhodes, de Palma and Coulihan. We're partners, Marshy. Put 'er there, pardner. You'll be drawing five hundred a week for openers."

"What have you boys been smoking?" I said.

"It's a shoo-in, Marcia." De Palma took over in that sure, slick, black-knit-tie, bright-young-senior way he had. You could see him being the most enterprising prexy the Psi U's ever had. "Lonesome is the biggest thing in home entertainment today. His Nielsen is seventeen point nine. His penetration is . . ."

"Marshy," Lonesome said. "In three years I'm going to be a lousy millionaire. I'm going to have half a dozen cars. I'll have two hundred suits. I'll have a private railroad car and a yacht, maybe a plane and a big place in the country. And I'll tell the people what to eat and who to help and what to think."

"The most authentic voice of the people since Will Rogers," said Tommy de Palma.

"Bigger'n Rogers," Lonesome said. "I got more mediums to be big on. The biggest."

"The greatest," said Tommy de Palma.

"And without you, Marshy," Lonesome said, "—and that's the reason I wanted you to come over—without you, why kid myself?—I'd still be a bum."

"Let's face it," I said. "With me you're still a bum. A bum with a corny magic touch. A bum with money."

"I do a lot of good," Lonesome said. "The charities. The BK. I'm gonna start plugging a Lonesome Rhodes Summer Camp for poor city kids. Before I'm through with 'em every sucker in the country is gonna love me."

"Mrs. Rhodes doesn't love you," I said.

"That bag," he said. "That bad dream. My nemesis. She just called me."

"Some simple soul," I said. "Some spokesman for the good family life. Next time you propose to anybody you might consider getting unmarried first."

"Marshy, so help me God, I got a divorce in Mexico, but the judge got indicted for fraud, so my ex claims it didn't take. Now she thinks she's got a gun at my head. Well, OK, I'll give 'er her stinkin' three thousand a month —anything to get her off my neck. I'm nuts about you, Marshy. I can't live without you."

"On the cigar-box guitar it might sound good," I said.

De Palma rose, straightened his creases and said, "Gotta run, kiddies. Early-morning golf game with Mr. Peerless himself. Here's a good-night drink to Rhodes, de Palma and Coulihan. Dat's how dynasties are born."

Lonesome and I did a little Indian wrestling on the couch. It's a good thing I have muscles from my tennis days.

"Larry," I said, "the marriage department is one of the things I never fool with. Next thing you know we're all in one great mess. Bad for us, and not too healthy for Rhodes, de Palma and Coulihan, either."

"Then you're comin' along?"

Well, I suppose I was. If a girl is going in for careers she might as well make it a good one. It looked as if I had found a home with Lonesome Rhodes, Inc.

"Thanks, Marshy," Lonesome said. "I wouldn't tell this to anybody else, but sometimes early in the morning I get kind of scared, Marsh. Sure, I wanna be a success. I got the gimmees just about as bad as anybody, but, shucks, I never figgered on anything like this. The number-one rating and the column and the comic strip and the Grandpaw Bascom dolls and Lonesome Rhodes drinks this and smokes that and everybody hangin' on my opinion of how t' bring back the good ol' hundred-cent dollar. It's enough t' scare a fella."

Poor Lonesome. Of course these moments of self-doubt and humility were few and far between, early morning bottom-of-the-bottle lapses, but they were genuine enough while he was having them. Then they would lift like a bad headache and he'd be his old braggy, egocentric, happy St. Bernard self again. Lonesome just had a severe case of American success, that's all. I doubt if there was ever anything like it in the history of the world. For one thing it takes a free (and free-wheeling) society for a success like his, and for another it takes a particular hopped-up kind of free society. Our kind, God bless it. This is a real screwball country, if you stop to think about it. Where else would the girls be tearing the clothes off skinny, pasty-faced boys with neurotic voices like Frank Sinatra and Johnny Ray? Or making Lonesome Rhodes, an obvious concoction if ever there was one, their favorite lover-boy and social philosopher?

I tried to explain it to Lonesome, and to myself, that night. I came on with some of that stuff I had learned in school about the frontier. This country has a terrible hankering for its lost frontier, the way a mother forever mourns for a son run down by a truck when he was seven years old. The frontier song is ended, but oh how the melody lingers on. That's why we don't trust brain-trusters and professors. Lonesome said it perfectly on the air one day. "My Grandpaw Bascom never went to no school an' he was the smartest fella in the county. Everything I know I owe t' my Granddaddy Bascom who didn' know nuthin' either. But Grandpap Bascom, the ol' rascal, did say one thing . . ." And then Lonesome would sound off on some crackpot scheme and next thing I'd know there would be a bushel basket of letters to answer, saying as how it was a shame Lonesome wasn't in Washington teaching those fancy-talkin' politicians a little common sense. Once you get on that kind of a cracker-barrel American kick, you can only go up. Where it would all end I both dreaded and was fascinated to wonder.

I told him how it would be with us if I went on with him to New York. Strictly career, strictly the girl assistant, associate producer, maid of all work or whatever I was.

"I've gotta have you with me one way or another, Marshy," he said. "I know I'm great and America needs me, but without you I'd be back in Nowhereville where I came from. You're my . . ."

"Anchor," I said. "Nursemaid. Ballast. The salt in your stew."

"You can laugh," he said. "When you get way out in front like I am you need a friendly face. Without you, I'm up there all by my lonesome. I'm all alone."

"You can't sing it on the air," I said, "until I clear the rights with Berlin."

"Marshy, stay all night," he pleaded. "Twin beds. I promise I won't lay a finger on you. Brother 'n sister."

"I wouldn't trust you," I told him, "if we were lying side by side in twin coffins."

"I'm a baad boy," he said, with all his heavy charm.

"You're Huck Finn with a psychoneurosis," I scolded. "God, if your public only knew what a slender reed they were leaning on."

"That's our little secret, Marshy," he said, and gave it the deep-belly haw-haw.

I finally got away and he said, "Good night, pardner," and went back to suck on his bottle. America's Uncle Lonesome, Big Brother to all the world.

II

We moved on to New York, into a humble seven-room suite in the Waldorf Towers. There was so much work to do that I had to hire an assistant, and pretty soon she had to have an assistant. Lonesome made the cover of *Life,* with a two-page spread on Riddle, Arkansas, and one of those Luce think-pieces on "The Meaning of Lonesome Rhodes." America, in this complex age of supergovernment, overtaxation and atomic anxieties, was harking back to the simple wisdoms that had made her great, said *Life*. The mass swing to Lonesome was a sign of this harking.

Lonesome was the indisputable king of television now and his daily column, written by two of his abler press agents, was syndicated in three hundred papers. There were Lonesome Rhodes hand puppets for the kiddies and the cigar-box guitar was rapidly becoming our national instrument. The Waldorf Towers layout made Bedlam seem like Arcadia. We had a staff of writers now to devise the folksy anecdotes that Lonesome delivered so spontaneously. And there were TV and radio executives under foot all the time. And the sponsors' people, and the advertising supernumeraries, and job seekers, and the theatrical reporters, and of course the press agents. They formed their own not-so-little group of court favorites around Lonesome. They laughed at his witticisms and marveled at the way he could hold his liquor and wondered out loud if show business had ever had such a philanthropical, sagacious and all-around-helluva-fella. Lonesome's ego expanded like a giant melon. It became very difficult and rare for him to stop talking about Lonesome Rhodes. He would hold the press agents spellbound with tales of Lonesome Rhodes Foundation benevolences: how he helped a whole village of Maine fishermen starving from seasonal unemployment by setting up a cigar-box guitar factory— the fishermen were using their surplus gut and wire leaders for strings—and how he had saved the land of a sixty-year-old farmer with arthritis who was being dispossessed.

"Shucks, neighbors," he'd run off at the mouth, forgetting that these were just the hangers-on and not his great American public, "if us plain ordinary simple folks 'd just help each other a little more—think about a good-neighbor policy at home instead of way down there in those banana republics that hate our guts, anyway—why heck we wouldn't need all this alphabet soup we got in Washington. As Grandpaw Bascom used t' put it, what we need is a little more good old-fashioned Christianity and a whole lot less of this new fangled bee-you-rock-racy." Lonesome never went to church himself—Sunday mornings were always spent in what he called Hangovertown —but he was a great one for telling everybody else to get up out of bed and "show the Fellow Upstairs you haven't forgotten Him." It was as on the level as a nine-dollar bill, but at least half a dozen sects made him an Honorary Elder, and Interdenominational Faith Conferences were always presenting him with plaques and diplomas. We've got one whole closet full of the stuff. It was all done for a purpose, Lonesome's purpose, but even though behind the scenes I could see what it really was, I had to admit that he did a lot of good in his own egotistical way. The Lonesome Rhodes Summer Camp for underprivileged kids of mixed races and faiths became quite a thing. Lonesome Rhodes was far from an unmixed evil or an unmixed blessing. He had a kind of mixed-up evil genius for doing good, along with a warm-hearted gift for working evil.

Even if he had been a lot more stable than he was, it would have been superhuman for him to keep his balance with Tommy de Palma and the rest of the Towers coterie constantly at his elbow inflating his already dangerously stretched self-esteem. Lonesome only had to mention something casually into the mike, or hold it in his hand as if by accident, and the product was made. One night he happened to mention that he liked to play acey-deucey to relax from the pressure of TV rehearsals, and presto, acey-deucey started replacing canasta as the latest civilian fad. He happened to toss off the phrase "as cocky as a teen-ager driving a Jaguar" and next morning there was a brand-new Mark 7 Jag at the door, free and clear. Every gadget company in the Republic had their

scouts roaming the corridors of the Waldorf hoping to in-
veigle Lonesome into giving them a little accidental or ac-
cidentallike publicity on the air. Everything in the world
he wanted in the way of wine, women, fast cars and fire-
arms (he had become a big gun collector with a wall full
of Kentucky rifles at $400 a throw) was ponied up for
him by grateful or hopeful anglers. There were always
half a dozen models loping around. They used to make
me feel pretty dowdy, sometimes, those numbers. Our
suite with money and wine and women and worried executives and slave writers and stooges was just about as
close as you can get in this country and this century to the
ancient splendors of the Persian kings. I didn't know
whether to laugh or cry every time I heard Lonesome
(with his Cadillac and his Jaguar and his Waldorf Towers
and his advertising company and his stocks and bonds and
his complexes) telling his credulous listeners, "A-course I
may not know what I'm a-talkin' about, I'm just one of
these Arkansas farm boys with the dirt still on me. . . ."
That wasn't dirt, that was money sticking to him.

The only thing the press agents and the sponsors couldn't
give him was me. Not that he needed me, God knows,
with all those good-looking dolls floating around, but he
had got it into his greedy little head that he did. Because
I was the only one who didn't come crawling and scraping,
I suppose. Because I was just as sassy with him as the
first day he shuffled in way back there in Fox, Wyoming,
with holes in his shoes. Because I was the only one who
would tell him off when he got out of line. He had fallen
into the habit of going around half-crocked all the time
and after one performance when he had held forth on
the homespun American virtues in a voice that was un-
mistakably thick-tongued, I chewed him out for being a
sloppy unprofessional, and threatened to walk off the job
if he didn't pull himself together. We played one of
those late, feverish, "I'd straighten up and fly right if only

you married me" scenes. He said it looked like his agreement with the first Mrs. Rhodes was going through. She
was down in the Virgin Islands having a divorce.
I said maybe. I said wait and see. I said he was a hand-
ful and there were troubles enough being his business
associate without taking on the personal responsibility,
too. He said he wanted a farm to get his sense of values
back, to get away from the squirrel cage of television. He
said he thought if he was married and settled down and
had a farm, raised Black Angus and some kids, he wouldn't
drink so much and be such a bastard. He said he knew I
was ready to write him off as a slob but it was just this
crazy pace and the fame coming down on him before he
knew what hit him. He told me how he suffered from in-
somnia and how he talked about himself too much because deep down he knew he wasn't as great as Tommy de
Palma and the rest of them talked him up. Nobody was.
Deep down, he said, he was really a shy and sensitive guy.
He said the brag act and the Great-I-Am bit was just a
cover-up for the real Larry Rhodes. I was the only one
he could admit that to, he said, and that's why he needed
me and had to marry me. He'd take a high dive off the
window ledge if I said no. Early hour hairdowns like
this, I could almost be persuaded; there was that nice,
warm St. Bernard side to him, even if it was a pretty
neurotic St. Bernard. I told him I didn't warm to this
high dive into no water idea. I didn't like the responsibility. I told him anybody who kept making those threats
and meant them ought to have his brains examined. I
even gave him the name of an analyst friend of mine.
He walked me to the door and kissed me fondly.
"Marshy," he said, "if you marry me I may even soften
up in my old age and get kinda liberal."
That had become a running gag with us. My common
man with his two-hundred-dollar suits and his twelve-
dollar neckties was about as liberal as William Howard

Taft. He was all for scrapping the UN and for going back to the open shop. I used to kid him that one of these days he'd run for President, Arkansas accent, cigar-box *git*-tar and all, on a platform of child labor and the sixteen-hour day. "Shucks, back in Riddle, my Uncle Bloomer went to work in the distillery when he was seven and it sure made a man of him in a hurry. By the time he was nine his daddy made him take the pledge. Yessir, nothin' like child labor, folks, t' build self-reliance." That's my boy.

On Lonesome's next show he made a pitch about the Amurican home that was really a beaut. He sang "Home Sweet Home" and there wasn't a dry eye in the house. Nobody had done so much for the marriage business since Edward VIII tossed a kingdom away for "the woman I love." Lonesome even had Lonesome weeping. Of course if anyone had analyzed the tears he would have found them high in alcohol content. Still, Lonesome could cry with the best of them. He was one of those magnificent fakes who could overwhelm himself with his own sincerity.

The night of this telecast he flew out to Arkansas to see a football game and to judge the State drum-majorette contest. I should have mentioned—and you might have guessed—that among Lonesome's cultural hobbies was a passionate enthusiasm for drum-majoring and drum-majoretting. He was rather an accomplished amateur baton twirler himself and he had announced that he would bring the lucky winner back to appear on his program with him.

Monday morning I went out to meet the incoming plane, but Lonesome wasn't on it. I tried to phone him at his Little Rock hotel, but he had checked out. And of course he was due for a program rehearsal at three. He never showed. I could have killed him. I had to scurry around and hurry up a substitute. About fifteen minutes

before we went on I got a wire from Lonesome. He was
in Juarez, Mexico. He said Mary-Mae Fleckum, the winning drum-majorette, had just done him the honor of
becoming Mrs. Rhodes. He added something about
holding the fort.

Three days later he planed in with his Mary-Mae. She
was a trim little corn-fed blonde with a provocative little
can, a syrupy purr and a way of being dumb that seemed
almost calculated, it was so extreme. Mary-Mae became
part of the folk program. She'd appear in tight-fitting
rompers, doing her cakewalk and throwing her bottom
and her baton around. She could also yodel. Lonesome
had really found himself a hunk of talent in this Fleckum
kid. He drooled over her on and off the program. He
called her his little Arkansas sweet potato.

I went in and said it was about time I took a vacation
and at the end of my vacation I thought I would resign.
There were any number of good TV jobs open for me
now, less money but also less Lonesome Rhodes.

Lonesome took me into his private study, which looked
like a medium-sized arsenal, and said he had wanted to
have a heart-to-heart talk ever since he got back. I said,
"Let's make it a heart talk because I can just barely make
out one heart between the two of us."

"Now Marshy, now Marshy honey," he kept saying.
He said it had been on his conscience to explain how he
happened to marry Mary-Mae instead of me. He was
afraid to marry me, he said. Last week he had been
afraid not to, I reminded him. They were both true, he
said, but I overawed him. I knew more than he did and
I was terribly critical. I didn't really approve of him. I
made him feel small. Mary-Mae was just the opposite.
Mary-Mae adored and worshipped him. For Mary-Mae
being the wife of Lonesome Rhodes and living in this
Waldorf penthouse with him was a Cinderella dream
come true. I said, "Mary-Mae is your public in one cute

little package. This is the logical culmination of the great twentieth-century love affair between Lonesome Rhodes and his mass audience."

"She's a little honey," Lonesome said.

"Sweet potatoes and honey," I said. "That's a mighty rich diet."

"I wish you weren't so bitter," Lonesome said. "You're a darned good-looking girl and you can be a lot of fun but you've got a chip on your shoulder."

"I didn't come in here to discuss my personality," I said. "That's my problem. I came to tell you good-bye and I want out."

"You can have the vacation," he said, "but then you've got to come back and work with me on a regular business basis. This thing is too big for you to quit. Lonesome Rhodes, Inc., is good for over a million a year now. Not to mention Rhodes, de Palma and Coulihan."

"It can be just Rhodes and de Palma," I said. "You two barefoot boys can buy me out. I think I'll take a job with 'Author Meets the Critics'."

"Books," he said. Lonesome Rhodes the oracle felt he was well read when he got through the *News* and *Mirror*. "Who reads books?"

"Just a few of us," I said. "Just a few hundred thousand die-hards."

"Have fun, Marshy," Lonesome said. "Blow your stack and come on back. But don't get stuck on anybody or I'll get jealous."

Just then Mary-Mae burst in. She did a kind of jazzy military strut even when she wasn't on. "Loancie," she purred, snaking her firm golden arms around him, "I want you to take Mary-Mae down to Schrafft's for a cherry ice-cream soda with oodles of whipped-cream on top."

Lonesome patted her with distracted appreciation. "Tell Tommy to have them send you one up here right away, sweetie. Now beat it, sugar, this is business."

"I'm leaving anyway," I said. "I'm off for the Islands. So why don't you do the big thing and take her to Schrafft's? She probably never has had a chance to see life as it is lived dangerously and fatteningly on Fifth Avenue."

Mary-Mae giggled. "I can never get enough cherry ice-cream sodas."

"That's how Lonesome is about drum-majorettes," I said, wishing I could have resisted being a cat. "The two of you should be very happy."

"Thank you very much I'm sure," I heard Mrs. Rhodes say as I went out the door with my very best posture.

I went down to Cuba, to a nice informal Cuban hotel on the beach at Veradero. It was pleasure to be away from that madhouse in the Waldorf Towers and to be rid of Lonesome Rhodes. I even met a man who interested me for the first time in years. He was one of the editors of the New York *Times* Magazine and he was well read and I liked his mind and at the same time he could be fun. We both liked the same kind of vacation, going barefoot and wearing any old thing and we went fishing together and had good talks on the beach and in the thatch-roof bars. I wondered if I had had to get Lonesome out of my life before anything could happen to me with any other man. I wondered if an analyst would have told me that Lonesome had been a kind of father figure in my life. I was half in love with him and half driven to get rid of him. And kick him in the teeth for farewell. Anyway now that Lonesome wasn't around like a giant sponge to suck me up into his life along with all the others, I was getting along nicely.

When we went up to Havana to make the rounds one evening I ran across a copy of *Time* and that's how I saw the latest development on Lonesome. He had delivered one of his Open Letters To VIP's—this one to Churchill, telling him Great Britain should get off our gravy train and warning him that Lonesome was ready to give up on the British and advise the American people to close them out just as we would any other bankrupt outfit. America would be better off, he had told his thirty million viewers and listeners, when she stood alone, "just as we stood in the days of the war against England when we first gained our independence." If I had been around I never would have let that go through. I had been doing a fair job of x-ing out the most extreme of Lonesome's antediluvian views. And in the second place I could have told him that we weren't exactly alone in 1776. There was Lafayette, and the Polish boys Pulaski and Kosciusko. Not to mention France and Spain and half of Europe lined up against the Redcoats all over the world. It was amazing and frightening how Lonesome, this cigar-box gondolier, would sound off on global issues without the vaguest knowledge of factual or historical background. A bold know-nothing who, in the courage of his ignorance, hadn't the slightest hesitation in getting up and telling his "neighbors"—which was just everybody in America—how to run their own and the nation's business.

But what was startling about this down-with-England pitch was the official response it drew. A Labor leader in the British Parliament got up and demanded that Churchill ask Lonesome to apologize for his intemperate remarks. There was a full debate on the floor which aired Labor and Conservative views on American relations. Churchill said it was preposterous for the English even to consider interfering with American freedom of speech, although naturally he deplored Mr. Lonesome Rhodes' rather uncharitable view of his British cousins. "Apparently he thinks us of an even lower order than his relations in Riddle," said the Prime Minister, thereby spreading the fame of Grandpaw Bascom and Cousin Abernathy to the far side of the Atlantic. New York papers had it on their front pages for nearly a week. Lonesome had become the darling of the Chicago *Trib*, the New York *Journal* and the *Daily News* while the *Times* and the New York *Trib* were writing polite editorials suggesting that Lonesome go home to Riddle for a while and rest up from international affairs.

One night, it must have been around three in the morning, I was enjoying one of those deep Caribbean sleeps, with the fresh warm air blowing in from the sea, when I heard someone knocking on my door. "Telayphone, pleece, long deestance." I jumped up and threw a robe around me and hurried down to the desk phone in the lobby. I was scared to death it was my old man. He hadn't been very well. But it wasn't my father. It was Lonesome Rhodes. "Lonesome, how did you know where I was staying?" That was easy, he had seen the card I had sent my assistant from Veradero and he had simply gone down the list of hotels. "Marshy," he said, "how soon can you get back to New York? You've gotta come back right away."

"Hah," I said, "or should I say *haw?*"

"No kiddin', I need ya bad, Marshy girl, I need ya real bad."

"What's happened, England declare war on you?"

"Those limey bastards. The hell with them. You shoulda heard me tonight—I really gave Churchill a piece of my mind. If there's any war declarin' t' do, I'm the one who's gonna do it. But I'll come to that in a minute. That's not why I need ya, Marshy. I need ya to live with me."

"You and I and the drum-majorette—that will be cozy."

"Mary-Mae, she's no good, Marshy. She's nuthin' but a good-for-nuthin' little tramp, Marshy. I just kicked her little ass right the hell out of here. The hell with her. It was you I wanted all the time, Marshy. I can't live without you."

"Then I'm afraid your days are numbered, Larry," I said.

"Please, Marshmallow. I'm on my knees. Right here in front of the telephone. I'm on my knees."

"If you had some white gloves you could sing 'Mammy,' " I said.

"There's a window right behind me. If you don't promise you'll come back on the next plane I'll jump out the window tonight."

"Oh, jump," I said.

"You don't believe me," he said. "You think I haven't got the guts. Well I've got the window open right now, what do you think of that? And I swear to God I am gonna use it if you don't promise to catch the next plane back."

"Lonesome," I told him, "listen. I found someone down here. The first one who's made sense to me since I got out of school. It's serious. I have a feeling it's going to work."

"Oh Jesus," Lonesome was blubbering, "what've I done that everybody should be against me? I won't be able to live if some bastard takes you away from me. I'll jump. I'll jump. I wanna die."

I thought of all the three A.M. alarms I had answered. I thought, This is a poker game and all the money is in the pot now and now is the time to call him. There was a terrible curiosity in me to see what would happen if I didn't come running. If this time I stood my own ground. I had made it too easy for him. He was an extreme personality from his shoelaces to the careless lock of hair over his forehead, and I had cushioned it for him all the way. I had toned down the views that would have made him sound like a sweet-talking Father Coughlin, and I had provided a line of emotional continuity between ex-wives and models and new wives and assorted tramps. I had been home plate, or rather the locker room where you ease up after the game, win or lose. And I had been the little cog of efficiency without which the great streamlined express breaks down. Lonesome Rhodes had been my career, my Frankenstein, my crime.

"So jump, jump," I said. "Get out of my life. Get out of everybody's life."

"Okey-doke," he shouted. "If you tell me to do it, I'll do it. It'll be your fault."

"Jump, jump, jump," I couldn't stop saying, in a broken rage. I would never forgive him if he did, and of course I could never forgive him if he didn't.

"All right," he said. "All right. You told me, Marshy. Never forget you were the one who told me. I can't decide whether to do it tonight or wait until after my broadcast tomorrow. I have a very important broadcast tomorrow. I am going to declare war."

"Just you? Without even bothering to inform Congress?"

"The people will inform Congress," he explained. "I've had enough of these Russkies and Chinks and foreigners pushin' us around. I say it's better to get it over with now while we're strong than wait for decay to set in. Like my Cousin Abernathy used t' say . . ."

"Please," I said, "on the great American public you get away with it, but don't perpetrate that fake cousin on me."

He believed he had a Cousin Abernathy, that was the frightening part. And now he believed he *could* declare war, that was even more frightening. The screw that always had been loose in him had worked itself free and the motor was coming apart. He was saying, "If I tell the people to declare war they will flood the White House and their congressmen with letters and telegrams. The GI's will insist on going into action. Volunteer militias will rise in every town and hamlet in America. The people listen to Lonesome Rhodes. The people act with Lonesome Rhodes."

It frightened me. Maybe he was only bluffing. Trying

to get a rise out of me. He knew how I felt about irresponsible amateurs with mass followings sounding off on international crises. He knew where I stood on these oracles who flunk the most elementary course in human relations but never hesitate to tell us how we could have saved those three hundred million Chinese from Communism or how to turn back the tides of Africa. So maybe this idea of declaring war was his idea of how to have fun with Marshy. But what if it was what he said it was? He had been able to bring the British to a boil. What was to stop him from bringing the whole world to the popping point? "In the Event of an Enemy Attack"—I saw those ominous billboards showing up among soft-drink and cigarette ads along American highways. I saw the fatal mushroom of atomic ruin rising above gutted, faceless cities. I saw Lonesome Rhodes as a gum-chewing Nero strumming his cigar-box *git*-tar and easing into the commercials while civilization burned.

"All right," I said. "Don't jump. I'll come. On one condition. That you hold off your war until I get there."

"Don't think you can talk me out of it, Marshy baby," he said. "I'm fed up. I'm loaded for bear."

"You're loaded, there's not much doubt about that," I said. "Now go to bed. Cool off. Sleep on the war."

"I'm sick 'n tired o' being stalled," he said. "The night before last I tried to get Joe Stalin on the phone. I figgered if Joe and I could get out behind the old woodshed together we might be able to work something out. But the big bum thinks he's too high 'n mighty to talk to me. Okay, sez I, I got an army of fifty million viewers back o' me, ready to march when I blow the whistle. I'll settle his hash."

"Take a hot bath," I said. "And then two empirin and a phenobarbital. And stay in bed and rest until I get in."

I flew in early the next afternoon and went right to the Waldorf. Lonesome was in a terrible state. He hadn't shaved in three or four days and there was so much Irish whiskey in him that he smelled like a branch of Jameson's. Whiskey had stained his bathrobe and empty bottles made a slum of his penthouse suite.

"Marshy honey, bless you, baby," he said when I came in. "Stay here and marry me and you'll be the first lady of America. Lonesome Rhodes Clubs all over the country want me to run for President. But I'm not sure I want it. I can't do everything myself."

"Please," I said. "Just no war today. I'm simply not ready for war today."

"Marshy, honey, for you I'll do anything. I should have had my head examined for marrying that little baton-twirler from North Little Rock. The kid sure could twirl, though. One in each hand and play the harmonica at the same time. She could even do it on her toes. But I need someone worthy of me. Someone with a brain who I c'n talk to." He reached for the bottle and I could see how his hand was trembling. "Damn it, nobody hates war more'n I do. But they got me mad now. Why do I have to have all the responsibility? But if Washington is too lily-livered to act . . ."

He gulped the whiskey and staggered to his desk, pushing a jumble of papers, clippings and letters aside to find something he was looking for.

"I woulda jumped," he said. "You didn' believe me. Here—here's the note I wrote to leave behind." He picked it up and read it to me in a hoarse, maudlin voice. It told of his grief for the fine American boys having to sacrifice themselves in foreign lands. He said he was sorrowing for all his American neighbors threatened with extinction in another terrible war. "For me this whole great country of ours is just Riddle, Arkansas, multiplied," he wound it up. "Every one of you is my Cousin Abernathy, my Aunt Lucybelle, my Grandpaw Bascom. God bless you and keep you all, my beloved kinfolk and neighbors."

"But you told me you were going out the window for

my sake," I protested. "Why do you drag in this other routine?"

He gave me one of those slow, inebriated winks. "My public," he said. "This is high-level BK stuff. The highest possible level. They gotta believe I love 'em to the end. Get it?"

"Yes," I said. "I think I get it."

"Smart girl," he said. "Why don't we have one more drink and then you crawl into the sack with me? The hell with everybody."

"That's not what I came back for," I said.

"Hell with everybody," he shouted. "Hell with you too if you don't be a good little girl and play house with Poppa."

His face was flushed and his eyes were crazy.

I said, "Larry, get into bed and I'll get you some sleeping pills. And for God's sake, stop drinking. I'll have the doctor come and give you a shot if you won't stop."

"Gotta put on a show at nine o'clock," he said. "Gotta declare war. *War!*" he shouted. "This means *war!*"

"Shhhh," I said, "you've got to lie down. You've got to be quiet for a while. I'll get Bert Wheeler or someone to take your place tonight. You need some sleep. Rest. Peace. Shhhhh."

He reached out his arm for me and almost lost his balance. I put my hand on his elbow to steady him. He grabbed me and we tottered together. He tried to force his mouth against mine. "Larry, for God's sake, let me go," I said. I broke away and ran down the hall. Lonesome came running heavily after me. "Hey Marshy, quit runnin'. Let's roll in the hay together." His big voice was right behind me. I had reached the marble steps leading down to the entrance hallway of the duplex suite. I ran down two steps at a time.

"Hey Marshy, let's . . ."

Then an ugly sound of hopeless protest came out of him. The staggering bulk of him had lost its balance on the top step and was floundering, hurling, thudding down. I could feel the back of his head striking the marble ledge of each step as he lurched to the bottom landing.

He made a low, broken moan and lay still. I was afraid to move him. I ran to the phone and called Tommy de Palma. When I told him what had happened, Tommy took the name of our Lord in vain, but quite solemnly. Then he said, "Listen, Marcia. You get the hell out of there. I'll be right over and take care of everything. And never tell anybody—I mean *anybody*—how it happened."

A few hours later it was all over for Lonesome Rhodes, at least the corporeal part. A compound fracture of the skull had removed his name from the Nielsen ratings. He had become a living legend even before he lost his balance on that top step and now Tommy de Palma did a beautiful job of rounding out the myth. On all the front pages it said that Lonesome's death was due to collapsing on the stairs from overwork on his way to deliver a message of tremendous importance to his vast radio-TV audience. "We begged him to slow down, but as long as his great heart kept pumping he had to keep pitching for his fellow-Americans," Tommy was quoted. Tommy had found the suicide note and without mentioning the window business he had used the sure-fire stuff about grieving and sorrowing for the fine American boys and his fellow countrymen. "I was with him at the end and I will remember his last words as long as I live," Tommy said. I'll remember those words too, but not quite the way Tommy reported them. He used that "great country of ours is just Riddle multiplied" line and wound up with the "bless you and keep you, my beloved kinfolk and neighbors" bit.

Tommy announced that the Lonesome Rhodes Foundation would continue as a lasting memorial to this simple American. Immediately thousands of dollars poured in from all over the country to keep up the good works. Plans were drawn up for a monument to Lonesome in Riddle with his famous last words inscribed at the base of a vast likeness in bronze. Well, Tommy can have his last words. They're a little more fit for public examination than what the man really said when he was chasing me down those steps.

The funeral was the most impressive thing of its kind I have ever seen. Traffic was suspended on Fifth Avenue and the great thoroughfare was jammed for twenty blocks. Half a million people tried to pass the bier. Women grew hysterical and fainted. The Mayor was there, and General MacArthur, and a Marine Honor Guard and Ike sent personal condolences. The entire population of Riddle, Arkansas, was flown in by the publicity department of our TV network. A cowhand from Arkansas sang, "Oh Bury Me Not on the Lone Prairie." A bishop spoke on the spiritual essence in Lonesome Rhodes. "He was a man of the people," said the bishop, "because he was, in the simplest and deepest and best sense, a man of God."

It was a shame Lonesome Rhodes couldn't have been there. He would have loved it. It was his kind of stuff, exactly as if it had been written for him and directed by him. He was an influence, there is no doubt of that. Look at the half-dozen minor imitators already trying to fill his boots. The film companies have started bidding for the movie rights. Already columnists are speculating as to who could play it. John Wayne? Will Rogers, Jr.? Paul Douglas? The Lonesome Rhodes Foundation is to have a considerable share of the profits. As Tommy de Palma would say, "Dat's how legends are born."

After the funeral, I walked around the corner to a bar and went in to think it over. While I had never given myself to Lonesome Rhodes, I had belonged to him. I had had a hand in shaping that legend. How could I disown it now without having to answer for myself?

A SHORT DIGEST OF A LONG NOVEL

Her legs were shapely and firm and when she crossed them and smiled with the self-assurance that always delighted him, he thought she was the only person he knew in the world who was unblemished. Not lifelike but an improvement on life, as a work of art, her delicate features were chiseled from a solid block. The wood-sculpture image came easy to him because her particular shade of blonde always suggested maple polished to a golden grain. As it had been from the moment he stood in awe and amazement in front of the glass window where she was first exhibited, the sight of her made him philosophical. Some of us appear in beautiful colors, too, or with beautiful grains, but we develop imperfections. Inspect us very closely and you find we're damaged by the elements. Sometimes we're only nicked with cynicism.

Sometimes we're cracked with disillusionment. Or we're split with fear.

When she began to speak, he leaned forward, eager for the words that were like good music, profundity expressed in terms that pleased the ear while challenging the mind. "Everybody likes me," she said. "Absolutely everybody." It was not that she was conceited. It was simply that she was only three. No one had ever taken her with sweet and whispered promises that turned into morning-after lies, ugly and cold as unwashed dishes from last night's dinner lying in the sink. She had never heard a dictator rock her country to sleep with peaceful lullabies one day and rock it with bombs the next. She was undeceived. Her father ran his hands reverently through her soft yellow hair. She is virgin, he thought, for this is the true virginity, that brief moment in the time of your life before your mind or your body has been defiled by acts of treachery.

It was just before Christmas and she was sitting on her little chair, her lips pressed together in concentration, writing a last-minute letter to Santa Claus. The words were written in some language of her own invention but she obligingly translated as she went along.

Dear Santa, I am a very good girl and everybody likes me. So please don't forget to bring me a set of dishes, a doll that goes to sleep and wakes up again, and a washing machine. I need the washing machine because Raggedy Ann's dress is so dirty.

After she had finished her letter, folded it, and asked him to address it, he tossed her up in the air, caught her and tossed her again, to hear her giggle. "Higher, Daddy, higher," she instructed. His mind embraced her sentimentally: She is a virgin island in a lewd world. She is a winged seed of innocence blown through the wasteland.

If only she could root somewhere. If only she could grow like this.

"Let me down, Daddy," she said when she decided that she had indulged him long enough, "I have to mail my letter to Santa."

"But didn't you see him this afternoon?" he asked. "Didn't you ask for everything you wanted? Mommy said she took you up to meet him and you sat on his lap."

"I just wanted to remind him," she said. "There were so many other children."

He fought down the impulse to laugh, because she was not something to laugh at. And he was obsessed with the idea that to hurt her feelings with laughter was to nick her, to blemish the perfection.

"Daddy can't catch me-ee," she sang out, and the old chase was on, following the pattern that had become so familiar to them, the same wild shrieks and the same scream of pretended anguish at the inevitable result. Two laps around the dining-room table was the established course before he caught her in the kitchen. He swung her up from the floor and set her down on the kitchen table. She stood on the edge, poised confidently for another of their games. But this was no panting, giggling game like tag or hide-and-seek. This game was ceremonial. The table was several feet higher than she was. "Jump, jump, and Daddy will catch you," he would challenge. They would count together, *one, two* and on *three* she would leap out into the air. He would not even hold out his arms to her until the last possible moment. But he would always catch her. They had played the game for more than a year and the experience never failed to exhilarate them. You see, I am always here to catch you when you are falling, it said to them, and each time she jumped, her confidence increased and their bond deepened.

They were going through the ceremony when the woman

next door came in with her five-year-old son, Billy. "Hello, Mr. Steevers," she said. "Would you mind if I left Bill with you for an hour while I go do my marketing?"

"No, of course not, glad to have him," he said and he mussed Billy's hair playfully. "How's the boy, Billy?"

But his heart wasn't in it. This was his only afternoon of the week with her and he resented the intrusion. And then too, he was convinced that Billy was going to grow up into the type of man for whom he had a particular resentment. A sturdy, good-looking boy, big for his age, aggressively unchildlike, a malicious, arrogant, insensitive extrovert. I can just see him drunk and red-faced and pulling up girls' dresses at Legion Conventions, Mr. Steevers would think. And the worst of it was, his daughter seemed blind to Billy's faults. The moment she saw him she forgot about their game.

"Hello, Billy-Boy," she called and ran over to hug him.

"I want a cookie," said Billy.

"Oh, yes, a cookie; some animal crackers, Daddy."

She had her hostess face on and as he went into the pantry, he could hear the treble of her musical laughter against the premature baritone of Billy's guffaws.

He swung open the pantry door with the animal crackers in his hand just in time to see it. She was poised on the edge of the table. Billy was standing below her, as he had seen her father do. "Jump and I'll catch you," he was saying.

Smiling, confident and unblemished, she jumped. But no hands reached out to break her flight. With a cynical grin on his face, Billy stepped back and watched her fall.

Watching from the doorway, her father felt the horror that possessed him the time he saw a parachutist smashed like a bug on a windshield when his chute failed to open. She was lying there, crying, not so much in pain as in disillusionment. He ran forward to pick her up and he would never forget the expression on her face, the *new* expression, unchildlike, unvirginal, embittered.

"I hate you, I hate you," she was screaming at Billy through hysterical sobs.

Well, now she knows, thought her father, the facts of life. Now she's one of us. Now she knows treachery and fear. Now she must learn to replace innocence with courage.

She was still bawling. He knew these tears were as natural and as necessary as those she shed at birth, but that could not overcome entirely the heavy sadness that enveloped him. Finally, when he spoke, he said, a little more harshly than he had intended, "Now, now, stop crying. Stand up and act like a big girl. A little fall like that can't hurt you."

A TABLE AT CIRO'S

At half-past five Ciro's looks like a woman sitting before her dressing table just beginning to make up for the evening. The waiters are setting up the tables for the dinner trade, the cigarette and hat-check girls are changing from slacks to the abbreviated can-can costumes which are their work clothes, and an undiscovered Rosemary Clooney making her debut tonight is rehearsing. *Don't let the stars get in your eyes* . . .

A telephone rings and the operator, who is suffering from delusions of looking like Ava Gardner, answers, "Ci-ro's. A table for Mr. Nathan? For six. His usual table?" This was not what she had come to Hollywood for, to take reservations over the telephone, but even the small part she played in A. D. Nathan's plans for the evening brought her a little closer to the Hollywood that was like a mirage, always in sight but never within reach. For, like everyone else in Hollywood, the telephone operator at Ciro's had a dream. Once upon a time, ran this one, there was a Famous Movie Producer (called Goldwyn, Zanuck or A. D. Nathan) and one evening this FMP was in Ciro's placing a million-dollar telephone call when he happened to catch a glimpse of her at the switchboard. "Young lady," he would say, "you are wasting your time at that switchboard. You may not realize it, but you *are* Naomi in my forthcoming farm epic, *Sow the Wild Oat!*"

Reluctantly the operator plugged out her dream and sent word of Nathan's reservation to André. André belonged to that great International Race, head waiters, whose flag is an unreadable menu and whose language is French with an accent. Head waiters are diplomats who happened to be born with silver spoons in their hands instead of their mouths. André would have been a typical head waiter. But he had been in Hollywood too long. Which meant that no matter how good a head waiter he was, he was no longer satisfied to be one. André wanted to be a screen writer. In fact, after working only three years, André had managed to finish a screenplay, entitled, surprisingly enough, *Confessions of a Hollywood Waiter.* He had written it all by himself, in English.

With casual deliberateness (hadn't Jimmy Starr called him the poor man's Adolphe Menjou?) André picked out a table one row removed from the dance floor for Mr. Nathan. The waiter, whose ringside table was A. D. Nathan's "usual," raised a protest not entirely motivated by sentiment. In Waiter's Local 67, A. D. Nathan's fame was based not so much on his pictures as on his tips. "Mr. Nathan will have to be satisfied with this table," André explained. "All the ringside tables are already reserved."

André had to smile at his own cleverness. A. D. Nathan did not know it yet, but from the beginning André had had him in mind as the producer of his scenario. A. D. seemed the logical contact because he remembered André

as an ordinary waiter in Henry's back in the days before
pictures could talk. But André knew he needed something
stronger than nostalgia to bring himself to A.D.'s attention. Every Saturday night Nathan presided at the same
table overlooking the floor. Tonight André would make
him take a back seat. Nathan would threaten and grum-
ble and André would flash his suave head-waiter smile
and be *so sorry M'sieur Nathan, if there were only something I could do* . . . Then, at the opportune moment,
just as the floor show was about to begin, André would discover that something could be done. And when Nathan
would try to thank André with a crisp green bill for giving him the table André had been saving for him all
evening, André's voice would take on an injured tone.
*Merci beaucoup, M'sieur Nathan, thank you just the same,
but André is glad to do a favor for an old friend.*

André thought of the scene in terms of a scenario.
That was the dialogue, just roughed in, of course. Then
the business of Nathan insisting on rewarding André for
his efforts. And a close-up of André, shyly dropping his
eyes as he tells M'sieur Nathan that if he really wants to
reward André he could read *Confessions of a Hollywood
Waiter* by André de Selco.

So that was André's dream and he dreamt it all the
while he was fussing over last-minute details like a nervous hostess getting ready for a big party.

By the time Nathan's party arrived, the big room with
the cyclamen drapes and pale-green walls of tufted satin
was full of laughter, music, shop talk and an inner-circle
intimacy that hung over the place like the smoke that
rose from lipsticked cigarettes and expensive cigars. Everyone turned to stare at the newcomers, for Hollywood
celebrities have a way of gaping at each other with the
same wide-eyed curiosity as their supposedly less sophisticated brothers waiting for autographs outside.

Nathan entered with assurance, conscious of the way

"There's A. D." was breathed through the room. His figure was slight but imposing, for he carried himself with the air of a man who was used to commanding authority. There was something ghostly about him, with his white hair and pale, clean, faintly pink skin, but his eyes were intensely alive, dark eyes that never softened, even when he smiled. As he followed André toward the dance floor, actors, agents, directors and fellow-producers were anxious to catch his eye. It was "Hello, A. D. How are you tonight, A. D.?," and he would acknowledge them with a word or a nod, knowing how to strike just the right balance between dignity and cordiality.

At his side was his wife, a tall brunette with sculpture-perfect features, hardened by a willful disposition. Some still remembered her as Lita Lawlor, who seemed on the verge of stardom not so many years ago. But she had sacrificed her screen career for love, or so the fan magazines had put it, though gossippers would have you believe that Lita was just swapping one career for another that promised somewhat more permanent security.

Accompanying the Nathans were a plain, middle-aged couple whom no one in Ciro's could identify, an undiscovered girl of seventeen who was beautiful in an undistinguished way, and Bruce Spencer, a young man whom Nathan was grooming as the next Robert Taylor. And grooming was just the word, for this male ingénue pranced and tossed his curly black mane like a horse on exhibition.

André led the party to the inferior table he had picked out for them.

"Wait a minute. André, this isn't my table," Nathan protested.

He frowned at André's silky explanations. He was in no mood to be crossed this evening. It seemed as if everything was out of sync today. First his three-thousand-dollar-a-week writer had turned in a dime-a-dozen script.

Then he had decided that what he needed was an evening alone with something young and new like this Jenny Robbins, and instead here he was with his wife, that young ham of hers, and those Carterets he'd been ducking for months. And to top everything, there was that business in New York.

Impatiently Nathan beckoned the waiter. "A magnum of Cordon Rouge, 1935."

1935, Nathan thought. That was the year he almost lost his job. It was a funny thing. All these people hoping to be tossed a bone never thought of A. D. Nathan as a man with a job to hold. But that year, when the panic struck and the banks moved in, he had had to think fast to hold onto that big office and that long title. He wondered what would have become of him if he had lost out. He thought of some of the magic names of the past, like Colonel Selig and J. C. Blackburn, who could walk into Ciro's now without causing a head to turn. And he thought how frightening it would be to enter Ciro's without the salaaming reception he always complained about but would have felt lost without.

But he mustn't worry. His psychiatrist had told him not to worry. He looked across at Jenny with that incredibly young face, so pretty and soft, like a marmalade kitten, he thought. A little wearily, he raised his glass to her. He wondered what she was like, what she was thinking, whether she would. Then he looked at Mimi Carteret. How old she and Lew had become. He could remember when they were the regulars at the Embassy Club and the Coconut Grove. Now their eyes were shining like tourists' because it had been such a long time since their last evening in Ciro's.

"Is the wine all right, Lew?" Nathan asked.

Lew Carteret looked up, his face flushed. "All right! I haven't had wine like this . . ." He paused to think. "In a long time," he said.

There was a silence, and Nathan felt embarrassed for him. He was glad when Mimi broke in with the anecdote about the time during Prohibition when they were leaving for Europe with their Western star, Tex Bradley, and Tex insisted on bringing his own Scotch along because he was afraid to trust those foreign bootleggers.

Nathan was only half-listening, though he joined in the laughter. When is Carteret going to put the bite on me for that job he wants?, he was thinking. And what will I have to give the little marmalade kitten? And though he could not divine André's plans, or guess how he figured in the dreams of the telephone operator who looked like Ava Gardner, he could not help feeling that Ciro's was a solar system in which he was the sun and around which all these satellites revolved.

"André," he beckoned, "will you please tell the operator I'm expecting a very important long-distance call?" An empty feeling of excitement rose inside him, but he fought it down. The dancers were swaying to a tango. Nathan saw Spencer and Lita, whirling like professionals, conscious of how well they looked together. He looked at Jenny, and he thought, with a twinge of weariness, of all the Jennys he had looked at this way. "Would you like to dance, my dear?"

He was an old man to Jenny, an old man she hardly knew, and it seemed to her that everybody in the room must be saying, "There goes A. D. with another one." But she tried to smile, tried to be having a terribly good time, thinking, If I want to be an actress, this is part of the job. And if I can't look as if I'm getting the thrill of my life out of dancing with this old fossil, what kind of an actress am I anyway?

Nathan could have told her what kind of an actress she was. He had expressed himself rather vividly on that subject after seeing her test that afternoon.

"Robbins stinks," he had told his assistants as the lights

came on in the projection room. "She has a cute figure and a pretty face, but not unusual enough, and her acting is from Hollywood High School."

That's what he should have told her. But he needed to be surrounded by Jenny Robbinses. Even though the analyst had told him what that was, he went on tossing them just enough crumbs of encouragement to keep their hopes alive.

"Enjoying yourself, Jenny?" he said as he led her back to the table.

"Oh, I'm having an elegant time, Mr. Nathan," she said. She tried to say it with personality, her eyes bright and her smile fixed. She felt as if she were back on the set going through the ordeal of making that test again.

"After dancing a tango together, the least we could do is call each other by our first names," he said.

He tried to remember the first time he had used that line; on Betty Bronson he thought it was. But Jenny laughed as if he had said something terribly witty. She laughed with all her ambition if not with all her heart.

Her heart—or so she thought—had been left behind at 1441½ Orange Grove Avenue. That's where Bill Mason lived. Bill worked as a grip on Nathan's lot. The grip is the guy who does the dirty work on a movie set. Or, as Bill liked to explain it, "I'm the guy who carries the set on his back. I may not be the power behind the throne but I'm sure the power *under* it."

Jenny thought of the way she and Bill had planned to spend this evening, down at the Venice Amusement Pier. They usually had a pretty good time down there together Saturday nights. It was their night. Until A. D. Nathan had telephoned, in person.

"Oh, Mr. Nathan, how lovely of you to call! I do have an appointment, but . . ."

"I wish you could cancel it, dear," Nathan had said.

"There's . . . there's something I'd like to talk to you about. I thought, over a drink at Ciro's . . ."

Jenny had never been to Ciro's, but she could describe every corner of it. It was her idea of what heaven must be like, with producers for gods and agents as their angels.

"Sorry to keep you waiting, Mac," Bill had called from the door a little later. "But that Old Bag" (referring to one of the screen's most glamorous personalities) "blew her lines in the big love scene fifteen straight times. I thought one of the juicers was going to drop a lamp on her." He looked at Jenny in the sequin dress, the pin-up model. "Hmmm, not bad. But a little fancy for roller-coasting, isn't it, honey?"

"Bill, I know I'm a monster," she had said, watching his face carefully, "but I've got to see Mr. Nathan tonight. I'd've given anything to get out of it, but, well, I don't want to sound dramatic but . . . my whole career may depend on it."

"Listen, Mac," Bill had said. "You may be kidding yourself, but you can't kid me. I was on the set when you made that test. If I'm ever going to be your husband I might as well begin right by telling you the truth. You were NG."

"I suppose you know more about acting than Mr. Nathan," she said, hating Bill, hating the Venice Pier, hating being nobody. "Mr. Nathan told me himself he wanted to keep my test to look at again."

"Are you sure it's the test he wants to keep?" Bill said.

Here in Ciro's the waiter was filling her glass again, and she was laughing at something funny and off-color that Bruce Spencer had just said. But she couldn't forget what she had done to Bill, how she had slapped him and handed back the ring, and how, like a scene from a bad B picture, they had parted forever.

For almost fifteen minutes Jenny had cried because

Bill was a wonderful fellow and she was going to miss him. And then she had stopped crying and started making up her face for A. D. Nathan because she had read too many movie magazines. This is what makes a great actress, she thought, sorrow and sacrifice of your personal happiness, and she saw herself years later as a great star, running into Bill in Ciro's after he had become a famous cameraman. "Bill," she would say, "perhaps it is not too late. Each of us had to follow our own path until they crossed again."

"Oh, by the way, Lita," A. D. had told his wife when she came into his dressing room to find out if he had any plans for the evening, "there's a little actress I'd like to take along to Ciro's tonight. Trying to build her up. So we'll need an extra man."

"We might still be able to get hold of Bruce," Lita said. "He said something about being free when we left the club this afternoon."

Nathan knew they could get hold of Bruce. Lita and Bruce were giving the Hollywood wives something to talk about over their canasta these afternoons. Sometimes he dreamt of putting an end to it. But that meant killing two birds with bad publicity. And they were both his birds, his wife and his leading man.

"All right," he said, "I'll give Spence a ring. Might not be a bad idea for the Robbins girl to be seen with him."

Lita pecked him on the cheek. Bruce was dying to get that star-making part in *Wagons Westward*. This might be the evening to talk A. D. into it.

And then, since the four of them might look too obvious, Nathan had wanted an extra couple. He tried several, but it was too late to get anybody in demand, and that's how, at the last minute, he had happened to think of the Carterets.

When you talked about old-time directors you had to

mention Lew Carteret in the same breath with D. W. Griffith and Mickey Neilan. Carteret and Nathan had been a famous combination until sound pictures and the jug had knocked Carteret out of the running. The last job he had had was a quickie Western more than a year ago. And a year in Hollywood is at least a decade anywhere else. A. D. had forgotten all about Carteret until he received a letter from him a few months ago, just a friendly letter, suggesting dinner some evening to cut up touches about old times. But A. D. knew those friendly dinners, knew he owed Carteret a debt he was reluctant to repay, and so, somehow, the letter had gone unanswered. But in spite of himself, his conscience had filed it away for further reference.

"I know who we'll get. The Lew Carterets. Been meaning to take them to dinner for months."

"Oh, God," Lita said, as she drew on a pair of long white gloves that set off her firm tanned arms, "why don't we get John Bunny and Flora Finch?"

"It might not be so bad," Nathan said, giving way to the sentimentality that thrives in his profession. "Mimi Carteret used to be a lot of fun."

"I can just imagine," said Lita. "I'll bet she does a mean Turkey Trot."

"Lew, do you think this means he's going to give you a chance again?" Mimi Carteret whispered as they walked off the dance floor together, "Easy on the wine, darling. We just can't let anything go wrong tonight."

"Don't worry, sweetheart," he answered. "I'm watching. I'm waiting for the right moment to talk to him."

Lita and Bruce were dancing again and Jenny was alone with A. D. at the table when the Carterets returned. It was the moment Jenny had been working toward. She could hardly wait to know what he thought of the test.

"I don't think it does you justice," Nathan was saying. "The cameraman didn't know how to light you at all. I think you have great possibilities."

Jenny smiled happily, the wine and encouragement going to her head, and Nathan reached over and patted her hand in what was ·meant to seem a fatherly gesture, though he lingered a moment too long. But Jenny hardly noticed, swept along in the dream.

Lew Carteret looked at his watch nervously. It was almost time for the floor show. There wouldn't be much chance to talk during the acts, and after that, the party would be over. He looked across at Mimi, trying to find the courage to put it up to A. D. If only A. D. would give him an opening. Lita and Bruce were watching too, wondering when to bring up *Wagons Westward*. And André, behind the head waiter's mask was thinking, Only ten more minutes and I will ,be speaking to A. D. about my scenario.

"André," Nathan called, and the head waiter snapped to attention. "Are you sure there hasn't been a call for me?"

"No, m'sieur. I would call you right away, m'sieur."

Nathan frowned. "Well, make sure. It should have been here by now." He felt angry with himself for losing his patience. There was no reason to be so upset. This was just another long-distance call. He had talked to New York a thousand times before—about matters just as serious.

But when André came running with the message that New York was on the wire, he could not keep the old fear from knotting his stomach and he jostled the table in his anxiety to rise.

"You may take it in the second booth on the left, Mr. Nathan," said Ava Gardner, as she looked up from her switchboard with a prefabricated smile. But he merely brushed by her and slammed the door of the booth behind him. The telephone girl looked after him with the

dream in her eyes. When he comes out I'll hafta think
of something arresting to sayta him, she decided. God,
wouldn't it be funny if he did notice me!

Five minutes later she heard the door of the booth
sliding open and she looked up and smiled. "Was the
connection clear, Mr. Nathan?"

That might do for a starter, she thought. But he didn't
even look up. "Yes. I heard very well. Thank you," he
said. He put half a dollar down and walked on. He felt
heavy, heavy all over, his body too heavy for his legs to
support and his eyes too heavy for the sockets to hold. He
walked back to the table without seeing the people who
tried to catch his glance.

"Everything all right?" his wife asked.

"Yes. Yes," he said. "Everything."

Was that his voice? It didn't sound like his voice. It
sounded more like Lew Carteret's voice. Poor old Lew.
Those were great old times when we ran World-Wide to-
gether. And that time I lost my shirt in the market and
Lew loaned me 50 G's. Wonder what ever happened to
Lew.

Then he realized this *was* Lew Carteret, and that he
was listening to Lew's voice. "A. D., this has sure been
a tonic for Mimi and me. I know we didn't come here
to talk shop, but—well, you always used to have faith in
me, and . . ."

"Sure, sure, Lew," A. D. said. "Here, you're one behind. Let me pour it. For old times."

He could feel an imperceptible trembling in his hand
as he poured the wine.

Under the table a small, slender leg moved slowly,
with a surreptitious life of its own, until it pressed mean-
ingfully against his. Jenny had never slept with anybody
except Bill. She was frightened, but not as frightened
as she was of living the rest of her life in Hollywood as
the wife of a grip in a bungalow court.

Bruce flipped open his cigarette case—the silver one

that Lita had given him for his birthday—and lit a cigarette confidently. "By the way, A. D., Lita let me read the script on *Wagons*. That's a terrific part, that bank clerk who has to go west for his health and falls in with a gang of rustlers. Wonderfully written. Who's going to play it?"

"Any leading man in Hollywood except you," Nathan said.

Bruce looked undressed without his assurance. The silence was terrible.

Lita said, "But, A. D., that part was written for Bruce."

All the rest of his face seemed to be sagging, but Nathan's hard black eyes watched them with bitter amusement. "There isn't a part in the studio that's written for Bruce. The only thing that kept Bruce from being fired months ago was me. And now there's no longer me."

Lita looked up, really frightened now. "A. D. What do you mean?"

"I mean I'm out," he said. "Finished. Washed up. Through. Hudson called to say the Board voted to ask for my resignation."

"What are you going to do now?" she said.

He thought of the thing he had promised himself to do when his time came, drop out of sight, break it off clean. Hollywood had no use for anticlimaxes on or off the screen. But as he sat there he knew what would really happen. Move over, Colonel Selig and J. C. Blackburn, he thought. Make room for another ghost.

The floor show was just starting. The undiscovered Rosemary Clooney was putting everything she had into her number, and playing right to A. D.'s table. *Don't let the stars get in your eyes* . . .

And as she sang, André smiled in anticipation. So far everything had gone just as he had planned. And now the time had come to move A. D. up to that ringside table.

MEMORY IN WHITE

He always used to stand at the entrance of the Grand
Street gymnasium, a little yellow man in an immaculate
white suit, white Panama hat, white shoes, white tie.
This was Jose Fuentes.

If you remember him at all, and you must be an old-
timer at the fight clubs if you do, you remember a tough
little Mexican kid with a wild left hook, weak on brains
but strong on heart. Young Pancho Villa the Third, he used
to call himself. No champion, never in the big money, just
another one of the kids who come along for a while, who
only know how to throw roundhouse punches with either
hand and to bounce up after a knockdown without bothering to take their count and get their wind. The kind the
fans go crazy about for a year or two and then don't recognize when they're buying peanuts or papers from them
outside the stadium a year or two later.

Club fighters, they're called, a dime a dozen, easy to hit and hard to hurt. At least, hard to knock out. Plenty of hurt, sure, plenty of pain, but that all comes later, when they can't seem to get fights any more, when they start hanging around the gym. Not training, not working, just sort of hanging around.

Now there are plenty of bums hanging around the gym every day in the week. A bum is any boxer who thinks he's going to be on Easy Street when he hangs up his gloves, and winds up on Silly Avenue instead. After that, they just hang around. They hang around waiting for another break, another manager, or a chance to pick up two, three dollars a round sparring with somebody's prospect, or a job as a second, or to put the bite on an old friend or a cocky youngster who wants to feel like a big shot. The gym is the only place they know, so all they can do is hang around and hope to make a dollar.

But no one ever hung around like Young Pancho Villa the Third. Young Pancho went into the occupation of hanging around the gym as if it were a serious and respectable profession. None of this sitting around all day on the long wooden benches with your legs stretched out in front of you as if life were one long rest period between rounds. No loitering for a man who calls himself Young Pancho Villa the Third, in honor of the Indian *guerrilla* whom the *compañeros* in the *cantinas* still sing that *corrido* about. And his valiant little namesake who lost his flyweight championship in a San Francisco ring, and, some hours later, his life in a San Francisco hospital. No panhandling for a man with a name like that. No, Young Pancho Villa the Third had a vision. He was going to get somewhere in the world. He was going to be an announcer.

For it was a funny thing, whenever he tried to think back to his days in the ring, all those fights, even that high point in his career, that main event at the Legion when Pete Sarmiento had him down nine times but couldn't put him away, all those beatings, all those rounds, all those punches he threw and the ones he caught, the whole thing seemed to run together. He would start thinking how it was in that tenth round against Sarmiento, hanging onto Pete to keep from going down, and instead he would be hanging onto Frankie Grandetta, or was it Baby Arizmendi? The memories kept spilling over and running together.

There was only one memory that stood out sharply, refusing to blend with the others. It was a memory in white, the memory of a man in a very white suit, a very important man with a megaphone who used to climb through the ropes while Young Pancho and his opponent were sitting in their corners, and say in a very important voice to which everybody listened in respectful silence, "Lay-deez and gen-tle-men . . ."

A white suit, a megaphone and everybody listening. That was the vision. Young Pancho Villa the Third, the stocky little Mex with a child's face hammered flat as an English bulldog's, walked down Main Street in pursuit of a vision, a white-linen, double-breasted vision that floated ahead of him, leading him past the burleycue houses and the pool parlors, the nickel flophouses, the dime flophouses and the exclusive clean-sheets-every-week two-bit flophouses, leading him past the saloons with their threadbare elegance, the gaudy juke boxes, the gaudy and threadbare B-girls, past all those wonderful and tempting ways to spend his money. But Young Pancho kept his thick little hands in his pockets until he came to Manny (Nothing Over Five Dollars) Liebowitz' High Class Clothing Store for Men.

None of the other guys who hung around the gym were getting any gold stars on their report cards for neatness. Most of them wore suits that looked as if they had been used to mop up the floors of Happy Harry's saloon on the corner. So Pancho was going to be smart. Pancho was going to look like class if it cost him a fortune. That suit in the window, for instance, that brand-new white linen suit, that was for Pancho. "Five Dollars," a large card pinned to the coat beckoned to Pancho. "Five Dollars," said another on the pants.

"I take suit in window," Pancho said.

"Wudja say, *amigo?*" asked Mr. Liebowitz.

Pancho's voice was husky and his words bumped against one another. Too many collisions between his brain and someone else's fist had thickened his natural accent to an almost inarticulate jargon. "Punch-patter," some of the boys described it.

"I take suit in window," Pancho said, pointing a short, chunky finger at the one he wanted.

"And what a bargain!" Mr. Liebowitz began. "In all of Los Angeles show me another genuine linen for ten dollars."

"Ten dollars?" said Pancho. "In window it say only five."

"Five dollars," said Mr. Liebowitz agreeably. "Sure, five dollars. Five for the coat and five for the pants. Just like it says in the window."

Pancho went out into the street and gazed at the suit again. He pressed his nose against the window and then stepped back and appraised it like a connoisseur studying a work of art. It was so beautiful. It was so white and so dapper. For a luxury maybe ten dollars was awfully steep. But this was no luxury. This was an investment. This was the uniform Young Pancho Villa the Third would need in his chosen profession.

"You have my size?" he said. "Must fit very good."

"Don't take my word for it," said Mr. Liebowitz. "My motto is Suit Yourself. *Suit*—Yourself. Get it?"

The suit might have been a good fit when Pancho was still making the featherweight limit. But he was almost a middleweight now and the coat button strained against his belly, the seat of his pants stretched skin-tight across his rump.

"Ugh, too tight," Pancho gasped. "Got him bigger?" "Bigger?" said Mr. Liebowitz. "You want to be in style, don't you? That is just the way the college boys is wearing them this season. Just off the campus from UCLA!"

Young Pancho Villa the Third looked over his shoulder into the mirror. Not so bad at that. Nice and form-fitting. Not soiled and baggy like the pants on those bums around the gym.

Then he tried on the shoes. Pointed white shoes with special heels built up, almost like a girl's. "Those are absolutely genuine imitation buck," Mr. Liebowitz explained. "Marked down from four-fifty to one-ninety-nine."

Young Pancho Villa the Third walked down Main Street in his white linen suit, a clean shirt, a white cotton tie, genuine imitation-buck shoes and a Panama hat worn at a rakish angle over one eye. The outfit had set him back thirteen ninety-nine, nearly all the money he had, but it was worth it. Then he went into a pawnshop and asked to look at megaphones. "I want biggest megaphone you got in place," he said.

The pawnbroker handed a bulky, battered megaphone over the counter.

"Now I am fight announcer," Young Pancho announced. He caressed the megaphone, raised it to his lips and shouted excitedly, "Een-tro-ducing Young Pancho Villa the Third, the chomp-peen announcer of the worrrrrld!"

The first day Pancho showed up at the gym in his new role he got his money's worth out of that megaphone. When he put it to his mouth, he lifted his head and closed his eyes like a concert artist. He stood there in the corner by the entrance shouting his announcements into that megaphone, thrilled with the sound of the beautiful deep voice that rose from his lips like organ music. Or at least, so it seemed to him, as he paused to listen to it reverberating through the big, high-ceilinged room full of serious boys with narrow waists and glistening skins, bending, stretching, skipping, shadow-boxing, punching the bags or listening earnestly to the instructions of men with fat bellies, boneless noses, ulcers, dirty sweatshirts, brown hats pushed back from sweaty foreheads, the trainers, the managers, the experts.

In the center ring Ceferino Garcia, the Pride of the Islands, was throwing punches at the air, ducking and weaving as he crowded an imaginary opponent to the ropes.

Young Pancho Villa the Third held his megaphone high and shouted, "Een-tro-ducing, ot one hon-dred and seexty pounds, that tareefic boy from the Phil-ha-peens . . ."

He spread his legs and bellowed. He was the greatest announcer in the world. Only nobody could understand him. The accent and a speech motor sputtering along on half its cylinders produced a kind of guttural doubletalk. Eddie Gibbs, the bald, irritable little guy who ran the gym, went over to Pancho and said, "What do you think *you're* doing?"

"Me announce," Pancho said. "Me announce very fine. Work here in gym every day."

"Go on," Gibbs said. "What the hell is there to announce around here? You're punchy."

That was a fighting word and Pancho felt the blood rush to his head. Anger brought his thick lips to a childish pout. "Ponchy. Who ponchy? Me no ponchy. Those boms over there, maybe they ponchy. Me have job. Me announcer."

Jerry La Pan, who had the best string of boys in town, stopped to listen on his way in. Jerry was a great ribber and he worked at it all the time. He flipped Pancho four bits and said, "That's for the commercial. I wanna buy the next fifteen minutes."

Pancho raised his megaphone solemnly. "Een-tro-duc-ing, Jerry La Pon, thot great mon-ager of thot coming heavyweight chom-peen . . ."

All the boys got a bang out of that, so Gibbs let Pancho hang around for laughs. After the third day it didn't seem so funny any more, not even to Jerry La Pan, but Pancho went right on announcing. He couldn't have been more conscientious about it if Gibbs had put him on the payroll. Every day Pancho would check in at noon, announce until two, take half an hour off for lunch and go back to his megaphone again until the last tired fighter hit the showers at six.

He was something of a genius in his own way. He could keep up a steady stream of announcements for six hours and succeed in saying nothing that anybody could understand. He kept it up so long that after a while the sound of his voice seemed to blend into the other sounds that made the rhythm of the place—the slapping of the small bag, the thudding of the big, the clicking of the jump ropes, and the rumbling of the canvas-covered boards under the weight of the boxers' dancing feet.

The first few days, all the boys thought the announcing was the funniest thing they ever saw. Then, when they were running low on wisecracks, they began to pretend he wasn't there. And finally they didn't have to pretend any more. Pancho and his white suit and megaphone were on the job all day long and no one even bothered to look around.

No one, that is, but Soldier Conlon. The Soldier was one of those characters who used to do a little boxing and has nothing to show for it but a couple of cauliflower ears and a cauliflower brain. After hanging up his gloves, he worked the corners for a couple of years, but one of the fights he worked looked so wrong that the commission had to take somebody's license away to save its face, and, of course, the Soldier was their man.

So now the Soldier just hung around, as the boys say, making himself useless. If he got hold of a couple of bucks he picked up a hand in one of the poker games in the back room. If things got so bad that he had to go to work, he'd promote himself a little dough, finding tankers for some new bum they were trying to build up. The Soldier was never what the boys call a vicious character. He didn't have the guts or the brains to kill somebody or rob a bank. The Soldier was strictly alley-fighting and two-bit larceny.

Soldier Conlon would have been just another Grand Street hanger-onner, if it hadn't been for one thing. His sense of humor. Especially where Young Pancho Villa the Third was concerned. For instance it didn't take him any time at all to find out what a nut Pancho was on the subject of keeping his white outfit spotless. So every time Soldier Conlon would come into the gym he'd stick his hand out and say, "Hiya, Pancho, how's the kid today?" And when he drew his hand back there would be a big black smudge on Pancho's sleeve where the Soldier had drawn the end of a burnt match across it with the other hand.

And when Pancho finally got wise to the hand-shaking gag, the Soldier would come by and say, "Glad to see ya puttin' your best foot forward, Pancho, old boy," and he'd stamp on Pancho's white imitation-buck shoes, leaving a dirty smear across the toe.

After a while it got so every time Pancho saw Conlon coming he'd run for the high stool near the entrance and draw up his feet and wrap his arms around himself and pull in his head like a turtle. "Stay 'way, stay 'way now," Pancho would plead. And the Soldier's answer would be a grin, showing wide orange gums and a mouth full of cheap store teeth. "Whatsa matter, Pancho? We pals, ain't we, Pancho o' kid, o' kid?" Then he'd turn around and wink at whoever happened to be standing around, to make sure they were getting the joke.

One day Eddie Gibbs decided to put on an amateur boxing show. As soon as Pancho heard about it he got all excited and ran up to Gibbs' office. "Missa Geebs," he said. "You put on beeg show, you need a-numma-one announcer."

Well, at first Gibbs told Pancho what to do with his megaphone. But Pancho kept hollering until finally Gibbs began to see the possibilities of it. Young Pancho Villa the Third, the greatest doubletalk announcer in the world. The louder he talked, the less you understood. They could throw him in once in a while just for laughs. So Gibbs said, "Sure, Pancho. You're in. I'll even put your name in the program."

There was no holding Pancho after that. He strutted around the gym like a bantam rooster. He was announcing everything that went on in a very impressive and inarticulate way. The boys said he even announced when Eddie Gibbs took a leak.

But the day before the amateur show, the boxers had to struggle along without their announcing. "How about givin' out with some of them announcements, Pancho?" Soupy Jones, the colored lightweight, laughed.

"Is better to save voice for beeg show tomorrow night," Pancho explained.

The next afternoon Pancho didn't show up at the gym at all. He was lying down in his room resting for his personal appearance. He left a call at the desk for seven o'clock.

"Get up yourself, you bum," said the manager. Pancho was three weeks behind in his rent.

At seven o'clock, Pancho rose, tested his megaphone, and went down to the end of the hall to wash his hands so he wouldn't leave any dirty fingerprints on his clothes.

He had washed and ironed his white shirt, chalked his shoes, and had given the Chinaman down the street ן buck to clean and press the suit and block his Panama hat.

He went over to the gym half an hour early. He felt good inside, the way he used to feel when he was walking down the aisle to the ring and the *compañeros* in the peanut gallery were yelling *Viva, Pancho Villa!* He went around glad-handing everybody outside, wanting to make sure all the boys saw him. In the gym the seats were full, and a lot of the boys were standing around the ring making bets and talking it over. Pancho wandered among them, careful not to brush his white linen against anybody's dirty suit. Someone let a stream of tobacco juice go and it narrowly missed Pancho's feet. "Hey, you look where you spitting," Pancho scolded.

He went over to the ring and picked up a program. He read through it eagerly, running his finger along the lines, until he found his name. It made him tingle all over when he saw it: "Special Announcer: Young Pancho Villa III." Eddie Gibbs was leaning against the ring with a pencil over his ear, going over the line-up for the evening with the referee. Pancho walked toward him briskly. He had better check over the program with Eddie and make sure just when he was to go on, he thought to himself. He went over to Gibbs with self-conscious importance.

Suddenly he stopped. Soldier Conlon was looking over Gibbs' shoulder. Pancho didn't think Conlon had seen him. He turned and tried to lose himself in the crowd. He edged behind two bigger men and started working his way around the ring. Then he heard the voice behind him, "Hey, Pancho. Hey, big shot."

There had never been anything in the ring that frightened him like the sound of the Soldier's voice. Everything cramped inside him when he heard it. He must keep his suit clean tonight, he thought, he must keep his shoes white. And though he did not know the words, the fear of them throbbed in him: he must not be *violated* tonight. He must not be *sullied*.

The Soldier watched this fear come into Pancho's face, and Pancho saw the orange grin with the false teeth. The Soldier took a step toward him. Pancho backed away.

"Hey, big shot. C'mere. I wanna talk to ya."

Pancho ducked behind the seats. The Soldier moved after him, laughing as he went. Pancho walked faster. He could feel the sweat prickling under his collar. He broke into a trot. So did the Soldier. Pancho ran around the seats, and when he saw the Soldier still coming, he hurried up the stairs to the gallery. So did the Soldier. They were running now. They ran all the way around the balcony. Pancho's legs were short and the tight white suit checked his stride. The Soldier grinned as he ran. He was having a great time and he was gaining. "Hey, big shot," he kept calling. "Hey, big shot."

Pancho raced past the door to the fire escape, wheeled and darted out. He tried to hold the door from the outside, but the Soldier was too strong and the door pulled away from him. The orange gums and the false teeth and the crazy laugh were right behind him now. Pancho looked down the dizzying descent of fire escape that fell away to the narrow alley behind the gym. A feverish prayer beat in his mind. . . . Then his small, neat feet broke into a Bill Robinson tap dance down the metal steps.

Still laughing, the Soldier reached down and grabbed the edge of Pancho's coat. For a moment Pancho dangled there in the Soldier's firm grip. With his hands swinging wildly into the air and his short legs pumping up and down in a futile effort to tear himself from the Soldier's grasp, he looked like a mechanical doll.

Then suddenly his left fist shot out, the old left hook. All his body was behind that fist, and all his life. The force of it spun him around, toward the Soldier. It caught the Soldier full in the mouth, smashing the laugh. The Soldier let go of Pancho's coat and snapped instinctively to the fighter's stance, the left arm straight out for the jab, the right cocked under the lowered jaw.

The Soldier's left drove like a piston at Pancho's face. Pancho reeled backward. For a moment he was looking up at the sky above the roof of the gym, then at the narrowing darkness of the alley below, as he struggled to break his fall. He grabbed for the railing twice and it wasn't there, but the third time it was. He hung on desperately with his right hand. The Soldier was coming at him again. Pancho squeezed his left fist tighter and crouched.

He was in the ring now, crowded into a corner, holding the top rung of the rope with his right hand to steady himself, lashing out with his left. The old hook, the wild left hook. The Soldier's face came down to meet the punch and his head snapped back. All that Pancho remembered was the look of surprise on the Soldier's face before he tumbled gracelessly down the metal steps to melt into the darkness below.

Young Pancho Villa the Third brushed himself off and walked back into the gym again. He was saved. That was all he could think about. He was saved from Soldier Conlon. There was nobody now to stop him from climbing into that ring under the glare of the overhead lights and raising his megaphone to his lips.

Swinging his megaphone proudly, Pancho went down the aisle to the ring. Old-timers smiled to see this little brown man in the snappy white suit strutting by them like a pouter pigeon. Their voices followed him down the aisle in good-natured banter, "Hiya, Pancho, geev it to heem!—Well look who's here, our favorite announcer . . ." Pancho acknowledged his fans with an important little nod and kept on going toward the ring.

Eddie Gibbs was in the ring, introducing a couple of old champs. After the champs had lumbered into the ring, mitted the crowd and lumbered out again, Gibbs grinned down at Pancho and announced, "Introducing next that distinguished personage of the boxing game, the Joe Humphreys of the West Coast, Young Pancho Villa the Third!"

It got a laugh from the crowd. Some of the boys stuck out their tongues and gave it the razzberry. Others cupped their hands to their mouths and yelled witty remarks. But this isn't what Pancho heard. Young Pancho Villa the Third, standing under the arc light with the big megaphone in his hand, heard acclaim. He was up there at last where he had always wanted to be, a white suit, a megaphone and everybody listening.

He was shining. His oily black hair was shining. His eyes were black and oily and shining too. His smiling face shone in the glow of the overhead lights.

He bowed to his audience, just a little half-bow it was, performed with dignity, lifted the end of the megaphone high in the air, and let his words roll through it louder than they ever had before: "Lay-deez and gen-tle-men, it geeves me grrreat pleasure to be here weeth you tonight . . ."

Someone yelled, "But how much pleasure does it give us?" and the room rocked with laughter again. But Pancho went right on. He heard nothing but the sound of his own voice. He saw nothing but the metal-rimmed mouth of his megaphone, into which he was pouring his life. He no longer saw the faces laughing at him. Or the two men in dark-blue uniforms who had just entered quietly and stood waiting against the door in the rear. He still didn't know anything was wrong when Eddie Gibbs reached up to him through the ropes and handed him a folded piece of paper. He simply opened it with an official gesture, raised his megaphone again and made a formal announcement: "Your atten-shun, pleece: Pancho —the cops are waiteeng for you at the entrance in co-neck-shun weeth the killeeng of Soldier Con-lon."

The crowd had already begun to laugh, but it caught itself, and a hush fell over the place. The absence of sound made Pancho stop and gulp for breath as if sound had taken the place of oxygen in his world. He read the message again, this time to himself. Then he climbed through the ropes and went slowly up the aisle toward the officers, swinging his megaphone as he walked.

T H E   B R E A K I N G   P O I N T

"Well, honey, they're here all right," Brad said. "I just ran into Fefe in town. Says the fellow he took out yesterday got five sails. We've got a date with those babies in the morning."

Martha looked up from the hotel bed and the magazine she was reading and stared at him. She saw a big man who had once been handsome, who had once been her lover and for a long time now had been her husband. She saw a ruddy complexion that women considered attractive and that derived almost in equal parts from outdoor living and indoor drinking.

"You saw Fefe, and you also saw the bottom of a glass," she said.

"Oh, Christ, are you going to start that again?"

She felt the same way about it, but the pattern that enclosed them would not let her rest. "I'm not starting it.

You started it when you broke your neck to get into town to have that first drink. In the hotel twenty minutes, and you can't wait to go into town and get stinking."

She hated that word. She always used it when she felt like this.

"I'm not stinking. Four, five drinks with Fefe—you call that stinking?"

She watched him take his shirt and pants off and stretch out on the bed. "Not stinking," he mumbled. "Uncle Brad doesn't get stinking that easy. Just sleepy. Little sleepy, tha's all."

Martha said nothing. She had decided to drop the case. It wasn't the charge she would have liked to convict him on anyway. She knew what the charge really was. It was the fishing in the morning. It was the fact that he never even bothered to ask her if she felt like going fishing in the morning. Their first day back in Acapulco after five years, after the long cruise, maybe she felt like just lounging around the hotel. Maybe she felt like strolling through town, noting the changes, or looking up the people who had been most hospitable to them on their honeymoon. But Brad would never know. Brad would never ask her. Brad would just go on being Brad, the big spoiled boy, the son of the chairman of the board, who never grew up, who thought everything was put there for his amusement—the sailfish, the native ports, Martha . . .

He was lying on his back with his mouth slightly open, his breathing punctuated by the familiar sound of his snoring. If she were to come into a dormitory of a thousand sleeping men, Martha felt sure she would recognize that snoring. How many nights had it disturbed her reading? How many early mornings had its monotonous insistence penetrated sleep? How many nervous hours had she listened to it, and how many mornings had it provided the sound track for her first sight of the new day?

The rhythm of his snoring was broken by a violent snort. He is like a bull, she thought, with no more romance or even human passion in him than the stud bulls we've seen on ranches. He never asks me if I want to make love, he never asks me if I want to go fishing, he never asks me if I want to go to the bullfights; no, he just holds up two tickets—"They soaked me two hundred pesos apiece for these but I've got 'em!" And then, at the bullfights, there was always that business of the horses . . . Oh, she knew her Hemingway; she knew that the business of the horses is neither good nor bad, is not important, is merely a necessary, momentary unpleasantness that should not distract one from the real issue—the integrity with which the *torero* is preparing his bull for death. But Brad there, laughing at the jerky movements of that skinny horse's leg after the bull had refused to take the point of the *pica* for his answer, *laughing* and telling her to take her hands away from her face. My God, how close are sympathy and selfishness, she thought. When I cry for the horse, the innocent bystander crushed to earth, I cry for myself, trembling against the impact of the dark beast.

Once, after a particularly cruel bullfight, she had refused to speak to him for the rest of the afternoon. And up in the hotel room before dressing for dinner, the time he always liked, she would not give herself to him—not so soon after the business of the horse.

He had tossed his head then, with a bull's rage and a bull's stubbornness, and had roared out into the hall, on his way to the bar, with a familiar threat that disgusted her, that made her want to remove herself forever from the path of his charge. She had stood at the window looking down into the great avenue, her mind already hurrying ahead to her suitcase, her clothes, the note she would leave . . . but when he came in several hours later, listing slightly with his overload of tequila, and threw himself down on the bed and began to snore, she was still there, trapped like a bird that has come in through an opening it can no longer find.

As she watched and listened to him sleep that other evening she had wanted to blame her failure to leave him on the rigidity of her Boston family tradition, a background that shrank from scandal and the public charge-and-countercharge that delighted tabloid readers. But she knew herself too well to accept this as any more than the hard outer shell of the frailty of flesh and spirit that would not let her act. It was almost an illness, this passivity. The symptoms went back at least twenty years, for she could still remember coming home from first grade and saying, "Mummy, the girl across the aisle from me holds my hand all the time. The whole recess she holds my hand and I don't want her to." "But, darling, don't give her your hand if you don't like to," Mummy had said. But of course it was never as simple as that, for Martha didn't know how to tell the girl—and so that stronger girl had gone on holding Martha's hand throughout the rest of the term.

It was the same with Brad. She could not get her hand away from his. "Just tell him you've had enough," Martha's one close friend would tell her. But it was always easier to put off the final break, to wait until the trip was over, to make sure she wasn't pregnant . . . and sometimes when she was sure she was ready, Brad would tap some hidden spring of intuition, and, then for a while he would soften to the man she thought she had married. He would bring her the special flowers she liked and be gentle with her—the way only the very cruel know how to be gentle—and so, for a short time she would forget, wanting so much to forget. And by the time his bogus little courtship had worn thin, her determination, fragile as spun glass, would have shattered.

If only he would perform one final act that could set her off, she thought. Yes, she was like the rusty trigger of a gun he had forgotten was loaded. It would take all his strength to bring the hammer down on the striking point. But even as she feared it, she waited for it.

Next morning they reached the docks at eight instead of seven-thirty because Martha had taken too long in the bathroom. Brad had been needling her with a sharp minute hand from the time he awoke. It was her bitter knowledge that an appointment with a fishing boat was the only thing he took seriously. He had had his picture in quite a few magazines as a master of giant game fish. It was the best thing he did.

The boat wasn't a clean boat, not even by Mexican standards, and the native skipper merely muttered something without smiling when they came aboard. "He's sore because we're late," Brad said. "They like to get out there before the sun's up too high."

Martha didn't say anything. She really didn't care what effect the extra time had on the moods of his pockmarked Mexican. She was watching the mate. He had a cadaverous face covered by an unkempt beard. Normally he should have been about five feet tall, but a slight hump, or rather a ridge running between his shoulders, bent him over until he was hardly more than four feet high.

They went out past Hornos, the beach that the Acapulqueños frequent at sunset, and Martha could remember her first swim there with Brad when the flaming red sun lit the waters around them with cool fire and the palm trees behind the beach stood out in brilliant silhouette against the purple sky. Had she loved him that evening long ago? She tried to remember: yes, she had, for his Irish good looks, for his gaiety, and for the elaborate charade of romance he had practiced on her.

She looked over at him now, as if to compare the sham she had briefly loved five years ago with this solid reality who was carefully unwrapping his fishing gear—the Hardy reel he had picked up in England and the O'Brien rod bought two seasons ago in Miami, the rod that had conquered yellowtail off Enseñada, tuna near Guaymas, marlin in the Caribbean, and tarpon in the channels through the mangrove swamps that lie off Key West. He was careless about most of his possessions, but not about this rod.

The boat slowed to trolling speed and Brad paid out his line. The hunchback had a pole for Martha and fixed the base of the rod in the socket of her chair.

"Well, *muchacha*," Brad said, "better get the big gaff ready. I feel lucky today."

If the hunchback heard the feminine ending, his face gave no sign. They had spent nearly all their winters in Latin countries, and Martha's Spanish was good enough to cause her to flinch from Brad's linguistic slips. But Brad took pride in his inability to speak foreign languages. And he was in too good a mood at the moment to care whether he called this deformed native a boy or a girl. There were really only a few occasions, Martha was thinking, when Brad's humor was so high—when he was starting to fish, when he came in with a fish bigger and gamer than anyone else's, when he had had more than two drinks but less than six, and when he was undressing for his pleasure before dinner.

"Come on, get on there, baby!" Brad was talking to them somewhere under the sea. "Let's get a big one for Uncle Brad."

When nothing happened for a while, the hunchback threw out some chum, live bait of fairly good size, to draw the larger fish. In a few moments a sea gull appeared, maneuvering in over the wake of the boat to dive for the small fish.

"*Gaviota*," the hunchback muttered. "Damn *gaviota*."

A second gull came in overhead, and then another, coasting or winging easily over the stern. They were a small variety, very white, and Martha enjoyed their grace as they floated overhead.

"Damn *gaviota*," the hunchback muttered again. He reached into a paper bag for a small stone—Martha realized that he must have brought the stones along for that purpose—and tossed it up at them. It fell short of the birds.

"Come on, *muchacha*," Brad laughed. "Where's the old pitching arm?"

The hunchback threw again, but his physical disability limited his throw. "I get hands on *gaviota*"—his English was almost unintelligible—"I—" Instead of a word here, he substituted a terrible cracking sound of tongue against teeth and a quick gesture of snapping down with both fists.

The sudden violence of it, rising out of this wretched little man, made Brad laugh. But it left Martha with a sinking feeling of discomfort.

After a while she felt a tug on her line, pulled her pole back the way Brad had taught her, and then lowered it at the same time she began reeling in.

"You got something there—doesn't look like too much," Brad said. He never liked anyone else to catch the first one.

But as the thing she had caught came closer to the boat, it broke surface, flapping its wings wildly and giving forth a shrill wail.

"Damn *gaviota*," the hunchback said. "Pull in, pull in."

Martha could feel the bird pulling against her line, thrashing the water with its wings as it fought for life.

"Here," she said, quickly handing her rod to the hunchback. "*No me gusta.*" She tried not to watch while the bird was pulled into the boat. But she had to listen to its screams; and when they suddenly became louder and more frightened, she knew it was held fast in the hunch-back's fierce, sun-blackened little hands. She was imagining what he would do to it—twist its neck or slam it against the side—when she heard the *sound* of what the hunchback was doing to it. It was not too different from the sound he had made with his tongue against his teeth when he had been pantomiming the act before. She kept her eyes away until she was sure it must be over, and then she turned around, just as the limp white body was flung into the sea.

It floated on top of the water with its wings spread out as if it were in flight. Then she saw the bird suddenly bunch forward in a furious effort to rise from itself.

"Brad, it's still living! It's alive! He didn't kill it!"

"Where've you been?" Brad said. "All he did was break its wings and throw it back."

She watched the stern pull away from the crippled bird bobbing in the boat's wake. The gull was silent now. Its silence seemed even more terrible to Martha than its shrieking.

"Why does he do that? Does he *have* to do that?"

Brad laughed. "He hates those things like poison. Says it teaches them a lesson."

The hunchback was setting her line out for her again. Four or five gulls were over the boat now. "I don't think I want to fish any more," she said.

"What do you want to do?" Brad reprimanded. "Let the *muchacha* fish for you?"

It was easier, she felt, just to sit there holding the line than to let him ride her all the way. She prayed she wouldn't catch another one, though. She didn't think she could stand another one.

She could not take her eyes from the white speck that bobbed in the distance. She could feel it struggling to rise with its helpless wings.

Suddenly Brad let out a cry of joy—"Sailfish!"—and the

boat came to life. The hunchback's face was animated with a gargoyle smile, and even the dark Indian mask that the skipper wore for a face was lit with fisherman's hope and eagerness for the catch.

"I got a good one," Brad called, fighting it happily. "A good one!"

The hunchback was jabbering at Martha, and Brad shot her an anxious glance, his face red with effort. "Damn it, reel in! Reel in, for Christ's sake!" he shouted.

Martha had been watching the drowning gull. The hunchback snatched her line from her and began winding frantically to get it in out of the way. But it was too late. The sailfish had drawn Brad's line across and back under Martha's and their lines were becoming hopelessly tangled.

No longer able to reel in, Brad gave himself to profanity. "Damn it, that's the first thing I ever told you! You goddam nipple-head!"

The tangled lines went slack as Brad's sailfish threw the hook. "He's gone," Brad said tragically. "Would've hit fifty, maybe sixty pounds . . ." And his words were a jumble of profanity again.

Because our lines were crossed, I ruined his day, Martha thought. Both lines were in the boat now, and the hunchback was working deliberately to loosen the knotted loops.

It was almost half an hour before they could fish again. The sun was directly overhead, beating down oppressively. A dozen gulls were following them now.

"*Gaviota*," the hunchback said. "Damn *gaviota*."

Just then several dived for Brad's line and his pole dipped sharply. "Sonofabitch. Now *I've* hooked one." He was so exasperated that he couldn't even reel in. "Here, *muchacha*, you handle it." In his defeat, he turned on Martha again. "God damn it, next time I hook into something big, reel in, reel in like I told you."

The gull that had been hooked left the water and flew up over the boat with the line trailing from its beak. Martha could see it flapping directly overhead, pulling against the hook and crying as the metal point ripped the lining of its throat. As the hunchback reeled it in, it flew around wildly over their heads. Martha screamed, and the gull screamed with her. What a horrible female chorus, she thought.

With a neat gesture, the hunchback reached up and snatched the bird.

"Don't," Martha said. "Please don't."

"Wait a minute," Brad said. "Let me have it."

Thank you, Brad, Martha thought, thank you, thank you. Do it quickly.

Brad took the bird, exactly as he had seen the hunchback do it, snapped its wings in his big hands and tossed it back into the sea.

"That the way you do it, *muchacha?*" he said, laughing.

She watched Brad's gull flounder and then rise in a series of desperate convulsions. He had not even done this as the hunchback had, through hatred of everything more perfect than himself. It was merely something he had never done before.

She put her fingers to her throat to feel the throbbing. She shut her eyes against the glare on the water. Oh God, she thought, seeing in her mind the image of her dead father, the time has come at last, has come. Dear Father, give me strength . . .

THE FACE OF HOLLYWOOD

When I first met Doc he was working in the drug store on the corner, just outside the studio. That is, he was employed there, for he never seemed to be working. Doc treated the place as a sort of salon. He always managed to look more like a man of the world than a hired clerk. He had the dapper, creased appearance of a carbon-copy Man of Distinction. His face was florid and had begun to bulge over his high stiff collar. His eyes were always laughing at everything.

I was sent to the drug store on one of those annoying errands to get a physic for our associate producer, Harry Small.

Doc came forward in a flashy double-breasted suit with a red carnation in his buttonhole.

"I would like some kind of physic," I whispered.

There are usually two ways to discuss a physic. Either you speak of it in hushed tones, or you stand your ground and blurt it out. But Doc was the kind of man who could lend as much dignity to the peddling of a physic as to the selling of rare manuscripts.

"And may I ask for whom it is for?" he said.

"You just did—it's for Mr. Small."

"Oh," said Doc. "Why didn't you say so in the first place?"

"What's the diff?" I asked. "Producers need the same physics as the rest of us. Even supermen like Harry Small. Give."

"Why does he need it?" Doc persisted.

"Listen," I said, "he's in the projection room now cutting his new picture. Why don't you break in and ask him?"

Doc scolded me with a glance. "A physic is no laughing matter, young man," he said.

"Who's laughing?" I said. "Maybe he needs it because he got married last night and threw a big party for both his friends and all his enemies."

"In that case," said Doc solemnly, "I would suggest castor oil."

Doc's eyes pled sincerity, but as I looked at him I got the feeling that he wasn't as dumb as he looked, that all this pomp and circumstance were just a joke, a very funny joke Doc was playing on the world. He was actually humoring you into thinking you were important, and what you were doing was important. All he seemed to want out of life was to make you feel that every second was a crisis in the world.

As Doc wrapped up the castor oil he inquired about Harry Small's wife as if he were about to say, "Next time you see her, give her my very best." Doc made you believe that being a drug-store salesman was just a hobby. I am sure that if President Eisenhower had ever ordered a toothbrush from him, he would have delivered it to the White House himself, saying, "I just dropped in a moment to be sure Mamie is taking care of her teeth—and what's new with the wages and hours bill?"

"What sort of lady is Mrs. Small?" he asked.

"I can't answer that," I said, "because I never heard her called that before."

"I hear she's stacked," Doc said.

Like all the great actors in the world, most of them never appearing on stage or screen, Doc could shift his moods like gears. His dignity was just so much grease paint that melted off in the heat of conversation, especially conversation about women. There was a touch of Casanova and plenty of traveling salesman in him.

"Give me that castor oil," I said. "Mr. Small may need it when he gets through running his new picture."

"I've been thinking about that marriage," said Doc, propping his chin up on the castor-oil box.

"Don't worry about Harry," I said. "The only man in Hollywood who ever stood in his way was a traffic cop— and Harry ran him down. . . . Now give me my change. If I know my Harry, I'll be among the unemployed if I don't get back in two minutes flat."

I finally got my package and started off as if there were a pack of mad supervisors at my heels.

"Let me know how he makes out with it," Doc called. "You might ring me up at home. I'll be worried."

"Listen," I yelled back, "the way you carry on, you oughta join the Screen Actors Guild."

"I am a member," he answered. "I picked up a day at Metro last week, working with Greer."

That's how Doc got his big chance in the studio, acting, but not in a picture. Instead, he starred himself in a little life drama called *Feeling Sorry for Harry*. It so happened that Harry was reaching that stage where the sobs of his commiserators was his favorite sound track. He was beginning to believe the things they wrote about him in the local trade papers, about his being A Martyr to Our Business.

One morning a tragic editorial sobbed its way through a column and a half of the *Hollywood Recorder*. It was full of genuine concern for the men who almost sacrifice their lives to become heads of great studios. In its unique prose style, it began:

Go into the executive chambers and you will see producers all fagged out, tired almost to complete exhaustion, physically and mentally out, yes, even sick.

Naturally Doc read this, as he followed the trade papers faithfully in order to keep his finger on the pulse of the industry. Naturally, he took this message to heart. He ran straight to the phone and called Mr. Small.

"I'm sorry," said Harry's secretary sweetly but firmly, "Mr. Small is in a Board meeting. He can't talk to anyone."

"But this is a matter of life and death," Doc begged, his voice breaking with emotion.

Small got on the phone. "Harry Small speaking," he said aggressively. "Whose life and death are you talking about?"

"Yours," said Doc emphatically. "I just read that warning about you, Mr. Small."

"What warning?" asked Harry, ready to hang up.

"In the *Recorder*," said Doc tearfully. "About producers working themselves to death. They meant you. It isn't safe."

"Well I'll be damned," said Harry. He was softening.

"We can't afford to lose you," said Doc. "If I were you I'd keep some adrenalin in your desk all the time, old man."

"Thanks," said Harry, "I'll have my secretary get me some."

"I'll rush it right over myself," Doc said.

Three minutes later he loped into the office like an Eskimo dog rushing serum to stricken Nome.

The next morning Doc was the new studio receptionist. He sat proudly behind the desk at the main door. I found him enthroned there when I was making my mail round.

He told me Mr. Small had given him the job because a good receptionist should anticipate people's wishes, he should be able to size people up quickly enough to separate the wheat of desirable visitors from the usual sightseeing chaff, he should have tact, patience, insight, humor and intuition.

"I see," I said. "A receptionist is something like God, only he's on the payroll."

"It's the most fascinating job in the studio," Doc confided. "It means you have to know something about every department—as the first contact outsiders meet, I am the Face of the Studio, as it were."

From the moment Doc became the Face of the Studio, the reception room was charged with excitement, importance and intrigue. Every stranger who asked for an interview pass was treated as a potential spy determined to dynamite the sound stages. Any visitor of importance whom Doc recognized would be salaamed and announced like a nobleman entering a royal house. Job seekers no longer under his suspicion would receive lengthy advice about their future in the studio, or Doc would inquire into their background, decide they were not yet ready and urge them to look for more experience elsewhere first.

One morning a delegation of high-school students from Atlanta, Georgia, bore down on the studio fifty strong.

"We cahm from G'ogia," said the animated schoolteacher who led them, "and we'd sho' like to see one of these studios."

Doc called Small's office and the answer was, "Let them march through Georgia—not here."

It was a tense moment.

"I'm sho' sorry," he said. "The studio is closed fo' the day. But if you all'll jes sit yo'self down, I'll be mighty glahd to tell you-all about it."

I kept going through the reception room for an hour, and Doc never stopped talking. The schoolteacher was so glad to find somebody from Dixie that she hung on every magnolia-scented word.

Word of this triumph got back to Harry Small, and he puffed a thick smoke screen of pride around him with his Havana-Havana.

"That man has push," he said. "He deserves something. Raise his salary to a hundred-and-seventy-five a month."

But Harry Small could never understand people except in terms of himself. Doc didn't have the push of a snail. He wasn't playing to win. It was just good clean fun, and an irresistible urge to take care of it, to build it up, to treat little acorns as if they were great oaks.

As Doc grew more accustomed to his job, this urge began to get out of hand. Small's secretary, Judy, noticed it first. Doc called her one day and told her to call a Mr. Carteret as soon as Mr. Small came in.

"But I know Mr. Small doesn't want to talk to him," Judy said.

"But you have to tell him," Doc said, "for my sake."

"What's it got to do with you?" she asked.

"I gave Mr. Carteret my word of honor Mr. Small would call him," Doc answered. "You wouldn't let me down, would you?"

"Listen," Judy said, "will you relax?"

I was just the office boy, so I could tell her, but she didn't have Doc right, either. It was like asking the Statue of Liberty to relax. They both had their part to play, it was their place in the world.

Carteret was an old director, famous in silent days, who had suddenly appeared at the reception desk one day. He had one of those faces that say: I haven't worked in years. His face was trellised with purple veins from too much drinking and not enough forgetting. He turned out, to his surprise, to be an old friend of Doc's.

"Hello, Lew," Doc said, "haven't seen you since Shirley Temple was a pup. What can I do you for?"

"I thought I might try going back to work for a change," Carteret said, too desperate to sound very funny. "What's new over here?"

Doc told him everything he knew, and he hadn't chatted with secretaries and read notes upside down on executives' desks for nothing.

"It looks like we're going to make a big American cavalcade epic," Doc concluded.

"Yeah?" Carteret said. "I'm the guy who produced the biggest cavalcade before talking pictures—*Like Father, Like Son.*"

"Of course Harry didn't exactly tell me," Doc said, "but one of our readers has been reading in the American historical wing of the public library for the past two weeks and three vets from the old soldiers' home came through here yesterday."

"That's the break I need," Carteret said.

"I'll take care of it," Doc said.

He called Judy and made an appointment for him. Carteret only had to wait an hour and fifteen minutes.

"Thanks, old boy," he said to Doc gratefully as he was called in. "You certainly have a pull around here."

Five minutes later Carteret came out. His face was red and perspiration was dripping down onto his only clean shirt.

"What did Harry say?" Doc asked.

"Listen," said Carteret grimly, "he told me you popped out with the studio secret of the year. He warned me that if his idea ever gets out, he'll run us both out of the industry. I practically bought myself a one-way ticket to starvation."

Doc had his salary reduced to forty a week after that. But that didn't stop him from playing his role. Every afternoon, for instance, he dropped in for a spot of tea at the commissary. If any of us office boys were grabbing a cup of coffee we used to dread seeing him because it would mean the end of our service. Doc was the idol of the waitresses. The moment he crossed the threshold the girls would drop everything they were doing and race each other to the door for the privilege of waiting on him. He had a way of looking a girl up and down without making her feel cheap. He knew how to make them laugh, he knew how to charge the air about them with importance. He was sort of like King Midas, only instead of gold, everything he touched became dramatic.

One girl in particular became one of the most important women in the world. She was a plump girl with large dimples. Her name was Emily. Emily hardly ever said anything. She was constantly singing snatches of popular songs absent-mindedly.

"*Oh, the merry go round broke down,*" she would sing. "What will you have?"

"Hello, little pigeon," Doc said to her as he came in one day, "from the back I thought you were Lana Turner."

"Sure," she said, "and I know you—Clark Gable."

"Sit down and take a load off your mind," he said to her when she brought his tea.

"Thanks," said Emily, "and do I need it! I got the jitters—don't tell anybody, but when I brought Mr. Small his lunch today, that little beetle made a pass at me."

"Well, that's too bad," said Doc solicitously, "and Harry just married."

"Because You're Mine," Emily hummed. "He's had three of the girls fired already for turning him down flatter than a carpet."

"Listen," said Doc, "if he tries anything again, let yours truly take care of it—tell him we're engaged."

"You listen," Emily said, "in the first place, when you help a lady in distress, keep your eyes off her legs, and in the second place, you got your own job to worry about."

"Baby," said Doc, "I got this job for life."

"Yeah," she said as she picked his saucer up, "but this is one pen where they let you out for *bad* behavior."

For a big, healthy girl, Emily was pretty psychic. It all began when Doc surpassed every former effort for taking care of it. Everybody on the lot was agog over the search for a brand new female personality to play in Harry's cavalcade, which was to be one generation longer than any cavalcade every filmed. The writers had concocted a central character that was expected to make Scarlett O'Hara look like Pollyanna. Harry Small said it was a star-making part, and so did everybody else after they heard him.

Doc had read the script and was devoting all his energies to casting the role of this heoine, Starr Maple. He even sent Harry Small a note telling him he thought he had a second cousin in East Orange, New Jersey, who would be perfect for it if she could only have her front teeth straightened.

One day a gorgeous redhead walked in. She was stately and poised, and her features were classic but not stony. She was what every man thinks about for those one-way trips to desert islands.

"I would like to see Mr. Small," she sighed.

"Have you an appointment?" Doc asked.

"It's about the role of Starr Maple," she explained.

"Have you a girl in mind for the part?" Doc asked.

"I'm hoping to play it," she said. "My name is Rosemary Laine."

Doc looked her over from head to foot, especially foot.

"Rosie," he said, "you look like too nice a girl to waste your time here. You don't seem to know anything about the Starr character. I've got the script right here. She's ten years older than you. She's a brunette—and very short, she has to be real short for a story point."

"But—are you sure?"

"Look at the last ten tests," said Doc authoritatively. "Frances Connell, Jerry Baretti, Mary Alister, all of them brunettes, in their late twenties and not one of them over five-two."

"If my agent gave me a bum steer, I'll cut his throat," Miss Laine said sweetly.

"You'd better go back and see him quick, sister," Doc advised.

The next day Doc was called into Mr. Small's office.

"Maybe I'm going up to a hundred a week," Doc said, as he went in.

Judy opened her mouth and said absolutely nothing.

Harry Small was slumped in his chair as if he were hiding from Doc under his enormous desk. Doc had never been in there before. He suddenly felt dwarfed, the way he had felt on the floor of Yosemite Valley.

"Doc," said Harry tensely, "do you remember seeing a girl by the name of Rosemary Laine?"

"Laine," said Doc musingly. "Sounds familiar."

"I wish she were more familiar," Harry said. "Her agent promised she'd see me before she signed anywhere and Paramount nabbed her this morning. I just called him up and gave him hell for not sending her to me first and he tries to tell me he did—and she came back discouraged. Six weeks from starting date we let the perfect Starr Maple slip out of our fingers."

"Starr Maple," said Doc. "The script says Starr is a little brunette and the Laine kid was a great big redhead."

Harry jumped to his feet. No prosecutor ever pointed a more accusing finger. "Then you did see her!"

"Now that you mention it, I did," said Doc, a little less sure of himself. "She was here yesterday. But I could tell she wasn't the type and I didn't want to waste your time."

"That's damned nice of you," Harry screamed. "The best bet of the year and you didn't want to waste my time with her! Maybe we were going to change the part to fit her! Maybe you should stop running my business. Why must this happen to me, Harry Small, who never did nothing to nobody!"

"I'm sorry, Mr. Small," said Doc, "I won't do it again."

"And I know why," said Harry. "Because you're fired. You're getting out of here. Tonight."

Doc went back to his desk very quietly. He didn't even stop for his habitual gallantry to Judy. I noticed there was something wrong with him when I picked up the mail at his desk. He told me what had happened. It was tough. Doc loved that reception desk. I guess it was all the power he ever wanted in the world.

I helped him clean out his desk. In the middle drawer there was a comb, some hair tonic, a hand mirror, a marked script of the disastrous cavalcade epic and a *Motion Picture Almanac*. He took his things out slowly, one by one, as if he never wanted to finish.

"Maybe I should hang around a couple of days, to break the new man in," he said.

"Where are you going from here?" I asked.

"I don't know," he said. "South America, Australia— I've got a soldier's pension waiting for me there."

A blonde woman with perfect skin and a placid, satisfied face came in.

"Would you call Mr. Small for me," she said quietly. Doc fell into his act. "Have you an appointment?" he asked stiffly.

"I'm Mrs. Small," she said.

Doc jumped up from his desk and bowed.

"Then you *have* an appointment," he said emphatically, "an appointment for life." He opened the door for her with a click of his heels.

She swished through and Doc saw me watching him bow. He straightened up quickly and looked away.

He just couldn't help going through with it, even when he was all washed up.

Emily came through. She blew Doc a kiss. "See you in the morning, Doc," she trilled.

"Good night, little pigeon," Doc said.

"Oh, seven lonely days make one lonely week," she hummed as she went out.

Doc pulled out the bottom drawer and drew out a huge blue volume, *The History of the Movies,* and a lot of loose typewritten pages.

"I was starting to write a book about Mr. Small," he explained, "but now that I'm leaving so soon I guess I'll have to make it a short story."

He was ready to go.

"I still think that Rosemary Laine would have ruined Harry's picture," he said. "Someday maybe he'll call me in and thank me and give me back my job."

I didn't hear a word about Doc after he walked out that night. The new man who took his place at the reception desk was efficient, and knew his place, which meant that all the fizz had gone out of the job.

One day I was sent to deliver a message to Mr. Small's home in Bel Air. There is a big sign on Sunset, right on the corner of the road leading up to Mr. Small's, that reads, "Visit the Movie Stars." A man was barking through a megaphone to an insignificant young couple. The man was speaking to them as if they were a very large crowd. "Peek into the intimate nooks and crannies of Hollywood," he was declaring. "Be the special guest of a man who knows Hollywood from the inside, who has actually decided the destinies of movie stars. See the glamorous homes of Betty Grable, Bob Taylor, the new Paramount star Rosemary Laine, and the famous Norman castle of my very good friend Harry Small. And if you have any questions, any little whim your Hollywood guide can satisfy, I'll take care of it."

It was Doc! I jumped out of the car and rushed over to him. Before he could shake my hand he had to excuse himself grandiloquently from his audience.

"Doc—as I live, breathe and run errands," I said, "how long have you been doing this?"

"Started yesterday," he said. "Had a long vacation, you know. Took me several months to decide on the proper vocation. But now I've really found it!"

He had his important face on. "It's a job with a real responsibility," he continued. "As the first contact outsiders meet, I am the Face of Hollywood, as it were."

As I drove off, he called to me, "Give my best to Harry," loud enough for his pale little couple to hear. "He's a swell little guy, but I'll never cast another picture for him as long as I live."

Driving on up the canyon to Small's house, I couldn't make up my mind whether to envy or feel sorry for Doc. He was either one of the greatest dead-pan comics or one of the most comical tragedians of our time. Or maybe he was closer to it than I would ever realize, maybe he really was the Face of Hollywood.

A FOXHOLE IN WASHINGTON

When Captain Schofield, a Signal Corps officer, and Lieutenant Colonel Pierce, just out of AMG school, first met
each other, at one of the beverage bars in the Pentagon
Building, they were just about to go overseas. Running
into each other a few evenings later at the Mayflower
Hotel was an occasion, the Lieutenant Colonel insisted,
that called for a drink.

"Well, are you all set, Colonel?" Schofield asked.

"As ready as a sixteen-year-old bride," Pierce said.

That was not the way Pierce normally talked, but ever
since he had bought his uniforms he had felt he was on
an outing. And now this going overseas any minute. It
was the most exciting thing that had happened to him
since he had hit one over the fence with three men on,
for good old Washington U. of St. Louis, nearly thirty
years before. He was a paunchy man with thinning gray

hair—the remains of a good-looking fellow, Captain Schofield decided. Pierce ordered two old-fashioneds, one without sugar for himself. The without sugar was a concession
to the rigors of Army life. While they were waiting for
the drinks, Lieutenant Colonel Pierce revealed that he
was an income-tax expert from St. Louis who was going
to have something to do with finance in occupied territory. He didn't tell Captain Schofield where he was going,
exactly, and Schofield kept his destination hush-hush too.
All they let each other know was that it was a matter of
days now—minutes, maybe. And both of them understood, though they didn't tell each other, exactly, that
their departure had something to do with the Main Show,
as Pierce had heard it described by his BG in the Pentagon.

"Well, here's luck to you, sir," Schofield said when the
drinks arrived. They clinked glasses with self-conscious
ceremony. "That goes for you too, Captain," Pierce said.
Every morning for twenty-five years he had gone down to
the office at nine and come home at five-thirty and he
wished his wife Agnes and the folks in St. Louis could
see him now. Like in the movies. The last few drinks and
jokes with a fellow-officer before going over and getting
into it.

Captain Schofield was a quiet, boyish man, a teacher in
a boys' school in Massachusetts. He was reserved and unemotional because his schools had taught him to be reserved and unemotional, but deep down he felt edgy about
this overseas business too. That last-supper feeling. That
last drink.

That evening at the Mayflower the two men liked
each other, or at least they liked the idea of each other.
"A damn nice fellow," each one thought, and "God knows
what the poor chap is getting in for." They drank with
the proper note of gay desperation and everything that
each of them had to say was of great interest to the other.

"Here's a toast to the Jap Navy," Schofield said when the waiter brought the second round of drinks. "Bottoms up!" He had picked that up from a group of women Marines at the table next to him in a restaurant the night before. Pierce repeated it, laughing. Schofield thought it was rather good too. After all, they were both leaving any moment for overseas.

When they met in the Mayflower Lounge a few nights later it was a great joke. "Still here, Captain?" "Why, Colonel, I thought by this time you'd be God knows where!" They both laughed. The realization that this minute they might be having a drink together in a Washington hotel, the next minute be dropped down in the middle of a war, was titillating. They had three or four drinks, toasting each other's forthcoming adventures again, and the Lieutenant Colonel began to observe the legs of the women coming down the steps.

"How about those over there?" he said. "Those aren't too bad. Though god dammit, you don't see legs the way they ought to be any more! These little ones coming up look like they're set on bean poles. The way I like 'em is when you grab 'em above the knee you know you got something."

Captain Schofield had never talked about women this way and he didn't like drunks, but this was all right, this was war, the way he had heard of it, and the Lieutenant Colonel, for all his vulgarity, was certainly a square shooter. They had another drink and when they said good-bye they both felt the seriousness of the gesture.

"Well, old man, lots of luck to you again," Pierce said.

"Thank you, Colonel. Maybe we'll run into each other on the other side sometime."

Lieutenant Colonel Pierce was into his third old-fashioned when Captain Schofield showed up two evenings later. "Hello, Captain," said Pierce. "Haven't I seen you somewhere before?" This time, when Schofield's drink arrived, they didn't bother with the toasts.

"Well, any news?" Pierce said.

"Something seems to be holding it up on the other end," Schofield said. "Should be coming through any day, though. How about you, Colonel?"

"Oh, just the usual red tape, I guess. Ironing out wrinkles in AMG policy or something. Might take a few more days."

The two officers looked at each other suspiciously.

"Maybe they're saving us for the invasion," Pierce suggested.

"Or maybe they're saving the invasion for us," Schofield said.

Pierce asked Schofield if he were married. Schofield said he was. "I've been hitched to the same woman for twenty-three years," Pierce announced. They didn't come any finer than Mrs. Pierce, he said. And his son, a shavetail in the Marine Corps, was a regular chip off the old block. One of his daughters was married to an insurance man in Minneapolis who cleared fifteen thousand in '43. "Not that money means anything, the way this government is going."

Pierce signaled to the waiter with his empty glass. "I tell you, Captain," he said, "I'm old enough to be your father, so I know what I'm talking about. No matter how much jack you've got in the bank you're a pauper if you haven't got the love of your own family."

He reached into his billfold and pulled out a snapshot of a family group. Mrs. Pierce reminded Schofield of the typical Brookline matron. "Mrs. Pierce is a very handsome woman," he said, and held the photograph the polite length of time before handing it back.

A Wac lieutenant appeared. She was small and rather plain, with a figure that was tidy if not pin-up. Pierce studied it critically. "I hear these service gals around Washington don't mind giving it away if you're going overseas," he said.

Captain Schofield smiled to show that he was one of the boys, but his mind was far away from Lieutenant Colonel Pierce and his observations on wartime morality. He was thinking about his wife, Mignon, in Greenmeadow, Massachusetts. He was wondering if perhaps he weren't going to be around long enough to make it worth-while for Mignon to come down and stay with him. Pierce was again talking about legs. A beribboned Free French officer with a slight, erect figure limped stylishly down the steps.

"Sort of gives me a kick to see the Free French here in the Mayflower," Schofield said.

"I still don't trust 'em," Pierce said. "From de Gaulle up or down."

Schofield said nothing. He was not an argumentative man and things he felt strongly about he preferred not to discuss with Lieutenant Colonel Pierce. The future of the civilized world lies in our trusting those fellows and their trusting us, he thought.

"Now that's the kind of legs I was talking about," said Pierce, eyeing a pair that were moving past the table.

After a while, when Lieutenant Colonel Pierce and Captain Schofield kept on meeting at the Mayflower, they stopped joking about still being in Washington. They stopped talking about the war because they weren't heroes any more. They didn't talk politics because after all there was no sense getting into an argument. They just sat down with each other because people don't like to sit down alone these days and there weren't many other men in Washington they knew to sit down with. Like a couple of fellows who find themselves thrown together in the same foxhole, Schofield thought. The Mayflower Lounge was a Washington foxhole papered with dollar bills, where officers going overseas any minute or any year were sweating out the war.

"I know what let's do," Pierce said one evening after a longer silence than usual. "Let's play a game. I'll bet I can count six silver leafs entering this place before you count twelve bars. And the loser picks up the check."

"Fine!" Schofield said. He thought of Mignon, pregnant in Greenmeadow, Massachusetts. He thought of the invasion and when it would open up and how much he wanted to be there in time for it, not because he aspired to heroism but because this was going to be the biggest fire the world had ever seen and men are still small boys chasing after fires. He wondered how much longer he would have to sit around the Mayflower while the orchestra played something called "Mairzy Doats" and Lieutenant Colonel Pierce tossed off old-fashioneds without sugar and commented on the good legs and the bad legs passing back and forth.

A youthful Air Force Captain with a string of ribbons, a young lady and a cane, appeared on the landing. Schofield pulled out a pencil and drew a cross on his paper napkin. "That puts me in the lead," he said. "One to nothing, Colonel."

The Colonel was watching the Wac lieutenant he had been eyeing for days. He rose so suddenly that he spilled a little of Schofield's drink into the captain's lap.

"The hell with this," he announced. "I'm gonna go over and see if I can get into that Wac's drawers."

For a moment, as the two men looked at each other, one of those private little wars within wars was being waged.

"And the hell with you, Captain, you prim, pious son of a bitch," Pierce said. Then he straightened his uniform, making sure his home-front ribbons were in place, and walked away.

Schofield checked an impulse to call after him, "I hope

I never see you again." Instead he toyed with his drink and thought of Mignon and the waiting French and the petty careering that would always blemish the nobility of war.

"We'll win something out of this in spite of you, you silly bastard," he actually said under his breath. And then, feeling a little better, he ordered another drink and went on waiting.

THE PRIDE OF TONY COLUCCI

No, nothing for me thanks. You boys go ahead, I'll just sit and talk with you a coupla minutes. Say, listen, I'm not *on* the wagon, I'm *driving* the God-damn thing. For life? If I wanna have any life left, the doc says. Yeah, ulcers. You know, the old belly bite. Oh that reminds me, I ain't had my milk yet today. That's a laugh, huh, Rocky Evans on the cow juice. Well let me tell you, chums, this here ulcer is no joke. I'd take cancer and seven points any day in the week. The hell it is my own fault. Well maybe I was pretty much of a sauce-hound in my day, but so was my old man, he still has to have his quart a day or he don't feel like he's accomplished anything. And you never seen an *alter kocker* in better shape than my old man. No boys, it ain't the amber that give me ulcers. It's the fight business. The aggravation. The mockies you got to deal with every day. The crooks all the time trying to pull a fast one on you, with one hand on your shoulder and the other in your pocket. And the bums, oh Jesus, how I wish I had as much money as I can't stand them bums. They are so ignorant, so unsensitive, like a bunch of mules. No wonder I got the bite in the bread-basket, now, Rocky Evans, a man who went three years to high school, a fella what has associated with plenty of class people in my time, screwing around with a bunch of stumblebums.

For instance, you want to know why I got ulcers, you take one of my bums, Tony Colucci, for instance. Every time I think of Tony, I want to get out of the fight business. There must be an easier way, I says to myself. You beat your brains out trying to make a dollar for yourself and your bum and what happens? Your bum turns out to be an ingrate who almost gets you run out of the business. Like this Tony Colucci I started to tell you about. The first time I caught Tony in the amateurs, it must be ten, twelve years ago, I almost broke a leg trying to beat the other managers back to the dressing room. Rocky, you old bastard I says to myself when the kid tells me nobody in the business has got to him yet, all aboard for the gravy train. He was a good-looking kid then, six-three or four, weighing around two-twenty, shoulders that went from here to over there, and not too heavy in the legs. It looked too good to be true.

Yeah, and that's just the way it works out. I win a couple with Tony out of town, and then when I bring him in I shoot my mouth off all over the street how I got the coming world's champion, so what does Tony do to repay me? He gets himself knocked out in the first round. So it turns out all I got is another bum on my hands. One of those big clumsy guys with two left feet and a right hook that's so wild every time he throws it I expect to see him knock himself out. Sure, you'll hear a lot of fellas around here tell you that Tony was a great prospect and might of got somewhere if I hadn't brought him along too fast and thrown him in with Louis and Charles and boys like that before he was ready. But that is strictly b.s. The way I figure it, Tony was just one of those guys God put on this earth to be punished, I can't see no other reason, because Tony couldn't of beat boys like Joe and Ez if they was dying of old age. So maybe he was overmatched. Only it's like I say, a guy as dumb as Tony is born to be overmatched, and I don't see how it makes much difference whether he winds up on Queer Street next year, or the year after next.

One thing I will say for Tony, he didn't seem to care how soon he got there. He would just get out there in the middle of the ring and lead with his jaw and stand there and grin and get his eyes cut and his lips split and his nose busted and keep on grinning until the other guy would finally take mercy on him and put him away. Oh what a bum! Sometimes I'd see the dames sitting ringside holding their programs up in front of their faces because they couldn't stand the slaughter. Well there were plenty of times when I wanted to hide my face, too, only it wasn't because I was a sissy, it was because I was so ashamed at the disgrace of having to be known as the manager of such a poor excuse for a fighter.

After a while I didn't have to worry very much about that, though, because I couldn't get matches for Tony any more. They said I'd have to wait for the next generation of heavyweights to grow up so we'd have somebody new to beat us. So the only work I could get for Tony was sparring with some of the name boys in the gym, three, four dollars a round. A little tough on his profile, maybe, but pretty good money for Tony if he worked every day.

That's where Tony was when I got my brainstorm, an inspiration I guess you'll have to call it, so when I tell you what happened you can see why I got so sore at the dope for almost throwing away the first chance we have to get ahold of a little folding money in over a year.

God-damn it, when I just think about it I get my bowels in such an uproar I . . . Hey, waiter, it's bad enough you got to drink milk without you should wait all day for it.

Well, as I was saying, that was the year they was beating the drums for Chief Firebird, the Apache Assassin they were ballyhooing into a spot for the title match. The Chief had a couple of real money boys behind him with connections, but the best, and they were touring around the country, piling up a knockout record that would read good in the books and give the p.a.'s something to suck the public in on.

So as soon as the idea hits me I hotfoot it over to see Bad News Harry Hoffman, who is one of the Chief's half a dozen managers.

Harry and I have a powder together, for old times' sake, because we used to do quite a bit of business together, and then another one and pretty soon we are feeling pretty chummy and I am ready to begin.

"Harry," I says, "I hear where you are taking the Chief out to K.C. next month," I says.

"Well," he says to me, "I been thinking about it, if I can make the right match."

So I says, "How does the champeen of Italy sound?" I says.

"The champeen of Italy," he says. "Who the hell is the champeen of Italy?"

I look him straight in the eye and I says, "Tony Colucci," I says.

"Tony Colucci," he says. "You mean that broken-down bum of yours? Since when has he been the champeen of Italy?" he says.

"Since I sat down with you," I says. "Harry, we know each other too long to fart around. I am not one of these shyster managers who would rather make a crooked dime than an honest dollar. When you talk to Rocky Evans you know you are talking with a man of his word," I says. "Put it to music and send it to me on a record," he says. But I know I've got him going. "Even the dopes will know he ain't the champeen of Italy," he says.

Then I give him the convincer, I says, "Do you know who the champeen of Italy is?" I says.

"Nah," he says.

"Then how do you know it *ain't* Tony Colucci?" I says. I got him on the ropes now. He's weakening fast. "And if you, a smart guy in the business, don't know," I says, "how in Christ's sweet sake do you expect the dopes in K.C. to know the difference?"

So we do business. Two-fifty for the fight and a G on the side to splash in the third round. I run right over to the gym to tell Tony the good news. Tony was stretched out on a rubbing table with his eyes closed. There was an egg over one eye and his kidneys looked like a rare cut of roast beef. "That new fella from Chicago was tryin' out his left hook," says the jig rubber. "From the way Tony drops, it looks like the fella is back workin' in the slaughter-house."

"Tony'll feel better when he gets a load of the match I just made for him," I says, and I tell the rubber to park his fat ass somewhere else. Then I pull Tony up to a sitting position and rub the back of his neck to bring him around. He lets his legs dangle over the side of the table and holds his head in his hands.

"Jesus," he says. "That sonofabitch can bang."

"Cheer up, kid," I says. "We hit the jackpot again. Twelve hundred and fifty smackeroos to box Chief Firebird in K.C."

"Twelve-fifty?" He raised his head slowly and looked up at me. I'm a sentimental bastard, I guess, but I couldn't help thinking how different he looked from the first time I seen him, back in the amateurs. He was a pretty good-looking kid then, high, straight nose, shiny, black eyes, always kind of, well, kind of proud-looking. Kind of cocky, the way he carried himself, only not the kind to annoy you, cocky and quiet at the same time, like he was saying, Look, I don't want to sound like I'm boasting, it simply happens to be a fact that I am the next champeen of the world. And I guess the dope really believed that too, before I brought him into town and he started kissing the canvas like it was his only girl. That Roman schnoz with the high bridge is fallen down now, he's got an ear on him that would look like a cauliflower even to a cauliflower and his eyes is sunken in and pulled back kind of Chink style the way most the boys' eyes get after they been in the business awhile. He is something to scare babies with if I ever seen one. Only the inside of his eyes is the same, the eyeballs, big and kind of moist-looking, and he's got a way of looking at you too long with them, sort of proud-like and melancholy that makes you want to look away. That's the way he was looking at me now when he says, "Twelve-fifty?" he says. "For twelve-fifty I gotta do tricks. What tricks I gotta do for twelve-fifty?"

"A trick that is already second nature to you," I says. "All you got to do is look for a nice soft place to fall and take a little nap in the third," I says.

Tony don't say nothing. "Twelve hundred and fifty bucks," I says. "A shyster manager would take two-thirds, but with Rocky Evans we split it down the middle. Twelve-fifty divided by two goes six, two into five is two and one over, two into ten is five even, leaves you six hundred and twenty-five fish," I says.

Tony pulls off his trunks, his jock and his cup and throws them in the corner like he's sore.

"Money talks," I says. "Even if you don't. Six hundred and twenty-five talkers."

Tony picks a towel up off the floor and slings it over his shoulder. "Tell 'em to go stick it up," he says.

"Tony," I says to him, "you remember me. This is Rocky Evans, your manager. That fella must of shook you up pretty bad."

"He's got nothing to do with it," Tony says. "Go back and tell 'em they can shove it. Chief Firebird ain't going to knock me out," he says.

He goes into the showers and I stand outside, yelling in, trying to put some sense into him. I says to him, I says, "Since when have you become a primy donna, you big bum? What record do you think you're protecting, for Christ's sweet sake? To hear you talk you never took a dive before. Why, you been in the tank so long you're starting to grow fins," I says.

He just goes on taking his shower. Then when he steps out and starts to dry himself, he says, "I don't care what I done. I ain't going to take no dive for that overrated sonofabitch," he says.

And you ask me why I got ulcers. That is the kind of aggravation you got to put up with from the punchy stumblebums in my business. "Look who's talking about what he is or ain't doing," I says. "Why, you big schlemozzel, you're lucky you got to eat. You was all washed up three years ago. If it wasn't you was tied up with a smart guy like me you wouldn't make six hundred and twenty-five dollars the rest of your life," I says.

"I ain't going to let no overrated bum like this Chief Firebird knock me out," Tony says.

Well there I was, up piss creek without a paddle. Of course there were other ways of handling it, I could slip Tony a mickey the day of the fight, but that's not the kind of fella I am. I been in this business almost twenny years and nobody ever tabbed me as a wrongo yet.

So in mortification I go back to Bad News Harry Hoffman. "Listen," I says to Harry, I says, "my bum, that Tony Colucci, I always thought he was slightly punchy, but now he has gone a hundred per cent off his nut. He don't want any part of that extra G," I says. "He won't lay down," I says.

Harry just yawns like he's bored. "Listen, Rocky," he says, "I'm a busy man. Chief Firebird ain't a fighter, he's a million-dollar corporation, and he's in my lap. All you gotta do is handle one punchy spar-boy. Go handle him," he says, like that's all there was to it.

"But Harry," I says. "Believe me all of a sudden the boy's got a screw loose somewhere. Like a mule he's so stubborn, I never seen him like this before," I says.

But Harry is not what I would call an understanding individual. "They are already putting up the billboards in K.C.," he says. "If that friggin' champeen of Italy of yours don't fold in three, this will not be a very healthy business for you," he says.

So that's the way it is when we go into training and when I take Tony out to K.C. and Harry has the drums beat like I never seen them beat before, and all the papers is talking about how Tony Colucci, the Champeen of Italy, is the one remaining hurdle in the path of Chief Firebird, the Apache Assassin who threatens to do with his fists what his ancestors failed to do with bow and arrow, establish supremacy over the white race. You know, the jive. All this time I can feel my ulcers multiplying like rabbits because I do not know what is going on in the mind of the Champeen of Italy, and I think maybe this p.a. jive about his being the one remaining hurdle etcetera may be going to his head. And all the time we are in training nothing has been settled between he and I because I think maybe I will work a little of this here psychology on Tony, so I don't say nothing to Tony until the day before the fight, and then, when we are taking a little walk around the block after supper, I says to him quick-like, "Now look Tony, stay in close to him for two rounds and around the middle of the third stick your

chin out a little and let him tag you with one, and, remember, don't go down before he tags you like you done
that time in Scranton, when they had to call the cops," I
says.

Tony just looks at me with them sad eyes of his and
says, "I ain't going to take no dive for that overrated
bum," he says.

"Tony," I says, "for Christ's sweet sake, the fix is already in. You got to take this dive. If you don't take this
dive you might as well hang up your gloves. You'll never
eat again. I promise you, you'll starve to death," I says,
"if Bad News Harry Hoffman don't find a quicker way,"
I says.

"I don't care what they do to me," Tony says. "I ain't
going to take no dive for that overrated bum."

"You dirty double-crossing no-good mother-lovin' bastard," I says. "So that's the gratitude I get for putting you in
touch with a good thing. I could of got plenty other bums.
I didn't have to pick you. I thought I was doing you a
favor," I says.

"Up your favors," Tony says. "I tell you I ain't going
to take no dive."

I am so mad I feel like I am busting a blood vessel.
"And just what is so special about this dive, may I ask?"
I says.

"That Chief is a bum," Tony says. "I seen him work in
the gym. He can't punch his way outa a paper bag," he
says.

"And just what has that got to do with our twelve-
fifty?" I says.

"He's a bum," Tony says. "He's a bigger bum 'n me.
I'd feel like a God-damn fairy going in three. I wouldn't
like for my girl to have to read about it," he says.

"Your girl," I says, "is that all that's stopping you,
your girl? You call that fugitive from a notch-joint your
girl?"

"Evelyn is okay," he says. "Don't you go making no remarks about Evelyn."

"Sure Evelyn is okay," I says. "But if I know Evelyn, and you come back with six hundred and twenty-five fish, she'll be able to stand the disgrace of how it looks in the papers."

Then Tony says, "What's this bum got that I ain't got? If you'd a took me along slow and fed me a bunch of setups like they're doing with him, instead of letting them belt me out before I got started, maybe I could of made money like this for winning my fights instead of throwing them."

That's what you're up against in this business, some back-knifing sonofabitch of a shyster manager always filling your boy full of wrong ideas. So I have all I can do to keep my patience, and I says to him, I says, "Listen, deadhead, let's not open up that can of tomato juice again. The question is, are you going to go in three tomorrow night or ain't you?" I says.

"I ain't," Tony says. "I got my pride."

Is that not but funny enough to be held over another week? "Your what?" I says. "You ought to get down on your knees and thank Christ you get your three squares and a mattress under you and you have to have pride yet?" I says.

But the dope won't listen to reason. He won't lay down. It is enough to drive a nervous man to the laughing academy. Twenty-four hours before the fight and the fix is in and my bum won't co-operate. There is nothing to do but to go back to Harry Hoffman. He has the best lay-out in the place on the top floor. The room is full of expensive cigar smoke coming from reporters and hot air coming from Bad News Harry.

"Hello, Harry," I says. "I gotta talk to you."

He looks at me like we are not even doing business together. "Listen, Evans," he says, "if you came up to bet your man against mine, my price is still the same, nine to five."

I think maybe everyone in the world is going crazy except me. Only maybe Harry is not so crazy. After the boys from the paper see that they have drunk all the amber and smoked all the Havana they are getting from Harry, they disappear, and Harry says to me, "For Christ's sake, Rocky, you ought to know better than that. Don't come in here and talk like we was brothers or sleeping together or something. You might as well come right out and tell them Tony Colucci is doing a swan in the third round tomorrow night."

"But that's just the trouble," I says. "He ain't."

Anybody else but Harry would of blown up, I guess. Maybe that's why Harry is a big shot and I got nothing out of the game but my bellyful of ulcers. I could see Harry was steamed, but he didn't throw a punch, he didn't even raise his voice at me. Getting sore is a luxury he didn't have time for, he says to me later, something fancy like that. All he says to me now is, "Send the boy to me," just, "Send the boy to me," like Lionel Barrymore playing the boss of a college or something.

So I finally get Tony up to see him, and God knows what the hell they said to each other because Harry told me to go down to the bar and have myself a powder. About half an hour later Tony comes downstairs and I say, "What happened?" and he says, "He told me not to say," and I says, "Everything all right?" and he says, "That Mr. Hoffman is a pretty sharp fella."

So I am as much in the dark as the paying customers until we get into the dressing room and Tony starts to get ready. Then he takes me aside and says, "Rocky, I want you to go out and get me a little piece of chicken wire," he says.

"What in hell do you want with chicken wire?" I says.

"Get it," he says, like he was the manager and I was the bum.

So a couple of minutes later I come back with the chicken wire. The semi-windup is on and they tell us to get ready to go in.

"Now come into the can with me," Tony says, "and bring a pair of pliers."

We crowd into the john together. "Now cut off a little piece," Tony says.

"How small?" I says.

"Small enough to fit into my mouth," Tony says.

"What the hell?" I says.

"Now slip the wire into something that will keep it from sliding out," Tony says. "A piece of rubber . . ."

"Rubber," I says. "Wait a minute." I pull out my wallet. I always carry a couple along, just in case. "How's this?" I says.

"Okay," he says, "now put the rubber up against my teeth, under the mouthpiece."

So that's the way it is when the fight begins. I don't see what's cooking right away, but it's a little clearer the first time the Chief holds his left in Tony's face. The blood starts right away. It begins to trickle out of one corner of Tony's mouth. But it don't seem to bother Tony and he fights back. He is holding his own. He always had a punch in his left hand and he lets it go a couple of times, spinning the Chief around. The customers stand up and yell. It looks like Tony can take him. The only trouble is that every time the Chief gets that left in Tony's face, there's more blood. By the end of the round he looks like he's been hit in the mush with a ripe tomato. It is dripping down his chin and onto his chest. The Chief don't even have to hit him. All he has to do is press that left glove against Tony's mouth and the chicken wire takes care of the rest.

I do what I can to stop the cuts between rounds, but they are up on the gums and tough to get at. The first jab starts them going again. Tony makes the Chief grunt with that left to the belly but the blood is beginning to bother him now. It pours out of his mouth like a faucet and it begins to look like he's ducked his head in it because the Chief's gloves smear his mouth across his face. After a while his mouth and the Chief's glove are so soggy it makes a squashy sound when they come together. But Tony keeps boring in, spraying the ref and the press-row seats with blood every time he swings.

When he comes back to his corner I says, "How you feel, Tony boy?" and he just shakes his head, he can't say nothing, he's swallowed so much blood. There's nothing much we can do for him now, and when the boys come up for round three Tony is bleeding so bad some of the ringsiders start to yell, "Stop the fight, stop the fight." I find out later Harry has them planted there for that, but he could of saved his dough, for them people don't need nobody to start them yelling, the referee's white shirt looked like it was dyed red, Tony was slowing up a little and the Chief was whipping hard lefts and rights to the mouth until it was flowing like a bloody fountain. Pretty soon everybody in the house was up on their feet yelling "Stop the fight, stop the fight," and finally the ref stepped in between them and raised the Chief's arm.

Tony was pretty sick from swallowing all that blood, but the crowd gave him a better hand when he left the ring than the Chief himself and he mitted them and grinned and I guess he felt pretty good until the excitement wore off. I had the doc take a hinge at that mouth when we got back to the dressing room and I never saw anything like it in my life, the gums was all ripped to shreds like it was so much hamburger.

Well we had to have the doc come back about three o'clock in the morning, superficial hemorrhage I guess you call it, and next morning when Tony woke up his kisser was out like one of these Ubangis. He sounds like he's talking with a sponge in his mouth and it looks like he'll be eating out of a straw the rest of his life, but right away he wants to see the papers. He reads the first write-up and starts to grin and sends me for a razor so he can save it for his scrapbook.

"For Christ's sweet sake," I says, "if you ain't got no scruples about throwing the fight, why you should let him cut your mouth to ribbons for three rounds when you could just sink down to the canvas without even scraping an elbow is a mystery to me."

Tony just went on cutting out the clipping. "For three rounds last night," this here article says,

Tony Colucci absorbed a terrible beating from Chief Firebird, the heavyweight contender. But Tony carried the fight to the winner all the way and was still gamely on his feet when the referee stepped between them to save the gallant Colucci from further punishment.

"You don't understand," Tony says to me.

"Understand," I says. "You'd have to be crazy in the head to understand a choice like that."

And you ask me why I got ulcers? A punchy stumble-bum almost getting me run outa the business and then letting them tear his mouth to shreds when he could stretch out on that canvas nice and comfortable like he was home in bed. All I can say is, if you can figure that one out, you're a better man than I am. Well, thanks boys, now that I got the milk down, I guess a little one won't hurt me. . . .

A NOTE ON THE LITERARY LIFE

Kenneth Channing Baxter studied the young man who had answered his ad in *The Saturday Review*. He not only studied him but was conscious of doing so, for as readers of Kenneth Channing Baxter's famous novels knew, KCB was a great student of human nature. An adulatory profile in a national magazine had quoted the great man as saying that his vocation was also his avocation, for "I have a passion for studying people—reading their faces, their gestures, their silences; my fellow-man never ceases to fascinate, challenge and amuse me."

That was a characteristic observation of KCB's. His first novel had been an instantaneous success when he was only twenty-eight and for the past several decades he had failed only once in his admirable ambition to "give my public a novel every two years."

"In this most uncertain of enterprises," his happy publisher was fond of saying, "a Baxter novel is one of the few sure things. He's America's answer to Somerset Maugham."

America's answer leaned back in his dark-red leather writing chair, tenderly caressing the rich brown bowl of his Dunhill, and smiled reservedly on the young man who wished to become his secretary. It was a smile such as is sometimes seen on a sleek, well-cared-for cat while regarding the mouse she has trapped but has not yet molested.

In this case the mouse, or, rather, the young man was a decidedly unprepossessing creature. He was slight and pale and chinless and he wore an unpressed thirty-dollar suit bought in a small-town store on the occasion of his graduation from college. It was not even what Baxter would consider one of the real colleges—he was a Williams man himself, but one of his sons was at Princeton and the other was prepping at Lawrenceville. The young man was a graduate of the local state teachers' college, where he had done some proctoring while getting his master's in English literature. He seemed rather nervous, and in the course of Baxter's direct and somewhat blunt questioning (KCB prided himself on his "frankness") the young man would lick his lips and blink his eyes. He also, Baxter detected, had a tendency to stammer.

Baxter had doubts about him. Even the name, Sheldon Dicks, seemed a little odd and unworldly. A young lady from Bryn Mawr had impressed the author as far more efficient and presentable—a bit too much of the latter, in fact, and for that reason Baxter had passed her over. He had his own writing house directly on the lake, several hundred yards removed from the main house, and since it was sometimes his habit to dictate at night, neighbors might talk. People in the limelight were invariably victimized by vicious gossip. If he had had more time he would have liked to interview some others—but he was in something of a jam at the moment. His most recent novel, *My Father's House,* had not only soared right to the top of the best-seller lists, but had received an inordinate amount of critical acclaim. Reviewers were calling it "the most mature work this penetrating craftsman has given us." There were fan letters to answer, at the rate of about twenty a day, Baxter told the young man. And there were telephone calls. The young man would have to use his ingenuity in separating the nuisance calls from the real thing. And there was the lecture and public-appearance calendar to be kept up. And callers to be protected from—autograph hounds, publicity seekers, job wanters, salesmen, charity solicitors. "They would all crawl in and carry me off in little pieces if we didn't keep a strong bolt on the door."

Sheldon Dicks bore little resemblance to a strong bolt, but he said he would try. Baxter told his new secretary that it would also be his responsibility to see that the writing table was supplied with paper, typewriter ribbons, pencils, erasers and the like. "Two dozen pencils sharpened to a fine point ready at nine each morning— that has been my rule for over twenty years," said Kenneth Channing Baxter. The young man said, Very well, he would attend to all these details so capably that the illustrious author would be free to concentrate exclusively on the plot, theme and characters of his work in progress.

"And then there are the archives," the novelist said. "The Princeton Library has set aside a Baxter Room where all of my manuscripts, proofs, correspondence, reviews, notebooks and clippings are being collected. So you will also be in charge of what I immodestly call the Posterity Department."

Sheldon Dicks promised to take charge of Baxter's posterity.

"Now one final word," Baxter said in his fame-weary voice. "I see in your references here that you have published a few poems and things in college magazines. One of the banes of my career is the budding, would-be, never-will-be writer. Friends who beg me to look over the first three chapters of their young nephew's novel. Young men who write that they want nothing from me but half an hour of advice. Everybody in this world seems to have a manuscript. There's a literary diamond in the rough behind every bush and under every bed, so to speak . . ."

Sheldon Dicks observed that this sort of mixed metaphor was not unknown to Baxter's prose style, but his face remained expressionlessly earnest, a weapon of passive resistance he had developed to balance his sensitivity to incompetent or graceless speech and text.

"—so," Baxter was continuing, "if you have any literary ambitions, if you aspire to be another T. S. Eliot or William Faulkner or even poor K. C. Baxter, I say that is splendid—provided you do not cultivate this ambition on my time or with my knowledge. In other words, no grubby little manuscripts shoved under my nose with a sniveling 'If you like this enough I wondered if you'd be good enough to show it to your publisher.'"

Sheldon Dicks did have a manuscript, a number of them, in fact, and he couldn't help wondering how Kenneth Channing Baxter had got his start. Had he sprung fully blown as a famous novelist out of some publisher's brain? But he put the question and the impertinence out of his mind. A room of his own in the writing cottage and seventy-five dollars per week seemed a perfectly good reason for saying, "I promise not to inflict any manuscripts on you, Mr. Baxter."

Somewhat to Baxter's surprise, Sheldon Dicks turned out to be the most satisfactory secretary ever in his employ. He was efficient. He was unobtrusive. He was resourceful. He was able to answer the fan mail without even bothering to consult the author. And Baxter had to admit that the letters were every bit as good as if he had composed them himself. Before the end of the first year young Dicks, on his own initiative, was writing Baxter's lectures for him, and even magazine articles. It rather gave Baxter a start to be told by a friend of his at the Lotus Club that his article on "What I Think of Our Younger Novelists" was one of the finest bits of critical work the author had done. "Quite frankly, old boy," his friend had said with an ingenuous twinkle, "I was beginning to think you were going to seed, but this piece proves you have wit and vitality and ideas to spare."

In addition, Sheldon Dicks had rare gifts as a typist. In the course of transcribing a Baxter manuscript, he would tighten the sentences, improve the syntax, judiciously change a word or sharpen a phrase, so that when the finished copy was submitted to Baxter's publishers, the editor wrote that he was happy to see that "the old master, like fine wine, is definitely improving with age."

One day after Sheldon Dicks had been with Baxter for a number of years and was so firmly established in the Baxter ménage that he was referred to by Mrs. Baxter and the household staff as "The Shadow," he came into the author's study to inform his lord that it was time to dress for his radio interview and that he had a few letters to be signed. They made a rather nice composition, Baxter thought, the author in his dark-green smoking jacket against the wine-red leather of the writing chair and the mild-mannered ghost of a secretary bending over him in attentive submission. As Baxter signed the first letter, thanking a reader for calling him "his favorite writer since Galsworthy," an impulse prompted him to realize that in all these years, nearly seven it was now, Sheldon Dicks had never volunteered an opinion of any one of the three novels he had typed and proofread so conscientiously.

"By the way, Sheldon," Baxter said without looking up, "what do you think of the new book?"

Sheldon Dicks's sensitive, birdlike face betrayed no emotion. "I don't feel it my place to comment, sir," he said.

Baxter frowned. "But after all, Sheldon, we're—we're more than author and secretary now. I would say we've gotten to be friends."

It was true that Baxter had advanced Dicks as much as five hundred dollars on occasion, to meet such emergencies as the death of his mother and the collapse of one lung. And during the last year or so, Baxter had fallen into the habit of lunching with Dicks at the cottage, during which time he would relax from the rigors of his work by chatting with Dicks of politics, the state of literature, modern art, the aerial ruts of television and other subjects of the moment. Often he found that Dicks's ideas and phrases could be fitted quite neatly into his own work in progress. "Dicks has a nice mind," Baxter had conceded to his wife. "I would sooner talk with him than with half the writers and publishers I know."

So now Baxter looked up at his secretary and repeated his question. "Seriously, Sheldon, what is your honest opinion of *Moondays?*" When he noticed the younger man's hesitation, he added, "Go ahead, I won't bite your head off. I'm not insisting you tell me it's better than *War and Peace.*"

The wisp of humor seemed wasted on the young man. "Mr. Baxter, if you don't start now, you'll be late for your broadcast."

"Oh, bother the broadcast—I'll make it. Lloyd drives as if he's in the 500 at Indianapolis. But tell me now, I insist"—for suddenly he had to know—"what do you think of *Moondays?* And *Father's House?* And *Second Harvest?* And—what is your opinion of the body of my work? Of my place, shall we say, in American letters?"

There was a long and (what used to be called) pregnant pause.

"Mr. Baxter, since you insist on my telling you this—I do not think you have any place in American letters."

On Kenneth Channing Baxter's face there was no mark, but the look was that of a man who has been sharply flicked by a leather whip.

"My dear boy . . ."

"I think you are the most overrated writer in America today," the words of Sheldon Dicks poured through the vents that suddenly had been opened after having been sealed for years. "Every age has its forgotten heroes and its renowned nonentities. Their span is their own lifetime or a part of it and they flash in it with the spectacular impermanence of fireflies. When Melville was a neglected customs inspector, for instance, there were a whole covey of lady writers being discussed in the serious reviews as if they were the female counterparts of Tolstoy and Turgenev."

Except for the fact that his teeth clenched around the bit of his pipe more severely than usual, Baxter managed to look like the poised, confident man of letters who has received not one but a brace of Pulitzer Prizes.

"At least I admire your frankness. Naturally your—uh —subnormal estimate of my literary powers will not have the slightest bearing on our professional relationship."

Kenneth Channing Baxter believed that and thought of himself as adhering to this principle scrupulously. A few months later, when he found it necessary to dispense with the services of Sheldon Dicks, it was—he believed—for quite a different reason. It was for failure, after several warnings, to have the L key repaired on Baxter's favorite typewriter. The author's fourteenth novel had just been designated merely an alternate book-club selection and this, on top of Dicks's negligence in regard to the L key, had been just too much. After nearly seven years of conscientious and ghostlike servitude, Sheldon Dicks had been pushed out of the Baxter nest and into the wide, wide world.

He did not remain there long. A year later he was in Arizona with spots on his lung and the year after that he was dead. A five-line obituary in the *Times* notified its readers that the deceased had served as private secretary to the eminent author Kenneth Channing Baxter.

Whether or not the dismissal and passing away of Sheldon Dicks had anything to do with the decline of Baxter is one of those intangibles forever to be argued. But Baxter's next novel was not even a book-club alternate, and the one that followed was rather generally ridiculed as old-fashioned and contrived. Baxter went on grinding out novels, but the tide had turned, and he was left floundering in the wake of others' success. Most of the reviewers who had lavished columns of print on the new Galsworthy and the American Maugham were dead or retired. A whole new generation of critics placed Baxter somewhere between Zane Grey and Oliver Kirkwood. To add to Baxter's plight, his money ran out, a fate not uncommon to the fortunes of the get-famous-quick in America. In anticipation of recapturing his lost public he had continued to live in the grand manner with his lake, his private writing house, his green rolling lawns, his great parties and the expensive Mrs. Baxter, long after his books had failed to sustain this sort of living. At last he had to sell, for a fraction of its value, his charming landmark, Rolling Brook. He was faced with the prospect of living out his days ingloriously on a modest annuity.

One Sunday a few months after Mrs. Baxter had passed on, KCB walked around the corner from his small Greenwich Village apartment to pick up the morning papers. As had been his habit for some thirty years, he fingered through the bulky Sunday sections until he found the book review. On the front page was a two-column cut of a face he had hardly thought about in recent years.

Sheldon Dicks's. A banner line asked a provocative question: "An American Rimbaud?" A review by a distinguished English poet welcomed "to the thin ranks of first-line American writers a new poet of such brilliance, intensity, originality and depth as to suggest—but in no way imitate—the erratic French genius of Rimbaud."

Wandering along the street in an uneasy trance, Baxter read the strange facts behind the publication of Dicks's long narrative poem, "A Mass for the Living Dead." When Dicks had died in obscurity on a ranch in Arizona, he had left a request in writing that all his papers should be burned. But a high-school English teacher who had become his friend in the closing days of his life had been so impressed by the manuscript that he had not had the heart to carry out Dicks's instructions. After several years of soul-searching, the English teacher had written in his introduction, he had decided that a higher conscience demanded his giving Dicks's long poem to the world.

From his obscure window, Baxter watched incredulously as the circle of fame spread ever wider around the shadowy figure of his former employee. T. S. Eliot delivered a paper at Harvard on "God and Gods in Sheldon Dicks." In one feverish fall season there were no fewer than three learned, obscure critiques on Sheldon Dicks (*The Worlds of Sheldon Dicks; Sheldon Dicks: An Exploration of Myth as Metaphor; Underground Stream: Ethos and Decalogue in Sheldon Dicks.*) The *Atlantic Monthly* ran a symposium on Sheldon Dicks and new young poets were accused of trying to write like Sheldon Dicks and Sheldon Dicks's "symbolistic" view of society became the fashionable one for literary undergraduates. Some young Americans on the Left Bank shaved their beards and cropped their hair in imitation of Sheldon Dicks. There had been nothing like it since the Kafka boom.

Rummaging through his file for some odd pieces of

writing that might be fed into the all but dried up stream of his magazine market, Baxter found a few lines scribbled in the margin of an abandoned first chapter of a forgotten novel. "Pl. nt. sug. ch. w'l tp tn S.D." he read. It brought back to Kenneth Channing Baxter a lost moment from his old world of fame and prosperity when a mousy underling, in line of duty, had scribbled something Baxter would interpret as, "Please note suggested changes. Will type tonight. Sheldon Dicks."

At a fashionable rare-book store on 57th Street a distinguished-looking relic from the nineteenth century studied through his pince-nez the scribbled notation. Then, deliberately, he compared it with a letter written in the precious hand of Sheldon Dicks. "Yes, yes, this would seem to be quite genuine," he assured the old man in the worn, expensively cut tweeds. "Signed only with his initials and not with the full name it would be worth" —quickly he consulted an open catalogue—"shall we say, fifty dollars."

Baxter was glad to get the money. His annuity was small, and he was making out by disposing of odds and ends, first editions, paintings and the like. As he drifted toward the entrance, the title of a book on the first counter caught his eye: *American Writers: 1900-1952.*

With the incurable vanity of the once famous he could not resist riffling the index to see if his name was still included. Ah, there it was: "Baxter, Kenneth Channing, 67." As quickly as possible he turned to *his* page and read:

Baxter, Kenneth Channing; popular writer of 20's and 30's. Better known as employer of Sheldon Dicks. *See* Sheldon Dicks.

MY CHRISTMAS CAROL

When I was a little boy, I lived with my parents in what was then a small suburb of Los Angeles called Hollywood. My father was general manager in charge of production for Firmament-Famous Artists-Lewin. It was a mouthful, but I used to have to remember the whole thing for the your-father-my-father arguments I was always having with a kid down the block whose old man was only an associate producer at Warner Brothers.

One of the things I remember most about Firmament-Famous Artists-Lewin was the way that studio and Christmas were all mixed up together in my mind. My earliest memory of the Christmas season is associated with a large studio truck, bearing the company's trademark, that always drove up to the house just before supper on Christmas Eve. I would stand outside the kitchen door with my little sister and watch the driver and his helper carry into our house armload after armload of wonderful red and green packages—all for us. Sometimes the gleaming handlebars of a tricycle or the shiny wheels of a miniature fire engine would break through their bright wrappers, and I'd shout, "I know what that is!" until my mother would lead me away. Santa Claus still had so many houses to visit, she'd say, that I mustn't get in the way of these two helpers of his. Then I'd go down the street to argue the respective merits of our two studios with the Warner Brothers kid, or pass the time tormenting my little sister, perfectly content in the thought that the Firmament-Famous Artist-Lewin truck was the standard vehicle of transportation for Santa Claus in semitropical climates like Southern California.

On Christmas morning I had the unfortunate habit of rising at five o'clock, rushing across the hallway to my sister's room in annual disobedience of my mother's request to rise quietly, and shouting, "Merry Christmas, Sandra! Let's wake Mommy and Daddy and open our presents."

We ran down the hall into the master bedroom with its canopied twin beds. "Merry Christmas!" we shouted together. My father groaned, rolled over and pulled the covers further up over his head. He was suffering the after-effects of the studio's annual all-day Christmas party from which he hadn't returned until after we had gone to sleep. I climbed up on the bed, crawling over him, and bounced up and down, chanting, "Merry Christmas, Merry Christmas. . . ."

"Oh-h-h . . ." Father said, and flipped over on his belly. Mother shook his shoulder gently. "Sol, I hate to wake you, but the children won't go down without you."

Father sat up slowly, muttering something about its being still dark outside and demanding to know who had taken his bathrobe. Mother picked it up where he had

dropped it and brought it to him. It was black and white
silk with an elegant embroidered monogram.

"The kids'll be opening presents for the next twelve
hours," my father said. "It seems God-damn silly to start
opening them at five o'clock in the morning."

Downstairs there were enough toys, it seemed, to fill all
the windows of a department store. The red car was a
perfect model of a Pierce-Arrow, and probably only
slightly less expensive, with a green leather seat wide
enough for Sandra to sit beside me, and real headlights
that turned on and off. There was a German electric
train that passed through an elaborate Bavarian village in
miniature. And a big scooter with rubber wheels and a
gear shift just like our Cadillac's. And dozens more that
I've forgotten. Sandra had a doll that was a life-size
replica of Baby Peggy, which was Early Twenties for
Margaret O'Brien, an imported silk Hungarian peasant
costume from Lord & Taylor, a six-ounce bottle of
French toilet water, and so many other things that we all
had to help her unwrap them.

Just when we were reaching the end of this supply,
people started arriving with more presents. That's the
way it had been every Christmas since I could remember,
men and women all dressed up dropping in all day long
with packages containing wonderful things that they'd
wait for us to unwrap. They'd sit around a while, laughing with my mother and father and lifting from James
the butler's tray a cold yellow drink that I wasn't allowed
to have, and then they'd pick us up and kiss us and tell
us we were as pretty as my mother or as intelligent as
my father and then there would be more laughing and
hugging and hand-shaking and God bless you and then
they'd be gone, and others would arrive to take their
place. Sometimes there must have been ten or twenty all
there at once and Sandra and I would be sort of sorry in

a way because Mother and Father would be too busy with their guests to play with us. But it was nice to get all those presents.

I remember one tall dark man with a little pointed mustache who kissed Mother's hand when he came in. His present was wrapped in beautiful silvery paper and the blue ribbon around it felt thick and soft like one of Mother's evening dresses. Inside was a second layer of thin white tissue paper and inside of that was a handsome silver comb-and-brush set, just like my father's. Tied to it was a little card that I could read because it was printed and I could read almost anything then as long as it wasn't handwriting: "Merry Christmas to my future boss from Uncle Norman."

"Mommy," I said, "is Uncle Norman my uncle? You never told me I had an Uncle Norman. I have an Uncle Dave and an Uncle Joe and an Uncle Sam, but I never knew I had an Uncle Norman."

I can still remember how white and even Norman's teeth looked when he smiled at me. "I'm a new uncle," he said. "Don't you remember the day your daddy brought you on my set and I signed your autograph book and I told you to call me Uncle Norman?"

I combed my hair with his silver comb suspiciously. "Did you give me this comb and brush . . . Uncle Norman?"

Norman drank down the last of the foamy yellow stuff and carefully wiped off his mustaches with his pale-blue breast-pocket handkerchief. "Yes, I did, sonny," he said.

I turned on my mother accusingly. "But you said Santa Claus gives us all these presents."

This all took place, as I found out later, at a crucial moment in my relationship with S. Claus, when a child's faith was beginning to crumble under the pressure of suspicions. Mother was trying to keep Santa Claus alive for us as long as possible, I learned subsequently, so that

Christmas would mean something more to us than a display of sycophancy on the part of Father's stars, directors, writers and job-seekers.

"Norman signed his name to your comb and brush because he is one of Santa Claus's helpers," Mother said. "Santa has so much work to do taking care of all the good little children in the world that he needs lots and lots of helpers."

My father offered one of his long, fat cigars to "Uncle" Norman and bit off the end of another one for himself.

"Daddy, is that true, what Mommy says?" I asked.

"You must always believe your mother, boy," my father said.

"I've got twenty-eleven presents already," Sandra said.

"You mean thirty-one," I said. "I've got thirty-two."

Sandra tore open a box that held an exquisite little gold ring, inlaid with amethyst, her birthstone.

"Let me read the card," I said. " 'Merry Christmas, Sandra darling, from your biggest fan, Aunt Ruth.' "

Ruth was the pretty lady who played opposite Uncle Norman in one of my father's recent pictures. I hadn't been allowed to see it, but I used to boast to that Warner Brothers kid about how much better it was than anything Warners' could make.

Sandra, being very young, tossed Aunt Ruth's gold ring away and turned slowly in her hand the little box it had come in. "Look, it says numbers on it," she said. "Why are the numbers, Chris?"

I studied it carefully. "Ninety-five. That looks like dollars," I said. "Ninety-five dollars. Where does Santa Claus get all his money, Daddy?"

My father gave my mother a questioning look. "Er . . . what's that, son?" I had to repeat the question. "Oh . . . those aren't dollars, no . . . That's just the number Santa puts on his toys to keep them from getting all mixed up before he sends them down from the North Pole," my father said, and then he took a deep breath and another gulp of that yellow drink.

More people kept coming in all afternoon. More presents. More uncles and aunts. More Santa Claus's helpers. I never realized he had so many helpers. All afternoon the phone kept ringing, too. "Sol, you might as well answer it, it must be for you," my mother would say, and then I could hear my father laughing on the phone: "Thanks, L.B., and a merry Christmas to you . . . Thanks, Joe . . . Thanks, Mary . . . Thanks, Doug . . . Merry Christmas, Pola . . ." Gifts kept arriving late into the day, sometimes in big limousines and town cars, carried in by chauffeurs in snappy uniforms. No matter how my father explained it, it seemed to me that Santa must be as rich as Mr. Zukor.

Just before supper, one of the biggest stars in Father's pictures drove up in a Rolls Royce roadster, the first one I had ever seen. She came in with a tall, broad-shouldered, sunburned man who laughed at anything anybody said. She was a very small lady and she wore her hair tight around her head like a boy's. She had on a tight yellow dress that only came down to the top of her knees. She and the man she was with had three presents for me and four for Sandra. She looked down at me and said, "Merry Christmas, you little darling," and before I could get away, she had picked me up and was kissing me. She smelled all funny, with perfumy sweetness mixed up with the way Father smelled when he came home from that Christmas party at the studio and leaned over my bed to kiss me when I was half asleep.

I didn't like people to kiss me, especially strangers. "Lemme go," I said.

"That's no way to act, Sonny," the strange man said.

"Why, right this minute every man in America would like to be in your shoes."

All the grownups laughed, but I kept squirming, trying to get away. "Aw, don't be that way, honey," the movie star said. "Why, I love men!"

They all laughed again. I didn't understand it so I started to cry. Then she put me down. "All right for you," she said, "if you don't want to be my boy friend."

After she left, when I was unwrapping her presents, I asked my father, "Who is she? Is she one of Santa Claus's helpers, too?" Father winked at Mother, turned his head away, put his hand to his mouth and laughed into it, but I saw him. Mother looked at him the way she did when she caught me taking a piece of candy just before supper. "Her name is Clara, dear," she said. "She's one of Santa Claus's helpers, too."

And that's the way Christmas was, until one Christmas when a funny thing happened. The big Firmament-Famous Artists-Lewin truck never showed up. I kept looking for it all afternoon, but it never came. When it got dark and it was time for me to have my supper and go to bed and still no truck, I got pretty worried. My mind ran back through the year trying to remember some bad thing I might have done that Santa was going to punish me for. I had done lots of bad things, like slapping my sister and breaking my father's fountain pen, but they were no worse than the stuff I had pulled the year before. Yet what other reason could there possibly be for that truck not showing up?

Another thing that seemed funny about that Christmas Eve was that my father didn't bother to go to his studio Christmas party. He stayed home all morning and read aloud to me from a Christmas present he let me open a day early, a big blue book called *Typee*. And late that night when I tiptoed halfway down the stairs to watch my mother trim the tree that Santa was supposed to decorate, my father was helping her string the colored lights. Another thing different about that Christmas was that when Sandra and I ran in shouting and laughing at five, as we always did, my father got up just as soon as my mother.

When we went downstairs, we found almost as many presents as on other Christmas mornings. There was a nice fire engine from Uncle Norman, a cowboy suit from Aunt Ruth, a Meccano set from Uncle Adolph, something, in fact, from every one of Santa Claus's helpers. No, it wasn't the presents that made this Christmas seem so different, it was how quiet everything was. Pierce-Arrows and Packards and Cadillacs didn't keep stopping by all day long with new presents for us. And none of the people like Norman and Ruth and Uncle Edgar, the famous director, and Aunt Betty, the rising ingenue, and Uncle Dick, the young star, and the scenario writer, Uncle Bill, none of them dropped in at all. James the butler was gone, too. For the first Christmas since I could remember, we had Father all to ourselves. Even the phone was quiet for a change. Except for a couple of real relatives, the only one who showed up at all was Clara. She came in around supper time with an old man whose hair was yellow at the temples and gray on top. Her face was very red and when she picked me up to kiss me, her breath reminded me of the Christmas before, only stronger. My father poured her and her friend the foamy yellow drink I wasn't allowed to have.

She held up her drink and said, "Merry Christmas, Sol. And may next Christmas be even merrier."

My father's voice sounded kind of funny, not laughing as he usually did. "Thanks, Clara," he said. "You're a pal."

"Nerts," Clara said. "Just because I don't wanna be a

fair-weather friend like some of these other Hollywood bas—"

"Shhh, the children," my mother reminded her.

"Oh hell, I'm sorry," Clara said. "But anyway, you know what I mean."

My mother looked from us to Clara and back to us again. "Chris, Sandra," she said. "Why don't you take your toys up to your own room and play? We'll be up later."

In three trips I carried up to my room all the important presents. I also took up a box full of cards that had been attached to the presents. As a bit of holiday homework, our penmanship teacher Miss Whitehead had suggested that we separate all Christmas-card signatures into those of Spencerian grace and those of cramp-fingered illegibility. I played with my Meccano set for a while, I practiced twirling my lasso and I made believe Sandra was an Indian, captured her and tied her to the bedstead as my hero Art Acord did in the movies. I captured Sandra three or four times and then I didn't know what to do with myself, so I spread all the Christmas cards out on the floor and began sorting them just as Miss Whitehead had asked.

I sorted half a dozen, all quite definitely non-Spencerian, but it wasn't until I had sorted ten or twelve that I began to notice something funny. It was all the same handwriting. Then I came to a card of my father's. I was just beginning to learn how to read handwriting, and I wasn't very good at it yet, but I could recognize the three little bunched-together letters that spelled *Dad*. I held my father's card close to my eyes and compared it with the one from Uncle Norman. It was the same handwriting. Then I compared them with the one from Uncle Adolph. All the same handwriting. Then I picked up one of Sandra's cards, from Aunt Ruth, and held that one up against my father's. I couldn't understand it. My father seemed to have written them all.

I didn't say anything to Sandra about this, or to the nurse when she gave us our supper and put us to bed. But when my mother came in to kiss me good night I asked her why my father's handwriting was on all the cards. My mother turned on the light and sat on the edge of the bed.

"You don't really believe in Santa Claus any more, do you?" she asked.

"No," I said. "Fred and Clyde told me all about it at school."

"Then I don't think it will hurt you to know the rest," my mother said. "Sooner or later you will have to know these things."

Then she told me what had happened. Between last Christmas and this one, my father had lost his job. He was trying to start his own company now. Lots of stars and directors had promised to go with him. But when the time had come to make good on their promises, they had backed out. Though I didn't fully understand it at the time, even in the simplified way my mother tried to explain it, I would say now that for most of those people the security of a major-company payroll had outweighed an adventure on Poverty Row—the name for the group of little studios where the independent producers struggled to survive.

So this had been a lean year for my father. We had sold one of the cars, let the butler go, and lived on a budget. As Christmas approached, Mother had cut our presents to a minimum.

"Anyway, the children will be taken care of," my father said. "The old gang will see to that."

The afternoon of Christmas Eve my father had had a business appointment, to see a banker about more financing for his program of pictures. When he came home,

Sandra and I had just gone to bed, and Mother was arranging the presents around the tree. There weren't many presents to arrange, just the few they themselves had bought. There were no presents at all from my so-called aunts and uncles.

"My pals," Father said. "My admirers. My loyal employees."

Even though he had the intelligence to understand why these people had always sent us those expensive presents, his vanity, or perhaps I can call it his good nature, had led him to believe they did it because they liked him and because they genuinely were fond of Sandra and me.

"I'm afraid the kids will wonder what happened to all those Santa Claus's helpers," my mother said.

"Wait a minute," my father said. "I've got an idea. Those bastards are going to be Santa Claus's helpers whether they know it or not."

Then he had rushed out to a toy store on Hollywood Boulevard and bought a gift for every one of the aunts and uncles who were so conspicuously absent.

I remember, when my mother finished explaining, how I bawled. I don't know whether it was out of belated gratitude to my old man or whether I was feeling sorry for myself because all those famous people didn't like me as much as I thought they did. Maybe I was only crying because that first, wonderful and ridiculous part of childhood was over. From now on I would have to face a world in which there was not only no Santa Claus, but very, very few on-the-level Santa Claus's helpers.

ENSIGN WEASEL

Those first days of naval training, no one, to use a land-lubber phrase, could see the trees for the forest. The only impression any of us had was of a new, overwhelming environment. I don't think any of us would have even remembered each other's faces if we had left there after forty-eight hours. It was something like being run down by an eight-wheel truck. You may get a quick look at the front end of the truck, but you're darned if you could ever recognize the face of the driver.

Except for a few Chiefs temporarily elevated to the level of Navy privilege and responsibility (as our new commission status was described to us), we were all erstwhile civilians who did not know enough to differentiate between "parade rest" and "at ease," or to translate three bells into our old Eastern Standard Time, or to explain the different functions of a stream anchor and a boat anchor. For nearly all of us those first hours were like the moment after the plunge from the high board into the pool when the diver is still going down, before he can begin to open his eyes and orient himself toward the surface. Unfamiliar subjects and unfamiliar systems of behavior were being thrown at us so fast that we had no chance to bring our surroundings into focus. We were still going down, but somehow, even in that dark confusion, we managed to respond to bells, bugles, commands and orders (we had just been told the distinction), for man, like his brother, the white rat, is highly susceptible to habit-suggestion.

Among us were men who turned out to be clever, men who proved slow, men who were quick to laugh, men who were sullen, men who had been college professors in sheltered academic communities and were shy among worldly men, and men who had been whiskey salesmen and knew how to make a Pullman washroom roar with laughter. But in the haze of strangeness that enveloped us those first days, we were all indistinguishable parts of one great beast that hit the deck at reveille, performed its calisthenics, went to chow, answered muster, attended class, formed for drill, marched, studied, fed, grew weary, shed its uniform, polished its shoes, doused its face and fell into its sack at taps.

It was procedure at the school, however, for our company to be commanded by a student officer from our own ranks. As Lieutenant Murdock, the young staff officer in charge of our metamorphosis informed us of this, there was a not quite imperceptible flinching back, the faceless mass not yet ready to assume responsibility, leadership, or even individual personalities. After all, we were not men. We were zombies in khaki. It seemed an affront to our conglomerate anonymity to attempt to single one of us out.

"We'll alternate the job of Company Commander so

that as many men as possible will have an opportunity to gain the experience," the staff officer said. "All right, now, who wants to lead off? Anybody here with previous military experience?"

There was another uneasy silence, and although all of us were staring straight ahead, we gave the impression of dropping our eyes and lowering our heads to avoid being seen.

The young staff officer gave a small smile of superiority that was meant to be sympathetic. "Come on now, don't be shy. You'll probably all have to do it sooner or later."

But we were not to be coaxed out from the protective herd.

"No previous military experience at all?"

Then, in the silence, a voice from somewhere in the rear spoke up. "I've had previous military experience, sir."

Irresistibly, all our heads turned. Every one of us had to mark for himself this first one to disassociate himself from the group.

"All right, eyes front," the staff officer snapped. "You men are still at attention." Then he turned to the man who had answered his question, and told him to come front and center.

Even in our stiffened attitudes of attention, I could feel all of us in the ranks leaning slightly forward in our eagerness to see the volunteer. A short, wiry fellow, with a face his mother must call alert but which impressed us as cocky, he stepped out smartly, executed his flank turn with clean movements and, when he had come within proper distance of the staff officer, threw him a salute with plenty of snap (we were supersensitive to things like this because we were just then learning how much more difficult proper saluting was than it looked at first glance). While he held his salute nicely until the staff officer returned it, I recognized this eager beaver as the little fellow who had the upper bunk right next to mine in the barracks.

"Your name, sir?"

"Wessel, sir."

"How much military training have you had, Wessel?"

"Naval ROTC in high school, sir."

Someone down the line snorted. The staff officer addressed us soberly. "I am going to appoint Mr. Wessel your first Student Commander. He will be in exactly the same authority here that I have been since you reported. You understand, men, the fact that he is a Student Officer like yourself in no way limits his authority for the period of his command. Any act of disrespect or disobedience toward him will be considered an act of insubordination under the Articles of War." He turned to Wessel and said officially, "Mr. Wessel, assume command."

Wessel saluted again, very salty, and faced us solemnly. I don't know if all of us did, but I think most of us could sense what was coming. By some law of compensation, men who are deprived of the natural means of self-expression and exchange of opinion can become so sensitized to each other that one can feel little silent waves of approval or apprehension or resentment running through an entire company. What we felt now had no approval in it. Something in the way Wessel looked, in the way he *changed* when he stepped forward to assume command, gave us a hint of what we were in for.

The bark of Wessel's commands was keyed to a self-conscious stridency as he dressed us off, brought us back to attention and then put us "at ease." Then he stepped forward and addressed us with exactly that tone of condescension that often passes for a confidential man-to-man talk from a ranking military leader to his men.

"Men," he began, "I couldn't help noticing a few moments ago that when I told Lieutenant Murdock I had had naval ROTC training, one of you laughed." He paused, for emphasis, and though I think every one of us in the ranks wanted to laugh again, we all waited dumbly with poker faces. "Maybe none of you realize that if you had all been in the naval ROTC, if our country had been more fully prepared, Pearl Harbor would never have happened. So when you laugh at naval ROTC you're casting aspersions on the Navy itself, and our flag."

If it had been a movie, a great Old Glory in technicolor would have unfurled majestically behind Wessel at this moment. Or perhaps phantom images of Roosevelt, Marshall and King would have grouped around him. But this was just Wessel all alone, a small figure against the high walls and towers of the fort. Lieutenant Murdock was looking on, but there was no way of telling from his young, carefully indoctrinated face which side he was on. In the silence, if there is any such thing as a hate-detector, our rising resentment would have sent it on past the danger point. But Wessel was too insulated by sudden power to feel the hate waves that rose from us and curled around him.

"Now I would like to ask that man who laughed to please step forward," he persisted.

No one moved. We all just stood there hating Wessel.

"Mr. Wessel," Lieutenant Murdock said, "if you wish to call a man out from the ranks officially, I suggest you bring your company to attention and give him the command, one step forward, march."

Now we knew where Lieutenant Murdock stood, and we regarded him as a human being for the first time since we had come to the fort. "Thank you, sir," Wessel said, and saluted. He was a little flustered. He gave the command, "Attention" and about half the company snapped to attention, but those of us who remembered what we had been taught the day before, that you don't have to respond to a command unless it is given properly, remained smugly 'at ease.' "*Company*, attention," Wessel

quickly corrected himself, and he glared at us for capi-
talizing on his mistake. He had not been out there in
front of us more than two minutes, but that had been
time enough for a declaration of war on both sides. We
had sighted each other and were moving forward to en-
gage each other, as we were learning to say.

"Now," Wessel faced us for the showdown, "the gen-
tleman who laughed, on his honor as a naval officer, one
step forward, *harch.*"

There was a split-second pause and then a large, red-
faced easygoing fellow with quite a belly on him stepped
forward. Wessel marched toward him with his back very
stiff, the expression on his face a small-fry imitation of
Admiral King's. He was a full head shorter than the
man he had called out, which lent a certain absurdity to
the severity with which he regarded him.

"Your name?"

"Finnegan . . . sir."

The way Finnegan added that dutiful monosyllable
would have had to be heard to be fully appreciated. It
slipped out in a kind of effeminate slur that met the official
requirements of respect while at the same time oozing
disrespect. Now, under the pressure of Wessel's reign, our
phalanx anonymity was giving way to individuality again.
We were beginning to have our villains and our heroes
and soon we would find our jesters, our drones, our wor-
riers, our politicians, our agitators, our rebels and our
Babbitts, like any other family of men. It was as if we
had all been lying together in a dark box like identical
matches, and now, struck against the flint of Student
Commander Wessel, we flared into flames of different
sizes, hues and intensity. By the end of this day, for instance, we would know that our friend Jim Finnegan was
a Hiram Walker distributor for Eastern New Jersey, that
he called his wife "Ginger," that he had played second-
string guard for Rutgers, that he was rather proud of his

imitation of Amos and Andy, with which he had once wowed a wholesale liquor convention, and that he liked to form barracks quartets to sing old ones like "I Want a Girl Just Like the Girl Who Married Dear Old Dad." But right now he was a one-man patrol feeling out the enemy in the first skirmish of one of those innumerable little wars that rage within larger wars that are fought within still larger wars.

Now Wessel was firing at point-blank range. "Didn't you understand Lieutenant Murdock when he explained that I was to receive exactly the same respect as if I were your regular Commanding Officer? If you were to laugh at a remark of your Commanding Officer, you would be guilty of insubordination and . . ."

"Excuse me . . . sir," Finnegan interrupted. "I laughed at you *before* you had taken command. Lieutenant Murdock hadn't appointed you yet."

None of us moved or made a sound, but we all smiled. That was one time when a generality like "the company smiled" would have been absolutely accurate.

"Mr. Wessel"—Lieutenant Murdock came into it—"I would suggest you return Mr. Finnegan to his squad without further reprimand. You are absolutely right to stress military discipline, and there is certainly no place for levity here. But in this initial stage of the indoctrination course, we can be a little more lenient with newly commissioned officers than we might be later on. After all, we must remember that they have not had your advantage of previous military training." All of us searched the proper face of the recent Annapolis graduate for some sign of sarcasm as he addressed his colleague from the naval ROTC. But we searched in vain. It was like looking for something you have dropped under the seat of your car. You are *sure* it must be there, but you can't find it. "Mr. Wessel," Lieutenant Murdock said, "I assume you are familiar with the commands and proper execution of close-order drill."

"Yes, sir," Wessel said emphatically.

"Then for the next forty-five minutes you will drill your men. Have them back here by 1600 and dismiss them for recreation and showers until chow call."

Then Lieutenant Murdock was gone. We had been delivered over to Mr. Wessel.

We were on our way out to the drill field, and doing pretty well for beginners, we thought, when Wessel gave the command, "Third platoon, to the rear, *harch.*" The entire company, with the exception of the inevitable two or three who forgot to turn at all, reversed its course. Wessel shouted "Company, halt," in an angry voice. "I gave you that command on purpose to see if you were on your toes," he scolded. "I distinctly said *third platoon,* not *company.* Now let's see you fellows get on the ball. You're being trained for a war, not a tea party."

It was a warm day and streaks of sweat had begun to stain our blouses. Wessel got us back in formation, turned us around and started us off again, counting cadence for us in his best military manner, "Hun, tuh, thr, fuh, heft, right . . ." Then, because some of us were out of step he gave the order for us all to count cadence in unison. It started somewhere in the rear squad, and spread forward, so in time with the cadence that it could hardly be distinguished. But it was there all right: "We—hate— Wes—sel—all—right . . ."

When Wessel finally detected this mutiny in the ranks an extra bit of color flushed his cheeks, but he fought back stubbornly. "All right, wise guys, knock it off." Then he countered with a "Change step, *harch.*" We hadn't been taught this yet, so the result was pretty much of a foul-up. We knew the only reason Wessel had given us this was to show off his military virtuosity, but another reason it made us mad was because we were just reaching that stage of indoctrination where we had begun to take pride in ourselves as a unit, enjoying the rhythm of doing things right.

"What's the matter with you joes, two left feet?" Wessel scolded again.

This time a lean, bony-faced, red-haired squad leader spoke up. "No, sir, it was your fault, sir. You were out of step."

We all looked at him gratefully, another individual added to our growing list. We had our villain, we had our hero, now we had our expert.

Wessel went up to him excitedly. "*I* was out of step? How could I be out of step? Aren't you supposed to keep in step with *my* count?"

"That command can only be given when the right foot touches the ground, so you can step out on the left foot, sir."

Wessel looked at him and frowned. He had counted on being the only drill man in the outfit. But he knew that answer was right out of the *Bluejackets' Manual*. "Where did you learn that?" he asked suspiciously.

"I've served two hitches in the Navy," the redhead said. This was a direct hit. "I've just been commissioned from Chief."

"Then why didn't you put your hand up when Lieutenant Murdock asked who had previous military experience?" Wessel demanded.

"Because I've been in the Navy long enough to learn to keep my mouth shut and never volunteer for anything, sir," this redhead said.

It was a broadside all right, and Wessel didn't have enough sense of humor to roll with it. He took it hard. All the rest of us laughed, though. The redhead had timed it beautifully. We had something there in that redhead.

"All right, knock it off, knock it off," Wessel screamed, his voice going high in frustration. He reassembled us again, barking his commands with an extra zip to make up for that right-foot business.

So far we figured we were out to an early lead. But it wasn't 1600 yet. By this time we were a good half-mile from the muster ground on the other side of the fort. It was time we started back. But instead of giving us an ordinary "Forward, march," Wessel gave us a double time. Nearly all of us still had the bodies of middle-class civilians in sedentary jobs and one hundred yards of that double time was just about our speed. But when we had run two hundred yards, Wessel still gave no sign of slowing down to ordinary cadence. We were a pretty sick-looking lot by that time. Gorham, a fat boy who had been recruited from an advertising agency and who had done all of his training at Toots Shor's bar, had to give up at the halfway mark. We didn't look back, but we could hear what he was doing as we left him behind. "We ought to rub that little bastard's nose in it," someone muttered.

The rest of us managed to finish, but it was pretty bad. It reminded me of a movie about the mad Czar of Russia I had seen when I was a kid. All about how Paul the First marched his soldiers up and down all day long until some of them dropped dead. Then, for laughs, he faced a squad toward a cliff, told them to forward march and then went in to have his dinner. Two soldiers who refused to commit themselves to the ravine as per Paul's command were shot for disobedience. That's what I was thinking about Wessel while I was trying to catch my breath. A couple of fellows had the heaves.

Only Flanders, the redheaded ex-Chief, and Gersh, the Jewish boy who had been a Brooklyn handball champion, and one or two others I hadn't noticed before were able to stand up without struggling for breath. We were too exhausted even to hate Wessel the way we were going to when we caught our breaths.

"Sixteen hundred to seventeen-thirty, turn to for recreation," Wessel announced. "Company dismissed."

"How about this for recreation?" Finnegan suggested to a couple of new friends as we headed wearily for the barracks. "Let's throw Wessel on his back and we'll all jump on him, in cadence, double time." In our weakened conditions, needing a safety valve for our anger, that seemed funny enough to be worth passing on to the entire company.

We all walked back to the barracks in two's and three's. Only Wessel walked alone, an erect, solitary little figure, feeling the weight of his responsibilities. That evening at mess no one would pass him anything and no one would speak to him. I think, in a way, we were all glad to have Wessel there to focus our anger on. A body of men in training needs something like that to break the monotony. Tojo and Der Führer were too far away. We were all wandering around blindfold and we needed something to pin the tail on. The existence of Wessel gave all of us our first chance to express ourselves. I made up a limerick about him which won me my first recognition. Finnegan worked up an imitation that proved very popular. Flanders called him "The Admiral," and that name pleased us for a while. Somebody else called him "Little Napoleon," and a serious high-school teacher from Troy amended that to "Napoleon the Fourth." Our imaginations seemed limitless, our wit endlessly resourceful where Wessel was concerned. Thanks to Wessel, we had our first sense of morale. That was the first evening that real laughter was heard in the mess hall. We began to discover that we were not just a line of mechanical men out of some blue-jacketed *RUR*. Each one of us had his own individual way of reacting to the tyranny of Student

Commander Wessel and we were drawn toward one another in the common cause.

Wessel and I had to undress in the same narrow space between the double-decker beds. "Sure wish we had a little more room to stow our gear, mate," he said. He talked as if he had been born in the navy. He was a salty little character, all right. I didn't say anything. Even if I had wanted to, I was silenced by the spontaneous unwritten law. There wasn't going to be any fraternization with the enemy.

After Wessel got undressed and came back from the head, he knelt on the stone floor against the sack under his and said his prayers. I was a little sorry to see him do this. It nicked the sharp edge of my indignation just a little bit. Not that I was sentimental about people saying their prayers. It was just that from my upper he looked awfully small and vulnerable down there. He didn't look quite formidable enough to be worth the emotion we were all expending. But even after taps, with the lights out, the war went on. Someone, I think it was Finnegan, but it might have been another wag, Cosgrove, began giving falsetto commands in an outrageous take-off of Wessel.

"All right, pipe down," Wessel called.

"Pipe down," the falsetto echoed. "Change step, *harch*," a high voice mimicked.

"Come on, knock it off," Wessel demanded.

But his military authority couldn't do him much good in the dark. "Knock it off, girls," a series of falsettos trilled through the barracks.

But next morning Wessel returned to the attack. At morning muster he laced into one platoon leader for not keeping his fingers together when he saluted on the "all present and accounted for." During the morning it began to drizzle and the uniform of the day was changed to include rain covers and raincoats. When we mustered after noon chow, Wessel's sharp eyes discovered that a small, somewhat comical ensign by the name of Botts was not wearing the plastic cover that fitted over our cloth hat covers. Botts was a pharmacist from Oxford, Mississippi, who had already come to Wessel's attention because of an inability to keep in step that was so consistent it appeared to be congenital. Wessel bore down on him now exactly as one has read the first Napoleon did, upbraiding his man for inattention to regulations. In his slow, naive drawl, Botts explained that rain covers had sold out at the PX before he could get one.

"That is no excuse," Wessel decided. "You should have had one with you when you reported aboard here."

We were still on land, of course, but Wessel had already caught the navy way. We half-expected him to sentence Botts to fifty lashes. He did put him on report, which meant two afternoons with the awkward squad that had to do half an hour of extra drilling during the recreation period.

"Ah doan hardly think that's fai-er, Mr. Weasel," Botts protested. The way he talked it was impossible to tell whether that was a sarcastic pun on Wessel's name or just a beautiful coincidence. Probably it was just accidental, for the chances are Botts was too simple a man to invent so ingenious an insult. A day before, hearing that writing had been my civilian profession, he had said, "We got one of them fellas in my town. Sleeps all day an' stays up all night an' is always comin' in for aspirin. Fella by the name o' Fo'kner." Anyway, whether it was dialect or inspiration, Botts' name for our nemesis supplanted all the others. From then on I never heard him called anything else but Weasel.

Right up to the last day of his temporary command, Weasel ran us ragged. He even put me on the awkward squad for mislaying one of my textbooks. When I had to go up to him and confess my crime, he said, "What do you mean, your *Watch Officers' Guide* is *lost?* You mean it's *adrift.*" On another occasion Finnegan, who was not our neatest officer, came to muster with one shirttail not quite tucked in behind. "You've got an Irish pennant," Weasel admonished him. Finnegan thought his racial stock was being insulted, but it turned out this was just navy for any loose end. Day after day, Weasel drove us crazy with that salty stuff. He caught Cosgrove saying, "I'm going upstairs," one time and made him come to attention and repeat "I'm going topside" twenty-five times.

But Weasel's behavior all during his command was human compared to his conduct the Saturday morning of the first captain's inspection. The commander of the company judged most exemplary was to become Battalion Commander for the following week and Weasel coveted that post feverishly. At our own company inspection at muster, a kind of dress rehearsal, Weasel fumed and fussed over us like the Prussian drill instructor to whom he was related in spirit. He detected a speck of dirt on several white hat covers and ordered the offenders to fall out and dust them with face powder or chalk. Poor Botts, a military man by Act of Congress but not of God, had turned up with a khaki hat cover when the uniform of the day called for white. Weasel gave him a tongue-lashing that would have been worthy of Admiral Halsey. Botts was put on report, which meant he would automatically be deprived of his first week-end liberty. Botts, Wrong-foot Botts, we called him affectionately, had become a sort of company mascot and terrible threats of revenge were muttered through our ranks. Someone was promising to beat the Weasel to a pulp after the war if he had to track him down halfway around the world. Botts was swearing that if he ever got on the same vessel with Weasel he would push him overboard at night.

Before we marched over to the main drill field where

the Commandant of the school and his staff officers were waiting to review us, Weasel gave us a real fighting man's pep talk. We were going over to do or die this morning for the honor of Company A. Weasel expected every man to be on his toes. Weasel had every confidence that we would be the smartest company on the field. Napoleon before Austerlitz couldn't have addressed his men with greater challenge.

We came up onto the main field with Weasel strutting out in front like a college-band drum major. We were a pretty smart-looking outfit at that, for a bunch of last week's civilians. But as our turn came to turn and pass the reviewing party, we were supposed to execute a left flank so the whole company could pass in two long lines. The first two platoons did a flank turn to perfection, but the third platoon, led by Finnegan, executed a column turn instead. Even if you never knew or have forgotten your close-order drill, you can probably imagine what a blow this would be to the military career of our first Student Commander. When Company C won the accolade, Weasel looked as if he had lost the big war all by himself instead of just this little Saturday-morning one.

We never knew for sure whether or not Finnegan's boner was an accidental or intentional thrust at Weasel's military ambitions, but whichever it was, it settled our first Student Commander's military star, at least there at the training school.

On Monday we had a new Student Commander, the ex-Chief, Flanders, who knew how to keep us in line without treading on our toes. By the end of that second week we were so absorbed with blinker, the names of the seven different mooring lines, the semaphore alphabet and the relative hauling power of whip-and-runner and jigger tackle, that we had neither time nor energy to hate Mr. Weasel in the manner to which he had become accustomed. By the end of the third week his name wasn't even mentioned any more. He was around, marching in the ranks with the rest of us, hitting the deck at 0600, standing watches and attending classes, but as Commander Weasel, the scourge of the company, he wasn't there at all. The only hangover left from our original indignation was the continuance of the silent treatment. It wasn't an active thing any longer, just a habit we had gotten into that first week and habits are hard to break when they become imbedded in a group like ours.

Near the end of the course I was sprawled out on the bunk next to Wessel's struggling over a navigation problem that included a double-running fix I was the last man in the class to master. Weasel was sitting on the edge of his sack and after a while he began looking over my shoulder. When he saw where I was making my mistake, he pointed it out to me. I thanked him and he moved in and worked out the rest of the problem for me. That saved me about half an hour at a time when I needed every minute I could get to cram for the final exams. Weasel knew his navigation, all right. No one else was as fast at plane recognition or receiving blinker, either. We talked a while after he brought my hypothetical ship into port. I didn't encourage him much, but it didn't take much. After all, man's a social animal who can starve for conversation just as he can for bread. I felt a little sorry for Weasel now, so I threw him a few crumbs of conversation.

I guess that was the first time anybody had talked to Weasel in the two months we had been there. We talked about Topic A, of course, what kind of orders we hoped to get when the course was finished. Each of us had been given forms to fill out that day indicating our choice of sea and shore jobs. They didn't promise to send us where we wanted to go, of course, but the Commandant had said our preferences would be "a guide to the final decisions." The jobs and types of vessels we listed were probably as good a guide to our characters as you could find. Flanders told us he had picked PT's. He liked small boats and after those two hitches he wanted to be his own boss. Gersh wanted to skipper a landing craft in European waters. He wanted a personal crack at Der Führer. I hoped to be assigned to Air Intelligence, one of those fellows on the carrier who gets the fliers' stories when they come in. Finnegan said it didn't matter what he put down. He had things all greased before he came in to be a four-striper's aide. Almost every job in the navy seemed to appeal to somebody—except that of Armed Guard. The Armed Guard officer was the one who commanded the navy gun crew on merchant ships. That job was on everybody's s-list. For one thing it was the merchant ships that were still catching it heaviest that season. They seemed to be losing one or two somewhere almost every day. And then there was all that friction between the navy and the merchant marine, another one of those wars within wars. There were the usual rumors of feuding and fighting between navy gun-crew commanders and the merchant skippers. Someone said an Armed Guard ensign had gone to Portsmouth for life for murdering a merchant four-striper who had made his life hell all the way to Oran. All of us thought about Armed Guard the way Russians must think of their Arctic forced labor camps.

So I told Weasel about my ambition to get on an LV or an LCV in the Atlantic (I wound up on a stinking submarine tender in the Pacific) and he told me he had put in for personnel work on a battleship. "I like that sixteen-inch armor plate on those BB's," he laughed. I thought this sounded a trifle cautious for an old sea dog like Weasel but I didn't say anything. I had already exchanged more words with Weasel than our entire company combined and I didn't want to overdo it.

On the day before the graduation exercises our orders

came through. We were in the barracks, after coming back from the classrooms where our final academic standings had been posted. Flanders, the acknowledged leader now, had placed first, the high-school mathematics teacher second and Weasel third. When we opened our orders, there were little whoops of triumph and little cries of defeat. Flanders was going to have his PT and Gersh was going to an anti-submarine school outside of Miami. I was supposed to report to the Potomac River Naval Command, apparently to write PRO stuff for the Bureau of Yards and Docks in Washington, exactly what I had hoped to avoid. Then there were the usual service foul-ups. Larrabee, a civilian radio engineer, had been short-circuited to a personnel job, and Finnegan, whose scientific knowledge did not extend beyond his ability to describe the ingredients of blended whiskey, had been assigned to a radar school at Harvard. Foster, a rich boy from the Cape who had been sailing all his life and who had joined the navy through an old-fashioned love of the sea, was assigned to an ordnance depot in Norman, Oklahoma.

But when I looked at Weasel, I saw the worst defeat of all. He was sitting on his bunk, staring at his orders. All the color had gone out of his face. I thought he was going to cry.

"What did you get, Wessel?"

He ran his hand over his forehead twice before he said it. It was hard for him to make the words come out. "Armed—Guard."

It got around the barracks the way a thing like that would. In less than a minute, Finnegan, Cosgrove and the other leaders of the fun were crowding around him. Botts was there, too, and the others who had had to take it from him in the beginning. It was as if they had all discovered Weasel again. For two months he had been practically forgotten, but now, in these last moments before we scattered literally to the seven seas, it all came back to us again, the ordeal of that double-time run back to the fort, the needlessly intricate drills, the sweaty hours we had spent on the awkward squad, the face of the Weasel as he shouted his commands at us. . . .

"Armed Guard," Finnegan said and he shook his head in mock-tragedy. "Well, good-bye, Weasel, it was nice knowing you."

"Did you read about that merchant ship that went down in the Gulf last week?" Cosgrove asked the crowd. "Damn sharks ate the entire personnel."

"Remember, Weasel, we expect you to live up to the highest traditions of the Navy," Flanders said. "Keep those guns blazing until you go down into the drink."

"Maybe you should have some last words handy," Gersh suggested. "Something that will go down in naval history like 'Don't Give up the Ship' or 'We Have Not Yet Begun to Fight.' "

"Ah hear those dirty old merchant marine skippers eat navy ensigns for breakfast," Botts drawled.

Weasel looked out at us from behind his white, stricken face. "Get away from me, you dirty bastards. Get away from me!"

His shame was public now. We had all seen the moisture in his eyes. By evening Finnegan was leading his quartet in one of those spontaneous little songs that sweep a barracks.

> Armed Guard—Armed Guard!
> Weasel takes it very hard.
> He came in salty as he could be,
> But when it came to going to sea—
> He'd rather send you, and he'd rather send me.

The taunts continued after taps again. A bass voice in the darkness offering "Rocked in the Cradle of the Deep" or Finnegan coming up with "To Commander Weasel, the Navy Cross—posthumous" was all the stimulus we needed for prolonged laughter. But no imperious commands to "knock it off" came from Weasel's sack now. I could see him lying on his back, mute and miserable. It almost seemed as if you could smell the fear oozing out of him as from an infected wound. Once I thought I heard a muffled sob, but I couldn't say for sure.

I didn't think anything more about Weasel until three or four months later when I went up to the BuPers office in the Navy Building to see what I could do about getting out of that PRO job. There he was, at a desk near the railing. When he saw me he smiled and came right over and wanted to shake hands. He was looking a lot happier than when I had seen him last.

"Hello there, mate." He smiled invitingly. "How's the navy treating you?"

"Four oh," I said, shoveling it back to him. "How long you been up here?"

"I got myself yanked out of that Armed Guard school after five days. I knew a three-striper from home up here."

"I thought you'd be a thousand miles out to sea by this time," I said, thinking of the time he had made me say *adrift* when my *Watch Officers' Guide* was lost.

"Well, a man might as well go where he can do the most good," he said. "After all, I was a CPA for six years. Paper work is my job. I can probably do more for the war effort right here than on a stinking merchant ship."

"And live longer too," I agreed.

"The Navy doesn't need any heroes," Weasel said. "It needs men who can do their jobs where they're best suited."

I looked at the papers on his desk. They seemed to be requests from officers for transfers from their present stations. They'd come to someone like Weasel for processing.

"I suppose you get quite a few requests for transfer from Armed Guard," I said.

"Anything I can do for you, just say the word," Weasel answered. "I got a pretty good in with the Old Man here. Might be able to expedite something for you."

"Weasel," I said, "the only expediting I'd like to see is your transference to a fighting ship that's going into action. I'm not like you, Weasel," I said. "I hate war. And one of the things I hate most about it is you and your kind of expediting."

There. I had said it. It is vitamin pills for the soul to make a speech like that. Weasel turned a little pale—but not as pale as he had turned when he got those original orders to Armed Guard—and went over to his desk and sat down with his papers.

I didn't see him again until after VJ Day, when I was back from the Pacific and had gone up to the Bureau of Supplies and Accounts to get my pay accounts straightened out. There was Weasel, at another desk. He was a Lieutenant Commander now, and his left side was covered with ribbons, the Victory, the American Theater, the Asiatic Theater, the Navy Commendation, and two different kinds for marksmanship.

He came over when he saw me and greeted me like an old shipmate. And of course he offered to expedite the endorsing of my orders and the back per-diem pay that was due me. There was quite a line in front of me and I was all hopped up inside to see the wife and kids for the first time in two years so I stifled what was left of my character after twenty months on that damned tender, behind the battle lines but under direct fire from mosquitoes, heat and boredom.

While we were waiting for the girl to bring my checks

up, Weasel told me a little about his war. He had been up in the Aleutians, after the Japs had been driven off, and out to Pearl after the war had moved on and he had spent four months in Rio, for some reason. "Boy, the *muchachas* down there!" he said with a touch of the continental he had acquired on his travels. The captain in charge of the office here was going to set up a private investment house in New York after his discharge and Weasel was going along as his assistant. It had been a pretty good war for Weasel all right.

It was almost three years before I bumped into Weasel again. It's seeing him again that has brought this whole thing back to me. I was down in Washington on a writing assignment the other day and I decided to drop in and say hello to Flanders whom I had seen a good deal of in the Pacific and who had stayed with the Navy on a regular commission. So I was on my way up the main stairs of the Navy Building when Weasel was coming down. He was in a plain gray business suit and did not look much like the Captain Bligh of the training school or the be-ribboned expediter of the Battle of Washington. The only way you could have spotted him for an ex-military man was from the miniature commendation ribbon in his buttonhole.

"Hello, mate," he said. "You here for the same reason I am?"

"I don't know—what are you here for?"

"I'm going back to active duty. I'll be a three-striper this time, boy."

Then he looked at me gravely and I saw the face I had first seen on the drill field of the training school, the little Napoleon, the leader of men, the man of action.

"Looks like we're getting ready for another one." He pressed his lips together into a hard line. "We've got to build the biggest, strongest navy in the world. I think every one of us navy veterans ought to come back in and start pulling his weight in the boat."

"Weasel," I said, "I guess the difference between you and me is that you're just a natural-born military man."

I could see him back in that training school, double-timing another batch of flabby civilians.

"But you've got to be patriotic," he said, a little on the defensive.

"Sure, patriotic," I said. But how could I tell him all the different colors and flavors and subtle variations of patriotism—all the way from shameless self-aggrandizement through the normal sense of self-protection to messianic self-sacrifice? How do you say those things to a little man like Weasel, ready with warlike exhortations and drill-instructor discipline to fight the war from desk to desk and from shore station to shore station, to the last rubber stamp, to the final endorsement?

T H E   D A R E

Paul Maxwell was staring out across the light-green sea. He was watching a small white outboard plowing up the water some hundred yards off the end of the pier. Skimming along behind in a golden blur was a water-skier. It was one of those things, Paul was thinking, for which you remember a vacation day when you're back in the city grind, the color of the sea sparkling green as champagne, the busy sound of the little outboard motor and its foamy white wake, and behind, the lithe human figure balanced gracefully on water skis that seemed to be flying over the surface of the sea.

Paul rose, and leaned on the railing of the pier to watch the sport. Only then did the yellow-brown halter above the deep-tan midriff inform him of the sex of the skier. Suddenly the outboard skidded to a daring turn and seemed to head directly toward him. It raced forward until he was sure it was too late to turn away. But in a last-moment swing of the stick, the small boat veered to safety by inches. But the girl behind, flying toward the pier—how could *she* possibly veer in time? It didn't seem real that anything so free, so perfect could come to such a brutal ending, but in his mind's panic he was already diving in to grope under water for the broken body. Then, close enough to Paul for him to see the smile on her face—more than a smile, a look of exhilaration—she calmly leaned out from her skis, in the opposite direction from what Paul would have thought logical, and shot away from the pier, streaking around the boat in a sweeping arc before coming back into position behind it again.

Twice more the boat and the skier made passes at the pier that seemed to make collision inevitable. But Paul was not to be taken in again and watched in fascination instead of panic as boat and girl dared themselves to see how close to the pier they could come without crashing into it.

"That first time I really thought they had it, General," Paul said to a little hard nut of a Cuban who looked as if he had been put in to bake and left too long. The General, who took care of renting boats and beach equipment, had won his rank in a now-forgotten South American war.

"Oh, that's Gerry Lawford. She's crazy." He said it as if everybody already knew it.

"What kind of crazy?" Paul asked, as he always did about words that had lost their original cutting edge.

"Real crazy," the General said. "Bats in the belfry crazy."

Paul did not have to ask the Cuban to enlarge on this. In these two weeks he had come to know the General.

"Always doing crazy things. Like last year, she tried to sail a dinghy to Cuba all by herself. The Coast Guard had to fish her out of the drink about thirty miles out. That crazy enough for you?"

Paul liked the story. Not being an adventurer himself, he always felt drawn to those who were.

"Who is she? Where'd she come from?"

"Oh, Gerry's been around Key West for years." The General's grin was an amiable slit in the burnt crust of his face. "Calls herself a fugitive from Palm Beach. Her folks have a big home up there. Real rich people, own a perfume business or something. 'Bout ten years ago they had her all set for one of those ritzy Palm Beach weddings. Supposed to marry a Prince Somebody-or-other. He's still around there, married to an automobile heiress. But anyway, the afternoon of the wedding, Gerry showed up down here. Came into this bar where I was working at the time. It's gone now. Just about all the old places are gone. Anyway, this girl Gerry, I'm telling you about. I can still remember what she said. 'Let him marry one of my sisters. They go in for that stuff. And he doesn't care which one it is as long as it comes equipped with a checkbook.'

"Well, the old checkbook wasn't much good to Gerry after she landed here. Old man cut her off without a cent. But it didn't seem to bother Gerry none. She just went on having one hell of a good time."

"But what'd she do? How'd she get by?" Paul was interested in things like this. In the dark hours he always wondered how he'd manage if he suddenly lost his knack for commercial illustrating.

The General considered a moment. "Gerry did—well, she just sort of did things nobody else could get away with. For a while she was a mate on a charter boat. I know that's a hell of a job for a girl, but somehow Gerry talked Red Merritt into it. Then she got on this WPA Artists' Project they had down here when things got so bad the whole town hadda go on relief. She paints real good when she feels like it. Then she came into some money—a trust fund or something the old man couldn't touch. She bought herself a sloop and just sailed around the islands until the money was gone. The kind of person Gerry is, you never have to worry about her and money. Last year she was a crew member in the yacht race to Havana. Her boat won and she stayed over in Havana with the millionaire and his wife who owned it. They staked her to five hundred dollars at the Casino and she came back here last fall with enough dough for the year." The General chuckled. "Even a year for Gerry."

Somebody had come up to rent a rowboat and the General was climbing agilely over the side to pull one toward the landing. While Paul had been listening to the General his eyes had been panning with the outboard and the tanned figure that soared in its wake. Now the boat was idling and Paul watched how the girl handed the skis up over the side and began swimming in toward the pier. She swam, as Paul had already come to expect her to, a capable Australian crawl, and he was fully prepared to believe that she had been a Woman's AAU free-style champion, maybe even an Olympic winner. For even before he had looked into her face, Paul was ready to accept her as one of those special people who perform the most amazing feats without breaking stride and for whom the improbable is merely routine.

He was watching her intently, at the same time trying to disguise the directness of his stare by occasionally glancing past her toward the outboard driver who was easing the boat toward shore. She scampered up the ladder to the pier, swinging herself up over the edge acrobatically. As he watched her lift her arms to shake the water from her shining hair, the image struck vividly in his mind: the tall, glistening, honey-brown figure with its long, smooth muscular symmetry, and the wet, gleaming face with the surprising Asiatic cast to the eyes.

He studied her movements with a professional ap-
praisal intensified by the challenge a man always feels when
he comes unexpectedly into the presence of a woman who
attracts him. But, a shy man in his manners, he would
have let her go silently if she hadn't looked up from shaking her head clear to grin at him. There was no flirtation
in it, he could see, no hint of coyness. It was just the
sudden *hello* one person flashes to another when they're
on the edge of the sea, when the sun is warming them
and they're both caught up in that sense of exquisite well-
being of a tropical island's winter day.

"How long have you been doing that?" he heard himself saying.

"The skiing?" Her voice was pitched low, charged
with excess energy, and the water was still shining on
her face. "I think I was born on those things. At least
I can't even remember learning how to do it."

He knew everything she had done—all the crazy things
—she had always done. She was one of those naturals.

"You make it look so easy."

"It is, for some people. I've seen others try for a month
and never even get up out of the water."

She gave a little laugh that Paul would remember.

The driver of the outboard was climbing up onto the
pier now and Paul was just wondering what he could
say that would leave things open to further possibilities
instead of closing them. But she solved his problem in
the most casual way: "If you're on the beach around ten
tomorrow, come out and try it." She paused, appraising
him. "Are you good at things?"

"Well, what kind of . . . ?"

"Oh, you know, regular skiing, skating, diving," and
then she added for fun, "tightrope walking, high tra-
peze . . ."

"Oh, sure," he replied. "Remember that fellow who
crossed Niagara Falls on a high wire . . . ?"

She laughed, and her lips, still moistened with sea water, made him think of the blood-red bougainvillaea after a sudden shower.

"Probably see you tomorrow then," she said, and he watched as she strode down the pier with another man. For that was the way it already seemed to him. Even though an unromantic little voice of reason told him this was just one of those vacation reveries. The other man was young, tall, handsomely made, tanned to a color that comes with years of moving in the sun rather than carefully exposing oneself to it for two or three weeks a year. With that sense of inferiority that city men have when confronted by the masculine great outdoors, Paul had to admit to himself that this bronzed Adonis, this sun god, was the perfect match for her. They were the two glorified figures in the cigarette ads, the bathing-suit displays. Good God, he should know them—for ten years he had made his living drawing them!

That evening, for the first time since he had come South, he put on his white linen suit, feeling a little foolish as he fussed with the bow an extra minute to get the ends even and checked the general effect in the full-length mirror of the bathroom door. Then he walked down to the Beach Club dance. His sense of foolishness, of a recapturing of college-prom excitement, increased as he saw the couples swaying slowly together in the open patio while the orchestra played what every orchestra seemed to be playing this season, "Because You're Mine . . ."

Gerry Lawford, who came skimming out of the sun and across the sparkling sea, did she really exist? Paul wondered. Or was she merely a city bachelor's sun-struck dream? And even if he were to find her here, what good would it do him if she were dancing in the arms of the sun god?

Then he saw her, all yellow gold, her hair swept up

into a crown of jet topped by a single flaming hibiscus. Paul watched as the tired strains of a worn-out hit tune were finally abandoned for a samba. With her cigarette-ad partner, Gerry danced it as a professional would have, or, perhaps better, as an inspired amateur, with a wild enthusiasm that made all the other dancers on the floor appear to be not so much dancing as pushing each other around.

Paul wondered what it would feel like to dance with her, and whether cutting in was a breach of Club etiquette, and while he wondered the music stopped and Gerry and her cigarette ad were on their way from the patio to the parking lot. Paul had no idea how nakedly his eyes must have been following them until the General, now doubling as a buffet waiter, mumbled to him, "That's the way she always is—comes in for one dance, maybe two, then she's off again, always on the move."

"Think they'll be back, General?"

The General chuckled. Gerry and her restless ways obviously served him as entertainment. "A crazy one like that, who knows? Right now she's probably on her way to the casino at the Casa Marina. Win a thousand, lose a thousand, who knows where she'll wind up tonight? Maybe flying to Cuba. Maybe trolling around the Keys with a kicker."

The General was amused. But Paul, with nothing to go on but a romantic imagination that was working overtime, knew he had to go on to the casino.

He walked around the tables until he found her at the craps layout. There were only a few people playing, so it was easy to edge in behind her. "Hi," she said when she saw him, as if it were perfectly natural that he should be there, "bet with me. I'm hot."

She had the dice and her point rolled ten. The odds were with the house, but she bet a hundred on herself and made the point on her third roll. Paul had backed her for five. She made three more passes, dragging all her winnings until she had run a hundred up to almost three thousand. Betting with her each time, but conservatively, Paul was around fifty ahead. The reckless way she played seemed to mock his conservatism and he felt suddenly depressed, as if this was a surer sign than any he had had before that this was a will o' the wisp.

She was still running the game, the dice doing everything she asked of them, when she suddenly lost interest. "I'm going to cash these in. Let's play roulette."

At the roulette table Paul watched with an amazement lined with admiration as she plunged on hunches, betting the limit on single numbers, all or nothing, 35-1, while he was putting five on red or black or settling for the short odds on groups of numbers. The wheel wasn't rolling for her and in less than ten minutes she had managed to throw away the big win she had taken from the other table. It hadn't been money at all, just little colored chips to fling across a board.

"That's tough luck," Paul said. "You should have quit when you were out there in front."

"Oh, what difference does it make?" Gerry said. "I'd just as soon lose it as win it."

That was beyond him, that kind of recklessness, that kind of wildness. Maybe that's why it attracted him so strongly. "Time for a drink," she said, and she led him into the bar, full of laughter, full of hell, full of something Paul had never had to cope with before and he remembered the General's answer, "What kind of crazy— bats in the belfry crazy." Well, what kind was that? It came in all sizes, from you and me to the straitjacket and the chair.

She drank the way he had seen her do all these other things, doubles, fast, ready to go further than anybody else, closer to the pier. And then, as abruptly as she had lost interest in the dance, the dice, she said, "Oh, the hell with this drinking. Who wants to go swimming?"

The cigarette ad, who had been at the bar when they reached it, said, "Oh, God, that again? I gave up moonlight swimming about the time I had my first hangover. Once a season holds me fine."

Paul was wondering if he could make his voice sound casual enough when he said it. "I'll go swimming with you."

"Swell. Are you a good swimmer?"

"Oh, good enough to paddle around."

"I feel like swimming tonight. I think I could swim to Cuba tonight."

Remembering the General's joke about Gerry and her impulsive night flights, Paul wondered about that last one. He wondered too if her escort was objecting to this improvised shift in the evening's pairing. Paul even started to mutter something about it, but the sun god was ahead of him. "Good God, I'm glad she's found a sucker she can entice into those inky waters. Otherwise I might have had to go myself."

Paul and Gerry sat on the end of the Club pier. The water was black and uninviting as it sloshed up under the pilings. It should have been moonlight, Paul was thinking.

"I never win long shots," he was saying. "And this afternoon, when I first saw you out there, it was an easy hundred to one against our ending up alone together like this."

"I like people who are ready to do things without planning them ahead," she said.

"Isn't Bob the ready kind?" he asked, meaning the sun god left standing on his clay feet at the hotel bar.

"Oh, Bob . . ." The way his name trailed off told practically everything. "Bob is something like me. Only he isn't quite up to me. So he bores me. And anyway, I like people who do something. All Bob did was inherit money. He . . ." Then she swung the rudder on the conversation. "What're we talking about Bob for? Bob's always around to talk about. How about you? You aren't just a rich kid. I know you do something."

"Eleven months a year I'm a commercial artist. A pretty good one. The other month, I go away somewhere, Tehuantepec last year, Key West this time, and try to paint for myself. A sailor rowing in Central Park. Awful one-sided compromise."

"But better than nothing," she said, and they talked a little about painting, nothing too flossy, about actual techniques, and the local problems with light and dampness, and the things she said were more businesslike and practical than he would have expected.

"You must have been painting a long time," he said. That WPA thing was a long way back now.

"I don't really paint," she said. And then after a moment of silence, "I don't do anything."

"But I thought you didn't like people who don't do anything?" Paul said. He had meant it for banter.

"Maybe I don't like myself."

Then, abruptly finished with conversation, she said, "The hell with it. Let's swim."

He saw her poise for a moment on the edge and then arch and knife cleanly into the dark water. He plunged in after her, expecting to tread water and splash around in the dark. But she was already moving off from the pier, her head bent low into the choppy sea as she executed her rapid crawl. Paul, an average swimmer, had to exert himself to keep up with her. Before they were fifty strokes out from the pier this swim had taken on a disconcerting quality. When they passed the first marker a hundred yards beyond the landing Paul knew this was no hilarious midnight escapade. There was an intensity about this swim out toward a dark, far horizon that made Paul realize he had gone beyond his depth into waters measured in other ways than merely in fathoms.

The sea water poured down his throat when he gasped for breath and his body ached to turn back. But he feared doing this might lose everything he had gained this evening, this strange, wonderful girl, this water-gypsy who had risen for him out of the sea. Yet there was a limit to his endurance and he was beginning, for the first time in his life, to reach the edges of it. His stomach tightened with the panicky feeling that his next stroke would double him up in a cramp of exhaustion. Alone with all the salt water, he was going to have to swallow his pride and turn back, slowly work his way into shore. Just then Gerry's face bobbed up close to his.

"Hello," she said. She looked fresh and impish, and the sight of her so close to him revived him a little.

"I'm hungry," she announced. "Let's go back."

His stomach felt too full of ocean water for an appetite, but when he finally managed to get back to the pier and climbed up beside Gerry he was suddenly exhilarated. Of course he was hungry. He was starved. He had kept up with Gerry Lawford, crazy Gerry Lawford, and he was ready for anything.

They went skipping down Duvall Street, actually skipping like a couple of crazy kids, and when they reached the all-night Cuban place, they both had two helpings of black beans and yellow rice, washed down with beer Gerry drank from the bottle. "An oral regression to infancy," she called it, and they both laughed. They were laughing at things that were funny only to them and Paul felt sorry for anyone who didn't have a Gerry Lawford in his life. The years before Gerry fell away to a flat, arid desert of monotony.

He walked her back to her hotel, the Southernmost House, it was called, an intriguing Victorian mansion of towers and great porches that dominated the point where the Atlantic met the Gulf. He stopped in for a nightcap at the old oak bar that looked out on the sea, and when they paused for a moment on the great balcony and listened to the waves, the night and what they had made of it suddenly gave him the courage, and he kissed her, feeling the recklessness, the restlessness passing from her lips to his. Then, with her kind of suddenness, she broke away.

"Let's go conching in the morning. Call for me early— say between eight and nine. I'll show you how the real conchs do it."

Her door closed him off from her so suddenly that he was left with the effect of her having vanished from his side in some metaphysical way. He could almost have believed this hadn't happened at all and that their evening had been simply an extension of his daydream. He walked back slowly to his hotel with his mind still flooded with the vision of that afternoon's golden sweep across the sunlit sea.

Every morning since he had come to Key West, Paul had slept late, counting that one of his chief vacation pleasures. But this next morning he was up in time to see the clouds opening up for the early sun to pour through. Even the pelicans were still asleep, drifting idly in small groups, rocking gently with the tide. Paul pulled on some ducks and a sport shirt and went down to the beach. Suddenly, as if by signal, all the pelicans rose together and went flapping out to sea on some urgent pelican business. Paul realized this was the first day since he had come to Key West that he was really alive. He thought about Gerry, and, for the first time, about her always being with him. The only trouble was, he couldn't quite see her in his tailored New York apartment. It was a little like bringing home to captivity some wild bird whose home is the open sea. He was in love with her, though, in a way he had not imagined a man of his temperament could be.

He walked down the beach to the Southernmost and when he didn't find her on the downstairs porch, he went up and knocked on her door.

"Come on in, Paul," she called and he entered to find her in white ducks with the legs rolled up to her knees, and an old sweatshirt. But somehow these had the effect of heightening rather than smothering her beauty. She was squatting on the floor finishing a hurried water color. Strangely, it was the scene Paul had been watching from the beach, the pelicans rising in formation from the rose water of the morning sea. It was done in swift, fluid strokes, and the rose color was redder, stronger than it had been. The peace and tranquillity of the scene that had impressed Paul on the beach was translated into disturbing colors and broken lines. Thumb-tacked on the walls were half a dozen other seascapes, all blurs and sudden strokes of color, suggesting rather than representing, all catching some of the recklessness and vitality that Gerry brought to everything she did.

"These are all yours?" It wasn't really a question, merely an opener.

"Just splashing around."

"But they're damn good."

"My God, Paul, I was only playing. Don't look so serious."

"But they're—they're big league. You should do something with them."

"I will, darling. I'll give them to you."

She jumped up, and with a little mock curtsey handed Paul the one she had just finished. "To remember me by." She laughed.

He took the picture, beginning to say something serious, trying to make it sound not too pompous, but she cut him off. "Hell with it. Let's go conching."

They walked down the street to the Negro "beach," a narrow, rocky promontory where the rowboats were pulled up. They carried the one they were going to use out over the rocks and pushed off. She showed him how to pole it, and then, when they were out a little way, she said, "Let's see if we can catch ourselves some crawfish first." He held the boat for her while she poised the long three-pronged spear over the surface and peered down through the single fathom of light-green water to the edge of the shoal at the bottom. Suddenly the spear shot into the water and when she pulled it up the prongs were fastened to a small speckled brown lobster. Paul tried it after that but even after he spied one on the bottom, the deceptive angle of the spear beneath the surface made him overshoot the target. It was much harder than it looked.

She tried it again, and when she brought up a larger one, lost interest in the spear.

"Conching's more fun," Gerry said. "I'll show you how we dive for them." Fixing a large circular glass to her eyes, she dived nimbly over the side. Paul was fascinated to watch her glide down through the twinkling green water to the rocks below. Watching her move along the bottom with slow-motion grace, he was reminded again of his earlier vision of her as a mermaid called up from the depths by his imagination.

But just then she popped up through the surface, crying, "Eureka!" triumphantly holding up a good-sized Queen conch.

She slithered over into the boat and handed Paul the goggles. "I know what let's do. Let's see who can stay down the longest." She said it as a child might, as a spur-of-the-moment dare. But Paul, remembering last night's swim, feared it might develop into more of an ordeal.

"But we haven't got a watch, Gerry."

"Oh, we can count, one-and-two-and . . ." She gave

him the beat. "Oh, come on. It's beautiful down there. It's fun to stay down."

Paul adjusted the goggles, inhaled until his temples began to pound, and dived. As Gerry had promised, he found himself enveloped in a shimmering green world more beautiful than he had imagined. He gripped a rock at the bottom to hold himself from rising and groped along, pleased with his unfolding ability to measure up to Gerry's adventures. He wondered how much time had passed. He had begun keeping track but a large octopus that turned out to be a massive undersea growth had frightened him off his count. Water was slowly seeping in under the rubber rims of the goggles and his eyes were beginning to smart. Then his ears were aching and he had a sense of being squeezed within green walls that were pressing down and in and up at him. He thought he saw a conch a few feet ahead of him, but that was too far now. His lungs were ready to explode. Why, a man could die, die down here to prove something. But what? What did it mean to Gerry? He was shooting up toward the surface now, flailing his arms with mounting frenzy as he wondered if he could make it in time.

Then his head was above water at last and he was breathing, breathing, that first and last of luxuries.

"Ninety-three," Gerry called. "Paul, I'm proud of you." The praise, the smile, the warm camaraderie completely erased his choking panic of a moment before.

"Now count for me . . ." She could hardly wait to get the goggles on and be over the side again. She was gone in a swift little dive that hardly disturbed the calm surface.

Fifty . . . He could see her gliding leisurely along the bottom. Seventy-five . . . ninety . . . Soon she had passed his record and he waited for her to pop to the surface, chortling over her triumph. But she was staying

down. One hundred . . . one hundred-and-twenty-five
. . . He peered down anxiously. She wasn't moving any
longer. Just seemed to be sitting there—the mermaid
again—at home on the bottom of the sea. One hundred-
and-fifty . . . sixty . . . seventy-five . . . And this count
slower than seconds—that was three minutes! The pulse
of panic began to thump in his throat . . . No one could
stay down that long . . . Suddenly he remembered those
nightmare stories of giant shellfish that clamp down on a
swimmer's hands . . . Somewhere he had read how a
Marine had been lost that way in the South Pacific . . .

In this same moment he dived, reached her, groped for
her and they shot up to the surface together.

"Gerry—Gerry—are you all right?"

"Of course." She laughed. "I was just getting ready to
come up. How high did you count?"

"One hundred-and-seventy-five."

"Dare me to stay down for two hundred?"

"Frankly," Paul said, "I've had enough diving for one
morning. You won't be satisfied till the Coast Guard drags
the bottom for you."

"Okay," she said, completely unconcerned. "Do you
like conch? The couple who run the Southernmost are
friends of mine. We can take these right in their kitchen
and start working on them. I lived on these things one
season down here when you could've turned me upside
down and shaken me and never found a nickel."

That day Paul felt as if he were gliding through life
on skis the way Gerry had skimmed the surface of the sea.
The lunch on the sun porch of the Southernmost, the
walk through town to the fishing docks; the long talk
on the beach; the cocktails at sunset, the fun of drinking
together and the marvelous sense of growing intimacy;
and finally the moonlight dance in the patio and Gerry
Lawford, this crazy, unpredictable, magical girl, in his
arms at last. His lips were against her golden cheeks and
even the smell of her was of some fresh wild berry that

one finds on the hills. Later tonight, or perhaps tomorrow, he would ask her. He was already trying it, phrasing it, like a stage bit player with one line to perfect: Gerry, you said you never turn down a dare. So, I dare you to marry me.

The song was still "Because You're Mine," only this time Paul was much more tolerant of its sentimentality. Her lips were brushing his ear—his skin tingled with the pleasure of it—she was going to kiss him. Only instead, she was whispering, "Darling, feel like going swimming? Let's go swimming again."

"Gerry," he said. "I'm still water-logged. Why don't we skip it tonight?"

"I want to go swimming," she said. "At night I love to go swimming."

"Baby, I—I just can't tonight. I love you. I'm lost in you. I want to marry you. But if we start swimming out tonight, you know what'll happen, you'll dare me to see which one of us can swim out the farthest. I'll bust a gut trying to keep up with you and . . ."

"All right, don't swim with me. I'll swim alone. I like to swim alone." She was glaring at him and the wildness was a new kind, and he thought he knew for the first time what the General meant.

"Gerry, why get so angry? Tonight let's just dance and have some drinks. Maybe tomorrow night we can swim."

"I don't want you to swim with me," she said. "I'm going swimming alone. I'm going now."

For a moment Paul considered following her. But then he thought, she's high-strung, she can't stay up at that pitch all the time without having these moods. I'll let her work her way out of it and send her flowers in the morning. By lunch time she'll be thinking up some new crazy stunt and daring me to follow.

The next morning Paul reverted and slept late. When he went downstairs to breakfast, everyone was talking about it. The Coast Guard was still searching for the body, he heard people say. But she was such a wonderful swimmer, he heard people say. She was always such a happy-go-lucky, such a high-spirited girl, it doesn't seem possible she'd do a thing like that, he heard people say.

He walked slowly out to the edge of the point and looked across the sea. The sun was high and the waters were smooth. He had no idea how long he had stood there, or when the truth first flashed for him, but when it did he was sure he had known it from that first moment of fear and wonder when she had seemed bent on crashing into the pier. It was so simple now. Gerry's courage had been fool's gold, not really courage at all. Only the wish to die. When he cupped his hands to light a cigarette he saw how they were trembling. He stood a long time that morning at the sea wall.

By the time the sun was lowering toward the horizon, the first shock was easing off into a kind of numb submission, a sense of inevitability, of having entered for a few stolen moments into a shadow-world. For he was no longer sure whether Gerry Lawford and their first day, their second, and their last, had really happened. Or whether a mermaid, a water-gypsy, turned mortal for a day, had merely swum home to the green depths out of which she had come.

THE ONE HE CALLED WINNIE

Between you and your childhood is a wall. You struggle with some half-remembered incident and it is like a loose stone in the wall. The loose stone may be a chance word or two or some almost forgotten person out of the past who jostles the memory—in this story the memory of a young man who thought he had forgotten the confining complexity of his four-year-old world. Tommy is eighteen now and his mind is busy with the present and the future. It isn't easy for him to point his mind back into the past when he was four years old and lived with three big people in a big city. He knew one as Mama and one as Daddy, but last and most important was the one he called Winnie.

Tommy remembered Winnie. Tommy remembered how he loved Winnie. When he was four years old he was pleased by the color of her. There was a sense of something that came down to him over the side of his bed, something soothing to him. It was the voice, a warm, quiet, affectionate voice, and a way of touching him that was both playful and respectful. Of course when Tommy was four years old he did not know that he wished to be respected. This only came to him when he was able to look back, as he was doing now. All he knew then was that a certain kind of contact made him laugh or smile or just feel good without having to smile. It was Winnie who knew best how to do this sort of thing. It was not what Mama and Daddy liked to do, which was to get a response out of him whether he felt like it or not. They liked to hear Tommy break out into a certain kind of laugh and often they would tickle him or fuss with him until they got him to make the kind of sound they were waiting for. Sometimes they would have him do this for their guests. It would make everybody laugh and then they would all go downstairs to their cocktails feeling satisfied.

Then Winnie would come. He would not see his parents again until the lights were out and he was almost too sleepy to know whether or not they had remembered their promise to come up and kiss him good night. Meanwhile he would have Winnie. Winnie with her assured way of talking to him, her way of knowing when to play or use playful talk and when to leave him alone to his thoughts. Winnie understood things like that. She made him feel like somebody, not just something to play with and show off to friends. For instance, if Tommy was examining a door knob, as he often liked to do, she would not gush all over him and say, "Ooh, Tommy likes the door knob? Tommy *likes* the door knob!" and then laugh absurdly. Winnie simply would say, "You see, Tommy, now you know how it works, and when you want to lock or unlock it you turn this latch up above—*here.*"

And she would show him once and expect him to know how to do it.

So it was all these things, the voice and the manner, her way of treating him as one human being to another, her soothing color—or maybe it was the many things he loved about Winnie that made the color seem nice, too.

He couldn't remember how far back he remembered the color, for Winnie had tended him in his crib and attended his graduation from the crib to his first real bed. In those first years with Winnie he didn't know—or he didn't know he knew—that there was anything special about the color of Winnie as compared with· the color of Mama and Daddy. Daddy was whitish except for his chin and the sides of his face that were a sort of bluish. Mama was a sort of pale pink with red lips and often she had some flaky white stuff on her nose and reddish-orange circles on her cheeks. But Winnie was the color of the coffee that Daddy liked to drink with the cream in it. Sometimes Daddy would let Tommy pour the cream. Tommy didn't know why, but it made him feel very important when he poured the cream into his daddy's coffee. One morning when he felt he was pouring especially well, he said, "Look, Daddy, I'm making a Winnie color."

Daddy made a face and looked around as if Tommy had said something bad. Tommy could not understand the look on Daddy's face. He always felt nervous when his father got that look on his face. Tommy knew he had done something wrong but he could not imagine what it could be.

Daddy looked at his son very solemnly. "Tommy, I want you to remember this," he said. "You must never *never* mention Winnie's color again. It is not nice to talk about people's color."

But that summer they had gone to the shore and Tommy remembered friends of Mama's telling her what a wonderful tan she had. Yes, and what about Daddy, picking Tommy up in his arms and saying, "Our little puppy—he's getting as brown as an Indian." What about Daddy? If it was all right to talk about people's color sometimes, why wasn't it . . .

He had been ready to point this out to Daddy, but his father would not let him talk.

"I want no argument about this, Tommy. Just remember, it is not nice, it is never good manners, to talk about people's color. Do you understand?"

"Yes, Daddy," Tommy said. He frowned very hard, the way he had seen his father do when he was listening to somebody he did not agree with. But frowning did not make it any clearer.

"Now run along and let Daddy read his paper."

Daddy mussed Tommy's "rat's nest," as Mama called his curly straw-colored hair, and smiled to show that he was no longer angry and that he considered the incident closed.

Tommy went up to his room to be alone with his thoughts. Why, oh why was it bad manners to mention the color of a person? It was only a year or so before that he had learned his colors and Mama had been very proud of how quick he was in telling blue from green and red from yellow. And then he would say, "That sheep is *white*," and, "That cow is *brown*," and Mama would hug him and say, "Wonderful, Tommy!" and have him do it all over again when Daddy came home from work. Now if it wasn't bad manners to know the color of a sheep or a cow, why was it so wrong to say the color of a person?

He thought he knew what his mother would say. Something like, "Now Tommy, you're too young to worry about such things, just do as Daddy says." So he decided to ask Winnie. Winnie was his friend and would tell him the truth if she knew.

That evening after Daddy and Mama had gone out

for dinner, he and Winnie were alone in the nursery and she was reading to him about Winnie the Pooh. He always thought that was very funny. Instead of Christopher, she would use his name in the story, so it would be Tommy Robin and Winnie the Pooh. That always made him laugh. Sometimes he would call her Winnie the Pooh. Usually, as soon as she had finished the story-poem, Tommy would say, "Oh, again! again!" Often Winnie would have to read it five or six times before he had had enough of it for one evening. But this time, when she had read through it once, he didn't say, "Again! Again!" He made a frown face like his daddy's and looked at Winnie, looked and looked at her without saying a word.

Finally Winnie gave a little laugh and said, "Tommy, what's wrong? Do you see something on my face?"

"You have a nice coffee-'n-cream-color face," Tommy said.

"Thank you, Tommy," Winnie said. "I'm glad you think it's a *nice* coffee-'n-cream-color face."

"But Winnie Pooh, why is it bad manners to say it's a nice coffee-color face?"

"What on earth are you talking about, Tommy boy?" she said. And she nibbled his ear a little bit. From the time when he was a little baby he had loved to have her nibble his ear.

He told her about pouring the cream on his daddy's coffee and what Daddy had said about never mentioning Winnie's color again. But he liked Winnie's color, he said. It was a lot prettier color than a pale white or a silly old pink. And it was true. He would always remember Winnie's color. It wasn't exactly cream-in-coffee. It was a light golden brown, something like honey color. It was—thought Tommy for many years—just the right color for skin to be.

Winnie took him on her lap. She raised her hand to squeeze his ear lobe gently—he always liked her to do *that* too—and he noticed, perhaps for the first time, that the palm of her hand was quite white, as white as Mama's. He felt confused by all this white-and-coffee-color difference. There was something about it, he was beginning to sense, that was very big, like the night and the sky and death, something that was outside of him and yet that he was a part of and would have to try and understand.

"Tommy, I wouldn't say this to every four-and-a-half-year-old boy," Winnie began, "but you have good sense. Some people can understand things at four that other people won't understand when they're forty-four. There's nothing really wrong with saying what color a person is. I don't mind being my color. I think it's a nice color, too. The reason why your daddy says it isn't nice to mention it is because most people are glad to be white. They're afraid their being white and my being coffee color will hurt my feelings. But there's nothing wrong with being coffee color. The only thing wrong is the way some people feel about other people being coffee color or chocolate brown or coal black."

"Chocolate brown is a nice color, too," Tommy said.

Winnie nuzzled his cheek and said, "Maybe the time will come when people will all be just people and won't pay no mind to whether they're coffee color or peppermint stripe."

"Peppermint stripe would be fun," Tommy giggled.

"Children are the nicest people," Winnie said. "Children just seem to start out knowing all the things that big people forget and sometimes never get to know again."

Tommy was pleased. While he understood this only a little better than what his daddy had said (and mostly not said) at breakfast, he knew that Winnie was trying to talk to him as a person, the same way she explained door knobs and other interesting things to him. He still felt pretty puzzled, but somehow he was reassured. He hugged Winnie and squirmed his face into her neck. "I wish I could grow up to be your color, Winnie Pooh," he said.

Winnie laughed, and then looked at him sadly, but with her eyes still smiling.

"You're a something," she said, as she often did, and the sound always pleased him, though he didn't know why. "You're really a something."

One evening when Tommy was almost five, Mama and Daddy came to his bedside to tell him they had to take a trip to California. They would be back as soon as possible and they hoped he would not mind.

"Is Winnie going?" Tommy wanted to know.

"Of course not, Tommy. Winnie will be here with you."

"As long as Winnie stays I don't care how long you'll be away," Tommy said.

Tommy's mother started to cry. She was so hurt that for a few minutes, until Daddy talked her out of it, she was saying that she would never be able to go and enjoy herself if she thought her baby no longer knew who his mother was. Tommy didn't want to make his mother cry, but it all seemed silly. He liked his mother tucking him in at night. But she wasn't Winnie. His mother was always going and coming and talking on the phone. She was terribly busy doing things that had nothing to do with Tommy. Winnie was with him all the time. All except one day a week when she went off somewhere and left him alone. She always brought him something when she came back. Tommy would run out and throw his arms around her and nuzzle into her neck and say, "Winnie, Winnie Pooh, what did you bring me?" And Winnie would say, "Oh, nothing, why? Do you think I have to bring you something every time I come back?" And Tommy would laugh and start hunting for his present, in the pocket of her coat, or in one of her clenched hands, or in her purse or even inside her gloves. It was one of their favorite games. It was great fun. It was always easy to find. Sometimes when Daddy played jokes like that he made it too hard to find and Tommy would get tired and his daddy would tell him he must learn not to give up so easily and then it wasn't fun any more.

About the best fun he ever had was the first week when he was alone with Winnie while Mama and Daddy were off in California. He had her all to himself at last. Though the memory of it would fade later on, he would never forget entirely the pleasure of being a small boy alone in the house with Winnie. He would remember how soft and warm Winnie felt in bed beside him and how good it was to curl up against her. Tommy liked to pull the covers right over both their heads and play tent and pretend there were wild bears prowling around in the forest of the bedroom. Winnie would play with him as long as he wanted and she was very good at pretending about bears. Most big people didn't know how to pretend, but Winnie did.

The first Sunday afternoon they were alone was Winnie's regular day off, but since she would be unable to have any time off until Tommy's people were back from California, Winnie decided to take Tommy with her for a visit to her sister and brother-in-law's. He noticed that Winnie's sister Cloretta wasn't light coffee brown like Winnie. She wasn't as pretty and warm-skin-looking at all. Why, she was as white as Mama and Daddy. When he realized that, he was glad in a way. Winnie was his special person and it seemed right that she should be a special color, the color of maple candy, taffy, honey and all the good things that he liked.

There were two people who asked him to call them his Aunt Cloretta and Uncle Floyd, both white and offering him candy and gum, and then there was a friend of the strange Uncle Floyd called George. George worked with Uncle Floyd in some kind of business. All during the afternoon George kept looking at Winnie. They thought Tommy was busy exploring and eating candy but he could see the way the man was looking at her. He kept looking at her, and even when the others were talking he kept looking at her.

George said he had a brand-new car and he wondered if Winnie would like to go for a turn around the block with him. Winnie looked at George and then at Tommy and acted as if she could not make up her mind between them. Her sister Cloretta said, "Go ahead, Winnie. I think it'll be nice for you. We'll keep an eye on Tommy for you until you get back." Tommy didn't want Winnie to go off and leave him, even with these people who gave him candy and gum. Tommy was very glad when he heard Winnie say, "I'd better not. I gave his folks my word I wouldn't let him out of my sight until they came home."

"Then let's take the kid with us," George said. "You'd like to go for an auto ride, wouldn't you, sonny?"

Years later Tommy would not recall what George looked like. But he would be able to recall how he had feared and distrusted this stranger, who was paying more attention to his Winnie than anyone ever had before.

When it was time for Winnie to take Tommy home, George said, "I sure envy you, kiddo. All alone in a house with a beautiful gal like that."

He was looking right at Winnie. Winnie told him to hush. Tommy couldn't tell whether Winnie was angry or pleased. George insisted on driving Winnie and Tommy home. George did all the talking. He told Winnie about his job and the things he wanted to do. He said he was a surveyor for the county, working under Floyd. When they saved up enough money they were thinking of going into private business together. George said he would like to live out of town—a little house in the country where he could keep a few chickens and grow his own vegetables—but first he had to find the right girl. Tommy did not like the way he kept looking at Winnie. Or the way he went on talking to Winnie, just as if Tommy wasn't there at all.

And it made him feel irritable that Winnie kept her head turned around toward this other man and was hardly bothering to look at *him*. He was used to having Winnie pay attention just to him and to nobody else.

As Tommy got out of the car he slipped and fell down. He lay on the sidewalk and bawled and felt terribly injured and Winnie had to pick him up and kiss the spot where he had hurt himself. George stood around helplessly, trying to tell Winnie, above Tommy's screaming, that he felt this was much more than a casual first meeting and that all he could think about was how soon he could see her again. Winnie hardly heard George, because she was so busy hugging Tommy and saying things to make him laugh so he would be himself again. She carried Tommy into the house and settled him down to his evening routine. In the bathtub Tommy laughed until he was almost hysterical because it had been a hard day and the man was gone and Tommy and Winnie were together again.

For the next few days Tommy did not notice anything different about Winnie. Then one night Tommy's lights were out—all but the one in the bathroom that was left to guide him through the darkness—and Tommy was supposed to be asleep, when he heard the murmur of grown-up talking. He thought maybe his mama and daddy had come home from California and he got up to find out what they had brought him. He hurried down into the living room and there was that man George talking to Winnie.

"Tommy, *Tommy*, it's after ten o'clock," Winnie said.

"I have a stomach ache," said Tommy.

"I think you're just tired and need your rest," Winnie said.

"No, it hurts me, it hurts me *here*." Jackie Coogan, in his most tragic moments, could not have pointed to his abdomen with a more piteous expression.

"I think he's a little faker," that man George said.

"But I can't take a chance," Winnie said. "He's like my own child."

"You'd be tougher on your own kid," George said.

All the while Tommy was whimpering as if trying to control himself while in great pain.

"I'm afraid all this is making him nervous," Winnie said.

"My God, you take care of him from daybreak until his bedtime, isn't that enough? Is he supposed to own you day and night? I think it's unwholesome."

"Shh, please George, don't upset him," Winnie begged.

"I'll see you Saturday night, Winnie," George said. And then he spoke to Tommy rather crossly. "Now you get over this bellyache business, son."

Tommy kept waking up and complaining so often of feeling funny in his tummy that Winnie let him sleep in her bed the rest of the night. "Tommy boy, maybe I am spoiling you, but you're my own little Tommy boy, aren't you, my own little Tommy boy." Tommy wished that night would never end and that he could just go on and on safely cuddled up against Winnie in Winnie's bed.

When Saturday night came Tommy got up an extra time to get a drink of water. Winnie came in to warn him not to use any more excuses for getting out of bed. He noticed something special about Winnie. She had red stuff on her lips like Mama and she was wearing a dark purple dress instead of one of the white or gray ones she always wore. And she had a flower in her hair. She looked very pretty with a flower in her hair, but Tommy knew what it meant. Tommy couldn't understand why she should pay so much attention to another grown-up when she was only supposed to look after Tommy.

After Winnie turned off his lights again and kissed him good night, he stayed awake on purpose. After a while he heard the front door opening and there was a little grown-up murmuring and then it got quiet again. He sat up and listened and then he swung himself carefully out of bed. It was double disobedience because he didn't even put his slippers on. He crept down the stairs and spied into the living room. Winnie was on the couch with that man George and he had his arm around her and she was letting him kiss her. She said in a funny kind of whisper, "George, George, stop," as if she were frightened, but he kept on holding her very hard and pushing his mouth against hers and she sort of sobbed as if she were crying, "Oh George, George darling, what are we going to do?" and he said in that definite way he had, "We're going to get married, that's what we're going to do." Then Winnie said, "George, I don't know, I know we love each other, but . . ."

George interrupted. Tommy was very conscious of it, because he had been warned so many times not to do that. His voice sounded awfully mean and angry to Tommy. "To hell with it. That doesn't worry me. I want you, Win, and I don't care how it looks to a lot of narrow-minded dopes." Winnie's answer was so much softer that Tommy could hardly hear it. "I know, I know, darling, if we could go away somewhere, but here in this country people would . . ."

"The hell with 'em," George kept saying. "I say the hell with 'em. The hell with 'em."

"If I looked like Cloretta," Winnie said. "If I could pass . . ."

"You're twice as beautiful as Cloretta," George said. "You're beautiful, Win. Just keep remembering that. You're beautiful and—and—a wonderful human being."

"George, I want to," she said. "You know I want to, but I want to think. I'm not sure. I'm afraid."

"Well, I'm not," George said. "I still say the hell with 'em." He started kissing her again.

Tommy went back to his room and started playing boat

in his bed and pretty soon he had all the blankets on the floor and then the sheets were pulled out from the mattress. He got to doing jumping tricks on the bare mattress and he pulled the pillow out of the pillow case and then he pulled the pillow case over his head and kept on jumping up and down higher and higher until he toppled off the bed and bumped his funny bone.

Winnie came running in and saw the tangle of bedclothes and Tommy suffering on the floor and this time she didn't feel sorry about the bump on his funny bone (which seemed to have spread to his head as well), she was angry at all this extra work he had made for her to do and she said, "Tommy, you're a little rascal. I'm really angry this time." Tommy looked up at her as if his time in this world was running out. "Has the man gone?" Then she got even angrier and she said, "That is no business of yours," and Tommy lost his temper and scratched her and she lashed out and slapped him for the first time in her life and Tommy got purple red in the face and bit her hard on the arm and she screamed and grappled with him and threw him down on the bed with all her might. Then they both cried hysterically.

Later he crept into her bed and she seemed glad he had come and kissed him and hugged him and called him her own darling little Tommy boy. Tommy thought about her kissing that grown-up George and he put his arms tight around her to keep her from getting away.

In the days after that Tommy noticed things about Winnie he did not always know he was noticing but that he would be able to remember later on when he was old enough to look back and see the whole thing as a life and not just as bits and pieces of the troubles and pleasures of being four. Winnie was very good to him, but she was edgy and moody. Once while she was rocking Tommy in her arms she started to cry for no reason at all. Tommy remembered snatches of a strange conversation in the kitchen between Cloretta and Winnie when he was supposed to be playing outside one afternoon. He couldn't remember all the words but he could remember that Cloretta wanted Winnie to marry their friend George. And Winnie said she couldn't make up her mind, because there would always be the problem of where they could live and what to do about children. Cloretta said she and Floyd had been afraid of that, too, and they were solving it by not taking any chances. Winnie shook her head and said she wasn't sure she could do that, she loved children and would love to have George's children, but something inside her told her it was wrong. Cloretta put her white arms around the creamy coffee-color shoulders of her sister and told her the right thing to do was the thing she, Winnie, wanted to do—that Winnie had always made herself too much of a doormat for the people she worked for—"like the way you work yourself to the bone for that little brat Tommy." It was time that Winifred Harris started living Winifred's life, Cloretta said, and wasn't just some white folks' Winnie. Tommy knew that Aunt Cloretta wasn't his aunt and that she was on George's side and that if they had their way they would take Winnie away from him forever. Tommy hated them and wished he could dump them all in the garbage truck, and he thought of all the horrible things he would like to do to them for trying to steal his one and only Winnie Pooh away from the Tommy she belonged to. He could not understand why grown-ups were so mean. Except for Winnie—and even she had been playing some no-fair tricks on him lately—there weren't any grown-ups in the world who really cared about Tommy.

One evening when Winnie was serving Tommy his tapioca pudding, he said, "Winnie, are you going to go away and leave me and marry that man and never come back here ever again?"

Winnie said, "Why, Tommy, you know I'd never leave you alone. What gave you that idea?"

"I heard you talking with Aunt Cloretta."

"Goodness me, little boys have big ears." Then she said, "Tommy, it's true that I'm thinking of marrying Mr. Higbee. I'm twenty-eight, and well, most people my age have been married for years. Your mama and daddy were married before they were twenty-eight and you, why you're going to be so handsome that some nice girl is sure to grab you long before you're twenty-eight. But don't you worry that I'm going to leave you until your mother and father are back and we've found someone else to take my place. I have a cousin called Emily who is awfully sweet and who would just love to take care of a nice little boy like you. And I'll bet pretty soon you'd forget all about your old Winnie and you'd love your new Emmy Pooh even more."

"I don't want you to leave me," Tommy said. "I want you to stay with me for ever and ever."

"I wish you couldn't hear through walls so well," Winnie said, "because this whole thing may never even happen at all. So there's no sense worrying about it ahead of time. I'm not going to leave you for a long, long time no matter what happens." Then she hugged him, squeezed his ear lobe and said, "I'll probably stay with you so long that you'll be the one who finally wants to get rid of me."

"I never never will, Winnie Pooh," Tommy said. "I want you to stay with me for ever and ever."

"Now eat your tapioca," she said. "You are a something. Only four years old and worrying about these grown-up things."

The big thing that happened to Winnie Tommy remembered very well. It was like the "Winnie-color" talk he had had with his daddy at breakfast. It was one of the things that made Tommy acutely conscious of Winnie as a color instead of just as a person with a kind of skin that seemed particularly pleasing to him. Maybe Tommy remembered this scene because it was so loud, even louder and more frightening than George had been. Or maybe it was because he had been old enough to realize—even at going on five—that his rivalry with George had come to its turning point.

Late that Sunday afternoon Winnie's mother and father had come to visit. He was a large man with a muscular paunch, reddish, gray-streaked hair and a mottled, orange-freckled face. She was shorter than Winnie and a little dumpy, but the color of her skin was almost exactly the same as Winnie's, only maybe just a shade darker, as when you're making chocolate milk and you put in a few extra drops to make it just a bit more chocolaty. They seemed to be polite, dignified people, and everything was perfectly peaceful and friendly until Winnie put Tommy to bed. Tommy had half-forgotten about George and he had run his legs off all day and he went off to sleep without even thinking of the second glass of water. But in the middle of the night a terrible grown-up shout from downstairs shook him out of his sleep and made him feel all trembly and scared inside.

"You're a *nigger!* Never forget you're a *nigger!*"

The strange, ugly word shook the house. Tommy sat up in bed, and though he had never heard the word before he knew in some instinctively wise way that it had something to do with his daddy's saying, "Never, *never* mention her color again." Tommy did not understand, but he knew there was some problem of one person being white and another person being coffee color that made grown-ups terribly nervous and angry and confused and violent.

Tommy crept halfway down the stairs and peered through the slats of the banister. He could see Winnie's father, but he could not see Winnie. Winnie's father was angrier than he had ever seen anybody in his life. He had seen Mama and Daddy arguing, but he had never seen one grown-up bawling out another one the way this big man with the freckled pumpkin-color face was bawling out poor Winnie the Pooh. "You're a nigger," he was shouting, and the word cut through the house like an angry whip. "Maybe you're ninety-nine and ninety-nine one-hundredths per cent white, but you're still a nigger. And niggers don't marry white men. Maybe in the last world and maybe in the next but not in this one, God damn it. What if your baby is white? He'll grow up to hate you! And what if he's black or high yeller like you? Your husband'll hate him. And what if you don't have any, like Cloretta? You'll end up hating each other. God damn it, I tell you, Winifred, we won't allow it. We don't want to see no more trouble in this miserable world than there's in it already. Look at me, a high-school education, but a redcap all my life because I got a drop or two of the wrong kind of blood in me. Somewhere back there in your great-granddaddy's time some white man started this thing and now we got a family that ain't black and ain't white, just a bunch o' poor miserable nigger in-betweeners. So I say, no, we won't let you. It's bad enough with Cloretta who we always feel funny about visiting because she's living white. But you've got color in your skin and you can't rub it off by marrying white."

Tommy didn't hear anything from Winnie. He heard Winnie's mother say in a honey-soft voice, "Baby, Papa's not mad at you. He's just mad at the way things happen sometimes. But he loves you like I do and he's trying to help you from getting into something that'll hurt you later on."

It wasn't her father's angry voice, but her mother's soft and loving one, that made her cry. She got crying the way Tommy did sometimes when he started choking on his sobs. It wasn't the soft, wet kind of crying, but the dry, hard kind that gets tighter and tighter in your throat. It sounded awful. It sounded as if she was dying. And when she ran out of the room and up the stairs she had her hands over her face and couldn't even see Tommy. She ran into her room and slammed the door and threw herself on the bed and cried that hard, dry cry for a long time into her pillow. It was awful hearing her cry like that. Tommy wanted to go in and see her, but he was afraid to. His daddy had been right to warn him. There was something powerful and evil about the color of a person. There was something about the color of a person's skin that was never, *never* to be mentioned in public.

Tommy crawled back into bed and thought about that. He thought about that harder than he had ever thought about anything in his whole life. Then he turned on his light to go to the bathroom and Winnie heard him and came in. She wasn't crying any more. There was a kind of set look to her face that made her look very serious. "Tommy, you don't have to worry," she said. "I'm not going away. I'm not going to get married. I'm going to stay here with you as long as you need me."

Boy, was Tommy happy! He jumped up and down on his bed and sang, "Winnie isn't leaving, Winnie isn't leaving, goodie, goodie, goo—ooodie, Winnie isn't leaving." Then he hugged her and bounced on her lap and chanted his kindergarten sing-song again and nuzzled into her neck. She nibbled on his ears and tried not to cry. He was so happy, so happy that it would take him many years to forget this moment of triumph. "Oh, goodie, oh, goodie, I knew you wouldn't leave me, I knew it, I knew it, I knew you wouldn't leave me," he sang. Winnie's eyes were wet with a strange, bitter kind of relief and she said, "Yes, I suppose I did too." Then she gave him a fond pat on the back flap of his Dr. Dentons. "Now scoot into bed. You should have been in bed hours ago. And I'm a little tired, too."

Tommy settled back in bed with the lights out, smiling

into the darkness and chanting, "I've got Winnie back, I've got Winnie back, I've got Winnie back . . ."

Tommy kept waiting for the night when George would come and Winnie would tell him. It would serve him right for all the things he had done to Tommy. He had made Tommy realize for the first time what it might feel like to lose somebody you loved very, very much. It served him right. It served him right.

But George never came to the house again. Whether Winnie phoned him or wrote him or just how she did it Tommy never knew. The little snapshot of George stayed on her dresser, but that was all. It stayed there for years. But later on Tommy would be able only vaguely to associate it with any actual person, much less an actual threat.

When Mama and Daddy came home from California they were pleased to find everything in order. Tommy was in good health and fine spirits and the house was spotless. "Well, I'm glad to find everything so peaceful," Mama said. "Did anything happen?" "No ma'am," Winnie said. "Oh, yes, one night when it rained we had a leak in the upstairs hallway. But except for that, you'll find everything just about the same."

Winnie stayed with Tommy's people for about nine more years, until Tommy was almost fourteen. When he was six they had had to scold Winnie for babying Tommy. She still tried to dress him when she should have known he was old enough to dress himself. Winnie couldn't seem to learn not to fuss around Tommy. She worried more than his mother about such things as his being out on drizzly days without his cap and rubbers.

When he was fourteen, Tommy said, "Mom, Winnie's driving me nuts. She's always picking at me to wear this or do that. I wish she'd mind her own beeswax and leave me alone."

Tommy's parents talked it over and decided, difficult as

it was to face, that Winnie had outlived her usefulness. She could not stop doing for him all those little things that no self-respecting teen-age boy can stand. "I dread having to tell her," Tommy's mother said. "She'll go off into one of those old-maid hysterics and I won't be able to stand it."

So they gave Winnie a six-weeks' summer vacation and near the end of it they wrote her a letter explaining the situation, giving her a liberal severance pay and promising to keep their eyes open for another position for her.

Early one fall when Tommy was getting ready to leave for college, Winnie came to call on them. She couldn't have picked a more inconvenient time, but she had meant something to them once and they didn't know how to turn her away without hurting her feelings. She said she hadn't seen Tommy since he was grown up and she hoped they wouldn't mind if she dropped in for just a few minutes, as she had loved him so much as a little boy that she just couldn't resist stopping in to see how he had turned out. Tommy was embarrassed at all this mushy stuff, but he remembered a few things about this old nurse of his, and as long as she didn't take too long he didn't really mind seeing her again. He couldn't remember too much about her, although now that he looked at her it began to come back to him about her high-yellow coloring. In the tinted picture in the family album she was quite handsome with her honey complexion and her dark, wavy hair dropping nicely to her shoulders. Her hair was streaky gray now and she wore it up in a rather severe, old-fashioned bun. Dad had said she had been "a knockout—a regular sun-tanned Loretta Young," but she looked faded and bony now, although she did have nice eyes.

"So you're Tommy," she said. "To think you're my own little Tommy boy."

Tommy squirmed. He wondered how long this was going to take. He tried to think of something to say. "Well, how are you these days, Winnie?"

She tried to make a joke of it. "Oh, all right, I guess. Still pretty spry for an old maid."

The words were like stones in the wall that stood between the eighteen-year-old Tom and the Tommy boy of his childhood. Loosening the stones that stood in the way of his remembering, he was thinking of his old Winnie, his Winnie Pooh, and once more he was stepping through into that dim yet feverish past when he had loved this coffee-colored stranger with all the narrow intensity that charges and confines a child's world.

E N O U G H

I thought I had run the gamut of command posts, from half-destroyed farmhouses to elegant castles on the Rhine —but this one was the pay-off: an ancient little convent on a hillside overlooking a gingerbread Alsatian village and the German lines beyond. A special recon outfit with the 7th Army lining up for the jump across the Rhine had moved in, but the sisters had not moved out, and so the two organizations were living side by side under the same roof, the French nuns industriously devoted to peace, the recon group industriously devoted to war. It was hard work, dangerous work, infiltrating enemy lines at night to determine troop movements and gun emplacements, but at evening mess most of the conversation was joke and banter, punctuated by the regular Jerry artillery fire that sounded as if it were passing directly overhead. "Alsace

Alice," the youthful CO said. "She's been trying to find us for a week. She isn't even close tonight."

The nun who served us conscientiously, silently, and without ever changing expression, as if she had lived all her life among American officers who sat down to dinner without taking off their .45's, refilled our empty coffee cups. The coffee was so good that nobody wanted to finish it, so we lingered over our cups, drawing slowly on the cigarettes or pipes we lit from the flickering candles that threw a soft yellow glow over the table. Everybody felt well fed and relaxed, the war, for the moment, wasn't breathing down our necks, and it was too early to crawl into our bed rolls. A good time for talking. At first we talked about the things that everybody in the ETO wanted to talk about that winter. How long the war would last, how long our guys would have to stay on after the supermen folded up, and what we'd do when we finally got back to the States again. I talked and the young CO talked and a lieutenant from Brooklyn, he talked plenty, and a former cavalry officer from Texas told us how he was going to open a riding academy in New York City.

But the captain didn't say a word. He had a grave, weather-beaten face, and a slow, deliberate way of eating, of moving and of listening to what was being said. All I knew about him was what the CO had told me, that he was a professional, a company commander with the 1st Division. What he was doing down here in Alsace I wasn't told. Conversation was beginning to run down when I happened to mention Aachen. I forgot just what I said, something about the unbelievable destruction that was still new to me, something about the unexpected docility of the people there.

Then, to draw him into the group, I asked the captain casually, "Let's see, the 1st Division was up around Aachen, wasn't it?"

The captain drew his cigarette from his mouth. "Yes, we were at Aachen," he said.

"Rough, rough, hey, Captain?" said the lieutenant from Brooklyn.

The captain waited so long that I thought that was the end of it. Finally he said, "My outfit was held up for sixty-four days outside of Aachen."

"Heavy losses?" the CO asked.

The captain drew another cigarette from his pack and offered the rest around. "By the time we got through, our battalion wasn't even a good-sized company. We finally got through it all right. But it was close, very close."

He inhaled slowly, took the cigarette out of his mouth with that poised deliberateness of his and again I thought this might be all there was to it. But all of a sudden he was into his story. He told it with such an economy of words and emotions that it wasn't until he had finished that I realized what kind of story he had told. There wasn't much more to say after the captain got through. The CO blew out the stubby melted candles. I went up-stairs into one of the cold, narrow bedrooms that the nuns had evacuated for us, stripped down to my long-johns and wriggled into my bed roll. I closed my eyes, but I was still thinking about the captain and his story. After a few minutes I reached out for my flashlight, a pencil and pad, and, at the risk of burning out my battery—which at night in a theater of war is like losing the sight of both eyes—I tried to put the story down as the captain had told it. Not word for word, for I do not have that kind of memory, but next morning, as soon as it was light enough, I read it over and I felt satisfied that it was as close as I would ever get it to the way the captain told it. So here it is, a little better spelled, a little more legible, better punctuated here and there, but otherwise exactly as I had scribbled it down that night in the convent with the Führer's artillery lobbing them systematically but futilely over our heads:

I don't remember exactly when I first noticed Shapiro. (That's not his name, but if you don't mind, that's what I'll call him, because in view of what finally happened I think it would be better just to call him Shapiro and let it go at that.) I think the first time he came to my attention was on the transport going up from Africa. I was a company commander at the time. Ordinarily the only men I would have come in contact with were the lieutenants who lead my platoons and the sergeants who lead the squads. But the first day out, this lad Shapiro, a new replacement, was brought to my attention. Yes, that's right, now that I think of it I remember it very well. Sergeant McCardle reported him. He caught Shapiro lighting a cigarette on deck after dark. The first time he warned him, just warned him, that's all. But the next night he caught him again. Those were the days when the Heinie U-boats were raising hell with our convoys, so this was no joke. The second time McCardle reported him to me. "Sir, if you want to know what I think, he's a smart-aleck Jew-boy from Brooklyn," said McCardle. "If he's a soldier, I'm a rabbi."

Now I hope I'm not offending anybody here with what I am about to say, but to tell the truth, I didn't look forward to the idea of having Jews in my outfit either. Not that I'm prejudiced or anything, I just had an idea that they weren't cut out for our kind of work. But of course I couldn't allow that sort of talk in my company. So I said, "Look here, McCardle, I'm not interested in a man's race or religion. All I care about is whether he toes the mark as a soldier or not." "Yes sir," said McCardle. He was a big, athletic, rugged-looking boy. A ball player from Boston. Two years in the National Guard.

One of the men I was going to be able to depend on to bolster my green replacements, I was pretty sure of that.

Well, we didn't hold a court-martial or anything but I threatened to throw the book at Shapiro, talked at him pretty hard, told him we were going to make a soldier out of him whether he liked the idea or not. As a matter of fact I never saw such a sad excuse for a soldier in my life. He was a small, bow-legged little guy who looked as if he didn't have strength enough to pick up an M1, much less fire it. But it wasn't the size that was so much against him. I've seen some little men from the Point who were the fightingest sons of bitches you ever saw—take our own little Terry Allen for instance. But this fellow Shapiro just didn't seem to have any soldier in him. His uniform was a mess. I had to make him tighten his tie and button the top button of his jacket. His shoes weren't shined. And when I called this to his attention, he said, "I know, Captain, the service on this ship is just terrible. I put my shoes out to be shined last night and they came back this morning looking just the way I left them."

Well, I handed Shapiro some sort of punishment, I forget just what it was now, but if I thought that was the last time I was going to have him in my hair, I was sadly mistaken. After we went to the staging area outside of London—I suppose there's no point in maintaining security on it any longer, but I just got in the habit of forgetting the name—I must've had more trouble with Shapiro than with all my other men put together. Sergeant McCardle was always turning him in. I knew that Mc-Cardle had this prejudice of course, the one I referred to before, so I always checked personally to make sure that Shapiro was really guilty of McCardle's charges. It was never anything big, you understand, just a string of irritating little things, taking his time to fall in, not keeping his weapons clean, going into places in town that were off limits and half a dozen other things I can't remember at the moment. We made him stand extra guard duty, cut down his passes to town, even had him in the guardhouse for a few days, but nothing seemed to change Shapiro. I'm afraid McCardle, for all his prejudice, had pegged him right. A smart-aleck Jew-boy from Brooklyn.

One Monday Shapiro failed to appear for morning muster. When he finally showed up, half a day AWOL on his week-end pass to London, I decided to get tough. I had him restricted to camp grounds for the duration of our training in England. We were working hard in those days and the boys counted pretty heavily on that thirty-six to London, but I was sick and tired of fooling with Shapiro.

One Sunday I came back from London early in the afternoon to write up some reports. There was Shapiro sitting on a bench in front of the CP. It was drizzling a little, you know, English weather, and Shapiro was just sitting there with his hands in his pockets and his neck pulled in, as sad-looking a joker as you ever want to see. When he saw me he stood up and saluted, so it looked like this restriction deal wasn't doing him any harm. "How are you getting along, Shapiro?" I said. "Lousy, sir," Shapiro says. "I don't know what to do with myself."

Well that was when I got the idea. As things turned out, it was one of the best ideas I had all the time I was in command of that company. "Why don't you go out on the range and do a little target practice? It won't do you any harm."

You see, Shapiro's marksmanship was one of the company's favorite jokes. He was the most hopeless shot I had ever seen, and believe me, in these days of civilian soldiers, I've seen some sad ones. So I told Shapiro that I would see to it that he got all the ammo he wanted if he spent his restricted week-ends out on the range.

Well, Shapiro had nothing better to do, so he went to work. After a while he got to like it. I saw it myself because a month or so later when I was working on some more reports—that's the only thing I don't like about the army, those damn reports—I went out on the range to do a little shooting with my .45 and there was Shapiro banging away. He had improved about 500 per cent. Every Sunday for the next six weeks while the rest of the company were sitting on their tails in their favorite pubs, Shapiro was out there on that range getting better and better. By the end of May, Lieutenant Ainsworth told me Shapiro was high man in his platoon. And he was still practicing every spare minute he had. Damn, when I gave him that ammo, I really started something.

About that time I could feel D-Day creeping up on us. I didn't know the date or the hour yet, but I had been in the army too long not to feel something in the wind. So I called Shapiro in to see me and I said, "Shapiro, I've decided to lift the restriction on you. This Saturday at 1800, you will receive a thirty-six-hour pass with the other men of your company. But if you are one minute absent over leave, Monday morning, by God, I'm going to throw the book at you with everything I've got behind it."

Well, Shapiro went down to London and he must've had quite a week-end. Ainsworth ran across him in one club that Saturday night, playing the bass fiddle with a limey jazz band. And Sunday night he must have celebrated right on through till Monday morning. But Monday morning there was Shapiro right on the dot. I remarked to his squad leader, Sergeant McCardle, on the improvement in Shapiro's behavior, as well as his amazing development as a marksman. But Mac still stuck to his guns. "Sir, if you'll pardon me for saying it," he said, "I still don't think you can make a soldier out of a Jew-boy."

I didn't think much about Shapiro those next few days. I had my own worries getting things ready for the move to the point of embarkation. We still hadn't been given the date, but it didn't take a West Point grind to know we had one foot on the boat. Then we went down to the coast, waited, got our LCI, and waited again until the fleet finally started forming up. But that is not what I wanted to tell you about. Let me tell you about Shapiro, and about McCardle, because in a way this story is about both of them.

Our outfit went in at Omaha Beach. If any of you fellows were there you know what that means. If you weren't there, you probably heard about it. Omaha was—well, it was the toughest thing the old Red One had hit yet, and if you remember the plums they picked for us in Africa and Sicily, you know what that means. The Jerries were all ready for us at Omaha, and they were looking down our throats and for a long long time that beach was so hot that I never will know how we managed to keep from getting pushed right back into the Channel. All we could do was dig in and hang on. The air was rattling with machine-gun fire and the Jerry artillery had us nicely spotted. It looked like we were going to have to sweat it out in those foxholes the rest of the war. All of a sudden I noticed somebody jump up about thirty-five yards in front of me. It was Shapiro. He was doing the damnedest thing I've ever seen on a battlefield. There didn't happen to be any latrines on Omaha at the time, so Shapiro was standing up there making a beautiful target of himself, calmly taking down his pants and attending to nature with bullets and shells cracking all around him. I guess you'd have to see it to 'believe it. I think it did something to everybody who saw it. Hell, if that kid can squat up there and take his own sweet time about it, they seemed to say, I guess we can take a chance.

When he was finished, he took off his helmet a moment, produced a ration packet of sanitary paper he had cached in the liner, then adjusted his uniform again, grabbed his M1 and ran forward. Everybody who saw Shapiro that day agreed with me that his work was magnificent.

Battle conditions didn't seem to have any effect on his shooting eye, except maybe to sharpen it a little. I was proud of every man in my company, but I don't think I was prouder of anybody than I was of Shapiro. When we finally weathered that first storm and fought our way up off the beach, I made Shapiro our company sniper. Everybody agreed he was the best man for the job. Everybody except maybe McCardle. McCardle had to agree that Shapiro had become a very talented soldier, but he wasn't sure how he'd stand up under the constant pressure. You see, McCardle had a prejudice, a set of preconceived notions as to how a fellow like Shapiro would operate, and once you get those notions in your head, it takes a lot of powder to blast them out.

Anyway, Shapiro fought like a madman all the way across France. I could tell you a hundred things he did, but it would take too long. Well, maybe this will give you some idea. One time late last summer we were dug in for the night in a field near the Meuse in Belgium. About three A.M. Shapiro woke up and looked over the edge of his foxhole. Parked smack in front of him, with the muzzle of its .88 extending right over Shapiro's foxhole, was an enemy tank, a Tiger. The funniest thing about it is that McCardle saw the whole thing, from his foxhole fifty or sixty feet away. Shapiro kept his head down and waited. He even tried not to breathe too loud, he told us later. It must have been a long wait for Shapiro, but finally the night began to lift. A few minutes later the first Jerry opened the hatch and climbed out. He was quickly followed by the rest of the crew. They were just climbing out for a morning stretch. They weren't more than thirty feet from Shapiro. In slow motion, the barrel of Shapiro's rifle inched over the edge of his foxhole. Even from where McCardle was, he could see that Shapiro's hand was trembling. But when he squeezed the trigger, a German fell. The others wheeled in surprise.

Shapiro had stopped trembling now, McCardle said. Before the tank crew knew what hit them, Shapiro had turned them all into "good Germans."

For that morning's work, Shapiro got the silver star and a boost to buck sergeant. "What do you think of your Jew-boy now?" I asked McCardle. "I don't know, sir," said McCardle. "I could be wrong I guess, could be." McCardle was a very stubborn Irishman.

We crossed the German border and moved up to Aachen. How those Jerries hung onto Aachen! The weather was bad and we had to sleep out in the rain and the mud night after night, waiting for the Jerries to break. But they didn't break. We figured we'd be in Aachen in a week, but a month went by and we hadn't moved. The outfit was taking a terrible shellacking. Night and day. Never any rest. The casualties were bad, very bad, every day. It was beginning to look as if none of us would ever get into Aachen alive. Except for the patrols that sneaked in at night, of course. Shapiro was in on a lot of them and always did a good job. On one of his missions he was nicked in the leg, but went on to carry out his assignment. Another time he brought in a man who stepped on a mine on the way back. I don't know how he managed it, the size of him, he just had it in him to be a very good soldier.

One evening I called McCardle and told him I wanted him to lead a patrol in force, not just reconnaissance, but to try and knock out some Jerry machine-gun positions that were guarding the approaches to the city. McCardle was a second lieutenant now, filling the shoes of an officer we lost three or four weeks before. "You can pick your own men," I told him. "Except for Shapiro. I want you to take Shapiro. He's the best man we've got."

Twenty minutes later, McCardle returned. "I can't take Shapiro, sir," he said. He had a handkerchief tied around his fingers and blood was beginning to spread through. "Why not Shapiro?" I said. Everybody's nerves were pulled pretty tight and I was a little sore. I thought maybe McCardle had fixed it so he wouldn't have to take Shapiro.

Then I found out what happened.

McCardle had called Shapiro in to the company CP, a half-destroyed farmhouse, and given him the order. As soon as Shapiro heard what he had to do, he ran out of the house. McCardle followed him. Shapiro ran around the farmhouse into the barn, where some of the boys were bunking, scrambled up into the hayloft and pulled a blanket over his head. McCardle could see his shoulders shaking underneath it, could hear him sobbing. McCardle went into the loft after him and put his hand on Shapiro's shoulder. Shapiro growled, like a wild animal, McCardle said, just like a wild animal, and shook his hand off. Then McCardle reached under the blanket for him. Shapiro made a horrible sound and bit McCardle's fingers. That's what the blood on the handkerchief was from.

I went out to the barn to see if I could do anything with Shapiro, but he wouldn't let me near him. Shapiro had had enough. He fought almost as hard against the medics as he had against the Jerries, but they finally got him down from the hayloft. That's a hell of a way for a good man to have to leave his outfit, but that's the way it is sometimes. Shapiro was a good man, but he had had enough.

McCardle and I walked back to the house and I briefed him on his mission. We didn't say anything more about what had happened until after he reported back early next morning. "Too bad about Shapiro," I said. "Yeah," he agreed. "No matter how good those Jew-boys are, guess they're too high-strung for this business."

The battle for Aachen dragged on. All of us saw our buddies getting killed, the best officers gone, more men getting it every day. That's when my platoon leaders came and told me they were afraid their men had had about enough. I knew from division G2 if we held out another week, two weeks, we were all right, because Aachen was too hot for the Jerries to hold forever. In fact, there were signs that some of the supermen were beginning to pull out. I decided to send another patrol down into town to find out just what was going on. I asked Lieutenant Ainsworth to send McCardle to me. In a few minutes Ainsworth came back with a funny look on his face. "I think you better come and talk to McCardle yourself, sir," he said.

I followed him down the steep wooden steps to the cellar. There was McCardle sprawled full length on the ground, stuffing his fingers into his mouth and sobbing like a baby. I put my hand on his arm and tried to reach him, but it wasn't any good. He couldn't stop crying. "I want Shapiro," he was sobbing. "I want Shapiro, that poor little son-of-a-bitch Shapiro."

McCardle had had enough. It was a terrible thing to see this big tough Irishman gnawing on his fingers and crying as if his heart would break, but there was nothing you could do about it. He had had enough. We had to send him back next morning with some other Section 8's.

We finally got into Aachen, or what was left of Aachen, a couple of days later. But I was sorry to have to get there without McCardle and Shapiro. They were two of the best men I ever soldiered with.

CROWD PLEASER

The guy on my left was a regular. Every Friday night since I could remember, he had sat in that same seat on the aisle. He was broad and beefy-faced, with a high-blood-pressure complexion and a big mouth. He was powerfully built, despite the pot belly and spreading rump of middle age. The first night he sat next to me he bought me a beer, told me to keep him in mind next time I bought a new car, and handed me his card. Name was Dempsey. "Edward J. (Champ) Dempsey," it said on the card. "No, no relation to Jack," he chuckled. "We went to different schools together."

His voice, deep in his throat, always sounded as if he had a cold. The laughter with which he punctuated everything he said was open-mouthed and prolonged, loud and unmusical. He had a ridiculous pride in his ability to keep up a running patter of public speech throughout any fight.

Years before he had appointed himself a sort of one-man claque to urge the fighters on to bloodier efforts, and whenever the boys in the ring decided to take it a little easy, coasting a round or feeling each other out, his throaty witticisms would pierce the dark and smoky silence: "Turn out the lights, they want to be alone!" or "Hey, girls, can I have the next dance?" Or if one of the boxers happened to be Jewish, he was quick to show what a linguist he was by yelling, "Hit him in the *kishges,*" or display his knowledge of geography by shouting, "Send him back to Jerusalem!"

The fellow who always sat on my right was George Rogers, a big-money lawyer, but his seat was empty tonight. "Well, looks like our old friend George is playing hooky tonight, ha ha ha," Dempsey said. Rogers was a white-haired old-timer who hardly ever said a word to either of us. Dempsey had been trying to sell him a car since early last summer.

Just before the first preliminary boys climbed through the ropes, the usher led to Rogers' seat a fellow I had never seen before. He was short, thin, nervous, somewhere in his middle thirties, but already beginning to stoop from the waist like a much older man. His skin was pallid, he wore glasses, and he needed only the green eyeshade to become my stereotype of a bookkeeper.

"Excuse me, sir," he said as he squeezed by. "I am sorry to disturb you."

That wasn't what they usually said when they shoved past you at the Arena. Dempsey looked at him the way a gang leader eyes a new kid who has just moved into the block.

"Where's my old pal George tonight?" he wanted to know.

The man was shy and his answer came in a thin voice. "Mr. Rogers is out of town on business, sir. He was good enough to give me his ticket."

"You in Rogers' office?" Dempsey appraised him with salesman's eyes.

The newcomer said yes, not too encouragingly, but it was enough for Dempsey to lean across me and display his professional smile. "Dempsey's the name. What's yours, fella?"

"Glover," the fellow said, but he did not seem very happy about it.

"Glover!" Dempsey shuffled quickly through thousands of calling cards in his mind. "Used to know a Charley Glover back in K.C. fifteen years ago. Any relation to old Charley?"

"I've never had any relatives in the Middle West," Glover answered.

"Well, I won't hold it against you, ha ha ha," Dempsey said. "Here, have a cigar."

Dempsey leaned across me to hand it to him. He hadn't offered me a cigar since the night I told him to stop trying to sell me a car, and let him know why.

Glover said he didn't smoke cigars, and Dempsey lit his, igniting the match with a flick of his thumbnail. "So you work for Rogers, huh," he went on. "Well, George is a very, very good friend of mine. What are you, a junior partner?"

"Oh, no," Glover said, and something that was almost a smile lit his face for a moment, as if at the impossibility of such a suggestion. "I am a stenographer."

Dempsey's smile, or rather, his clever imitation of a smile, wiped from his face mechanically, like a lantern slide. When he abandoned it suddenly like that, his face looked even more bloated and aggressive than usual.

"A stenographer! Ha ha ha. Are you kidding?"

"Mr. Rogers has employed nothing but male stenographers for over thirty years."

Dempsey looked disgusted and turned away.

The boys in the curtain raiser were entering the ring.

There was scattered applause for Sailor Gibbons, a rugged, battle-scarred veteran who had never graduated from the preliminary ranks. He bounded through the ropes with showy vigor and winked at a friend in the working press as he shuffled his feet in the rosin box. He was an old-timer getting ready to go to work, easy to hit but hard to stop, what the tub thumpers like to call a "crowd pleaser."

The boy who followed him through the ropes had the kind of figure and color that made everyone want to laugh. His 140 pounds were stretched over a six-foot frame and his skin was purple-black. His face was long and thin and solemn, and the ring-wise could detect nervousness in the way his muscles twitched in his legs as his handlers drew on his gloves. Over his shoulders was a bright orange bathrobe that identified him as a Golden Gloves Champion.

The moment Dempsey saw him, he began. "Ho ho! Look what we got with us tonight. A boogie! Boy, how I like to see them boogies get it!"

The announcer was introducing them. ". . . and at one hundred thirty-nine and a half, just up from the amateur ranks, the Pride of Central Avenue, Young Joe Gans."

Dempsey cupped his hands around his mouth. "Come on, Sailor, send him back to Central Avenue—in sections." Then, like a professional comedian, he looked around for his laugh. He got it.

The stadium lights dimmed out and the ring lights came on, molding the ring and the fighters together in one intense glow. You could feel the nervous excitement in the hushed crowd, five thousand men and women crouching there in the darkness waiting for the blood.

In the white glare the fighters, the pale stocky one and the dark slender one, moved toward each other with animal caution and touched gloves in that empty gesture of sportsmanship. Gibbons was an in-fighter, strong-legged, thick-shouldered, crouching, weaving, willing to take one on the jaw to get inside and club and push and rough his man against the ropes. Young Gans was the duelist, jabbing with a long spidery left and dancing away.

"Come on, Sailor!" Dempsey bellowed. "Let's get home early. Down below. They can't take 'em there."

As if responding to Dempsey's instructions, Gibbons brought a wild right up from the floor in the general direction of the colored boy's stomach. But Gans swayed away from it with the graceful precision of a bullfighter.

Next to me a small voice spoke out in a conversational tone. "Nice work, Gans," Glover said.

Dempsey turned and frowned. "You pulling for the boogie? What you pulling for the boogie for? Betting his corner?"

"I like his style of fighting," Glover said.

"Fighting!" Dempsey said. "You call that fighting? The boogie is a hit-and-run driver, that's what he is. Ha ha ha." He liked it so well he cupped his hands to his mouth again and gave it to his public. "Hey, ref, how about giving that shine a ticket for hit-and-run driving?"

Some of Dempsey's fans in front of him turned around to show him they were laughing. Gibbons lunged at Gans again, and the Negro flicked his left in the white man's face half a dozen times and skittered sideways out of danger.

"Attaboy, Gans," Glover said. "Give him a boxing lesson."

He didn't say it loud enough for the fighters to hear; it was really intended as a little encouragement for himself, but Dempsey heard it and glared at Glover again. He opened his mouth to put Glover in his place but turned back and yelled at the fighters instead.

"Don't hit him in the head, Sailor. You'll break your hands. In the breadbasket. That's where they don't like it."

The Negro feinted with his left, pulling the slowhinking Gibbons out of position, and scored with a short, ast right to the heart. Gibbons sagged, but his face spread n a big grin, and his legs pistoned rapidly up and down to how how light on his feet he was. He was hurt.

"He doesn't like them there, either," Glover said. "Nobody likes them there."

Dempsey was talking half to Glover and half to the fighters in the ring now. "But he took it. That's the way to take 'em, Sailor. Give the boogie some of that and watch him fold."

"I'm watching," Glover said. "All I can see is Gans's left in Gibbons' face." Suddenly he raised his voice, edged with excitement. "That's the way, Gans, jab him. Jab his head off." He was growing bolder as Gans piled up points.

Dempsey leaned forward, his fists tightly clenched, his shoulders moving in unison with Gibbons' as the Sailor tried to reach Gans with vicious haymakers; the colored fighter skillfully ducked and blocked and rolled until Gibbons was charging in with the crazed fury of a punished bull.

"Come on, eightball, why don't you fight?" Dempsey jeered.

"Good boy, Gans," Glover answered. "He hasn't hit you once this round."

When the bell rang, Gans dropped his hands automatically but Gibbons' right was cocked and while the sound of the bell was still *galong-galonging* through the arena, he let it go. You could see Gans stiffen and then sag as his body absorbed the pain for which it hadn't been prepared.

The blow made Dempsey laugh with excitement and relief. He always gave a short, nervous laugh when the fighter he was rooting against got hurt, but tonight he had someone special to laugh at. "That's the baby! What'd I tell you? He don't like 'em downstairs. Those boogies never do. One more like that and he'll quit cold."

"One more like that and Gibbons ought to be disqualified," Glover said.

"Aah, you nigger-lovers give me a pain," Dempsey said. "Always griping about those bastards getting gypped. That punch started before the bell."

"Well, he'll have to wait three minutes before he can hit him again," Glover said. "The only time Gibbons can hurt him is when Gans isn't looking."

"Oh, is that so? What the hell do you know about it? I been sitting in this same seat for eight years. I'll bet you ain't even seen a fight before."

"Do you have to see a skunk to recognize its smell?"

Dempsey tensed himself to rise. "Listen, you little shrimp, if you're trying to call me a skunk . . ."

Glover looked frightened. Dempsey had at least fifty pounds on him, and Glover didn't look as if he had had too much experience with his dukes. But the bell saved him, in reverse timing. The ten-second warning buzzer for round two made fans around us say, "Sit down. Down in front! We wanna watch the fight in the ring."

The two fighters leaned toward each other from their stools, feet set for the spring at the bell. Dempsey and Glover anticipated the bell too, sliding forward to the edges of their seats, their legs tensing under them as if they also expected to leap up as the round started. Dempsey made his hands into fists again and they trembled with eagerness to begin punching. In the shadows just beyond range of the ring lights, Glover's face was white and drawn. His right hand was doubled against his mouth in a nervous gesture of apprehension.

"All right, Sailor, this is the round," Dempsey shouted. "In the belly. In the belly."

"Come on, Gans," Glover countered, "box his ears off again."

At the bell, Gibbons ran across the ring and tried to nail the Negro in his corner before he was set. Glover

opened his mouth in fright, like a mother seeing her child
run down in the street. "Look—look out!"

Without changing the solemn expression with which he
had come into the ring, Young Gans stepped aside in what
looked almost like a gesture of politeness—"please, after
you"—and Gibbons plunged foolishly through the ropes.

"Where is he, Gibbons?" Glover said. "You can't even
find him, much less hit him."

"Why don't you stand up and fight, you yellow
bastard?" There was desperation in Dempsey's tone for
the first time.

Glover's voice became shrill with combativeness. "That's
the way to fight him, Gans. Keep that left in his face."

"Keep rushing him, Sailor. He can't hurt you. He
couldn't break an egg."

"What are you blinking for, Sailor? What are you
stopping for? I thought he couldn't hurt you."

"He's not hurt. A little nosebleed like that don't bother
him. Keep after him, Sailor. Make the boogie fight!"

Young Gans was making a monkey out of Gibbons, but
I was watching the fight between Glover and Dempsey
now. They were talking at each other but looking straight
ahead, straining forward for every movement and moment
of the bout in the ring. I didn't have to watch the fight.
There in the thin, hysterical voice of Glover and the bull-
frog fury of Dempsey, it was more vivid than even Jimmy
Powers or Bill Stern would have made it.

"How do you like that one? And that one? And that
one?" Glover flicked the jabs in Dempsey's face.

Dempsey shook them off and laughed. "Powderpuff
punches. All powderpuff punches. Hey! That's it! That's
it! Break the boogie in two!"

Glover clinched a moment to ride out the pain and
danced away again. "Who says you can't take 'em in the
belly?"

Their voices rose as the tiring fighters fought harder,

became more vulnerable now, more dangerous. But suddenly their shouting was lost in the giant roar that filled the place. The crowd was on its feet, screaming through its thousand wild mouths, screaming at the sight of a man, a black man, writhing convulsively on the canvas, bringing up his legs and clutching himself, twisting his long, serious face into a grotesque mask of agony.

Glover looked on in horror and futile anger. "Foul. Foul," he said. "He hit him low. I saw it. He hit him low."

There were others around him who saw it that way too and they took up the cry, "Foul, foul, foul . . ."

Dempsey was standing right next to me but his laughter sounded far away, as if the wave of voices breaking over us were carrying it off. "Ha ha ha ha ha," he said, and his face was distorted with terrible joy. "Foul, hell. Look at him dogging it. He wants to quit."

The referee had disregarded the cries of foul and taken up the count. Gans was fighting his sickness down, reaching out for a strand of the rope and clinging to it to keep the floor steady so he could rise from it again.

"Look at him dog it," Dempsey hollered. "He's yella. If that's a foul, he's got his crotch where his heart is."

A few people laughed and Dempsey winked at them. His sense of humor was coming back. He was feeling on top again. He looked over at Glover. Glover was badly shaken. Some of the strain of the Negro's torturous ascent had come into his face. "Well, wise guy, how do you like your nigger now?" Dempsey poured it on.

"All right, Gans," Glover pleaded, "coast through this round. You've won it on a foul anyway."

"Come on, Sailor, kill him, kill him, kill him!" Dempsey cheered.

The Negro was on his feet but he wasn't dancing around any more. It plainly hurt him to move now. His skin was a curious chalky color and his eyes turned toward his corner in distress.

Dempsey was laughing. "Look at him! he's so scared he's white! You're making a white man outa him, Sailor."

Gibbons rushed the crippled fighter into a corner and opened his cheek with a hard left hand.

"Ha ha ha. One more, Sailor. One more and he'll quit."

Glover was too full of injury to speak. Dempsey grinned over at him. "Wha'samatter, pal, lost your voice? Why, you was just full of chatter a minute ago."

Glover did not seem to hear. He sat back in his seat and looked straight ahead. His fighter leaned wearily against the ropes, too weak to hold his man off any longer.

"Let him drop," Dempsey was shouting. "Stand back and let the boogie drop!"

Then there was a loud laugh, even louder than usual, and the Negro crumpled in the corner and lay still.

Dempsey stood up and pulled the seat of his pants away where it had creased into his buttocks. "What did I tell you? Didn't I tell you he'd dog it if he got hurt? I never saw a boogie yet that could take it in the belly."

The ring was being cleared for the next bout, the band was rendering *Stars and Stripes Forever* and the next pair of fighters was coming down the aisle. But Glover didn't seem to be hearing or seeing. He just hung his head and held his hands together in his lap. How long would it take him, I wondered, to recover from this pain in Young Gans's groin?

THE LEGEND THAT WALKS
LIKE A MAN

There's quite a gang of us hangs out at Stage One. The moment the director says, "All right, wrap it up," and the assistant director (that's me) calls out, "Tomorrow morning we move over to the night-club set on Stage Seven, nine A.M. on the button," most of the company hightails it across the street to our favorite watering place.

Stage One isn't a dive, but it isn't Ciro's, either. We hardly ever get a big star in the joint and that's okay with us because we've seen enough of those so-and-so's from nine till six. Now don't get me wrong I've got nothing against the glamour department and a couple of those gals, Jean Harlow and Carole Lombard for two, were real good joes in anybody's league. It's just that in Stage One we kind of have our own crowd, assistant directors, second cameramen, juicers, grips, mixers, cutters, you know, the guys who actually do the work. I suppose if Frank

Capra or John Ford came in, we wouldn't toss 'em out exactly. It's just that we feel more relaxed by ourselves, you know how it is, we get a couple of drinks, unwind a little and pretty soon an assistant is telling us something extra-stupid his director did that day, and then maybe I chime in with my story of how much trouble a certain star gave me when I knocked on her dressing-room door to tell her we were ready to shoot and then the second cameraman gives us his peeve about what a prima donna the head cameraman is getting to be.

Making pictures is nothing but hard work, all of it under pressure, and since we have to keep our yaps shut all day there's nothing like bending an elbow at Stage One and blowing off a little steam.

The nice thing about the fellow who runs the joint, Larry White, Cecil B. himself could come in that place and Larry wouldn't pay him any more mind than he would one of us hundred-a-week guys. Not as much, probably, because Larry is pretty partial to us regular customers, runs the place more like a club than a commercial saloon and most of us who live at Stage One from the time our company breaks for the day until closing time are privileged charter members. Larry used to be quite a boy in the movie game himself, back in the silent days. He was a popular leading man for First National when Jack Mulhall and Dorothy Mackail were going great guns. If you don't believe it, just look at those stills behind the bar, that's Larry with Sue Carol, and Phyllis Haver and Sally O'Neill. He had a nice head of hair in those days. Larry got a tough break when sound came in. He had the same kind of voice as poor Jack Gilbert, a funny little squeak of a voice and overnight he was out of the money.

But Larry's done a lot better than most the old-timers. The way we flock around that bar, he'll never have to check in at the Motion Picture Relief Home like a lot of old kids I know who were pulling down five thousand a week without taxes twenty years ago.

I was saying a little while ago that we didn't have any celebrities in Stage One, but that isn't 100 per cent God's truth. We have Matty Moran, all right. Some of us aren't sure if Matty has any other address besides Stage One. He's there when we come in for a quick one at lunch and going strong when we come back at six and going even stronger when Larry finally starts locking up around one. Matty is a fixture, all right. I don't think any of us would feel the same way about the place if he should ever leave it.

Now maybe I'd better stop right here and take a reading on how many of you ever heard of Matty Moran. Because it's a funny thing about fame in this screwy business. One day you're recognized if you show up on a side street in Calcutta and the next day or the day after you can walk right down the middle of Hollywood Boulevard and nobody knows you from the street cleaner.

It sure was that way with Matty Moran. It wasn't so long ago that Matty was one of the biggest directors in the business. You said Griffith and you said De Mille and then you usually said Moran. Yes, sir, I can remember—I should, I was his assistant on a dozen pictures—when Matty was good for ten thousand clameroos a week. I'll bet Matty would like to have a dollar now for every grand he threw away.

Matty was the original star-maker in those days. I swear, kids would be willing to work in his pictures for nothing because he seemed to have a kind of magic when he touched them. This Sue Carol and Phyllis Haver I just mentioned, those kids weren't nothing till he sprinkled a little of that special Moran stardust on them. And a lot of them who are still going can thank Matty for the start. Gary Cooper for one, Claire Trevor for another.

Matty gave Larry White his chance, too. And more

than that, I guess he dug down and helped Larry over those bumps back in twenty-seven or eight. Then when things were on the other foot, Larry seemed to have an unlimited cuff where Matty was concerned. So you'd never guess that Matty was, well to put it harshly, a dead-broke bum from the way he's treated around Stage One. The city's finest may be looking for him for that last rubbery check, but he's strictly Special People once he steps inside Larry's place. And to look at the dapper way he keeps himself, you'd never know he was half a step ahead of the law and just as apt as not to spend that night as a guest of the county for drawing on a bank that has no relation to any actual bank either living or dead, as we say in those forewords.

One of the things that always got us about Matty is that he's managed to look just as prosperous these last few years as when he was sporting not one but two white Rolls Royces, one for himself and his lady love (of the moment), the other for his own private five-piece orchestra. The only reason it wasn't a ten-piece orchestra or a symphony-sized orchestra is that they wouldn't fit into that Rolls. Well as I was saying, Matty still managed to show up in a flashy double-breasted (maybe not this year's but still mighty sharp) and he's always sporting a jaunty bow tie and if he didn't have that fresh red carnation in his buttonhole we'd think it was some impostor. Another thing Matty always brings into Stage One with him is that mischievous red face and that cocky grin, just as if he had come straight from the Paramount lot where he was directing the most expensive production since *Ben Hur*. Is that amazing, a guy who hasn't had a real job in maybe fifteen years and he doesn't change a peg in looks or behavior? All the hard knocks and he's had them plenty can't stop him from acting like he owned the town. No kidding, Orson Welles in his cockiest moments (and that is something to see too) can't compete with Matty

Moran down and out and every studio door slammed in his face.

Yes, Matty still swaggers in and if he happens to spot me he says, "Evening, Red," and I say, "Evening, Mr. Moran," just as if I was still working assistant with him. And then maybe I say, "Will you join me in a little hair of the dog?" and the truth is probably that his tongue is hanging out for it, but he'll say, "Well maybe just one so you won't spread the word through the Junior Directors' Guild that Moran's gone high-hat." And then after we've had three or four, all "forced on him," like that first one, Matty will say, "Now I insist, young man" (I'm chasing him into the fifties but he's called me that from the time we were making Beery-Hatton comedies) "the next one is on me." And then you should see him order, like the King of England or L. B. Mayer, instead of a joker who couldn't buy his way into a dime movie on Main Street. "I say, Larry old boy, a spot of whiskey for my friend Farrell. And I might have just a touch myself to keep him company." Then he'd give me that wink, the wink that had charmed Pola Negri and Lya de Putti and Norma Talmadge out of their temperamental tantrums.

You've heard of this word "irrepressible"? That's the word for Matty Moran, all right. You probably wonder how a fella with Matty's reputation and talent and personality and energy-plus ever hit bottom. Well, one reason might be that the town got sort of scared of Matty's crazy ways. For instance, one time to celebrate the wind-up of a Jack Gilbert-Renée Adorée picture he gave a party on the set that lasted—I swear to Zanuck—five days. He had one orchestra from the Coconut Grove and another from the Plantation Club and a Hawaiian orchestra for in between. He'd been to a *louou* in the Islands the year before (had an ocean-going yacht in those days, natch) and he just decided to reproduce it in the studio. As I said, that party went on for five days and five nights and the boys and girls were so thirsty that Matty's boot-legger, Jerry Faye, had to send up a special boatload from Lower California. That party set Matty back somewheres in the neighborhood of ten thousand fish, ten thousand fish he should have salted away.

But that probably wouldn't have given Matty squatter's rights behind the eightball if he hadn't been such a wild man when he was shooting. Like D.W. and C.B., he came up out of the old school where the director was the whole cheese. For instance, one time he was telling Barbara La Marr how to play a scene and she said something under her breath and Matty heard it and bounced her right the hell off the picture. Matty's producer came crying that the picture was already sold as a Barbara La Marr starring ve-hicle and shooting her scenes over would cost an addi-tional ninety thousand, but Matty couldn't hear him. That's the way he was. The greatest guy in the world off a set, more laughs than a barrelful of ass-holes, but on the set it had to be done strictly Matty's way and no fool-ing. He didn't care what it cost or who it hurt. For in-stance one time he was directing a million-dollar cast with Wally Beery, Vic McLaglen, Charley Farrell and Buddy Rogers in one of the first big war epics. The cast got fool-ing around the way they will sometimes, clowning and getting sloppier and sloppier. Finally Matty said, "Look, sweeties, mess me up like that once more and I'll hop a boat for China."

Well, the next take they still hadn't settled down to business, so Matty just puts his megaphone down and walks off the set. The next morning he didn't show up at all. Or the next. I called his valet and he said Mr. Moran had packed a small bag and left without saying where he was going or when he'd be back. Two weeks later we get a cable from him and where do you think he is? Right the first time. Shanghai! And when he finally gets back, he's married to a gorgeous Russian-Chinese girl who turns out to be Sari Sanine, and of course Matty develops her into the most exotic foreign star since Dietrich.

But the all-time topper, until recently, I should add, was the time Matty was directing Sari. Sari was the hottest thing in pictures by this time and Matty was on the skids. In fact, it was general studio talk that the only reason Metro was keeping Matty on was because they were afraid of losing Sari. So what does Matty proceed to do? He gets into a knock-down-drag-out with Sari on the set as to how a certain love scene should be played. Sari wants it subtle. Matty wants it sex on the line. Sari says after all, she is a great dramatic actress. Matty says baloney, if she had to depend on her acting she wouldn't be worth five dollars a day. Well, they get going round and round in more and more of a hassel until finally Matty pulls the classic. He fires her off the picture! Bounces his own wife and Metro's biggest drawing card right off the set! I was right there when it happened or I wouldn't of believed it. Twenty minutes later Matty is taken off the picture. And this plus the trip to China plus a hundred-and-one other hotheaded stunts and Matty is just about washed up with the majors.

He does a couple of low-budget jobs for Republic and Monogram and then he's down to those shoestring deals on Poverty Row, but Matty is no good unless he's doing things in a big way. If he has a waterfall scene he's used to renting Niagara. If he was shooting a scene supposed to take place in Heaven he'd tell me to hire God. So he was no good trying to scale himself down to those thirty-set-ups-a-day, $150,000 quickies. It wasn't long before Matty lined up with the has-beens. Though you'd never know how tough the going was from talking to Matty. You know the old gag about never being unemployed, you're just "between pictures." Well Matty worked that one up to a high art. "I've just dropped in on my way back from Fox," he'd say, when we found him in his usual place at the far corner of Larry's bar. "It looks like Darryl is going to have something really big for me in a couple of months."

And then he'd offer to buy us a drink and come up with some funny story of the old days even I had never heard before and the way he'd talk shop and laugh with us you'd think it was his name that was up in lights instead of Jack Ford's or Johnny Huston's.

But lately, some of us began to notice that in spite of the prosperous front and the jokes and the winks and those "important jobs" he was always about to get, Matty was beginning to show signs of wear and tear. The suit was pressed, all right, but it was getting a little thread-bare. He still had those fifteen-dollar monogrammed shirts, but the cuffs were getting a little stringy. And then one night he called me and asked if he could stay at my place. Said they had just painted his room and the fumes were bothering him, but I didn't have to be a genius to know he had been bounced from his one lousy room in one of those cheap boarding houses between Hollywood Boulevard and Franklin. And that morning when I was going off to work I slipped him a fifty and he started to say, "Don't be silly, Red—well, I'll pay you back tomorrow," the way he usually did. But this time he did something I had never seen him do before. He stopped right in the middle and looked at that bill for what seemed like a full minute and then his eyes suddenly filled. Not knowing him the way I do, you probably would not be so affected, but for me, seeing him through all these years chipper and jaunty and so much more fun to be with than most the guys I knew who worked regularly, well I can't put it into words, but it was something, let me tell you.

I thought about it all morning on the set. And I guess when I've got something on my mind it shows on my stupid face because, when we broke for lunch, Vic Flanner, the director, and one of the best, came up and said, "What's the matter, Red?" So I told him about Matty.

Now Vic is an old-timer too. I guess he goes back as far as any of them, D.W. included, so right away he was interested. "I didn't know Matty Moran was still around," he said.

You see, that's why Hollywood is such a funny place. In some ways it's a small town, but it's built on a lot of different levels. All the big producers are buddy-buddies, and ditto the big directors, the assistants, the top writers and the bottom writers, but top is top and bottom is bottom and the twain don't meet very often. So it was perfectly possible for Matty to be right across the street all these years and Vic not know it because if he goes anywhere it's probably to Chasen's or Romanoff's or one of those places where they throw ten-dollar bills away like paper napkins.

Anyway, I give him an earful about Matty and he gets to thinking. His next picture is one of those super-duper epics called *San Juan Hill*. Now a picture like that is such a big deal that they use what they call a second-unit director to take some of the load off the regular director. The second-unit director usually shoots exterior backgrounds and tie-in shots, none of the important dialogue scenes, naturally, though sometimes he's allowed to handle routine dialogue, like when the butler says, "Just a minute, I'll see." You know, the odds and ends.

"I don't know why Matty couldn't shoot second unit on *San Juan*," Vic says. "I'll talk to the front office about it."

So that's the way, after fifteen years on the outside, Matty finally got back on a studio payroll again. $350 a week. He couldn't have kept himself in Alexander & Oviatt ties on that in the fat days, but all of us in Stage One had quite a ball the day the deal was definitely set. And you should have seen Matty. If he was full of beans under circumstances that would have driven most of us

to Suicide Bridge, there was no holding him on the
ground now.

He made an entrance into Stage One that put C.B. in
the piker class. "Larry," he ordered, using his hand like
it was some kind of a scepter, "buy everybody in the house
a drink and put it on my check." If Sari or one of his
other famous wives had shown up just then I would of
sworn that time was running backwards like those trick
shots in a Pete Smith short and that this was the Matty
Moran of twenty years ago.

Knowing his old ways, I couldn't help wondering how
this deal was going to work out, because Matty never
could play second fiddle to anybody. But I got a ringside seat when Vic Flanner switched me over as first assistant to the indefatigable Mr. M.

Well to everybody's amazement including yours truly,
Matty pitches in and does a whale of a job. The first
day out on location near San Berdoo he knocks off eight
setups, three more than I had figured, because everything
takes longer outside of the studio. He always was a fast
worker when he was in the mood (wrapped up a feature
in eleven days once), and this time he was keeping the
company on its toes like the old Moran and then some.
And of course all of us boys from Stage One, the grips,
the juicers, the camera crew and the sound men, were
really behind him, and that never hurt a director yet. In
five days' shooting he's two days ahead of schedule, and
that schedule wasn't one of those padded jobs, because I
made it out myself. I might of been tempted to feather it
a little to make Matty look good, but sure as taxes I'd of
had our hawk-eyed production manager on my neck. Anyway, the form Matty was showing, he didn't need any
special favors from anybody. He was like an old race
horse that's just been itching for someone to get him out
on the track and give him his head.

And it wasn't only speed. The rushes looked swell. Way above the average background and pickup stuff. Those rushes had mood and the timing was sharp and Matty was getting a lot of nice little touches in that weren't called for in the script. You could tell the way our producer, Oscar Mittels, talked to Matty after the second day's rushes that the old master was scoring. Mittels' secretary—you know the old studio grapevine—even told me she had heard the big boss mention to the studio manager that Matty had certainly seemed to've learned his lesson, and that it might be an idea to sign him to a low-salary contract as a regular second-unit man.

The second-unit schedule was seventeen days, and when Matty wrapped up his job in twelve he went to Vic and asked him if he could stay on the picture, taking over some of the minor dialogue scenes. Well, as usual, Vic was having his hands full with that bitch star of ours, Mona Moray, and Mittels' crying because he was two days behind schedule, so he told Matty to go ahead, and gave him his blessings.

On the first day Matty drew some unimportant scenes with a couple of twenty-five-dollar-a-day bit players and I must say everything went smoothly. They say a champ can never come back and usually that's as true for the movie racket as it is for the fight racket. But this time it sure looked like old Matty was crossing all the pessimists. "If you keep this up," I ribbed him, "us common people won't even let you in Stage One. You'll have to go over to Romanoff's with the big shots."

"Success never has gone to my head," Matty declared. "It's the great men who are truly humble."

"Amen," I said.

The next day Matty had his first scene of any importance. It was just a routine moment in the picture, but it called for the two leads, Grant Gibson and Mona Moray.

It was only a simple tie-in shot. A telegram arrives, Mona takes it and says, "It's for you, dear." That's all, just those four words and a little look at the end, the kind nobody has to tell Mona how to do. I figured we'd have it in the can in half an hour, master shot, close-up and all.

Well, Grant and Mona rehearse the scene once, and Matty doesn't like the reading. Where she'd said, "It's for *you*, dear," Matty thinks it ought to be "It's for you, *dear.*"

"I think that sounds too sarcastic," Mona says. "After all, I'm supposed to be sympathetic in this part."

"I'll tell you what you're supposed to be about it," Matty says. "After all, I'm directing this picture."

I see Mona look at Grant and they both look at me. I know what they're thinking—it's Vic Flanner who's directing this picture. Matty is just filling in with second unit.

Well, they don't get anywhere with the rehearsal, so Matty says, "All right, turn 'em, we'll go for a take," "Twirl 'em," I call out, "Quiet!" and my heart's in my throat. I can see that look on Matty's face. Live actors in front of him for the first time in all these years. Famous stars. Matty Moran is back in the big time.

They go through their little scene and Mona still says, "It's for *you*, dear."

"Cut," Matty said. And I see signs of that famous temperament flushing up his face. "You're ruining that line. Don't emphasize 'It's for *you* . . .' The lowest moron in the balcony knows it's for him. It's that '*dear*' I want you to work on. Not sarcastic. Just a little hint of cattiness around the edges. You can be catty, can't you, Mona?"

The script girl laughed. That was some question to ask the lot's champion feline. I could almost feel those beautifully painted claws reaching out to pin Matty for the kill.

"I'm an actress," Mona snapped. "I can be anything the script calls for. But we play these parts a little differently now from when you were doing them, Mr. Moran."

Matty's temperature, or should I say temperament, was rising. He never could stand backtalk from an actress. Would I ever forget that terrible moment when he bounced his own wife Sari off the set? Irrepressible, did I say? The word I was reaching for is incorrigible.

"That's the trouble with this business," Matty was shouting. "A bunch of hams who don't know how lucky they are to be eating every day trying to tell the director how to interpret their parts."

"Why you, you barbarian, you *has-been*," Mona screamed. "I'm going to play this part the way Vic Flanner tells me to play it."

"I'll let you in on a little secret." Matty threw it back in her teeth. "I'm a better director than Flanner. Maybe he knows how to get along with the front office better, but he never could touch me for real feeling."

Remember that old wheeze about signing your own death warrant? This sounded more like Matty was writing his own epitaph. I found myself already thinking of him as the late, departed Mr. Moran.

Mona Moray hadn't been talked to like this since she changed her name from Gertrude Schindler. "I refuse to stand here and be insulted by an—an old bum," Mona exclaimed in her best dramatic soprano. "Do you realize that one word from me to Mr. Mittels and you're back in—in the gutter?" Mona was one of those girls who sounded a lot better when she had someone writing her dialogue.

"Hams, hams, I'm surrounded by hams!" Matty shouted. "Now, are you going to play the scene my way, or do I have to get somebody else who can give me what I want?"

I just stood there with an awful silence in my mouth,

watching what I thought had been the comeback of Matty Moran go into reverse. Mittels had pulled every string he knew to sign Mona to a new contract and here was Matty, in on a pass, firing her!

"Just whom do you think you are?" Mona demanded. She never said *who* any more. It was beneath her.

"I think I'm Matty Moran," this character of mine shouted back, "and I've fired better actresses than you."

That's all, brother. Mona flounces off the set, and I begin getting hot-and-cold flashes.

Mona must have sprinted over to Mittels' office like Mrs. Blankers-Koen, for the next thing we knew the head man himself was on the phone. Mr. Moran was to go to his office immediately.

Well, five minutes, ten minutes pass, and the silence on the set is thicker than Beverly Hills smog. When I can't stand it any more I move across the street to Stage One to fortify myself.

A few minutes later in comes Matty, looking chipper as ever, grinning like his last picture has just been held over at the Music Hall.

"In?" I says.

He put his thumb out and turned it toward the floor in that ancient gesture of defeat.

"Oscar said he'd put me back on second unit, but first I had to apologize to Mona Moray."

"So?"

"So I say 'Oscar, m'boy, I'd rather turn myself in at the Motion Picture Home than take back anything I said to that bag!"

"Matty"—I'm so upset I'm calling him by his first name—"hasn't it ever occurred to you that eating a little humble pie has its virtues over not eating at all?"

"Red," he says, not even bothering to answer so foolish a question, "have you got a dime handy? I've got to call Goldwyn. Sam told me to be sure and get in touch with him when he went back into production. Don't be surprised if I step into an important assignment."

So now we've got Matty back in Stage One with us all the time. I should of known the Matty Morans of our town don't come back. They just go on being legends. So let's drink up to the fresh carnation and the ready grin of a legend that walks like a man.

THE TYPICAL GESTURE

OF COLONEL DUGGAN

When I was taking a quick look at a Broadway column the other day, my glance was caught by a boldface heading, "Typical gesture of Joshua Duggan's."

Now, Joshua Duggan happens to be an interesting fellow, any way you look at him, so I read with eagerness the little paragraph that followed.

Joshua Duggan, Broadway hero recently discharged from the army with the rank of full colonel and ribbons from here to Hoboken, has taken a precious week off from rehearsal of his new show to go to Zodiac, Illinois, to present a posthumous silver star to the widow of Master Sergeant Luther Bissell. Heartwarming story behind this item is that Luther, a hero of both world wars, used to be the doorman at the East Fortieth Street theatre where Duggan had his record run in *Blow the Man Down*, which probably would be running yet if Duggan hadn't volunteered for active duty six months before Pearl Harbor. A week out of a play rehearsal is time that never can be recaptured, and it's a long way from the Stork Club to Zodiac, but people who know Joshua Duggan and his oversize heart aren't surprised to find him putting the heart before the box office. In fact, this mission to Zodiac might be called a typical Duggan gesture.

Well, I thought, you knew Duggan, knew him pretty well. Surprised? I had to admit I wasn't. But it made me stop and think. About that Bissell thing, about the Duggan outfit, and how we all happened to get together.

The first time I met Duggan, and Bissell, too, for that matter, was back in the summer of '41 when I was the *Journal's* second-string drama critic, which, in my case, was a euphemism for glorified legman. This particular evening, for instance, I went backstage to interview Duggan for a Sunday feature. Duggan was an impressive character, of course, then as now, one of the few big talents in show business, an actor who could direct, a director who could write better stuff than most of the guys along the street who called themselves playwrights.

I had first seen Duggan when I was a kid, in a play called *My Brother's Keeper,* on which Duggan had collaborated with Laurence Stallings or somebody like that, pretty good stuff as I remember it, pretty daring for those days. After that I guess you might have called me a Duggan fan, for I went along with all of his hits, and even his flops were good flops.

So it was with considerable awe that I sat down in Duggan's dressing room. Duggan was sitting at his mirror, wiping the make-up off his face. He was a powerfully built man, with a dark, rugged face, restless, humorous eyes, and a mouth that looked as fascinating off stage as it did on. As I think back on it, it reminds me of Goering's mouth, with its quality of warm good nature that can change so suddenly to a hard line of anger and repressed cruelty. It was the quality that made Duggan able to play heroes and scoundrels with equal effectiveness, make you weep for his gentleness in one play and seethe against his villainies in the next.

There was almost always someone in his dressing room to interview him, usually a schoolgirl. This evening was no exception. In fact, there were two girls. They watched admiringly as he took off his make-up, and he responded to their admiration exactly right. I sat and smoked until the girls left.

"Glad to see you, Cumming," Duggan said to me then, pronouncing my name with an accuracy to which I was not accustomed, since everyone always insisted on adding an *s* on the end. The real Duggan seemed to have none of the blackhearted, ingrown, sadistic characteristics of the evil old sea captain he had just portrayed so convincingly on the stage.

Everything went along fine and easy. He is one of those fellows who interviews himself. He knew what he wanted to say, the points he wanted to make, and if my questions didn't bring them out he'd lead the conversation his way. He was a man of profound conceit, but egotism never disturbs me in a man who is really as creative as he feels himself to be, and Duggan's egotism had become such a tradition that you were inclined to accept it as one of the facts of theatre life.

I don't remember much about the professional side of our conversation that night, except maybe the phrase that I dutifully copied into my notes and that I happened to run across the other day when I was disinterring the remains of my prewar civilian career: "I became a director" (Duggan said) "because I was sick and tired of incompetent directors getting between me and my characterizations. I became a playwright because I became sick and tired of trying to delineate the stereotyped, foggy characterizations of stupid and incompetent playwrights. I became an actor because I was born that way."

We batted back and forth for a while the subject of why Duggan was the only authentic, dynamic voice left in the American theatre, a subject Duggan was well known to discuss with considerable intelligence and inexhaustible enthusiasm. And then, somehow, we got talking about the war. I think I must have asked Duggan how long he expected his current hit to run. Duggan turned around and gave me a long, deliberate, soul-searching look. "These days," he said slowly, with just a touch of that projection that made him so popular with the fans in the second balcony, "in these days," he repeated, "when the world balances on a bayonet, you begin to wonder just how important your own personal success is." He held me again with that famous Duggan look, and then, with a movement few men could make so significant, he picked up a copy of *Life* that had fallen on the floor. "Look at this," he said, with eloquent understatement, and I saw pictures of "the onrushing, blitzkrieging German panzers, driving the disorganized, panic-stricken Russian army out of Orel," and with the disorganized, panic-stricken *Life* editors Greek-chorusing, "Hitler will be in Moscow in three weeks." Duggan turned the pages tragically. "And on page 32," he said, "Rommel races for Suez." He took a long, thoughtful breath. "Cumming," he said, "this is absolutely off the record, man-to-man, but I've got it from—well, I can't tell you his name, but he's pretty high up on Marshall's staff—that we're liable to be in this thing sooner than most people realize." He slammed his great hand down on the dressing table. "And damn it, it can't be soon enough for me. Are we just going to sit around and worry about good notices and box-office successes while French actors and British actors and Russian actors and Jewish actors are ground to mincemeat?"

It may sound a little tired and corny now, but as I remembered it that night, against a backdrop of Nazi triumphs, congressional torpor, and general complacency, it sounded pretty exciting. Especially the last part, when he stood up and shouted: "The Duggans come from a long line of roughnecks and saloon fighters. I'm going to give you a real story, but you can't break it until I get the word from Washington."

"From Washington, Mr. Duggan?" I said.

"Just call me Josh," Duggan said. He rolled the copy of *Life* into a tight club. I wondered if it could be an unconscious gesture of rearmament. Then he wrinkled his brow and stared at me with a searching objectivity that was as disconcerting as it was intended to be. "Can you keep a secret?" he said.

"Why, sure I—"

"I don't mean the ordinary, Broadway secret. I mean a—military secret."

Later on, of course, the average "military secret" got to be a gag. But I still remember how it hit me that night, just the ordinary Broadway guy for whom military discipline and official secrets were strictly melodrama. The way Duggan said it, the way his mouth lingered over the phrase, the way his eyes challenged mine as he paused, made this a moment of great meaning. "I wouldn't trust you with this," Duggan continued, "if you didn't strike me as an all-right Joe."

Later I would have laughed. In fact, later I did laugh, plenty of times. But that night there was no getting around it. I was pleased. I was impressed. I was ready to step forward like Nathan Hale, to guard Joshua Duggan's secret with my life if necessary, my very life, as they say in the pulps.

"Well," Duggan said, dropping his voice an octave as if to make it difficult for enemy agents, "I've been asked by the top brass to form a psychological-warfare outfit. I don't know if you realize just how important that is. The

Nazis have won some of their biggest battles with psychological warfare. We have to beat them at their own game. That's why the army needs the best brains in the country in that department. And not just intellectuals. Men with guts. Because we'll have to be right on the front line with the infantry. Sometimes even behind enemy lines." Duggan paused and looked at me again, his behind-enemy-lines look.

"In times like this," Duggan went on, "personal values do one of these." A thick but expressive hand flipped over the other. "The playboy big shot with his hatful of dough becomes a bum. The little guy you wouldn't think of looking at a second time turns out to be the man you depend on. For instance—" Duggan drew me closer—"I'll give you a tip. Maybe you noticed the doorman when you came in. Maybe you didn't. The old codger with the specs who looks like he's half-asleep all the time?" I nodded, though I doubt if I could have picked him out from a dozen other doormen all around town. "Well, that's Luther Bissell. You may not believe it, but Luther's record in the last war was just as good as Sergeant York's. Stormed a Boche machine-gun nest with three slugs in him. When his ammunition ran out, he kept on going until he finally took care of the Heinie gun crew with his bayonet. He came out of the war with every combat medal there is. He doesn't know it yet, but if I can get him past the physical—he's practically blind in one eye—I'm going to take him into the outfit. Just the man to make soldiers of you Broadway guys."

Duggan was wiping the make-up base off his neck as he spoke. But in his mind he was already a soldier of democracy storming the fascist bastions. Looking into his large dressing-table mirror as he talked to me, he warmed to his subject. "There's the man you really ought to be interviewing: Luther Bissell. One of the troubles with this country is that we forget our heroes. We honor them for a brief moment like star football players whose names are lost in the next season's shuffle." Duggan rose, impressively, a big man who knew how to carry his weight, and moved toward me as I had seen him so often sweeping upstage toward the apron for a thunderous curtain speech. "Yesterday's hero may only be today's doorman, but how do we know that destiny hasn't singled him out for greater deeds in the struggle that lies ahead?"

As I say, it sounds a little overboard now, even for Duggan, who can get away with that sort of stuff. But those were the fever days when the press was talking about the invincibility of the Wehrmacht and the air was charged with the fear and excitement of approaching hostilities. Anyway, to a newspaperman, there did seem to be a story in Bissell. So I stopped to have a talk with him at the door. This was the first time I really got a good look at him. He was sitting on a chair near the stage door with his spectacles halfway down his nose, apparently absorbed in something he was reading. He was around fifty, I would have guessed, a mild-looking man with thinning hair and round, pink cheeks, a curious combination that gave me the impression of a perennial adolescent encased in the fatty frame of dormant middle age. As I drew closer to him I saw that the magazine in his lap was the *American Legion Magazine* and that his apparent absorption was informal slumber.

He awoke as I approached, however, nodding and smiling in an absent-minded, humble way. "Evenin', Mr. Cummings, didn't recognize you there for a moment. These old peepers of mine ain't gettin' any sharper."

"We were just talking about you, Luther," I said. "You seem to have quite a booster in Mr. Duggan."

Bissell pressed his lips together and shook his head reverently. "There's a wonderful man, sir, a wonderful man."

"Known him a long time?"

"Met him in France in the Great War—the first one, I mean. But I didn't see him again until '22, when he came to play a benefit in the hospital I was convalescing at. Mr. Duggan, he's been mighty good to me. If it wasn't for him, I'd never have no good job like this. And every Christmas it's: 'Here's ten dollars, Luth. Go out and get yourself ten good cigars. None of those cheap ones, now. Ten dollar cigars.' " Bissell chuckled. "That's Mr. Duggan for you. Never forgets Luther."

When it came to talking about what he had done in the war, Bissell wasn't one of those shucks-it-was-nothing fellows. He talked freely enough about the achievement side of it, the prisoners he had taken, the enemies he had killed, the honors he had won. He remembered it all the way a man remembers something he never succeeds in achieving again, with the dates of the battles, the obscure French places pronounced with surprising correctness, and the names of officers and comrades sharply retained and alive for him after more than twenty years.

"What about this time?" I said. "Feel like doing it again?"

"You bet," he said. "I'd like to get another crack at them Huns. But I don't know. I ain't as young as I was. The army might take one look at me and say, 'Luther, go on back to the old soldiers' home.' The mizzuz tells me I'm a darned fool even to think about it. But I don't know, it'd feel pretty good to be back in again. Mr. Duggan, he's goin' in, and maybe he can fix it for me. It sure would be a privilege to go along with a man like that!"

I did the story about Luther, the old-fire-horse angle, the kind of thing we all would have upchucked at the year before, but it went pretty good now, for war isn't only man's most ruthless activity but his most sentimental. I guess without the schmalz it would be just so damned painful and vicious that we couldn't take it. Smear a nice soft salve on the wound and it doesn't look so bad. Sprin-

kle a lot of Luther Bissells around, look back at them
through a gauze of pain-absorbent years, and a war doesn't
seem so bad at all.

I didn't hear from Duggan again until my piece on
Luther appeared. Then, to my surprise, he telephoned.
His voice was crisp and efficient and pitched a little differ-
ently. "Hello, Cumming," he said. "Duggan here. I'd like
you to come to my dressing room tonight at seven-thirty.
Don't say anything about this to anybody. See you then."

When I went through the stage door, a little early, Bissell stood up and greeted me, a little excited, I thought.
"Good evening, sir," he said. "Glad you came, sir."

"Listen, Luther," I said, "don't give me this sir treatment. I'm a country boy myself. And anyway you're old
enough to be my father."

"That doesn't matter, sir," Luther said. "One of my
best officers at Catigny was a young man just out of college.
Lieutenant Alvin Sabath. He was a fine soldier. Would
of been a fine man if he had lived."

I passed on through to Duggan's dressing room, feeling
as if I were all ready to be laid beside young Sabath in
some distant burial ground. I didn't realize until I got inside the door that I was attending a meeting. Lou Ross,
the press agent, Jack Woodridge, the young playwright,
Tom Lovell, the stage manager, and three or four others
were sitting around stiffly and expectantly, looking at Josh
Duggan in his brand-new tailored major's uniform. Duggan was striding up and down, with the kind of military
bearing most generals would like to have. Four ribbons on
his tunic gave him the appearance of an old war dog. He
wore the World War I Victory Ribbon, the First German
Occupation, the Brazilian Cruz de Sol, and the Mexican
Águila Azteca. He waited stiffly until all of us were settled. As on stage, he had the ability to make his silences
momentous.

"I think you all have a pretty good idea what I've called

you men together for," he began. "I've picked you out because I thought you were the best officer material Broadway had to offer. Being an officer is a responsibility and a
privilege. Your reward may be the highest honors this
country has to give. But the price may be high—the highest any man can pay. If any one of you men feel for one reason or another that you aren't ready to make that sacrifice,
this is the time to tell me. There's no disgrace in pulling
out now. I'd rather have you do that than come in with
any reservations."

Duggan looked into all of our faces, one by one. His
eyes were hard and yet understanding. The man-of-iron-
but-at-bottom-a-human-being type. All of us, Lou, Jack,
Tom, exchanged grim and self-conscious glances. A few
minutes before, I was wolfing a sturgeon sandwich at
Reuben's, Jack and Tom were laughing over coffee and
brandy with their wives at Sardi's. Now somehow, here in
this dressing room, we were already at war, already
breathing the heavy air of life-and-death decisions.

The gathering broke up with a soldierly: "Thank you,
men. I'll take your applications for commissions down to
Washington tomorrow and walk them through myself.
Nothing's official yet, of course, but off the record you can
start picking out your uniforms. If there are any hitches—
if they think you're too much of a pinko, for instance,
Ross, I'll take the matter up with George—er—General
Marshall—personally. All right, men, I'll be in touch with
you." He shook hands all around. I don't think there was
anybody there—even Jack, who's won the Critics' Award—
who didn't feel this was the most important thing that
ever had happened to him. When Duggan got to me he
said, "Don't go, Cumming. I've got a job for you." It was
my first order.

"I want you to work up a little news release, Cumming," he said when the others had left. "Something
about the Duggan Psychological Warfare Unit being or-

ganized in my dressing room. Not that I'm looking for any personal publicity, you understand. I've seen my name in enough papers to keep my ego happy. But I figured it would be a good thing for the outfit."

It didn't take me long to throw something together, and then, since Duggan was still on stage, I wandered out to the stage door to see how Luther was getting along. He was half-dozing over a tabloid; but as I approached, he rose, very formally, almost as if he were going to come to attention.

"Well, how was the meeting, Mr. Cummings? The old man got you all signed up?"

"Yes," I said. "I just gone and done it."

Luther took my hand, pumped it seriously, and said: "Congratulations, Mr. Cummings, good luck and God bless you. There's nothing in this life for a man like answering the call to the colors. And it's a real honor to serve under a man like Major Duggan." Then the expression that always anticipated his childlike emotions concentrated in concern. "The—the old man—he didn't happen to say nothing about me, did he?"

I had to tell him that Duggan hadn't mentioned him.

His lips pushed out in what was very much like a little boy's pout. "That's funny, I thought—I kind of hoped he —Major Duggan—would ask me to the meeting. Said something to me about it over a week ago. But he's got so much on his mind these days, maybe he forgot. Or maybe this meeting was only for prospective officers. Yes, that must be it." He sucked on his bottom lip the way he had a habit of doing when he wasn't too sure of himself. Which was, in Luther's case, I'm afraid, a great deal of the time. "Say, Mr. Cummings, I realize I don't really know you good enough to ask a favor, but, well—if you could just put in a word for me with the old man, sort of find out how serious he is about taking me along, I sure would appreciate it a whole lot. I know the major don't mean to forget me, but thinking about so many things like he is all the time, it's kind of hard to pin him down sometimes. I sure hope he figures to take me."

I promised Luther I'd put it up to the old man—he was beginning to get me talking like that, too—but later in the evening, when Duggan and I were going over my copy in his dressing room, I couldn't get any farther with it than Luther had. "I'm working on Bissell," was all he'd say. "Nothing definite yet."

"He's sure knocking himself out to go," I said.

"Bissell would be a definite asset," Duggan said. "I hope I get him through."

"With his war record, and your pull in Washington," I said, "I should think it would be a cinch, Josh."

"By the way, Cumming," Duggan said, and from his tone I squared myself for a this-is-hurting-me-more-than-it-hurts-you speech, "I know last time you were here I asked you to call me Josh. Well, as far as I'm concerned personally, that still goes. But, well, now that I'm in this monkey suit," he said, with a smile to take the sting out of it, "I think it would be a better idea if you gave me the Major Duggan. Not that *I* give a damn, you understand. It's just the respect due the uniform, the rank, not the guy that's in it. When we're alone, of course, the Josh is good enough for me."

"Sold, Major," I said. "I'm just not used to it, but . . ."

"I understand," Duggan said, and he put his arm around me, very chummy, or I suppose now it should be very comradely. "And by the way, don't let Luther get you all up in the air about his case. As an old army man he ought to know better than to go outside of channels anyway. If he tries to pester you again, just tell him it's none of your business, Major Duggan is looking after that."

Duggan and I—Major Duggan, I should say—left together. Luther was still on the door. I could see from the way he opened his mouth and got ready to start talking

when he saw Duggan that he had his little speech all prepared. "Major Duggan, I'm sure I don't want to bother
you, but I just wonder whether it would be possible . . ."

It was too slow a windup, with too many words, and I
could see right away that Luther was never going to get
the pitch off.

"See you tomorrow, Luther. Good night," Duggan said,
not even slowing his pace, brushing him off so deftly that
it could have seemed as if he actually hadn't heard him at
all. "Great character, Luther," Duggan said when we
were out on the street. "The real killer type. Unobtrusive,
gentle, with real humility. I love him like my own
brother."

That was just a line from the Duggan script, of course.
Aroused to self-defense and abnormal struggle for sur-
vival, Luther probably did act very well that day at
Château-Thierry. But that was twenty-five years ago,
twenty-five anticlimactic and sedentary years, during
which time whatever combativeness had heated Luther's
nature had cooled to servility and impotence. Courage in
battle, you might say, is compounded partly of fearless
initiative, partly of blind obedience, and it was only the
selfless, blindly obedient Luther left sitting at the door.

Every time I passed Luther that next week or so, he'd
put the arm on me to talk to "the old man" about his
joining the outfit. But every time I tried to bring up the
subject to Duggan, he'd brush me off. It was hard to figure. If he had the pull with the War Department he
claimed to have—and the way our commissions were coming through that seemed to be on the level—it shouldn't
have been much trouble to push through some sort of
rating for an old soldier like Luther, bad eyes and all.
And if he knew he could do it, it hardly seemed possible
that he would be sadistic enough to keep Luther deliberately on the hook. Yet, I had to admit, that's the way it
seemed. As the day for the closing of the show and Dug-

gan's departure for Washington drew closer, Luther became too nervous even to take his customary snoozes. Whenever Dugan was off stage, Luther would keep an eye cocked toward the dressing room in hope of catching the major as he came out. But every time he started toward Duggan, stammering and blinking in his overanxiousness to make his plea, Duggan would parry him, sometimes even turning his back and walking off deliberately, leaving Luther standing there in a fog of frustration.

The way Luther looked at me the first time I showed up in uniform made me realize that I was going to have to talk to Duggan once more, no matter how hot he got. As soon as he saw me, Luther jumped up, put away his glasses, and went into his act, only it wasn't an act with Luther, it was just what happens to a man who dwells too long on past glories. "Good evening, Lieutenant," Luther said, and his hand rose in a half-salute. "You sure look fine in your uniform, sir. Only, if you're going in to see the old man, I might suggest, sir, that you square your cap a little bit—that's more like it." He stepped back and appraised me carefully. "And you're a little out of uniform, I'm afraid, sir. That button there on the right-hand pocket." He buttoned it for me and straightened my blouse a little in the back. "There you are, sir. All ready to present yourself. And by the way, Lieutenant, if you get a chance to . . ."

"I will, Luther," I promised. "I'll try to see what goes."

"Thank you, Lieutenant," he said, and I got that half-salute again.

Duggan was in his dressing room, with his uniform blouse off and his khaki shirt open at the neck. "Look me over, Maj," I said.

"Come to attention," Duggan said severely.

It seemed just a little silly, coming to attention in an actor's dressing room, but there I was.

"All right, carry on," Duggan said. He offered me a

cigarette. "Sit down, Lieutenant." Then he lapsed into his own self—or rather, since his plastic personality seemed to include so many selves—his previous self. "Don't let me frighten you with that 'Attention' stuff Al. Just because I've got these oak leaves on my collar, I know I don't belong to the WPPA, you know, the West Point Protective Association. But I just want to get you broken in so you'll know how to act in the presence of field-grade officers."

For a man who didn't give a damn about that sort of thing, it seemed to me Duggan was putting us through an awful lot of military hoops.

"Well, we're just about ready to report in Washington," Duggan said. "But before we do, I think it might be a good idea to have a couple of drill periods—just to brush up on our protocol a little bit, so we won't look so wet behind the ears when we report to Colonel Partridge. He's in charge of the whole PW Division, regular army, so we don't want to walk in like a bunch of Broadway wiseguys. So next week, every other night, I thought I'd have Luther put you boys through a little close-order drill."

"Luther," I said. "Did you get Luther through?"

"Well, I couldn't get him that warrant because his eyes were too bad," Duggan said. "But I guess the staff-sergeant rating will come through all right."

The way he said it I had the distinct feeling that he knew he could have got this all the time.

"But why don't you tell Luther?" I said. "This is the most important thing that's happened to him since he stormed that machine-gun nest."

"That's why I didn't want to break it to him until I was absolutely sure," Duggan said. "I felt it would be a little cruel to break it to him prematurely, just in case the thing fell through. Why, I wouldn't hurt Luther for anything in the world."

"Then if I may say so, Major," I said—I called him nothing but "Major" now, with a kind of perverse glee— "why don't you take him off the hook?"

"I'll notify him just as soon as I have word from Washington," Duggan said. "That will be all, Lieutenant."

Duggan's military conduct tended toward the complex, but, in relation to myself at least, I was beginning to recognize a pattern. When he liked me he called me Al. When he liked me but felt like playing soldier he called me Lieutenant. When he didn't like me and felt like playing soldier he called me Cumming. And when he just plain didn't like me he called me whatever came into his head, which was considerable.

Next afternoon, when I had to check with Duggan on the chart of chain of command I had to draw up for him, I found myself brushing by Luther myself. It was too hard to look at him. Duggan went over my chart punctiliously, as if it were the table of command of the entire American army, and then, when he had made the last small change, he said, "Oh, by the way, Lieutenant, tell Bissell the old man says front and center."

I did just as I was told. I said, "The old man says front and center." I wish you could have seen Luther come to life. He followed me in, as correct and on his toes as a Prussian corporal, and when he saw Duggan, even though he wasn't in uniform, he came to stiff attention, with his tail out and his nose up in the air like a bird dog.

"As you were," Duggan said.

Luther relaxed a little, but even at ease he looked more attentive than the rest of us did at attention. Then began the little pageant that Duggan must have been building up to all this time.

"Staff Sergeant Bissell," Duggan began, in a deep, March of Time intonation, "I have the honor to welcome you back into the Army of the United States."

Luther stepped forward like a West Point senior receiving his diploma. "Thank you, Major," he said, shook hands, stepped back and saluted.

"Sergeant Bissell," Duggan went on, "as your commanding officer I am proud to reactivate such an illustrious soldier. And as your friend of long standing, I want to express my personal pleasure at seeing you back in the ranks as my comrade in arms."

There was even more to it than that, I think, but that will give you a rough idea. If I had been out front, at least I could have applauded when the scene was over, or walked out or something, but there I was, trapped in my uniform, having to stand by and watch.

If ever there were two hams cut out to play straight for each other, I thought, here they were. The only trouble was that Luther was too much on the level. There were tears in his eyes when he left the room. I can't say what was in Duggan's eyes, because I couldn't look.

A few nights later Major Duggan's Psychological Warfare Unit assembled for the first time in all its military glory, on the empty stage of Duggan's theatre. None of us fooled anybody in our uniforms. Somehow I couldn't seem to get mine to look like a uniform. Tom's had been made specially for him by his tailor. He even had pleats in his trousers. Lou's was at least two sizes too large. In fact, there was only one man in the hall who really looked like a soldier, and that was Sergeant Bissell. There was something about the way Luther fitted into that uniform that made you take him almost as seriously as he took himself. Buried somewhere in that uniform, with combat ribbons covering his breast and the service stripes running up his arm, was the pink-cheeked doorman with the soft body and the sleepy face. Even with his specs, the peaches-and-cream complexion, and the gentle expression, Luther managed to create the illusion of a martial figure. It was almost as if his uniform and cap sternly squared away were like a coat of mail behind which the most insignificant and timid of men could present a formidable front.

For the next half-hour we sweated through the alien intricacies of close-order drill, and under Luther's expert command we were surprised to find ourselves, grown men and relatively sophisticated, taking absurd delight in keeping in step with one another or carrying out a flanking motion. The tediousness of it for me, I know, was dissipated by the fascination of being in on Luther's metamorphosis.

Then Major Duggan appeared. Luther brought us to attention, saluted smartly, said, in his new sergeant's voice, "The platoon is ready for inspection, sir," returned Duggan's salute with a snap, and fell into step behind him as Duggan started the rounds of his first inspection.

They were both playing it for deadly earnest, with Duggan stopping to inspect this man's tie, another man's shoes, while Luther, always a pace behind and in perfect step, produced from somewhere (there was no bulge in his uniform to indicate it) a little black notebook in which he scribbled obediently the Major's comments.

Then Luther gave us "at ease," and Duggan gave us his inaugural address. It was the kind of fight talk a commanding officer probably gives his men on the eve of battle, or rather, the kind he would give if he had the talent and imagination of Joshua Duggan. "Tonight," he said, "we hold our first inspection in an empty theatre in the heart of New York City. But who knows in what theatre of war our final inspection will be held? Who can tell what ordeals we will be compelled to undergo in the fulfillment of our duties, and who can tell which ones of us will be called upon to make the final sacrifice before the last 'fall out' is given?"

I looked at Lou, and Lou winked at Tom, and almost every one of us, I think, fought back the impulse to break up, but when I looked at Luther, standing there with his braid and his medals, unbelievably transformed into a figure of importance, the whole show seemed to be like nothing more than a marvelously acted and costumed charade.

One week after the do-or-die inaugural, we embarked for the Munitions Building, where, except for the protocol kept alive by Duggan and Luther, we all found ourselves with our bottoms planted in swivel chairs, doing pretty much the same kind of work we previously had been doing in striped ties and tweeds. It was our job to work up propaganda schemes to undermine the Japanese will to fight. Since it was the kind of brainwork only slightly removed from our civilian activities, all of us soon found ourselves relapsing into the relaxed postures and attitudes of pre-military creation. To Luther, whose heart was set on maintaining smart military discipline, these aberrations from standard operating procedure were a source of constant shock and frustration. And Duggan, of course, took everything with solemnity.

The feeling between the two camps, Duggan and Luther against the rest of us, was more or less an armed truce most of the time, with Luther the butt of most of our comedy and Duggan coming in for our more profound observations. Only once in a great while did it flare into the open. One Saturday morning, for instance, Luther gave the order to fall in for inspection. Jack, who always had a tendency to be nervous when he worked, was trying to finish a script that was supposed to have a noon deadline. "For God's sake, I'm trying to knock out a script. Do we have to play soldier all the time?"

Luther just looked at him unbelievingly, with deep hurt in his eyes.

At this moment Duggan, who had happened to overhear this mutiny, strode up. "Sergeant," he said, "put this officer on report for disciplinary action."

Jack got by with nothing more than what Duggan called "an official reprimand," which was little more than an opportunity for Duggan to play a scene from his favorite drama—himself. An hour later I'm sure both Duggan and Jack had forgotten all about it, but Luther was still brooding about it. When work was over for the day—retreat, Luther called it—he caught up with Jack in the hallway. "I'm sure sorry, sir, if I got you in the doghouse with the old man," Luther said. "I was just trying to do my duty, sir. I'm sure glad the old man let you off with a reprimand. That won't show on your service record, sir."

But despite these differences of orientation between Luther and the rest of us, this must have been the happiest period of his life. Whenever he was in the presence of Duggan I'm sure he had the feeling that he was living life deeply, significantly, and efficiently. I'm sure he had not the slightest idea what we were supposed to be doing, but, trusting Duggan with blind devotion, he was ready to follow him around the globe and serve him around the clock. He called for Duggan at his hotel in the mornings. He took him home in the evenings. He took his uniforms to be cleaned. He saddle-soaped his boots. He made and served coffee for him every afternoon. There seemed to be no errand too menial for Luther to perform gladly, as long as it was "for the old man." And not only perform them, but lend to them a sense of eminence, a sense of importance. Going out to the snack bar to get cigarettes for Duggan seemed to become in his mind, and perhaps in Duggan's, too, a courageous penetration into enemy territory.

In spite of all kidding, the interruptions, and the occasional irritation, I found myself missing Luther when he flew out with Duggan for the New Britain invasion. He had been grim and warrior-like about the adventure. Duggan, of course, had taken leave of us like a man who was going to parachute alone into Tokyo itself. But Lou was offering two-to-one the pair never would get beyond Honolulu, and getting no takers.

When word came that they actually had shoved off for New Britain, though, I think we all felt a little lumpy. We told one another that Duggan, for all the comedy, was a pre-Pearl Harbor volunteer when most men his age were sitting back and letting their kids run the show. And at the thought of anything happening to Luther, everyone got a little moist.

But a few weeks later, the New Britain fighting still in the headlines, they were back. Duggan, now a lieutenant colonel, was wearing a new Purple Heart and the Legion of Merit and had a tremendous tale to tell. They had gone in with the first wave, it seemed (though it was never really explained what they were doing there), and Duggan had been hit in the knee with shrapnel and would have bled to death if Sergeant Bissell hadn't carried him back to an emergency aid station. The story and Duggan's wound grew with each telling, although for a man who had been at death's door such a short time before, he looked remarkably fit. I tried to get Luther alone and pin him down, but either he had received a thorough briefing from Duggan or he had heard the old man tell the story so often he had come to believe it. "Believe me, you would have been proud of the old man," he told me. "I must have carried him almost a mile to the beach, and not a peep out of him."

"Luther, are you sure this whole thing didn't take place in a bar in Honolulu?" Tom wanted to know. "Maybe it was the Royal Hawaiian you carried him to."

Luther just waited with his pained face until the laughter died down. "Gentlemen," he said, "before this thing is over, I hope you'll all get a chance to go up front with the old man."

During their fourteen-day leave, Duggan took Luther to 21, a place he had always wanted to go, and introduced him to Jack and Mac, to Quent Reynolds, to John O'Hara, to *everybody* as "the man who saved my life."

Lennie Lyons devoted a paragraph to Luther, and Adela Rogers St. John gushed over two columns on the inseparable bond between these two Broadway heroes.

Eventually the excitement wore off and we all plugged away again, with all the jokes about the chair-borne soldiers and wearing the red-and-black ribbon for action with a typewriter. Once in a while, of course, work halted for military ceremonies, like the Saturday morning Duggan presented Luther with his second bronze star. For this event Luther's wife came all the way from Brooklyn. She was a sweet-faced, homey-looking woman who never should have tried to get dressed up. For the occasion she was wearing an orchid corsage Duggan had sent her. The three of them smiled for the news photographers. I still have a picture of it clipped from the *Daily News*, with Duggan upstaging Luther a little as he pins the medal on him, while Mrs. Bissell looks on proudly.

Then all of a sudden our entire outfit, penned up so long that the real war seemed as if it were being fought on another planet, got the word that we were moving out to the Pacific. Duggan, on his last trip out, had made a number with MacArthur (that's how these things were done, I came to find), and as a result we were all going to work the Philippines invasion, beaming radio messages to Filipino resistance groups.

The week before we shoved off, a strange thing happened. Mrs. Bissell came in and asked to see Duggan alone. She was in there a long time, maybe twenty minutes, and when she came out she walked right on through without even stopping to nod at those of us she had met. I happened to follow her into Duggan's office, for a regular conference. He held forth for four or five minutes, as he often did, about the importance of the work we were doing, and then, with an expression of martyrdom, he said, "You know, sometimes I'm disappointed in human nature. So few people ever measure up to their responsibilities. Take Mrs. Bissell, for instance. She just asked me not to take Luther back overseas, because, she says, he isn't what he used to be."

"So what did you say, Colonel?" I said.

"What could I say?" Duggan wanted to know. "Why, it would break Luther's heart to be left behind. I just wouldn't tell an old campaigner like Luther that he was going to have to miss out on the Philippines show."

Just to keep the records straight I grabbed a cup of coffee with Luther at the snack bar one morning and put the question to him about our expedition.

"Well, I don't know," Luther said, and I thought there was more weariness in his voice than usual. "I seen a lot of places and a lot of fighting in my time. And I already been to the Pacific. Them islands is all the same. But if the old man thinks he needs me . . ."

The old man needs you to make his coffee, snap to attention, and hang up his breeches, I thought to myself.

But no matter how anxious or reluctant Luther was to return to the wars, he played his part to the hilt all the way over. On the C-54 going to Honolulu, when Tom, who had had a hard night in San Francisco, dropped into the first of two reclining seats (it was a bucket job), Luther spoke right up. "The Colonel isn't aboard yet, Captain," he reminded Tom. "Don't you think you'd better wait and see where the old man wants to ride?"

And when we landed at Hickam, Luther wanted to line us up and call the roll, even though there weren't a dozen of us. But after bouncing around on those buckets for twenty-four hours, we were in no mood for military sport, not even to indulge Sergeant Bissell.

But it was when we shoved off from the staging area with regular components of the 6th Army that Duggan and Luther really began to express themselves. Any way you looked at it we were a freak outfit, not slated to hit the beach until after it had been secured; and in cases like that, when you're among fighting men tuning up for an invasion, discretion is not only the better but the only part of valor. But the way Duggan and Luther behaved, and no doubt felt, the Colonel (he had made his full colonelcy) and the Sergeant were MacArthur and his chief of staff about to throw their army into the jaws of death. At Luther's suggestion, several inspections were held on the afterdeck, with thousands of jeering GI's on hand to watch the comic opera. Every time we passed Duggan on deck we were supposed to salute, although even combat officers were dispensing with the formality except upon first greeting in the morning. But the pay-off came when Duggan called us together for instruction from Luther on hand-to-hand combat.

"These Japs are tricky," Duggan said, standing on a hatch with the sun highlighting his strong face like a baby spot. "Even if we're back in Headquarters territory, you can never tell when the Nips will make a surprise night raid. I want every one of my men to know how to defend himself if necessary. I don't want to have to live with myself after this show is over if I have to think I lost a man through carelessness. So every afternoon until we land I've asked Sergeant Bissell to give you an hour of routine judo."

"Can you show us how to wrest a typewriter from a Jap in hand-to-hand psychological warfare?" Jack called.

Everybody laughed except Duggan and Luther. "You can save the comedy for when you go back to Lindy's," Duggan said. "Whether you realize it or not, gentlemen, this is a matter of life and death."

Everybody passed whispered jokes around to everybody else. It was like hearing Duggan in one of his plays telling another character that some hoked-up situation was life or death. He made it sound convincing because he read his lines so well. But actually you knew that this was just a theatre and that the character, if he did, subsequently, fall lifeless across the apron, would rise again the moment the curtain was down.

We got to Leyte with very little trouble. The Kamikazes gave some of the ships around us a shaking up, but the landing turned out to be easier than anybody expected. The first five waves went in with practically no opposition. Our outfit went in with the sixth, all except Duggan and Luther, who were waiting to go in with MacArthur and Osmena.

Even though resistance was light, there was plenty of confusion on the beach as the various HQ's tried to set themselves up. We had a portable radio transmitter and started beaming our stuff as soon as we got ashore. Duggan and Luther showed up a couple of hours later. I didn't have time to ask whether Luther had saved his life yet or not. Duggan and Luther inspected our position, and then a terrible thing was discovered. Luther had forgotten the coffee, the "joe," as he and Duggan called it. Luther was ordered back to the Quartermaster tent to get some more. It was growing dark by that time. There wasn't too much happening on the beach. It looked more like the aftermath of a Rose Bowl game than a battle, with jeeps, trucks, half-tracks, tanks, everything the army had that moved pouring out of LST's and getting snarled in traffic jams as the beachmasters muffed their signals in the dark. Out at sea a terrific naval battle seemed to be going on, but the only casualties I saw on the beach were from occasional snipers in the palm trees. There was one sniper who winged a couple near our transmitter before somebody picked him off. He fell practically at Duggan's feet, a little man with a face we would have called cute if he had been a houseboy.

"Maybe we've moved up a little too close, Al," Duggan said. His voice sounded unnaturally high and the careful enunciation was gone.

I was scared, too, even though this was still a long way

from actual combat, but I said, "Close? This isn't close. Not for an outfit that's supposed to be ready for action behind enemy lines."

"It's not myself I'm thinking about," Duggan said. "It's the equipment. And none of you men has been exposed to battle conditions before."

A few minutes later Colonel Talley happened to pass by in a jeep. He was on MacArthur's staff, one of the men through whom Duggan worked the deal that got us here. "We've just taken the airstrip, Josh," Talley said. From the way he said it you could see that he enjoyed the intimacy of calling a stage celebrity Josh. "I'm flying back to Guam on the first plane out. Be back in a day or so. Want to come along?"

Duggan looked at the dead Jap, looked out at the darkening night with the lightninglike flashes on the horizon, and then addressed us all without looking directly into any one face. "Might not be a bad idea for me to hop over to Guam," he said. "I've been wanting to have a talk with Colonel Partridge. Tom, you'll be in command until I return. Carry on, men. And God bless you!"

About an hour later Luther came. He had the coffee but he had had a hard time finding us in the dark. When he came into our transmitting shack, he was breathing hard, and his face looked old.

"Well, it was tough going, but I got the old man's coffee, Lieutenant," he said. Then, when he didn't see him, "By the way, where is the Colonel?"

"He's gone back to Guam," I said.

"No kidding, Lieutenant, where is he?" Luther said.

"I said he's gone back to Guam, Luther," I said.

He looked around like a little boy who's lost his parents in a department store. "But he—the old man—he wouldn't go without me."

"He left with Colonel Talley," Tom said. "Maybe you can still catch him at MacArthur's HQ."

"Sure, that's it, that's it," Luther said. "He's probably waiting for me up there. Hell, the old man wouldn't go anywhere without me." He stood up, and for the first time since I had known him I saw that he was deeply shaken. His face had gone very white, and his head was almost imperceptibly shaking like an old man's. It wasn't that he was frightened. He was undermined, humiliated, deeply embarrassed. We were all sitting around the shack, in the most informal dress and position—just a bunch of radio guys who happened to draw a somewhat inconvenient assignment. But Luther came to attention, saluted us just like a scene from *Journey's End*, and said: "Thank you for the information, sir. Good night, gentlemen."

We kept knocking out our radio stuff all night, telling Filipino guerrillas what was happening and where they could tie in to our advance patrols, and about five A.M., while we were trying to keep awake with the help of that coffee Luther had brought for Duggan the night before, an MP came to the door and said he wanted an officer from the radio outfit to follow him. I followed him down the beach, threading my way through ack-ack outfits, stalled jeeps, supply dumps, and all the rest of the amazing gear that man drags with him onto enemy beaches, until at last we came to a little clump of sandbrush, where Luther was lying.

"One of your men?" the MP said.

Sprawled there on his side with his smashed spectacles lying near by, he didn't look very impressive any more. He didn't look the way a hero is supposed to look. He just looked crumpled, deflated, like a doorman who falls asleep on the job.

"A sniper?" I said.

"No, one of our trucks," the MP said. "Ran into him last night in the dark. The driver wasn't using his lights, of course, and I guess the old man couldn't see so good, anyway. Thought maybe since he was one of your guys you'd want to take him up to your camp and bury him."

I don't remember what I thought about as I carried him back. I don't remember thinking anything one way or another. I just carried him back. We dug a grave for him in the sand, and then we lowered him down, facing the USA. Then, since nobody had anything to say, we all just stood at attention for one minute of silence. Luther should have seen us. It was the most military moment of our entire pseudomilitary careers.

I suppose the one thought in all our minds was, Thank God, Duggan isn't here to give us the curtain speech. But if Luther had to go, too bad he couldn't have gone in style, storming a Jap machine-gun nest. Well, by the time Duggan got back to "21" he was sure to have Luther storming a half dozen machine-gun nests.

Saluting the grave and listening to the bugler blow his tinny requiem, I couldn't help thinking: This isn't on the level. We're really back on that empty Broadway stage and my show-business mind is jumping way ahead of Duggan's inaugural address. After all, nobody dies in an outfit like ours. Nobody is supposed to die. We wear soldier suits and we salute and call each other by our military titles. But it's all a charade, the kind of charade that only Duggan and Luther really know how to play—the kind of charade that Colonel Duggan, on his way to Zodiac, Illinois, to decorate Luther's widow, has to go on playing alone, now that the soft and faithful flesh of Luther Bissell lies in its sandy and unnecessary grave.

MEAL TICKET

The old man had just come in off the docks with Eddie
and they were drinking beer in the kitchen. The old lady
didn't like them drinking beer in her kitchen—precious
little work space in these cold-water flats—but it was better than having them drink themselves into the blind
staggers down at Paddy's Waterfront Bar & Grill. She
didn't like them sitting there slopping it down until they
were too full to stand up straight and she'd have to shake
some life into them so Pop could grope his way to bed
while Eddie wandered out into the night in search of such
evils as only the Devil knew.

Eddie was saying, "Pop, what gives with our West Side
boys these days—can't punch their way outa a paper bag.
Last night that Mickey Cochrane, a real chumpola, and
he's supposed to be the pride of the West Side. Harlem—

Little Italy—that's where they got the fighters now. Jeez, in my day . . ."

The old lady looked up from the meat loaf she was preparing, but she didn't say anything. She had heard all she wanted to hear about his day. She remembered all too well the days of glory for Eddie (Honeyboy) Finneran. He had been the "crowd-pleasing kayo artist from the West Side" then, making three, sometimes four thousand dollars a fight. In his best year, '42, he had earned nearly thirty thousand. Quite a take for the son of a longshoreman who had worked hard all his life for his two or three thousand a year. Ma hadn't gone for the fighting. She hadn't been impressed when Eddie said, "Just think, Ma, in forty-five minutes Friday night I'll make more money than the old man makes in a whole year."

Pop would go to the fights, and their older daughter Molly and her husband Leo, but not Ma. She'd stay home with Vince, the baby of the family, and wait for the excitement to be over. One night when Eddie was fighting Joey Kaplan, his East Side rival, and she was worried for him because the sports writers had wondered if Honeyboy Finneran wasn't "being taken along too fast," that night she had turned on the radio for a minute and she heard: "Finneran's got a bad gash over his right eye— but he keeps boring in—lots of heart—and another hard right hand to Finneran's eye!" She had heard the hoarse, blood-thirsty yowl of the crowd and that was enough. She had snapped the radio off and waited. Pop came home late and very drunk because the referee had stopped the fight in the ninth to save Honeyboy from further punishment. "'Magine a skinny little sheeney from the East Side lickin' our Honeyboy," the old man said. For days he had stayed away from his favorite saloons, he was that ashamed. And Eddie had hid out in a hotel until his face looked good enough for him to come home. Stayed up in a hotel and belted whiskey with all the trash of the neighborhood, man and woman alike, who were perfectly content to tell Eddie how he would have beaten the little East Side Jew-boy if only for some lousy breaks, all the while helping Eddie get rid of his more-money-in-forty-five-minutes-than-Pop-made-in-a-year.

Oh yes, Ma remembered *his* days all right. She remembered how he made thirty thousand in the ring and lost it in the horse rooms. And she remembered how Pop quit work because Eddie was a main-eventer at the Garden and what was the sense of making a lousy ten dollars a day when Eddie had a grand on him all the time. She remembered how Pop spent nearly all his waking time in the bars buying drinks for his longshore pals and reviewing Honeyboy's triumphs round by round. And she remembered how a cold-water flat wasn't good enough for the Finnerans any more, how Eddie insisted they move away from their old block between 10th and 11th, even over Ma's objections. She had lived there since before Eddie was born and if she needed help or company there was always Mrs. Boyle and Mrs. Hanrahan right in the building, and Fred the janitor was a friend of theirs, and she liked to know that Father Corcoran was just around the corner. But they had moved because Eddie was proud and the money was burning his pocket, and because Pop and Molly had argued that if Eddie was so famous why shouldn't they have a taste of better things? Yes, and Ma remembered, not with bitterness but with a sense of realism, how long those better things had lasted. Less than two years after Eddie's retirement Pop was back in the shape-up again, kicking back to the hiring boss to make sure of a day's pay, and the Finnerans were back in their railroad flat. And what did Eddie—their briefly famous Honeyboy—have to show for it but a flattened nose and one bad eye and a state of mind that wasn't exactly punchy, but wasn't quite up to normal, either? Eddie was excitable, unstable, with fits of delusion, and his vision was turned in upon the past. He lived more in *his* day than in the present and he had no capacity for work. The quick big money of his ring purses had spoiled him for ordinary living. A docker's wage was sucker's work. Not vicious enough for crime or conscientious enough for honest labor, he had drifted through the years of his retirement in search of a soft touch—working for the books, doing a little gambling, tied into the numbers racket on the waterfront. Ma hated to think the word, for she had tried to bring her children up to fear God and honor their responsibilities, but Eddie Finneran was a bum. So she said nothing while they sat at the table talking fights and the dearth of good Irish fighters on the West Side and the glories of the old days when the wearers of the green dominated the ring, Mickey Walker and Tommy Loughran, Jimmy McLarnin and Billy Conn.

Ma felt better when she heard the door creak open and Vince come in. Vince—she never looked at him or thought about him without adding automatically: Vince is a good boy. Like day and night, she would think, comparing Vince with Eddie. Her youngest was a quiet, serious boy who worked hard and minded his own business. He was making a good record at St. Xavier's. Well, at least one Finneran was going to finish high school. Vince was her baby, her prize; somehow she had managed to keep him off the streets and out of Eddie's circle of street-corner admirers who still thought it was something special to be an ex-pug whose name had once flashed from the Garden marquee. Vince never had a dirty mouth like Eddie and his crowd. Vince didn't call every girl a broad and leer at every passing skirt with heavy-humored obscenities. Vince was good in chemistry. His teacher thought he should specialize in it and become a teacher or a laboratory technician.

Vince came up behind his mother, spun her around and

kissed her. "Well, Mom, we beat St. Tom's, fifty-two–forty-nine, a basket in the last thirty seconds."

"And I bet I know who made the basket," his mother said.

"I got lucky," Vince said. He was tall for his age, nearly six feet, and thin and wiry, only a hundred and forty pounds; he was captain of the school basketball team and an all-around athlete, with speed and timing, though lacking Eddie's aggressiveness.

It made her feel proud, Pop on the docks, just as her old man had been, and Eddie, who never even finished high school, roaming around up to no good, nobody on either side of the family who even saw four years of high school, and now Vince going through with honors. She looked at the tall, slender boy with the serious eyes and the thoughtful, remote way of wandering in and settling down with a book, apparently unaware of the same old conversation (Did Pop remember Eddie's fight with Red Collins? and was Marciano going to give it to Walcott again? and could Armstrong have taken Sugar Ray if they had met in '38 instead of '43?).

Vince was settling down to some homework when Eddie came over and squatted on the edge of his chair.

"How's the muscle, kid?"

"No complaints, Eddie."

"How you feel about the Golden Gloves?"

"The Golden Gloves?"

"Yeah, I entered you."

"Me in the Golden Gloves? You might've asked me, Eddie. You might've asked."

Eddie had been sparring with Vince ever since the kid brother was old enough to hold his hands up. Eddie was proud of the way Vince had learned to jab, to cross with his right and to slip punches.

"Against those amateur punks you'll be a cinch," Eddie

said. "Just do what I learned you and you'll be a shoo-in. You'll have height and reach on 'em. You c'n stand back 'n pepper 'em."

"I never said I wanted to box in the Golden Gloves," Vince said.

The old man got into it. "You go in there and knock their blocks off, Vinnie m'boy. Show 'em the Finnerans are scrappers." With one punch the old man finished off an imaginary opponent.

Ma moved in. "What's all this talk about scrappers?"

"It's just the amateurs, Ma. We entered Vinnie in the Gloves."

"You leave Vince alone," Ma said. "Vince is gonna amount to something. Vince plays basketball, a nice clean game. Who wants him in the filthy prize fights?"

"It ain't a prize fight, Ma," Eddie argued. "A prize fight's for money. For blood. Three-minute rounds. Small gloves. This is for sport, see? Jus' three two-minute rounds, gloves like pillows, and the contest" (he remembered, like the announcers, not to say "fight") "is stopped at the first sign of a scratch. Nobody gets hurt in the amateurs."

Mrs. Finneran looked at Vince. Vince wasn't saying anything. "Vince, is this something you want to do?"

Vince's old man looked at him hard. A good student, that was all very well, but you couldn't buy a round at Paddy's on the strength of a B-plus in chemistry. But another fighter in the family. That was something to throw out your chest about.

Vince looked at his old man and felt the pressure of it. He wanted to please Ma and get through St. Xavier's, but he wanted his Pop to be proud of him, too. The summer was coming on and he had a half-day job. He wouldn't have to train too hard for the amateurs. He was in pretty good shape from the basketball season.

"I'll get you down to the C.Y.O. and I'll work out with

you." Eddie talked fast. "It'll do me good too. Get this blubber off me. You'll be a cinch, kid, a cinch. The talk o' the neighborhood."

"Well, I guess it can't do me any harm," Vince said.

"All right, all right, now leave him alone, let 'im do his homework." Ma broke it up.

Eddie was on time for his training dates with Vince at the C.Y.O. It was the only thing he had ever been on time for, except his own fights. He taught the kid how to stand and move, how to tie up an opponent in the clinches and how to turn his right toe in a little and get his body into it when he threw the right. He taught him to punch, not in single blows but in combinations, to an inner rhythm. He taught him how to weave and feint and pick off punches with his gloves, how to suck an opponent into leading and how to counter. Vince didn't look like a natural fighter. He had never loved and lived fighting on the streets as Eddie had. But he studied his brother's instructions the same way he tackled math or chemistry. And he was lithe and quick. Eddie saw he would never be as aggressive as he himself had been, but he had a faster, more accurate left hand, and by following Eddie's tips on punching power he could hurt you with a right hand.

A perfectionist, Vince found himself enjoying the mastery of a new sport. It was good exercise, something like fencing. You fenced for an opening, you tried to draw your opponent off guard. It was fun to make him miss and step in to nail him before he recovered. There was something to it all right. It wasn't just sock and be socked. It was science. It wasn't so different from chemistry, in a way. You worked out a formula and then you experimented on the basis of it and then you adjusted the formula to the new facts. In a month he was stepping around Eddie, reddening his brother's nose with his snaky lefts and smothering his bull-like rushes.

Eddie lost weight, looked younger, was beginning to

find himself. For the first time since he had hung up the gloves, his life began to have focus. He would be the discoverer, the trainer, the manager of Vinnie Finneran, successor to the old, crowd-pleasing Honeyboy.

It was the talk of the neighborhood the way Vinnie breezed through the Golden Gloves, how he went eight straight bouts without dropping a round. He was a shade of the old Irish boxing masters, Slattery and Loughran and Tunney and McLarnin. In the City Finals he met a strong Puerto Rican boy who crowded him but every time the other boy rushed in Vinnie peppered him until finally a faint streak of red trickled from the Puerto Rican's cheekbone and the bout was stopped. Eddie lifted Vinnie up and carried him around the ring and Pop climbed through the ropes and hugged him and shook his big hands together to salute friends in the crowd.

That night in the Finnerans' flat it was like old times. Too much like them to please Ma. There were cronies of Pop's, and Eddie and his crowd in their striped T-shirts, and Molly and her husband Leo, and Sally, the younger daughter, with a boy friend, all of them telling each other just how good Vinnie was and what he had done to this boy and that, as if they had not all been there and seen it with their own eyes. Drinking beer and wallowing in this new little puddle of glory, Eddie had the center of the stage. It reminded him of the days when he was a winning fighter and the guys made a circle around him to hear what he had to say. Even if this was only amateur stuff, they were beginning to listen again as Eddie talked up the prowess of his kid brother. "He did just like I told 'im, he's got class, he's cute, he could turn pro and make a bundle, a second Billy Graham."

Then everybody was talking at once, each with his or her own small life made to seem a little larger through the magnifying glass of success. Eddie with his taste of the old prestige, and Pop crowing over his pals and feeling less of a failure for being able to show around the winning wristwatch with the inscription on the back. The brother-in-law Leo had brought a couple of his best customers to the fight—there was nothing like having a fighter in the family to help the liquor business. Everybody likes to know the fighters, an unconscious attraction to our brutal beginnings. Molly and Sally were enjoying it too; it was exciting, relief from the humdrum. Some of the silver light of Vinnie's local fame had begun to spill over onto them. People kept asking them how it felt to have a champion in the family.

The only quiet ones at the celebration that night were Vinnie and Ma. Vinnie didn't see what all the shouting was about. He had won, and it hadn't been too difficult but it didn't feel much different from coming home after a winning basketball game. He didn't feel like fighting the short rounds over and over again in conversation. He looked on with detached amusement as Eddie demonstrated to a crowd of admirers exactly how Vince had opened the other boy's cheek. "He'll go t' the top," he kept repeating in a kind of self-hypnosis, "if he keeps doin' like I show 'im he'll go right to the top, we could make a bundle if he ever turns pro."

Ma helped serve the beer and the coffee and was polite when she was spoken to, but she would have liked to have tossed the whole bunch of noisy fair-weather parasites out of the place. Backslappers and spongers. She remembered the flattery and the free loading when Eddie was in the money. Of course Vince had more common sense, more character, but she was afraid of this fight world with its quick fame and quick money. Oh, there was always Tunney to point to as the West Side boy who had made good, but right here in her own neighborhood, on the docks working alongside Pop and lounging around with Eddie she knew how many ex-pugs there were who had had a taste of four-figure money for a year or two and then had slipped back into the crowd, some of them with foolish gummy grins on their faces, and some like Eddie spoiled for everyday work at ordinary money.

Next morning Eddie clipped out of the paper the squib on the bottom of the third sports page: "Brother of Honeyboy Finneran, Ex-Boxer, Wins Amateur Title." Then he put on his sports jacket over his wine-colored T-shirt and went uptown to the Forrest Hotel to look up his old manager, Specs Golders. Specs was crying the usual managerial blues. Except for a Robinson or a Marciano, there were no big draws anymore. And no young blood. The kids you got didn't want to train; give them a few big wins and you couldn't tell them anything. "I'm so disgusted I'm ready to go into the shoe business with my brother-in-law," Specs summed it up.

Eddie told Specs about the kid brother and made it sound big. "You know I'd level with you, Specs. You know I ain't just shittin' ya 'cause he's the kid brud. Vince is sharper 'n blue blades. Like the good old days. How many good white boys around these days? Vince is money in the bank."

Specs said he was buddies with the Garden crowd again. Next time his light-heavyweight got a main event he could probably spot Vince in the six-round special.

"How much?"

"Five."

Five hundred. Honeyboy had started at fifty and clubbed his way up, but now with the Finneran name and Specs' connections it was half a G. Then a semi-windup, fifteen hundred, a few of those and up into the feature bout, three or four thousand, maybe five with the television. He keeps winning and he's fighting for a percentage, 20 per cent of $60,000, 30 per cent of $90,000, title fights, and maybe some day, if they got the breaks, a real pay night in six-figure money. Eddie would have tailor-made suits, $175 and up, a big suite in a plush hotel, fur coats and ice for the pick of the broads, big men would call him for tickets, Toots Shor would slap him on the back and insult him with affection, the columnists would press him to recall some favorite anecdotes, he'd take Vince to Paris to fight this Humez or whoever they had over there, there would be French broads and a Jaguar and champagne wine and a big night in the casino, there would be sucker tours against soft touches from Boston to Seattle, they'd move, they'd live, Eddie and Specs in partnership, good new kids would beg 'em to manage them, they'd find a heavyweight and finagle a jackpot.

"How's about we cut like this," Eddie said. "Fifty for Vince, twenny-five for you, twenny-five for me."

"For me, because you made money for me and you're a friend of mine, I'll only take one-third, point three three three," Specs said. "The rest you and the kid split as you see fit."

He and Vince could take the two-thirds and cut it down the middle, Eddie figured. After all, this was his idea. He was opening the doors. And he'd do the teaching, the worrying, the greasing. Vince was a careful kid, a saver. One third of five- and ten-thousand dollar purses would add up for him.

"A deal," Eddie said.

"And expenses off the top," Specs added.

"You would steal your own mother's glass eye," Eddie said, with admiration.

"If he's as good as you say, we'll make a few dollars," Specs said.

"On the head of my mother," Eddie said. "Right now he's better 'n I was when I was good."

"You were never good," Specs said. "You drew the money because they liked to see you laugh when you got hurt."

Eddie was hurt this time, too, so he laughed and they shook hands. "You watch, we'll make a bundle," Eddie said.

Eddie had to start working for his money right away. He had to go down and talk the kid brother into turning pro. Vince said, What about school? He had promised his mother to finish. He didn't like the idea of turning pro. In the long run a high-school education could even mean more money.

Eddie said, "Who's knocking the school? You go to school and you train in the afternoons. You can't read them books all the time. 'Stead of going out for basketball or something you spar 'n punch the bag. Fidel La Barba, the flyweight champion remember?, he went to college 'n boxed and you take this kid Vejar, he's at N.Y.U. right now and he's making nice money boxing. Look kid, here's the clincher, for one Garden main event—and Specs 'n me 'll get you there, believe me—you'll make more money than twelve months in a job."

"And you really think I'll have as easy a time in the pros and I did in the amateurs?"

"If you work," Eddie said, "if you keep practicing what I learn you, a breeze, a romp, there's nobody around c'n box anymore, you'll be too fast 'n too clever for 'em, they won't lay a glove on you."

"I guess the family could use the dough," Vince said.

"Now you're thinkin'," Eddie said. "I'll tell Specs to make the six-round Garden match for you. Don't worry, we'll dig up some crud to make you look good. And tell you what, kid, the first fight you take the whole purse, the whole five hundred except for expenses. After that Specs and I 'll take a regular cut."

"Five hundred," Vince said. "I wouldn't have to work after school."

"Peanuts," Eddie said. "When it rolls in it'll roll in big. Plenny for everybody."

Ma didn't want to believe it when she finally heard. She said she knew Eddie would try anything but she couldn't understand Vince. Vince said he was doing it partly for her. "Not for me," she said. All he had to do was finish high school for her. So he could amount to something. Vince said she didn't understand, he would only have enough fights to salt some money away and then he'd quit. Ma looked at him hard. "I know these leeches. Eddie and that chiselin' manager Specs. You win, you make money for them and they'll never let you go. Not until your face is beaten in like Eddie's and that good head you've got on your shoulders is . . ." A lump in her throat saved her having to say it.

"I won't be like Eddie," Vince said. "For one thing I'm a boxer, he was a slugger. I duck and slip away and pick the punches off with my gloves."

His mother said, "I don't want to hear about it. It's that Eddie. My own flesh and blood, but he's a no-good. You think he worries about you? You think he stays up nights worrying what might happen to you? He's thinking about silk shirts and winters in Miami. People who work for their money, he calls them suckers."

Just the same, the match was made and Vince went into training at the C.Y.O. gym. Vince was classy in the gym, he could make the light bag sound like a snare drum now and the sparring partners crowded him foolishly while he snapped their heads back with lightning jabs and moved in for rapid combinations.

Eddie went uptown and ordered a suit from Nat Lewis on the strength of Vinnie's promise. He felt good, full of bounce, no more street-corner loafer and fringer of the mob. He was the old Honeyboy. The way he came into places, he already looked like money. A few big wins and he could swagger into Shor's and get one of the choice tables against the front wall.

Pop was feeling pretty chipper, too. He wasn't bothering to shape for the afternoon shift because he was over at the gym every afternoon presiding over Vinnie's workouts. He'd take his pals with him, including Bart McGann, the business agent of his local and a political wheel. He had promised Bart a couple of ringsides. McGann was beginning to treat Pop like an equal now. "Well, with a chip off the old block fightin' in the Garden I don't expect we'll see you in the shape much longer, Finneran."

Old Man Finneran didn't expect so, either. Nice break having a neighborhood hero and a big breadwinner in the family again. Not that Pop would ask much of Vinnie. Just grub and beer money and maybe a little house in Florida to retire in after a while.

Leo, the brother-in-law, called Eddie to hold half a dozen ringside tickets for him; he was taking two good prospective customers and their wives. "If the kid is really as good as Eddie says," Leo told Vince's older sister, "I'm liable to double my sales. Take the boys out to the training camp, get Vinnie to have dinner with 'em at Moore's— it'll give my business a shot in the arm."

"I'll never forget the first time Eddie fought a main event in the Garden," Molly said. "He bought me my beaver coat. It's beat-up now but I still have to use it. I could sure do with a new coat."

And back in the Finnerans' cold-water flat, Sally, the sixteen-year-old, was dreaming her tough-minded little dreams, too. This dingy tenement, steaming in summer and bone-cold in winter, may be all right for Ma and Pop. But these days a young girl with her looks wanted something better. A nicer neighborhood, nicer boys, some place you wouldn't be ashamed to take a nice fellow if you should be lucky enough to find one. A five-room apartment on the Upper Drive. Maybe, if Vince turned out to be a drawing card, he'd do that for them. The sister of the champion.

In the Finneran household the tension mounted as with

an army facing invasion day. It was Fight minus eight, F minus seven, six. . . . Eddie was a busy man, working out with Specs the tactics for the fight, hovering over Vince and watching his diet, on the phone to friends wanting tickets, selling a block of seats around the neighborhood so the matchmaker would be impressed with Vinnie's following, buttonholing reporters in the restaurants and telling anybody and everybody what the kid brother was going to do to Georgie Packer.

Packer was a Negro veteran who had gone as far as small-club main events and then slid back into the preliminaries. He was slow and wild and his legs were used up after four rounds. He was rough and he was willing and his left hook could hurt you if it landed, but he was pretty well punched out now, his reflexes were gone and this was just another purse for him before he racked up. In public Eddie carried on about what a rugged test this was for Vinnie, but privately he told the chums that Spec had lined up a real soft touch so Vinnie could score in his pro debut. "Packer'll be packed up and shipped home to Palookaville before it goes halfway," Eddie promised.

As the days before the fight flew off like calendar sheets in an old movie, Ma was a ghost around the house, moving silently in a shroud of disapproval. She listened and she watched, and felt like throwing them all out of the house, Pop, Eddie, Sally, Molly, Leo, the whole selfish lot of them. She watched Vince closely, too. He listened to the advice Eddie kept telling him, nodding and going over it in his mind. He would look around as if the place were no longer familiar to him and he couldn't find a comfortable seat to settle himself in. In a sharp voice that didn't sound like his, he kept saying that he wasn't nervous, that he felt fine, why should he worry?, Eddie said he had met better boys than Packer in the amateurs, it was just another fight. But his nerves talked back: Who was he kidding? This was six three-minute rounds instead of three two's, hard six-ounce gloves instead of those sixteen-ounce pillows, and this Georgie Packer was an old war-horse with over seventy pro fights.

The day of the fight Ma was ready to do something about it. Something drastic. She thought of a lot of crazy things. Maybe there was something she could drop in Vince's tea to make him sick to his stomach so they would have to call off the fight. Or she would pretend she had a stroke so Vince would be too upset to report at the Garden. Then he'd be suspended and the bad dream would be over. She even had crazy visions of going to the other fighter and telling him Vince's weaknesses as she had picked them up from Eddie's loudmouthing. But, of course, she couldn't do that. That was just a whim of desperation. Finally she didn't do anything but go around the corner to see her favorite priest.

Father Corcoran was a neighborhood boy in his middle thirties who had made a name for himself standing up for the members of his waterfront parish against the mobbers on the docks. He was an old friend of Tunney's cousin, Ben, the longshore rank-and-filer, and he liked the fights, all right, but he couldn't see it for Vince. He was a realist and he thought the business was only for those who had nothing better to do. But how to stop it? He could try reasoning with Vince, though it probably wouldn't do much good if the boy won and found the going easy. Maybe all they could do was to pray that he lose and work it out of his system before the start of the fall term.

Ma went into the church and knelt before her saint, Veronica. "Oh, Sweet Saint Veronica, intercede with the Heavenly Father," she prayed. "I don't know if He knows anything about the boxing game. I don't know if there's any way for a boy to be thoroughly defeated without getting hurt. But if there is, please ask Him to bring that defeat to my Vince tonight. Lead him out of the valley of temptation. Give him the strength to turn his back on evil and to find that there are no easy ways and that every man should do a dollar's work for every dollar. Have him knocked out tonight, dear Lord, and may it not injure his sweet face but only the selfish spirits leeching to fatten on him. In the Name of the Father and the Son and the Holy Ghost, amen."

Vince was sitting stiff and strange in the bare dressing room. Eddie had been getting around giving the big hello to familiar faces and taking bows as the old Honey-boy. People remembered the great fight he had put up with Kaplan and listened respectfully when he talked up Vinnie. "Watch 'em t'night—tuhriffic—a year from now he's in with the title—a second McLarnin."

"Don't just sit there, kid," Eddie said. "Get up, move around, warm up, you're on next."

Vince did as he was told, but he felt stiff in his joints. Beyond the dressing-room door the roar of the crowd sounded like a waterfall that can be turned on and off. He tried not to listen. It had a strange effect on his stomach. It wasn't fear of Packer, but of something larger, something that made him feel small and helpless, as if he were a leaf carried along by a rushing torrent toward the waterfall.

The last four-rounder was over and the kid who had gone out bouncing on his toes and full of beans came in gasping for breath and leaking blood from one eye. Vince had no memory of being moved through the door down the long aisle to the ring. He was only numbly aware of being in the ring under the bright lights with Eddie rubbing encouraging circles into his back and winking at writers he recognized in the press row. He was only numbly aware of Georgie Packer, a short, squat, dark figure with a boneless nose and thickening scar tissue over the eyes. He was completely unaware of Pop, with the Mc-

Ganns, and Leo and Molly with the prospective customers, and Sally in a new dress, all looking for the win,
with front seats reserved on the bandwagon.

The bell rang and the place hushed. Vince crossed himself automatically and automatically moved out toward
the dark, bearlike form weaving in front of him. Packer
lunged and Vince flicked a jab and danced away. The
jabs irritated Packer like mosquito bites and he lunged
in to swat them away and Vince jab-jab-jabbed and skirted
sideways. Packer missed a vicious left hook at the bell.
Vince was more tired than he should have been when he
sat down. Maybe nerves. "Relax, relax, kid," Eddie said.
"It's all yours. Keep that left in his face but cross with the
right. You're not throwing enough punches. You got the
round but you gotta be more aggressive."

Round Two looked like a retake on Round One with
Vince jabbing and floating away. Packer wanted to fight,
but he couldn't. His fights were all in the record book
now. Vince's left hand and the footwork were fancy, but
he was reluctant to mix it with Packer. Packer was doing
all the leading and missing. Vince was countering, but in
a light-hitting, mechanically defensive way. The crowd
was stamping its feet in unison to show its boredom.
Packer, the old club fighter, answered the crowd's deri-
sion with a clumsy try, grabbing Vince with his left arm
and bringing up a looping right uppercut. It was a wild,
unorthodox punch, not the kind that Vince had been
trained to counter, and it flushed him on the side of the
jaw and knocked him sideways. Before Packer could follow it up the round was over.

Vince turned to a neutral corner instead of toward his
stool. The crowd laughed and shouted. Vince thought he
was in a basketball game and the other team had scored
a basket. Eddie ran out and rushed him to their corner.
The sharp tickle of smelling salts was in his nose and ice
burned into his neck. "Sucker punch . . . Don't let 'im

get set . . . Move around and throw more rights . . ."
He heard Eddie in his ear and then the mouthpiece was being pushed into his face, a wet sponge came down smack
on his head and many hands were lifting him to his feet
and shoving him toward the middle of the ring. Before he
could do any of the things Eddie had told him, Packer was
on him again, walking in and punching and brushing off
the jabs and hooking to the body. Packer was after him
and somehow none of the things that had held them off in
the amateurs would work on this one. Packer charged in
and bulled him into a corner with his body so the kid
couldn't dance around and use the footwork. Packer just
leaned his head on the kid's shoulder and banged away. It
wasn't a science, it wasn't an experiment, it was a fight,
and Vince felt cornered and helpless against the swarm
of punches. The mouthpiece was choking off his breathing, felt too big for his mouth, if he could get rid of the
mouthpiece he could suck the air in, get a fresh start . . .
Then wham something harder than a leather glove could
possibly be struck him in the mouth and the mouthpiece
flew out and Vince was sagging to his knees to look for it
when the bell rang at last.

Eddie and Specs ran across and dragged Vince back and
worked over him feverishly, Eddie wild-eyed, frantic, a
lose to a punched-out bum like Packer meant curtains, no
soap, no money, no ride, no meal ticket, back to the street
corners with the Hell's Kitchen cowboys. "Kid, you gotta
do it, you gotta do it, take the play away from him, punch
hard, baby, please kid, we're countin' on ya, Vinnie Vince
Vinnie can ya see me?, are ya listenin'?, don't let us down
Vinnie boy . . ."

Over Specs' and Eddie's shoulders the referee was leaning in to watch the boy's eyes. The handlers were so busy
pumping false strength and bogus courage into their be-
wildered fighter that they didn't notice the referee until, just as the ten-second warning buzzer sounded and

Vince was trying to find his feet, he staggered up into the arms of the official. "Sorry kid, that's all." He went over and raised Packer's hand.

An old sports writer turned to a colleague. "His name may be Finneran, but he's sure no Honeyboy. Honeyboy liked to fight."

"I saw this kid in the gym, he looked good," the other man said.

"A gymnasium fighter," the old sports writer said. "I've seen hundreds of 'em. They fight because someone teaches 'em how and everything they know goes out the window the first time they get tagged."

"I wonder if this new boy from St. Paul is any good," said the other writer, ready for the next fight.

Leo had planned to take the prospective buyers back to the dressing room to see Vince after the fight, but now he thought he'd forget the whole thing. He felt a little embarrassed in front of his customers for having done so much talking about the boy.

Pop was quiet too. McGann had been polite, but in a kind of laughing way, as he said, "Don't take it to heart, Finneran. One lad who can use his mitts and another with a head on his shoulders, that should be enough for any man." Pop nodded. It would be hard to go back to the Monday morning shape-up. Seven-thirty in the morning. The same old grind.

Specs stood outside the dressing-room door while Vince got dressed. "I suppose I could get him another fight, but I think I'd be wasting my time. The boy doesn't take much of a punch. He c'n box but he's got no heart for it. He's gonna get hurt and he won't make no money."

"Okay, okay, I got my eyesight, I could see it," Eddie said.

"I'm sorry, Honeyboy, it could of been a nice thing."

"The hell with that," Eddie said. Even the night he had

decided to hang up the gloves, he hadn't felt so lost, so empty and the hell with everything. "I'm gonna go out 'n drink whiskey."

The flat was quiet when Vince came in. Sitting there waiting was Ma and nobody else.

"Vince?"

"Yes, Ma."

"Let me see how you look."

She led him toward the lamp. There was a bruise on his jaw and a swelling around one eye.

"I lost, Ma. I was NG."

"I heard about it on the radio."

"Looks like I better keep that delivery job after school."

"That's right, Vince. Get into your pajamas. I'll make you a sandwich."

She went into the kitchen and she thought how Pop and Eddie and Leo and Molly and Sally must be feeling. Well, it served them right. It wasn't that easy. When would they ever learn it wasn't that easy?

Eddie didn't come in until after four when all the bars were closed. He had trouble finding his way to the bathroom in time to throw up.

"Eddie, is that you?" his mother called from the bedroom.

"Yeah, 's'me. Go t' sleep, Ma, I'm aw-right." Eddie felt very weak. He felt as if he was going to pitch head first into the can. He'd sleep it off and then go down to Paddy's for a beer. There was a kid washing dishes in there who was pretty handy with his dukes, Paddy said. Maybe Eddie could get a-hold of him and . . .

He threw up until his stomach was emptied and then he groped his way to the narrow bedroom he shared with Vince. He fell into bed, and in a little while he was snoring through his broken old fighter's nose and dreaming his ex-fighter dreams. The dishwasher at Paddy's was turning out to be a champ and Eddie was up there with the Nat Lewis sport shirts and the big suites and the fancy broads, and everybody was saying See if you c'n fix me up with a pair for Friday night, Eddie, Honeyboy, Eddie, old pal.

THIRD NIGHTCAP, WITH HISTORICAL FOOTNOTES

It was one o'clock and the waiters were wishing the two young men would go home when Mead came in and sat down. "Hello, Sheridan. Hello, Peters," he said, and paused for their invitation to join them.

Sheridan and Peters exchanged a look that said they were ready to leave, but would have to linger. After all, who were they, young writers who had written a mediocre Broadway success in collaboration, to walk out on the author of *The Days Beyond?* That play had been required reading in Baker's course when they were at Yale ten years ago.

Mead saw the look in their eyes, for he was a student of looks and eyes, but he didn't care. It was late and he was lonely. Bending his tall, unathletic body to the table, he slid into the booth. His dark, heavy-lidded eyes twitched behind their thick lenses as he observed his youthful, not yet twitching companions. His long, nervous fingers reached out for things with which to occupy themselves, arranging the water glass, a fork and several matches into various designs.

"Have a drink, Mead?" Sheridan said, trying to keep the scholastic awe out of his voice.

"Thanks," said Mead. "Maybe one. A nightcap."

Sheridan beckoned the waiter and caught Peters' eye again. To such a man we owe a debt, he signaled. Even two drinks and twenty minutes' conversation is not too much.

"Can you imagine?" said Mead. "They don't even know who Firdausi is. Can you imagine living in a town fifteen years where they never even heard of Firdausi?"

"You mean Joe Firdausi, the agent?" Peters said. They were writing a farce comedy at the moment and keyed for wit.

"An agent they would have known," Mead said. "Up at Vonn's party, I'm talking about, playing *Who Am I?* So I take Firdausi, you know, the Persian epic poet, and everybody screams it shouldn't count because he's too obscure."

Mead drank the straight Scotch the waiter brought him without asking, and it was only when he tried to raise the glass to his lips that Sheridan and Peters saw how drunk he was.

" 'Obscure!,' I told them," Mead continued, " 'So obscure the encyclopedia gives him a full page, that's how obscure!' So then Birdie Slocum, that noted historical scholar, says, 'I never heard of such a man.' So I told Birdie, 'That's because his name has never been in the *Hollywood Reporter.'* "

"Did you really tell her that?" Sheridan asked.

Birdie Slocum was the wife of Mead's producer. Mead twirled the empty whiskey glass idly. The young men looked at each other guiltily. They knew his reputation for post-facto courage.

"I don't know how to play that game in this town," Mead said. "If you pick Churchill or Eisenhower they get sore because they think you're insulting their intelligence. And if you pick anything tougher than that, they think you're trying to show off."

Peters and Sheridan said nothing. They were afraid Mead was going to ask them if they knew who Firdausi was. "Have another?" Sheridan urged.

"Well, all right," said Mead. "But this *is* the nightcap. Firdausi. The greatest poet in the history of Persia. The author of *The Book of Kings*. Even the savage tribesmen in the hills recite Firdausi."

The waiter brought Mead his drink and he raised it in toast. "To Firdausi," he said, "whom Birdie Slocum will never know."

"And last week it was Tilly," Mead was saying into his empty glass. "And Vonn wouldn't count him either. Can you beat that, a German and he never heard of Tilly? Tilly, the Catholic general. The Thirty Years' War. It's like an American not knowing Washington." He removed his glasses and rubbed his red eyes irritably. "And the week before that, Vico, the Italian philosopher. And before that, Timothy Dwight."

Mead studied the two young men with pensive amusement. His face looked as if it had been drawn on an egg, the narrowing side down, the forehead broad and bulbous.

"Fifteen years in a town that never heard of Firdausi or Tilly or Vico or Dwight," said Mead.

"Have another one," Sheridan said.

"But this really has to be the nightcap," Mead said. "I've got a conference with Slocum at ten."

After the third nightcap, Mead said, "When I was your age, at least I used to stand for something. I was a Socialist. I voted for Debs. Now I haven't got enough freedom of speech to talk back to Birdie Slocum."

The young men were ready to call it a night, but neither would make a move. After all it wasn't every day in the week that they could sit down with Elliot Mead, former historical scholar, now thirty-five hundred a week.

The waiter yawned and turned off as many lights as he could with ostentatious discretion. The old writer and the two young ones sat there in the empty bar.

"Don't make so much noise turning off those lights," Mead reprimanded. "Remember, there are people here trying to sleep."

The waiter laughed joylessly and Sheridan and Peters looked at each other in mutual acknowledgment of Mead's reputation for repeatable quips.

Mead smiled with them. He was not going to keep that ten o'clock date in the morning. He was going to sit up with these boys, impress them with his wit and knowledge, get good and drunk, and have his secretary call the studio to say he was sick.

"I know what let's do," Mead suggested. "Let's play one quick game. I am somebody whose name begins with C. Now, who am I?"

"Are you a brilliant French economist of the mercantile period?" Sheridan began, reaching back into freshman history.

"No," Mead said, smiling, warming to the game, "I am not Jean Baptiste Colbert. . . ."

OUR WHITE DEER

One afternoon, early last fall, we were back at the far end of our property having a meeting in our underground clubhouse. My brother Davy and I had dug it out that past summer and covered it over with pine branches and tar paper. We were just climbing out of our secret tunnel when along came Mr. Jeliffe on horseback, riding his side of the fence. Mr. Jeliffe is very rich and has a mustache and a big red face and a house that's about ten times as big as ours.

People around where we live don't put on much dog; they just do their writing or their painting, stuff like that, and mess around in their gardens and go for long walks across the fields. The simple life, that's what we always hear them calling it. Well, Mr. Jeliffe, he leads the simple life in a pretty rich kind of a way. I mean he rides to the hounds and gives hunt breakfasts and big deals like that. It's sort of funny in a way because when he first came out here only two or three years ago he couldn't even ride a horse. He still flops around on his *buhwhosis* but nobody laughs at him to his face because he's so rich. He cornered the market on copper or cotton or something like that when the army needed it real bad to win the war and Dad says that's about the only way to get rich any more. You'd think that having all that money would make a fella nicer, that he'd sort of relax and smile at everybody and just enjoy his money. But not Mr. Jeliffe. Mr. Jeliffe is—even if Dad says he wishes we wouldn't use the word—a jerk.

Like the time he caught us in his orchard eating a few of his apples. Dad says it doesn't pay to spray our orchard so our apples are all wormy. That's why, once in a while, we have to go over and try some of Mr. Jeliffe's apples. They're Mackintosh, and I guess all the worms must have come over to our place because they sure don't mess around with Mr. Jeliffe's apples. Well, this time Mr. Jeliffe caught us—red-apple-handed, says Dave, who's ten years old and still likes to pun. He reined in his horse and looked bigger than God and he said, "Boys, I don't think it's a very good idea for you to be over here. I raise Dobermans and they'd sooner bite you than look at you and I wouldn't be responsible for your safety."

See what we mean? He didn't come right out and tell us to get the H off his property or he'd sick the dogs on us. He made it sound like he was trying to do us a favor by getting us out of his lousy old orchard without those Dobermans eating us up. Lousy is another word Dad doesn't like us to use; in fact he fines us a nickel every time he hears it, only there are some words that are bad words but there just aren't any good words that mean the same thing. Like the jerky way Mr. Jeliffe went about ordering us out of his orchard.

Well, anyway, we were just climbing out of our clubhouse, which is a swell hideaway nearly four feet deep and just big enough for the three members of our club, when there sits Mr. Jeliffe on his big white horse Captain, making like he's Teddy Roosevelt or something.

"Howdy, boys," he says. He's getting pretty Western since he's been riding around on that horse. He's about to ride on and then he remembers something and leans his horse around.

"Say, Steve, that ram of yours—does he have any horns?"

Davy and I looked at each other and shook our heads. "Not that we ever noticed, why?"

"Well, maybe I was imagining things but seems to me when I was riding along your meadow fence the other day, I thought I saw a white ram with a beautiful set of horns, trotting right along with the ewes. Of course I was about a hundred yards away, so . . ."

"Sure, maybe it just looked like it, an optical delusion or something." I looked at Davy and we were both embarrassed because everyone knew Mr. Jeliffe liked his whiskey—that's the way Mom says it—and from what I hear you can see some pretty strange sights when too much whiskey gets inside of you.

"I'll admit it was only for a second I saw him and then he saw me and took off pronto. But still, I was pretty sure . . ." He broke off and suddenly guffawed for no good reason. "Maybe it was one of Schofield's rams got in with your flock. Well, I was just wondering—you don't think it could've been a white deer, do you? The head of a ten-point white buck would look pretty nice over the mantlepiece in my study."

He dug his heels into the big belly of his horse and rode off. Davy put his thumb to his nose and wiggled his fingers at him. A *white* deer, and over *his* mantlepiece! In the first place every autumn since we were little kids someone has told us about someone else who's pretty sure he's seen a white deer. But I am almost twelve years old now and I had never seen one and I had still to meet anybody who had honest and truly seen one with his own eyes.

And in the second place, if that thousand-to-one shot came in and there really-truly was a white deer wandering around our place, what would his head be doing over Mr. Jeliffe's mantelpiece? He was in our meadow with our sheep, wasn't he? If there was such a thing as a white deer, and if he was anybody's white deer, he was ours, wasn't he? Mr. Jeliffe just better keep his greedy old hands off him. Even if our white deer didn't exist, we didn't like Mr. Jeliffe even thinking about him.

We spread more pine branches over the tar-paper roof and filled the tunnel up so nobody would know we had a clubhouse there at all and then we ambled over to the lower pasture where there was an old dead apple tree that had been our first clubhouse when Davy was still going to nursery school. Our initials were carved in that tree, and the secret sign of our club, and we still used the ladder to the tree-house to climb up once in a while to see if any enemy was approaching. Well, this time as soon as we got to the tree we noticed something funny. Where the carving had been, the trunk was almost bare and there were slash-marks all up and down this one side, as if—we looked at each other and wondered—as if the horns of some animal had been slicing at it to sharpen his points. Plenty of times we had seen bulls do that, and rams—but we didn't have any bulls and our ram Hector had only those two little hard bulges where his horns ought to be. And yet these slashed-off places on the tree were fresh as anything.

Well, naturally we knew better than to pay attention to anything Mr. Jeliffe had to say, but just to make double-sure we kept checking on the flock. We watched them come in every evening and quite a few times we even went out after supper and walked up as far as the pine woods that run along the west line of our place and the Jeliffes'. But we didn't see any white deer. In fact we had just about given up and decided that Mr. Jeliffe was talking through his hat, as usual, when we happened to be picking up some groceries for Mom at the country store. Billy, whose pop runs the store, is a big kid, maybe fifteen or sixteen, and a pretty good friend of ours. He lets us go with him when he sets out his muskrat traps and he lets us play with his hunting dogs and once in a while he even takes us along when he goes gunning. Billy was an Eagle Scout and he pitches on the school baseball team and when he says something you can bet it's true. Well, anyway, while Billy is picking out some oranges for us, he says, "Say, you fellers haven't got a new ram up at your place, have you?"

Davy and I looked at each other. This was getting mysterious and kind of exciting. "Uh-uh. Why, Billy?"

"Well, when I was setting up traps last night, I thought I saw a ram in your meadow, with great big horns."

"Billy, could it've been a deer—a white buck?"

"Well, it ain't exactly impossible. They do turn up every now and again. My old man saw one around here when I was a kid, maybe ten or twelve years ago."

That white deer—how can I explain it?—he was our white deer. Whether he was for real, or just a fragment of our imagination, like Dad says sometimes, he belonged to us. We wanted to see him and try to make a pet out of him. We didn't want anybody to hurt him. Mr. Jeliffe just better keep his dirty hands to himself.

"Say, Billy, this white deer, when gunning season starts, you don't think anybody'd try to shoot him, do you?"

"Well, I wouldn't, for one," Billy said. "You know what they say about killing a white deer? It's twice as unlucky as bustin' a mirror."

"Mr. Jeliffe better remember that."

"That joker," Billy said. "Last season I saw him open up on a hen pheasant on the ground. He's from the city and I guess he don't know any better. He's liable to do anything."

"Well, he better stay away from our white deer or I'll

shoot him in the kiester with my bee-bee gun," Davy said. Davy likes to use words like that.

"Let me know if you spot 'im, fellers," Billy said as he handed us the grocery bags.

We went out after supper that night and we looked and looked and we got in so late that Mom said what on earth were we doing out there in the meadow two hours after our bedtime. We didn't tell anybody but we set our alarm for three o'clock, with the clock under our pillow so it wouldn't ring but just buzz in our ear. There was almost a full moon and it sure was beautiful, only a little chilly when the wind came up, and finally we had to go in without seeing anything that even looked like a white deer. We did the same thing the next night and the next and the next and we were getting so pooped that we were yawning all over the place and Davy fell asleep right in the middle of his arithmetic. But we still hadn't seen our white deer.

That Friday after school we asked permission to go up to our clubhouse and camp out overnight. The moon was full and awfully close, like it was out there to light the meadow for us so we'd be sure not to miss him if he came down. We made up stories to tell each other to keep ourselves awake but by around one o'clock Davy was so sleepy that he'd slip off into little cat naps while he was talking. We were just about to call it a night and crawl into the clubhouse when all of a sudden I saw something that looked like branches moving out of the woods.

"Davy, look! Look over there!"

You could only see his antlers and the front of his head poking out of the woods, but there wasn't any doubt about it—the head was white. It was our white deer all right.

Davy shouted, "Oh, boy, there he is—isn't he a beaut!" and sort of clapped his hands without meaning to. The head of the white buck popped back into the pines and we could hear him taking off through the woods.

The next night we were all ready for him. We took some corn from the crib and made a trail of it from the pine woods to the middle of the meadow. Then we got down behind the fence and we tried not to move, even when we itched. The moon threw a path of light across the meadow and the stars looked cold and bright. The only sound in the world was the breeze blowing in from the river. We kept our eyes on the spot where we had seen him poke through the night before. Maybe two hours went by, or maybe it was only twenty minutes. It was hard to tell, out there in the moonlight with Davy and me not saying a word to each other and hardly even breathing. And then, there he was again, in the same spot where we had seen him the night before.

This time we didn't say a word and we didn't move a peg. We froze like hunting dogs and now we were really holding our breaths. He pushed his head out and looked around, and then we could see his neck and his haunches, and they were *white,* as white as first snow in December. He nibbled the nearest ear of corn and we held our breaths as long as we could and loved the sight of him. With another slow and careful look he moved on to the next ear of corn. Now, for the first time, we could see all of him. He was big and lean as a racehorse and you could see how proud he was of those wonderful antlers. Davy swore he was a sixteen-pointer, and he had at least twelve, anyhow, and the way they stood out in the moonlight against the black green of the pines was one of the most elegant sights we ever hope to see. He stood right out there in front of us for at least five minutes, or it could have been half an hour, and he moved with his head high, wearing those antlers as proud as a king. We stood still, so still that we ached, and then Davy couldn't hold it any more and shifted his feet.

Snowy—that's what we had decided to call him—jerked his head and sniffed the air and looked straight at us, right into our eyes, it seemed, and the moonlight made his eyes glow like a lit-up reindeer we had seen in the window of a big city store at Christmas time. He watched us for maybe a minute and we watched him, and then he was off, sailing over the meadow, a white streak of deer-speed that would have outrun Man o' War.

Every night after that we left corn for Snowy and almost every night he came down from the pine woods. Each time he was a little bolder and more sure of himself. I think he knew we were there. I think he was sort of showing off for us. He would finish the corn and look over to where he had seen us the first time and lower his head two or three times as if he was bowing to us. We planned to get closer and closer to him, and one of these days, when he learned where his food came from and who his friends were, we hoped maybe we could get him to eat right out of our hands. Yes, and maybe we would have, if the darned gunning season hadn't come along.

We hadn't told anybody about our white deer, not even Mom or Dad or Billy, for fear the news would get back to Mr. Jeliffe and he'd get after Snowy with his rifle and try to bag him for that mantelpiece in his den. It didn't seem right that anything as proud and handsome as Snowy's twelve- or fourteen-point antlers should end up on the wall of a loudmouth like Mr. Jeliffe. So every time we heard a shot up on the hill we were awfully nervous, for we knew that Mr. Jeliffe and some of his friends were gunning over there near the pine woods. We asked Dad not to let Mr. Jeliffe gun on our side of the line but Dad said that was rather hard to do because after all we were neighbors and it was local custom for neighbors to gun each other's places even when they were posted. So all we could do was hope and pray and that night when we snuck down to the meadow we felt like cheering out loud because Snowy showed up as usual. The night was a little darker now because the moon was beginning to shrink again but he was still one beautiful sight. We watched him go trotting off into the woods proud as a king and I think if Mr. Jeliffe had showed up with his gun just then and shot old Snowy down, we'd of grabbed that gun away from him and murdered him in cold blood.

Late the next afternoon we heard a shot up in the woods, from the far end of our line and we ran out with our fingers crossed and our hearts twisting up. There at the boundary line of our place and his was Mr. Jeliffe, peering into the woods.

"So you kids didn't believe we had a white deer up here?" he said. "Well, I just got a shot at him and I think I nicked him but he ran off into the woods. You c'n come along and help me look for him if you want to. He might be dying somewhere in there. How would you like a nice venison steak to bring home to Dad?"

He thought he was so great, standing up there with his gun.

"Don't you know it's bad luck shooting a white deer, Mr. Jeliffe? Billy Yeager says it's even worse'n busting a mirror."

Mr. Jeliffe laughed. "Those silly superstitions. Don't tell me two intelligent boys like you won't pass under a ladder and are scared of black cats."

As a matter of fact we weren't a bit superstitious and we used to tease Billy because he'd turn around whenever he saw a black cat. But all of a sudden we were awfully superstitious about Snowy. We knew it was bad luck to kill Snowy. Anybody deserved bad luck if he even thought of killing anything as handsome and proud and beautiful as Snowy was when he ventured into the meadow that first evening and pointed his antlers at the moon.

So our hearts kept twisting up as we walked along with Mr. Jeliffe searching for Snowy's body on the piny floor of the woods. His dogs kept sniffing, stopping and then running forward and any second we were afraid they would lead us to the fallen body of poor Snowy. But he wasn't to be found. He had disappeared somewhere into the woods. Mr. Jeliffe got angry and said some bad words. "I'm going to get that S.O.B. of a buck yet," he said. It made Davy and me feel pretty bad to hear Snowy, our beautiful white deer Snowy, called a name like that.

We worried about him all that night. We slipped out to the pasture but he wasn't there. It was snowing a little bit, and mighty cold, but we waited as long as we could, until Davy's teeth got to chattering so loud we had to go in.

That night I dreamt about Snowy. There was a terrible wound from a bullet in his sleek white chest and then he was gone and Davy and I were following a trail of blood across the white fields beyond the woods. I woke up half bawling and I heard Davy say, "What's the matter, Steve?" He wasn't in his bed. He was sitting on the window ledge staring out at the snow. I told him about my dream and he said he had woke himself up with a dream too. He dreamt that the two of us had gone hunting for Mr. Jeliffe and we had shot him right between the eyes and his head was mounted over the mantel of our fireplace with the bullet holes in his forehead making him look like a man with four eyes.

We kept leaving corn for Snowy night after night and we stayed up as late as we could on school nights in the hope of seeing him again, but it looked like he must have crawled off into the woods and died somewhere. We sure missed him. He wasn't like our dog Toro or our cat Quaker; we had never fed him or patted him or even so much as touched him. But Snowy was a pet to us just as much as if we had ridden him or taught him to sit up and shake hands. He was the only white deer we ever had and it felt like a knife inside to think of him dead and gone or crawling off to a lonely death. Every night, with less and less hope, we kept a lookout for him, until the last day of gunning season. That was a Saturday, so Davy and I decided to take a long hike through the woods and across a stream to an old deserted, broken-down stone house we used for an emergency headquarters. At the stream we had just stopped to kick the ice in and have a drink when suddenly Davy grabbed me by the shoulder and pointed. It was Snowy all right, big as life and twice as spry, having a drink about twenty-five yards upstream. Boy, we felt so good we could have thrown our arms around him and kissed him, only by that time he was gone, flying up over the rocks and away from the stream as if he had wings on his feet.

So the last day of gunning was coming to an end and Snowy was still in one piece, kinging it over the woods. We should have known Mr. Jeliffe was just sounding off when he claimed to have hit him. Mr. Jeliffe liked to talk about his trophies, but he wasn't much of a shot. The way Billy put it, his aim was so poor he couldn't hit the water if he fell out of a boat.

That evening, exactly a month from the time we had first seen him, we went up to the meadow again to see if Snowy would come down to visit us again. The moon was like a big white balloon hanging over our head in the cold sky. We had stopped putting corn out because we figured it was healthier for Snowy not to be lured out of the woods. But now we reckoned it was safe again so we tried our old trick of dropping a trail of corn into the middle of the meadow. If we could get Snowy to make a habit of coming down, we would have time to train him now. After a while we could get him to eat out of our hands. He would get used to us and let us lead him around. Maybe we could tame him to the point where we could bed him down in the barn. Wouldn't that be something to show the kids at school, a fourteen-point white buck for a pet! We'd be about the most famous kids in the county, and the luckiest, because if it's bad luck to shoot a white deer it must be good luck to help one keep from getting shot and to turn him into a pet.

That's what Davy and I were whispering to each other when I'll be six kinds of a jack-rabbit if Snowy doesn't poke his head out of the woods, just the way he did the first time; poke his head out, take a good, slow, thoughtful look around and then mosey on into the meadow to nibble the corn, just as peaceful and unconcerned as if he was Hector the ram.

We were watching him and thinking how noble and magnificent he looked when we heard a sharp whisper behind us—"Shh—quiet—and keep your heads down, boys." Mr. Jeliffe, with his damn gun, had come creeping up like an Indian. The moon was making a regular spotlight for Snowy and we saw Mr. Jeliffe raise his gun and take aim.

I yelled, "Davy, Davy, chase him into the woods!" Davy and I started running forward and Snowy took off across the fields as if his tail was on fire. We'll never forget how beautiful he looked racing along the fence separating our place from the Jeliffe's, closer and closer to the dark pines. Mr. Jeliffe could never hit a target moving at that speed but somehow we couldn't stop running and shouting and waving our hands. Now he was almost to the woods, in the far corner of our property, only a few yards from the sheltering woods where Mr. Jeliffe could never get him. His speed must have been fifty or sixty miles an hour, and then, in one terrible moment, he wasn't moving forward at all. He was crashing down through the small-branch and tar-paper roof of our clubhouse; into the four-foot drop we had tunneled out as a secret meeting place. We ran up to the hole and looked in, feeling trembly all over, feeling sick. Snowy was thrashing around on the dirt floor of our clubhouse. We saw him struggle up nearly to a standing position on three legs and then topple over again.

"God damn it," I said. "His leg is broke."

When he rolled over on his side and tried to raise again you could see where his rear left leg was hanging loose. He looked up at us and we had never seen him so close, so close that we could touch him. His eyes were wild and sort of pleading and terribly angry and sad as death.

Mr. Jeliffe came up behind us and looked in. "Well, looks like you trapped him, boys."

I said to Mr. Jeliffe, "Go ahead shoot him. His leg is broke. You better shoot him quick."

It made an awful noise. Davy and I didn't want to look, but finally we couldn't help it; we had to look. Snowy was lying all white and still and terribly dead at the bottom of our clubhouse.

Mr. Jeliffe said, "Well, looks like we'll all be eating venison for a month."

We didn't say anything. We just stood there thinking what kind of a man Mr. Jeliffe was and what a wonderful sight Snowy made the first time he lifted his antlers to the moon in our meadow.

Mr. Jeliffe said, "Tell your dad I'll have my man hang him and butcher him for both of us. But if you boys don't mind I'd still like to have that head for the wall of my den."

Davy, who says those things faster than I do, said just one word. It was the one he has to pay fifteen cents for every time Dad hears him saying it.

Mr. Jeliffe said, "Keep your hands off that carcass, boys. I'll send my man over to carry it back."

Davy and I didn't say anything. We both knew at the same time what we had to do. We went to the edge of the pines and broke off as many branches as we could carry. We covered Snowy with them and went back for another load.

We had to work fast because Jeliffe's man would be coming back any minute. Then, while Davy went on piling fallen branches and dead wood on top of the pine, I double-timed it back to the house for some matches. By the time I got back Davy had done a good job. It was a regular funeral pyre. I held a match to some of the pine branches and they caught like paper. We stood back and watched the flames leaping up.

When Snowy was once more ash and dust and bone we would fill in our clubhouse with dirt and trample it down hard, so the dead would be safe from dogs and buzzards and Mr. Jeliffe. We would set up a cross with Snowy's name on it. He was our white deer. Never again would Snowy come trotting into our pasture bearing his antlers like the crown of a king. But by God, neither was Mr. Jeliffe going to have Snowy's wonderful white head mounted on his wall.

A NOTE ON THE AUTHOR

Budd Schulberg has written some of the most powerful and popular novels of the twentieth century, including *What Makes Sammy Run?*, *The Harder They Fall*, and *The Disenchanted*, and the screenplays for *On the Waterfront* and *A Face in the Crowd* (adapted from his short story "Your Arkansas Traveler"). His other books include *Loser and Still Champion: Muhammad Ali*, *Sanctuary V*, *Moving Pictures*, *Sparring with Hemingway*, and *Ringside*. Mr. Schulberg was born in New York City, the son of Hollywood film pioneer B. P. Schulberg, and was educated at Los Angeles High School, Deerfield Academy, and Dartmouth College. After a brief stint as a screenwriter in Hollywood, he served in the United States Navy during World War II and was in charge of photographic evidence for the Nuremberg Trials. Through the years his writing on boxing has received several awards. He lives in Long Island, New York.